"I came by to see whether you want me now." There was a slight pause, then Alex added, "For the sketch."

"Uh, sure. Now is great."

But when Alex walked into the studio, and Gen got a good look at him, she wasn't so certain this was a good time after all. His light gray T-shirt clung to the muscled contours of his chest. Imagining the play of muscles beneath the thin cotton had Gen's throat constricting. She swallowed hard. "Um, would you mind taking off your shirt?" she asked, appalled at the betraying huskiness of her voice.

He grinned mischievously. Grabbing the hem of his shirt, he slowly began peeling it off of his torso.

Riveted, Gen watched as inch by inch his tanned body was revealed.

"I think this is a bad idea," she whispered. "A really bad idea."

Alex's smile widened and the pulsing heat inside her quickened. "Have I told you yet that you're a rotten liar, Genevieve Monaghan?" He murmured as his hands reached up to frame her face. Aware only that she was breathless with desire, breathless for him, Gen's lips parted.

Also by Laura Moore

NIGHT SWIMMING

IN YOUR EYES

LAURA MOORE

BALLANTINE BOOKS • NEW YORK

An Ivy Book
Published by The Random House Publishing Group

Copyright © 2004 by Laura Moore

All rights reserved under International and Pan-American Copyright Conventions. Published in the United States by Ivy Books, an imprint of The Random House Publishing Group, a division of Random House, Inc., New York, and simultaneously in Canada by Random House of Canada Limited, Toronto.

Ivy Books and colophon are trademarks of Random House, Inc.

www.ballantinebooks.com

ISBN 0-8041-2005-6

Manufactured in the United States of America

First Edition: July 2004

OPM 10 9 8 7 6 5 4 3 2 1

To my brothers, Peter and Adam

ONE

Her breathless moans filled the darkened room, answering his every thrust. Alex felt her fingers curl, her nails raking the width of his back as she urged him on. Accommodating her unspoken demands, he drove himself deeper, harder still. Abruptly, her moans were transformed, channeled into a single, suspended cry that echoed off the walls of the spacious bedroom. He felt her convulse then melt around him.

No sooner had she recovered than Sydney arched against his pelvis, pressing close. "More. Give me more," she panted as she wrapped her legs around his hips. Her hands shifted in a downward sweep, clutching feverishly.

His gaze swept over Sydney's flushed face. Her eyes were glazed, lost in a haze of passion. He flexed his hips, sheathing himself within her, then, in one fluid motion, slipped his arm beneath the small of her back and rolled, bringing her with him as they switched positions. He exhaled as her nails left his back, replaced by the smoothness of the bedsheets.

Clasping her hips, Alex guided her until she'd found

the rhythm, a slow grind that left her gasping, her head thrown back in rapture. His broad hands roamed, sliding over her sweat-dampened skin, stroking as they traveled upward to cup her swaying breasts. He swept his thumbs back and forth over her nipples.

Shuddering, Sydney moved against his hands, her breath catching then rushing out, ragged and quick. She was almost there, damn close to the edge, Alex thought. He shifted, raising his torso so his mouth could reach her. His teeth closed over her turgid nipple, biting down gently. As if on cue, Sydney exploded. Her inner muscles clenched violently, milking him.

Alex's cock responded. He tensed, swelling and growing inside her, his hands grasping as he surged into her slick heat one last time and found his release. With a low groan, his mouth closed over hers, swallowing her shattered scream.

Like a curtain lowering, postcoital quiet descended. The silence was broken when Sydney rolled over onto her side to face him. "No one can make me come like you do, Alex," she purred, skimming her fingers over the muscled contours of his chest. His pecs twitched involuntarily at the sudden memory of her nails scoring his flesh.

Sydney snuggled closer so she could press her lips to the base of his throat. With a soft sigh, she dropped her head back onto the pillow, seeming not to notice that Alex had neither replied nor offered a casual caress in return. He felt her sated body relax against his, and grow heavy as sleep claimed her. Her breathing slowed and deepened, fanning dry the sweat on his skin.

When he was certain she was fast asleep, he swung his legs over the bed and padded into the adjacent bathroom. Dropping his condom into the wastebasket, he flicked on the bathroom lights then blinked, accustoming his eyes to the sudden brightness. He turned to the sink and was abruptly confronted with his reflection in the mirrored medicine cabinet.

He stared dispassionately, cataloging the details of his face: dark blond hair, pale blue eyes, squared chin . . .

Yeah, he looked the same as ever. So what had changed? Why was it that the sex he'd just experienced left him cold and empty, with nothing more memorable to show for it than an aching head and a lacerated back? Why did he suddenly wish he were anywhere else in the world than here in this Central Park South penthouse with a beautiful woman lying naked and replete in his bed, a woman who'd climaxed three times in his arms? He didn't know what had triggered the change in him, but he knew for certain that the act that Sydney Raines and he had just performed was precisely that: an act. Empty and meaningless.

Filled with a sudden impatience, Alex yanked open the cabinet door, banishing his blue-eyed reflection. He rummaged among the first-aid creams and sprays and boxes of Band-Aids and gauze pads he kept stocked for visits from Sophie and Jamie, his niece and nephew, before finding the aspirin. He opened the bottle and with a quick toss of his head downed two of them, then bent over the faucet for a long drink of cold water. Shutting the cabinet, he carefully kept his gaze averted from its mirrored front. He'd had enough soul-searching for one night.

He walked over to the shower stall and pulled the glass door open. Reaching in, he turned the water on full blast. It didn't take long for the marble cubicle to fill with clouds of steam. He stepped inside and let the soft grayness envelop him. Arms braced against the tiles, he emptied his mind of everything except the lashing sting of hot water beating on his scored flesh, welcoming the pain like an old, familiar friend.

Alex didn't bother with sleep. As the clock's hands crept toward five, he pushed his chair away from his computer monitor, which glowed with numbers and deciles courtesy of the Nippon stock exchange, and wandered over to stand by the penthouse's oversize windows. Hands fisted inside his jeans pockets, he stared out at the park that lay stretched below, twenty-six stories down. An ever-changing quilt, this morning the fifty-some-block-long rectangle that delineated Central Park was dominated by light browns and grays and soft, pale greens. Near the southern end of the park, just below his bare feet, was a liberal smattering of bright pink that signaled the riotous bloom of the cherry trees.

Perhaps it was the angle of the dawn's light. Whatever the reason, Alex had a sudden urge to pull on his sweats and running shoes and go down to the park for his morning run. A voice inside his head chimed in, told him that if he went now—right now—he would see her, the mystery woman, flying down the hill near 102nd Street on her Rollerblades, her massive hound galloping flat out by her side.

The population of New York City was around ten million; densely packed Manhattan boasted close to two million. Yet there were moments when this teeming metropolis shrank to the size of a small town. Six o'clock in the morning in Central Park was one of those times. The people out then, whether running, cycling, or blading around the six-mile loop—however disparate their lives the other twenty-three hours of the day—were bound by their need to get that rush of endorphins racing through their systems.

The mystery woman belonged to this select group. Watching for her had become a ritual; an actual sighting never failed to brighten his mood. A New York miracle was how Alex thought of her. Each time he saw her, he was struck anew by how wild, how unfettered she seemed, a glorious contrast to the gritty cement and steel jungle that surrounded them . . . and Alex would find himself grinning, grateful to be alive right here and now, a witness to this brief, incredible spectacle.

It had taken nearly half a dozen sightings before he'd even been sure his hurtling Rollerblader was a woman. Bundled in a dark watch cap, fleece jacket, sweatpants, and thick gloves, she didn't exactly advertise her sex as she sped around the park. She was more a blur of long scissoring legs, the enormous dog beside her all flying fur and lolling tongue. Then, one morning he'd heard her laugh. Definitely a woman's laughter—light and musical—it had floated in the crisp dawn air as she acknowledged the awed, startled shout of "Holy shit!" from the two cyclists she'd flown past.

His fascination with the Rollerblader had grown with each sighting. Recently, he'd caught himself thinking of her at odd moments, as if she'd taken hold of his subconscious.

Which was why Alex couldn't, wouldn't permit himself to go out looking for her today. Not when he knew what lay ahead. It didn't matter that the woman from the park was destined to remain yet another anonymous New Yorker, one he wouldn't recognize or even look for anywhere else in the city. His personal code refused to entertain pleasurable albeit innocent thoughts of one woman when he was going to hurt another shortly.

Again. God, he'd done this so many times before, he should have the technique patented. The Alex Miller Method of breaking up. Guaranteed results.

He cursed softly and then stiffened. Unconsciously his mouth hardened in a grim line as from the bedroom behind him he heard the shrill ring of the alarm clock. Sydney would be out in a matter of minutes, ready to sit down with her *Wall Street Journal,* juice, and cappuccino. For a second, he was tempted to maintain his silence and put off the unpleasantness. But no, he couldn't. To do so would only delay the inevitable. It wasn't as if he needed more time to analyze his feelings or, more precisely, his lack of feelings.

A damned shame. Sydney Raines was beautiful, intelligent, and dynamic . . . and that was pretty much how Alex felt about his Aston Martin, too.

She deserved better than that.

* * *

Alex waited until they were seated at the oval marble table to break the news. Sydney stared, her cup of cappuccino poised in midair. "Excuse me, Alex, what did you say? I can't have heard you correctly. Did you just say, 'It's time we ended this. I'm not the man for you, Sydney'? If so, I'm afraid I don't share your sense of humor. It's a pretty bad joke." Her cool smile underscored her annoyance as she brought the cup to her lips.

"I'm sorry but I wasn't joking. It's over between us." Holding her gaze he saw her brown eyes widen as they filled with comprehension and outrage.

The cup was lowered with a clatter of porcelain, the noise magnified in the suddenly tense atmosphere. Sydney's slender throat worked until at last she managed a hoarse, "What do you mean, 'it's over'? How can it be over?"

Alex kept his tone calm. "I'm not interested in a deeper commitment. I care about you, Sydney, but—"

"You care about me, but you're breaking up with me? What kind of a line is that?" she cried. Jumping to her feet, she began pacing back and forth, her black kimono making a slippery sound, like the first breath of a storm. "You can't possibly be serious about ending our relationship. We've been together for almost six months. What we have is *good*—no, fantastic. How can you talk about ending it?"

"Sydney," Alex said and raked his hair in frustration. "None of this is your fault. It's mine. I'm a dead-end street. Not what you deserve."

She whirled, her glossy dark hair swinging about

her shoulders, and glared furiously. "I know *exactly* what I deserve. I deserve mar—"

"No, Sydney," Alex said, cutting her off before she could finish. "I told you from the very beginning, when we started seeing each other, I'm not interested in getting married. I would never have gotten involved if you'd said—"

"I've changed my mind!"

His eyebrows shot upward. Yes, that much was obvious. "Well, I'm afraid I haven't," he drawled coolly.

Sydney continued as if she hadn't heard him. "But instead of proposing, you intend to humiliate me in front of my friends and my clients! What will I say to them? Everyone thinks we're a couple. And Mother— she's already begun looking for hotels with dining rooms large enough to hold the wedding party!" Her voice cracked and she covered her face with her hands. Beneath the silk kimono, her shoulders shook.

Despite Sydney's distress, Alex felt a wave of relief wash over him. She hadn't once said she loved him. A rather glaring and telling omission under the circumstances. Obviously some part of her recognized the truth of it, that neither of them really loved the other. Alex knew he had faults aplenty. Hypocrisy wasn't one of them. He refused to marry someone he didn't truly love. Better that he behave like a bastard now than make false promises and destroy both Sydney and himself in a sham of a marriage.

Her shoulders were still shaking. "Come on, Sydney." At the sound of his voice, Sydney lifted her face from the shield of her hands. Her brown eyes, awash in tears, were fixed on him. "Come on," he repeated gently.

"Surely you're exaggerating. Your mother wouldn't be shopping for a place to hold a reception unless—" He broke off as her gaze slid away.

Oh, hell. He rubbed a hand across his brow. "You didn't," he said in a weary tone.

"Yes. Yes, I did," she fired back. "I told Mother you were bound to propose soon. We're practically living together, and you haven't looked twice at—oh, God," she cried, her voice filled with anguish. "That's it, isn't it?"

Alex shook his head. "No, Sydney, there's no one else."

Her face, tight with suspicion, searched his. Slowly, slowly she relaxed. "No, of course there's no one else," she repeated, as if to reassure herself.

Listening to her, Alex felt a surge of compassion. He could still recall the night when Sydney indulged in one too many martinis. Worried that she might inadvertently injure herself if left on her own, after the party was over, Alex had taken her back to his apartment.

By the time the night air hit her, she was barely able to stand, let alone undress herself. Alex had helped her out of her clothes, letting her fall against his bowed back as he dealt with her stockings and heels. For some reason, this simple act had caused an emotional meltdown. Bewildered, he'd carried a sobbing Sydney to his bed, then held her as she revealed in disjointed bits and pieces her deepest pain. That was the one and only time he'd heard her mention the name Richard Raines, the father who'd abandoned her and her mother when Sydney was eight years old to run off with another woman.

The tear-soaked tale had illuminated much about Sydney's personality, permitting Alex to understand what fueled her seemingly tireless ambition, her desire to be and to have the best. It all stemmed from a hopeless, twenty-year-long wish . . . a little girl's desperate and unfulfilled wish.

By breaking up with Sydney, Alex realized he was adding to the damage inflicted by her callous father. But however bad he felt for her, he couldn't continue the affair. "Listen, Sydney, I'm sorry, but we've got to end this. So you can find someone—"

"But, Alex, I don't want anyone else." Swiftly she crossed the room, dropping to her knees before his chair. Alex made to stand but she pressed her body against him, closing her hands over his thighs, flattening her lush breasts against his knees. He felt his muscles turn rock hard.

In the charged silence, he stared into her upturned face, taking in her flawless complexion, the way her mouth was parted in a sultry smile. In one distant corner of his brain he wondered what the hell was wrong with him. Sydney Raines was beautiful and smart. A million men would die to have her down on her knees, that temptress's light ablaze in her eyes.

As if sensing Alex's indecision, she rose and pressed her soft lips to his. Her perfume wafted in the air. "Alex, darling," she whispered. "Don't shut me out. I know you care for me. I know it. Nobody makes me feel like you do."

"Don't inflate sex into something it isn't, Sydney,"

he said bluntly. "The sex has been good between us, but there's got to be more to make a relationship last. Which we don't have."

"How can you be sure when you won't give us a chance?" Correctly reading the closed expression on his face, her tone grew mulish. "No, I refuse, I simply refuse to give you up!"

A chill stole through him at her words. "Let me ask you something, Sydney. You know how volatile the stock market is these days. What if I were to lose everything, every last penny? Would you still want to be with me?"

He watched carefully. Her face was close enough to catch the betraying flicker that crossed it. To her credit, Sydney recovered quickly, even managing a light laugh. "Don't be absurd, Alex."

"I try not to be."

"You're brilliant, a financial genius. That would never happen."

"Maybe, maybe not." He shrugged, no longer interested in the conversation. A glance at the light pouring in through the windows told him it was getting late. He stood and brushed past her kneeling form. "Listen, I'm going to be pretty busy with work these next few days. I'll leave a note for Rose telling her to let you in so you can pick up your things."

Rising gracefully to her feet, she approached him. "Sending me packing, Alex?" she asked. "I'm afraid it won't be that easy. I'm not a quitter. I won't give up on you—on us. I realize what I've done wrong—I haven't been paying you the right kind of attention. . . ." Her smile grew bold, full of her signature confidence.

Through the silk of her robe, Alex saw her nipples had hardened.

He shook his head. "No. Sex isn't going to work."

"I think it will," she contradicted huskily. "It doesn't matter what you say, Alex. I want you and I know I can make you want me."

"Sydney—"

"It's not like you can avoid me. We still have to confer on the decisions regarding the hospital wing. Then there's the party you're throwing for the Miller Group's companies . . ."

Damn, Alex cursed silently. When Sydney had volunteered to oversee the details for his firm's party months ago, he'd happily accepted her offer. It had seemed like a convenient, hassle-free solution, especially since her public relations company, Raines and Byrne Consulting, was already working for his philanthropic fund, TLM, and handling the day-to-day details for the wing he was donating to the Children's Hospital in Boston.

Alex knew that one of the main reasons Sydney and his relationship had lasted as long as it had was because they'd both maintained a strictly professional attitude to their business dealings. He hoped Sydney wasn't going to jeopardize that now. "Naturally we'll be seeing each other," he replied. "As business associates and friends—but nothing more."

She shrugged. "Very well, we'll play it your way. Perhaps you're right—a little break might be good for us, darling. That way, when you come to your senses, it'll be like our first time all over again." She leaned close and placed a chaste kiss on the corner of his mouth, then stepped back. As if by magic, the sash of her kimono came unknotted and the robe slipped silently to the floor. Naked, Sydney stretched sensuously, like a cat demanding to be stroked. Without bothering to retrieve her kimono, she turned, presenting Alex with a view of her backside, which was every inch as enticing as her front. As if knowing his eyes would be on her, she tossed him a provocative glance over her shoulder. "We should get going, lover. You have an eight o'clock meeting, remember?" Then, as if she hadn't a care in the world, she strolled off toward his bedroom.

The discarded kimono lay in a rumpled black heap on the pale beige carpet, mocking him. He stared at it for several minutes, going over the scene that had just transpired, realizing the enormity of his mistake. Not that he'd decided to call it quits with Sydney, but that he hadn't anticipated how tenacious she would be when faced with the prospect of losing him. And he should have. After all, it was her tenacity and unflagging drive that had won her the coveted account of handling the PR for Alex's interests. From the way she'd reacted this morning, it was clear that she wasn't going to make the breakup easy for either of them. He would have to give Sydney the cold shoulder until she realized once and for all that the relationship was over. So much for the Alex Miller Method of breaking up, he thought. Guaranteed results? Yeah, right. They were bloody spectacular.

TWO

Gen Monaghan squeezed the ancient Yugo into a parking spot a few doors down from the loft. A turn of the key and its motor died with a tubercular cough. Murphy sat up in the back, rumpling the Navajo blanket Gen used to cover the car's ripped upholstery.

"Yup, we're here," she confirmed as she grabbed the leather leash that lay beside her red backpack on the front passenger seat and snapped it onto Murphy's collar. Her fingers sank into his brindle coat as she leaned forward and dropped a kiss onto his hairy muzzle.

"Okay, let's go," she said, and heard his tail beat the back of the seat. "Oh, and Murph?" Gen added, giving her dog a stern look. "Don't jump on Jiri. You know he doesn't appreciate that kind of thing."

Eyes dark and solemn beneath the shaggy fringe, Murphy blinked and then scrambled his way to the front of the car.

"You're late," Jiri replied to Gen's call of 'hello' when she and Murphy entered the studio. As the door slammed behind them with a thud, Gen watched Murphy bound across the paint-splattered floor, making a beeline for Jiri. Skidding to a halt, Murphy stood up on his hind legs until he was almost eye to eye with him.

With his customary cry of disgust, Jiri shoved him away. The stream of Czech that followed Murphy as he wandered over to his cushioned dog bed by the small bookcase required no translation.

Murphy, having completed his third and final spin, circling the dog bed, lowered his shaggy body with a loud grunt. For a moment he stared back at the two humans. Then lifting his hind leg, he began grooming himself energetically.

Jiri gave a loud snort. "That," he said, switching to his heavily accented English and pointing an accusing finger at Gen's dog, "that revolting creature I will not miss."

"Ahh, but he'll miss you, Jiri. Loads," Gen replied good-naturedly. "Murphy's been watching you pack all week, getting sadder and sadder. I'm sorry we were late," she said, diplomatically switching topics. "The park was beautiful this morning, all crisp and fresh-smelling. Murphy couldn't bear to leave." She glanced around at the large wooden crates, their sides plastered with red and white FRAGILE! stickers. During the past month she and Jiri had spent hours of each day wrapping and packing his art. "So, what's left to do?" she asked.

"More drawings," Jiri informed her with a tilt of his salt-and-pepper head.

Gen glanced over to her side of the studio they'd shared for the past three years. On top of the long plywood plank supported by two sawhorses that Gen used as a worktable were four tall stacks of drawings. Alarmed, her gaze flew around the worktable. Her sculptures, her tools . . . where had they gone? Gen's jaw tightened when she found where Jiri had put them—next to the large trash bins. Her tools were stashed inside dust-coated milk crates. The stoneware jars that held her paintbrushes peeped over the rim of one. The brushes' bristles, some a dark mink brown, others originally a light blond but now permanently tinted with the remains of pigment, were listing drunkenly. But it was seeing her sculptures on the floor, in a place where they could be knocked over, that had Gen blinking rapidly against the hurt.

Jiri was perfectly aware of how delicate terra-cotta was. He knew, too, that these six pieces, three busts and three figurines, had been selected for her upcoming show. Moreover, it was Jiri himself who, when he invited Gen to work as an assistant in exchange for letting her share his loft space, had established the one and only rule in their studio: *Never touch.* "Never touch my art or my tools without my permission, Genevieve. Never," he'd repeated, his voice as heavy and inflexible as a judge's.

On any other day, Gen would have been tempted to say something, but not today. She didn't want to part with bad feelings between them. Jiri was obviously preoccupied with his return to his native Prague and in a rush to get his art safely packed, she told herself.

Otherwise he'd never have done something as inconsiderate as this. As she followed him over to the table, however, her eyes darted to her sculptures, trying to penetrate the plastic sheeting that enshrouded them and reassure herself that nothing was damaged.

As soon as Jiri's drawings are packed, I'll put everything back in order, she thought. *Why bother, Monaghan, when soon you'll have to pack up, too?* Resolutely Gen ignored the nasty voice inside her head. She'd deal with what was now a two-month-old headache, the futile search for an affordable studio space, after the group show had opened. Fixing a smile on her face, she pushed her worries to the back of her mind and walked over to the worktable.

The drawings were neatly stacked, sorted by size to ensure a precise fit in the archival boxes. "Which ones first?" she asked.

"The small ones," he replied, pulling the smallest of the specially designed boxes toward them. "We work quickly, okay? I have to pack rest of clothes."

"Sure thing, Jiri."

They worked systematically, building a multilayered sandwich of Jiri's drawings between protective layers of acid-free paper. Gen's previous bout of annoyance evaporated as she gazed at drawing after drawing, openly admiring the brilliance of Jiri's draftsmanship.

"God, I love this piece." Between her fingers she cradled a still life Jiri had executed in pastel. "The way you captured the light is so subtle. And this reflection of the delft vase of peonies against the silver tray is masterful."

He gave the drawing a passing glance. "That one is too sentimental, too pretty," he said dismissively.

"Oh, no, I don't think . . ." she began, but her words died away. She knew this would end like so many of the arguments they'd had recently, with Jiri criticizing her recent series of figure studies. He claimed it was a betrayal of all he'd taught her, this reveling in bourgeois subject matter. She was sullying the purity of her art, weakening it.

Gen hated the strain their clashes had introduced into the studio and realized, too, that the lingering tensions between them were the reason why she'd initially felt a huge sense of relief when Jiri had received and accepted the offer from the National Academy of Art in Prague to be its new director. Yet now that the moment for him to return to his native country was here, she was flooded with sadness. She was losing the man who'd been her teacher and mentor for years; she'd learned so much working by his side. More important, she was losing a friend who loved art as much as she.

Wistful, she picked up another drawing, a more recent one. A large work, the paper was nearly filled by swirling dark masses. In the center, a jagged streak of light ripped through the blackness, like a bolt of lightning briefly illuminating a world of chaos. There was such power here, awesome power. "The National Academy chose well, Jiri," she said with quiet sincerity. "You'll make a wonderful director and be a true inspiration for the students."

Jiri's angular face softened. Smiling, he wrapped an arm around her shoulder, squeezing it. "Ah, Genevieve, my angel, only if I am lucky enough to have students as gifted as you." He gave a slight cough, as though he were clearing his throat, and added, "I'm sorry I miss the show. . . ." His voice trailed off, leaving an uncomfortable silence.

Gen hurriedly filled it. "That's all right. I know you want to get settled in Prague and meet with your staff before the semester ends. And it's not like you haven't seen my work before," she said, laughing lightly.

Jiri looked relieved. "Afterward you come for visit and stay with me and Maminka?"

"That's kind of you, but . . ." she fumbled awkwardly, not wishing to make him feel bad, "but I'll have to see where I am in terms of finding a new studio."

An elegantly tapered hand waved that concern aside. "Prague not expensive city. Not like New York. There are plenty of studios in old factories. Big studios," he opened his arms for emphasis, "you get for nothing. . . ."

"Yes, well," Gen began, but before she could go further, the phone rang—as it always did, every morning at eight o'clock. Jiri strode over to the small telephone table by the wall.

"Allo, Maminka," he said before he plunged into a stream of Czech. The pattern of their conversation was the same as ever. Though an ocean separated them, Mrs. Novak kept close tabs on her only child. Never mind that he was a forty-five-year-old internationally acclaimed artist, she required a daily accounting from her adored "Jiriko."

As always, when Gen thought of Jiri's relationship

with his mother, she felt a rush of gratitude for her own large and loving family. Her parents had raised their twelve children in an atmosphere of unconditional support and encouragement. Gen knew her large and boisterous family was always there for her, ready to bolster her when she was discouraged, cheer her on when she triumphed. She couldn't wait to see them at the group show; the entire clan was flying in from Boston for the opening.

When Jiri replaced the phone in its base, he didn't return to help with the remaining drawings but instead walked through the narrow doorway on the left that led to his bedroom. A minute later Gen heard the metallic scratch of wire hangers scraping the metal rod of the coat rack that served as a closet. There was such a distressing finality to the sound, she thought, and her gaze dropped unseeing to the drawing before her.

Gen knew Jiri wanted her to go with him to Prague. He'd hinted broadly that arrangements could be made so she could teach at the academy and continue working as his assistant. This didn't have to be the end—all she had to do was say yes, and she could continue learning from him and sharing their mutual love of art. But something kept her from accepting his offer.

It was as if she'd come to a crossroads in her life, in her art. Quite possibly, Jiri's criticisms were right and the course her art was taking would ultimately prove shallow, too conventional to stand the test of time— yet it was a direction Gen nevertheless felt compelled to explore. If she failed, then so be it. But she wouldn't know one way or the other unless she first stepped out from the long shadow cast by Jiri Novak.

The drawings were all neatly boxed by the time Jiri reemerged, his hands weighed down by two new bulging leather suitcases. Neither he nor Gen uttered a word as they took the jerky, clanking ride in the old industrial-size elevator down to the lobby of the building.

The cab Jiri had called for pulled up alongside the curb within minutes, its squealing brakes rousing them from their oddly frozen state. Jiri turned to Gen and his slender hands reached out to cradle the sides of her face. His eyes were a deep solemn brown as he leaned forward and kissed her. When he pulled back, a melancholy smile curved his lips. "I will miss you, Genevieve. I will miss your bright spirit and your beautiful face. Perhaps I will even miss your odious beast. You come and work in Prague, okay?"

"Yes, maybe." His arms wrapped about her, gathered her close. Gen blinked back the tears that threatened and nodded shakily. "Take care of yourself, Jiri," she whispered.

She stepped back from his embrace and with a quavery smile waited as he settled himself in the cab, then raised her arm in a subdued farewell. The yellow taxi pulled away down Spring Street, weaving past double-parked cars and trucks unloading their wares, before rounding a corner and disappearing from sight.

Gen turned and headed back into the building. Bypassing the elevator, which would give her far too much time to cry, she instead raced up the four flights of stairs. Murphy was waiting, his head cocked when she unlocked the door. As if sensing her distress, he got up and trotted over to her. Gen dropped to her knees and buried her face in his wiry coat. "It's just you and me now, Murph."

THREE

The two men skidded, slammed, and grunted. Droplets of sweat flew from their faces and forearms and rained onto the scuffed white floor as they lunged for the tiny black missile ricocheting off the walls of the squash court. The game was going quickly. Usually Alex Miller and Sam Brody were evenly matched. Today it was a total wipeout.

After Alex won the particularly brutal match point, Sam Brody's racquet fell clattering to the floor. With an inarticulate exclamation of disgust, he dropped his head, braced his hands against his knees, and sucked in air. When at last he recovered his breath, he looked up at his friend and business associate. "Good game, Miller," he offered.

"Thanks," Alex replied and swiped at the sweat streaming down his face with his terry-cloth wristband.

"So, have the European markets been driving you crazy?"

Alex cast him a sideways glance as he continued walking in a tight circle, shaking his legs out. "No, I pretty much assumed we were in for a shaft this week. I made a few adjustments."

And from that modest remark, Sam guessed that Alex Miller was in the elite minority of investors who'd been able to walk away from the slick slide of the market with bulging pockets. Sam decided to cast his net wider. "The board of directors on one of your new companies been giving you the runaround? Some CEO been throwing a tantrum?"

Instead of replying, Alex went over to the two plastic water bottles resting against the court's narrow wooden door. He grabbed them, handed one to Sam, and then squeezed a long jet into his upturned mouth. Swallowing, he wiped his mouth with the back of his hand and leveled Sam with a piercing, blue-eyed gaze. "Mind telling me where you're going with this, Brody?"

"Simple idle curiosity." Sam spread his hands, all innocence. "I was just wondering whether there was any particular reason why you were trying to send that squash ball clear to China."

"Ahh, I see." Alex grinned. "Business is fine, Brody. Nope, sorry, there's no excuse for the eight points you dropped. Must be losing your touch, that's all."

"Wait till next week. I'll be wiping the court with you," Sam growled good-naturedly. "Come on, let's hit the steam room. This damned white box is making me claustrophobic."

"Funny how you only feel that way on days you lose," Alex remarked casually as he followed him out.

Alex's and Sam's lockers at the New York Athletic Club were located in the same section, on opposite sides of the worn narrow wooden bench. Thanks to the Friday-afternoon lull, they had the canyonlike row of blue metal to themselves. Opening his locker, Alex stuffed his racquet into its case and hung it on the metal hook, and then proceeded to peel off his sweat-drenched shorts and shirt. Wrapping a narrow white towel about his hips, he was about to see whether Brody was ready to head off to the steam room when Sam's low, drawn-out whistle froze him in place.

"Damn. You and Sydney Raines getting into some serious S and M these days?"

The muscles that Alex had managed to relax for the first time since his showdown with Sydney earlier that morning tightened with renewed tension. He bit back a curse. He'd forgotten about the long scratches Sydney had inflicted last night.

"Sydney neglected to trim her nails," he replied as he shut his locker door with a clang and set the combination dial spinning, only then turning around and meeting his friend's gaze. "However, she's been declawed. As of this morning."

Sam said nothing, merely quirked a dark brow.

But Brody had been a cop as well as a bodyguard in his former life, before creating his own security firm, a start-up company in which Alex had invested a fair amount of his own money. Sam was one of the most perceptive men Alex had ever met. Very few things slipped past those keen amber eyes. Fortunately he was as discreet as he was intelligent, another reason Alex valued his friendship. Outside of his family, there were very few people Alex trusted implicitly. Sam Brody was one of them.

Banks of hot steam floated thick and heavy in the tiled chamber, swirling about them as they made their way to the far side and dropped down on the tiled ledge. "You want to talk about it?" Sam asked quietly.

Alex absently rubbed the flat of his stomach and sighed. "Shit. I suppose so, yeah. It's times like these I miss my brother, Tom, the most. I'm sorry you never met him, Sam. You'd have liked him. A damned good man, loyal as the day is long. All day, I've been hearing Tom's voice inside my head, razzing me about Sydney. Christ, I was stupid enough to forget every one of Tom's cardinal rules concerning women, right down to the most important one: Extricate before the lady latches on. Sydney was thinking marriage, Sam. She told me her blasted mother was already reception shopping." He dropped his head back against the wall with a groan of self-disgust and closed his eyes.

Glancing at him, Sam saw the lines of tension etched around Alex's mouth, the weariness that hung about him, as tangible as the thick clouds of steam wafting about them. He shook his head.

He was sitting opposite the man who'd attained the stature of a god by age thirty-three. In the world of finance, people spoke Alex Miller's name with a hushed awe. It wasn't simply that Miller had had the genius to make himself a couple of fortunes within an astoundingly short period of time as a Wall Street bond trader. It was that he was a true phenomenon. A breed apart. After scaling the very top of the financial world's Mount Olympus as a bond trader, Alex Miller had stunned Wall Street by deciding to tackle a new challenge—as if the high-stakes gamble involved in anticipating the crest and fall of the world markets simply wasn't enough to satisfy him any longer. He had walked away from a corner office in one of the Street's most powerful firms to head a company of his own, only this time not as a trader, but as a venture capitalist.

Sam understood enough about the business world to realize that everyone had fully expected Alex to crash and burn. It was simple, fundamental, a law carved in stone: Bond traders weren't venture capitalists. The whole mind-set was different—from the training, to the background, to the gut instincts involved. So Miller was doomed, the vultures already circling high above, ready to swoop down and pick apart his sorry carcass.

But instead of going belly-up, Alex, along with three other wizards he'd invited to join him as partners in the Miller Group, had a tidy portfolio of twenty companies. And while everyone else in the business world was clutching their heads and bitching about the economy, Alex's firm was posting profits.

There was, however, a definite downside to Alex Miller's untrammeled success. It had made him a target for all the marriage-hungry women from coast to coast. Handsome, richer than Croesus, Alex was the most sought after bachelor in New York. Women fell over themselves in their maddened chase to catch him. In the two years since he and Alex had become friends and business associates, Sam had witnessed the scene many times. Sydney Raines was one of the more talented huntresses. She'd used her brains as well as her beauty to capture Alex's attention, first landing an account with his firm, and then a place in his bed. Sam didn't dislike Sydney herself, only the way she seemed to glory in her role as Alex Miller's lover, parading before the other women in her set like a lioness with her kill. He wasn't terribly surprised to learn that she'd decided it was time to solidify her exalted position by becoming Mrs. Alex Miller. "So how'd she take the news?" he asked.

"Sydney doesn't deal well with failure, Sam. The damnable thing is, despite my telling her it was over, she's acting as if nothing's changed between us. We had a meeting this afternoon to go over the schedule for the final phase of the wing TLM is donating to the Children's Hospital. When it was over, she invited me to dinner. At her place."

"Major denial, huh?"

"Yeah, I'd guess you'd call it that. Thank God I'll be spending time in the Hamptons this summer." Alex smiled. "Cassie and Caleb are coming up from Charlottesville and lending me the kids while they're at some horse shows in the area."

"Next time you talk to her, give your sister my best."

"I will. Thanks." Rubbing the stiffness from his neck, Alex said, "Yeah, it'll be great to see Cassie and the kids and get away from all this. . . . Sydney will have to give up her marital hopes fairly soon."

Sam's grunt held a wealth of skepticism. Alex couldn't blame him. He wasn't particularly optimistic, either. "Christ, Sam, I don't want to hurt her any more than I have. And I really don't want to add injury to insult by firing her—she's been great at dealing with all the minutiae between the hospital and my foundation."

"Sounds like a lousy situation."

"Yeah, I'd say that's a fair assessment. It's not as if she's in love with me, Sam. She's just settling because I happen to satisfy a few other requisites: success, money, the right background . . . all that bullshit."

"Well, you do make a hell of a consolation prize."

Alex managed a wry laugh. "Thanks, Brody. You really know how to cheer a guy up."

"You're more than welcome, pal. Let me know if there's any way I can help."

"I'll do that." Alex stood and went over to the metal door and held it open for Sam. After the junglelike humidity of the steam room, the air felt as if they'd stepped into a meat locker.

"So have you talked to the Duchess lately?" Sam inquired as he shrugged into his shirt and began buttoning it. "Still ruling the Hamptons?"

Chin raised, Alex paused in the midst of knotting his tie and grinned. As far as he knew, Grace Miller hadn't a single royal connection, but Sam's nickname for Alex's elderly aunt was apt. Sam was probably the only person on earth who'd ever get away with calling Grace Miller "Duchess" to her face. He and Alex's aunt had become fast friends when Alex sent him to her house in East Hampton to install one of his high-tech security systems. She'd ended up convincing Sam to give her computer lessons. Aunt Grace now surfed the Web almost as efficiently as Alex.

"She's terrific," he replied. "Busy as a whirlwind since I put her in charge of commissioning an artist to create a work for the new wing of the Children's Hospital. We spoke on the phone yesterday. She asked after you, of course. Demanded to know when you were going to come by for tea and chess."

"That sounds irresistible. Best offer I've had in some time."

Alex grinned. "Does this mean the beautiful divorcée Lizzie Osborne is still leading you on a merry chase?"

"Oh, yeah, she's putting her all into it, dodging left and right," Sam acknowledged wryly. "Maybe I'll mention Mrs. Miller's invitation to Lizzie. It'll do her good to know there's another woman in my life, one who clamors for my attention." His grin turned into a smile. "And if I tell her I'm also going to drop in on Ty and Steve Sheppard and check on my mare, Cassis, that should be enough to send her into a full-blown snit." Sam's light brown eyes gleamed with anticipation. "Lizzie is damned cute when she's mad."

Sam Brody was a lucky man, Alex thought. He'd found the woman he loved. Indeed, so confident was Sam in the strength of his feelings that none of the many obstacles Lizzie Osborne threw in his path fazed him. From what Alex had observed, Sam relished each and every challenge, since winning meant claiming the ultimate prize—the heart of tempestuous Ms. Lizzie Osborne.

Alex envied him. It seemed as if all of his own relationships had been like the one he'd just ended with Sydney: while the sex had been hot, his emotions had remained coolly detached. By this point Alex had accepted that he wasn't the type to make a deep, lasting connection with a woman. This recent affair with Sydney, a beautiful, intelligent woman, only confirmed what he knew—love just wasn't in the picture.

FOUR

The studio was nearly silent as Gen dragged her thickly loaded paintbrush over the rough weave of the canvas. Only the occasional whirfling of Murphy dreaming broke the quiet. Even the city sounds—the honks, the clangs, the hammerings and shouts of construction crews, the wailing sirens of ambulances and police cars—seemed muffled, as though coming from a distant land.

In the rare quietude, the buzz of the intercom resounded loudly. Murphy jumped up from the dog bed, tail extended, his hairy ears twitching expectantly. Gen ignored the sound, ignored everything but the brush in her hand and the blurred trail of black and gray paint she was applying to the stretch of canvas.

Only when she'd reached the very edge did she step back and examine the painting she'd been working on for the past three days. It was a passable beginning, but she had a long way to go before this latest work came close to resembling the image that filled her mind.

Patience, Gen, she thought, squashing the impulse to disregard the second, now more insistent peal of the intercom and reimmerse herself in her private world of color and form. Instead, she dropped the broad paintbrush into a water-filled coffee can and wiped her hands on the dishrag she'd tucked into the waistband of her jeans. She walked over to the intercom and, with an unconscious sigh, pressed the speaker button. A male voice barked the name of an international shipping company. They were here to pick up Jiri's art.

Seconds later, from the hallway, came the heavy rumble of the elevator starting. Murphy stared at the door, his tail wagging in anticipation.

Unfortunately, not everyone appreciated Murphy's meet-and-greet mode. Deciding to avoid a potential lawsuit, Gen went and kneeled by her backpack and dug out a smoked bone she'd bought at the pet store. It was nearly as long as her forearm. She held it out, baton style. "Hey, Murph . . ."

Murphy needed no further entreaty. Ears flattened, he trotted up, a wide grin splitting his enormous muzzle. Without breaking his stride, he wrapped his jaw around the bone. His body brushed hers, a body check of thanks as he returned to his bed and got down to business.

Gen was grateful that Murphy possessed a clear set of priorities, in which smoked bones ranked well above security issues. She only hoped the bone was big enough to keep him happily engaged while the movers tackled their job.

The crew entered the studio with a clang of metal

dollies bouncing over the loft's threshold, three burly men who looked like they'd just climbed off their choppers, with faded bandannas wrapped around the domes of their heads and colorful tattoos across their bulging biceps. Momentarily distracted by their appearance and busy contemplating various poses for a group portrait, Gen didn't notice the older woman who trailed in behind them, her sophisticated couture as different from these rough-hewn men as night from day.

So when a patch of pink entered her field of vision, Gen blinked, startled. With a cry of delight she rushed over and hugged the other woman.

"Phoebe! What are you doing here? When did you get back? It's wonderful to see you!"

"It's good to see you too, darling." Phoebe smiled. "I came in this morning. I had some news that I couldn't wait to tell you about. You've eaten already?"

Gen glanced at the large face of her wristwatch, astonished to find it was already 3 P.M. "Uh, I was just about to break and fix myself something," she said.

"No doubt," Phoebe returned skeptically. "I had George stop at Balducci's on my way here—just in case you'd forgotten to feed yourself again."

Gen glanced toward the open doorway, where four bulging, distinctively green-and-white paper bags lay propped against one another. Her stomach rumbled at the sight and she abruptly remembered that she'd missed breakfast too, having hurried back to her painting after taking Murphy out for his morning run.

"Hey, lady, d'you mind?" One of the movers, who Gen assumed was the foreman, tapped a clipboard with the back of his hand, an impatient drumroll. "We're kinda on a schedule here."

"Oh, yes! Sorry, let me get the list." Turning back to Phoebe, she said, "This shouldn't take long. Would you like some tea? I think there's some souchong in the cupboard."

Phoebe followed her over to the tiny kitchenette's countertop and watched as Gen scooped up the sheath of papers lying there. "Where's Jiri?"

"Oh, he's gone already. He left Friday."

"Leaving you to handle all this." Phoebe waved her manicured hand at the numerous crates.

Busy checking that she had the papers in order, Gen gave a distracted shrug. "It's no big deal—mainly tons of signatures and customs forms to fill out."

"Whatever will he do without you, love?"

Gen glanced up. "I'm sorry, what did you say?"

"Nothing. Go deal with these charming men. I'll make us lunch. A celebratory lunch," she added with a smile.

Gen sat at the table, its surface covered with the remains of Phoebe Hayes's shopping spree at Balducci's. There was still enough food left to feed an army but Gen had long finished eating. She was turning the pages of the exhibition catalog that Phoebe, with a magician's flourish, had pulled from her leather tote, offering a careless, "Look at what I picked up today at Alicia's" as she handed it to Gen.

"They did a terrific job with the transparencies," Gen murmured, gazing at a full-page reproduction of one of her paintings. Looking up, she grinned. "I just can't believe it! There I am."

"Indeed you are. Can't be too many Genevieve Monaghans in Manhattan who are exhibiting at a major gallery," Phoebe teased. "And high time, too, Gen. Do you remember that day, years ago, when you came for lunch and brought your portfolio with you? It was bursting apart with your drawings. You were, what, seventeen? You hadn't even started college and already you were so talented."

"Talented? I don't know about that, but I definitely had the fire in the belly, as Dad would say." Gen laughed.

"Robert's got the wrong body part—it's the lightning from your fingers when you create that sends shivers through the beholder. I only wish we could have included this latest work of yours in the catalog, too," Phoebe said, her gaze returning once again to the large canvas hanging on the wall. "At least Alicia will be able to have it in time for the opening—as the pièce de résistance."

"But, Phoebe, it's not finished. And I couldn't possibly ask Alicia to reconfigure the whole show to accommodate a work this large—"

"She'll be jumping at the chance once she sees the painting." Phoebe rose from the table and crossed the studio, coming to stand before the painting. "You know I'm not one to praise idly, Gen. Alicia will shoot you if you *don't* include this piece. Have you given it a title yet?"

"I'm calling it *Day One*."

Phoebe pivoted and regarded Gen, her gaze bright

and piercing. "Yes, that's very fitting," she said and turned back to the painting.

Gen kept her own eyes averted from the unfinished canvas. If she looked at it, she'd be compelled to grab her brushes and resume working until the image filling her mind became blurred, lost in a fog of exhaustion.

That Phoebe Hayes admired this recent work meant a great deal to her. In addition to being Gen's godmother, Phoebe was also a passionate art collector. Over the past thirty-five years, Phoebe had amassed one of the most important collections of contemporary art—including several Monaghans. Yet despite her encouraging words, Gen wavered. "Phoebe, I can't show this piece—it's not nearly where I want it to be."

"When did you start painting it?"

"Friday morning."

"Ahh, so that's why you haven't been answering the phone. This one's really got you in its grip, hasn't it? No wonder you've forgotten to eat and sleep. Thank God for Murphy." At his name, Murphy's tail thumped once, letting them know that even asleep he was on top of the situation.

A guilty flush stole over Gen's cheeks. Noting it, Phoebe laughed.

Okay, her godmother was right, Gen admitted silently. The only times she'd been out this past weekend were to give Murphy his exercise.

"Why don't you let Alicia see *Day One* so she can judge its strength," she suggested. "And since I know how much you hate promoting yourself, I'll give her a ring. You realize, of course, what a huge sacrifice this is on my part. If you exhibit *Day One,* it'll be snatched up opening night."

Gen laughed at Phoebe's outrageous prediction. "At Alicia's prices? No way. Remember, the majority of the people coming to see my work at the gallery opening will be poor-as-church-mice Monaghans."

An amused smile lifted the corners of Phoebe's lipsticked mouth. "I think you're in for a surprise. Word's spreading fast around town. Genevieve Monaghan is the new sensation."

Gen instinctively scrunched her face as if she'd caught a whiff of something unpleasant.

"Now, now," Phoebe chastised lightly. "You mustn't bite the hand that's going to feed you—which reminds me, I haven't told you about *my* big surprise; your painting made me forget. Hold on to your chair, dearie, you may fall out of it."

Gen grinned. "Okay, what's the surprise?"

"You're being considered for a commission. And from what I can tell, it's a very short list."

"Excuse me?" she said blankly.

"That's right," Phoebe said. "A commission. Do you remember my telling you about a woman named Grace Miller?"

"Yes, I think so." Gen's brows furrowed as she searched her memory. "She's an older lady, involved in the arts?"

Phoebe nodded. "Yes. I've known Grace forever. She and her husband, Alexander Miller, took me under their wing the summer after your mother and I graduated from college. After Tansy and Robert went off on their honeymoon, I was at loose ends without my two best friends. So Grace and Alexander invited me to travel with them to Europe. They introduced me to the artists, collectors, and art dealers they knew in Paris, London, Cologne. . . . It was thanks to the Millers that I started collecting. Alexander had such a wonderful eye. A true connoisseur—in addition to being quite a talented artist in his own right. He passed away several years ago." Phoebe's usually animated voice became laced with sadness. For a minute she was silent. Re-collecting herself, she said, "Where was I? Oh, yes! I was staying with Grace this weekend in her house in East Hampton. Naturally we spent most of the time talking about art. Well, I happened to have some slides of your work. . . ."

Gen smiled. She adored her godmother's unique attitude toward life. While other people carried snapshots of their kids in their wallets, Phoebe was never without her black leather case filled with her own precious "babies": slides and photos of her cherished art collection.

"Grace took one look at the slides from your Central Park series and nearly did a triple flip off the sofa. You see, Grace has been asked to find an artist for some philanthropic fund. She's a natural headhunter, what with her connections to the art world. But apparently it hasn't been easy. She's been scouring galleries and poring over dealers' collections for months without seeing anything that she really loved. Until your work." Phoebe laid a hand on Gen's forearm and squeezed it lightly. "Guess what? Grace asked me if you might be interested in creating a piece for the new wing of the Children's Hospital in Boston."

Gen stared at her godmother in disbelief. Just last month, she'd driven past the construction site. Her mother, who volunteered at the hospital, had raved so much about the new wing that Gen had agreed to drive into the city with her and take a look at the nearly completed building.

Her mom's boasts hadn't been idle. Gen had been awed by the dynamic glass structure. With its fluid and bold lines, it gave the impression of soaring—creating a painting that might complement such a space would be an incredible artistic challenge. Sudden goose bumps covered her arms.

"I can't believe they would consider me," she said softly.

"I can. But it *is* a wonderful opportunity. Listen to this, though. There's more," she said, smiling like a cat with a mouthful of cream. "I told Grace about how with Jiri leaving for Prague, you'd be losing your studio, and that it might take months before you found a suitable work space. Gen, Grace has offered you the use of Alexander's old studio."

"Me . . ." was all Gen managed.

"You'll enjoy living with Grace. She's delightful. Salty and energetic. I swear, she's got more energy than women half her age. We went for a two-hour walk on the beach, though 'march' might be a better term for it. You wouldn't believe the cramps in my calves by the time we got back to her house—I had to call up my massage therapist and schedule an appointment. Anyway, she's had a live-in companion, but Tilly's leaving next week to be with her daughter, who's confined to bed rest for the remainder of her pregnancy. So you'd be doing Grace a favor by staying with her. You wouldn't mind, darling, would you?"

Gen had gotten control of her breathing. "Mind? Are you kidding? I've been *dreading* having to look for a place," she confessed with a shaky laugh. "Especially since I knew I wouldn't find anything I could afford. And the cooperative studios are so hard to get into—the waiting lists stretch into eternity. Phoebe, you're magic, pure magic." Enthusiasm had Gen jumping from her chair, her feet doing a jig as she crossed the floor to hug her. "I feel positively sorry for Cinderella. All she got from her fairy godmother was some handsome prince. One flick of your wand, Phoebe, and I get the chance to make art *and* have a studio all to myself!"

"One thing at a time, darling," Phoebe murmured, returning her hug. "One thing at a time."

"No, Mother. I haven't seen Alex since Friday," Sydney replied, her tone worn flat from having answered essentially the same question for the past ten minutes. "No, he had some dinner engagements with clients. Why didn't I go, too?" she echoed, and a trace of desperation entered her voice as she said, "Perhaps because I wasn't wanted—No! No, of course not. Nothing's gone wrong between us. Yes, I'm sure I'll be seeing him soon. *Yes,* I'll call you. Good-bye, Mother." Slamming down the phone with a hard *clack,* she dropped her head into her hands.

"And how is Mommy dearest?" a voice asked.

Sydney started. Harry Byrne, her business partner, was standing in the doorway to the office they shared. Harry had flown to Boston at eight o'clock that morning for a meeting with the hospital's director of community relations. Raines and Byrne Consulting was helping the hospital put together a twenty-page bulletin for the new wing Alex Miller was donating. "Harry! I didn't expect you back so soon. Weren't you supposed to be having dinner with some old flame, Bitsy Something-or-other?"

Harry cocked his head and grinned at her. "Betsy *Stevens* is fine. Hasn't changed a bit, she's as cute as ever. We had a very pleasant lunch during which she made me promise to stay at her place the next time I was in Beantown. She was quite eager to renew our friendship." The devilish twinkle in his eyes was at total odds with his modest tone.

"Sounds a little desperate to me."

"Oh, no, not Betsy," he said, flashing a grin. Harry had the whitest teeth of anyone Sydney knew and a smile that women, young and old, found irresistible, Sydney included. "So what's Hilary on about now?" he asked, referring to Sydney's mother by her first name.

Sydney's mood, momentarily lightened by Harry's unexpected return, plummeted.

"Hey, Syd," he said, crossing the office swiftly. "What's the matter? What's happened?"

With an effort Sydney composed herself. She hadn't mentioned anything about Alex breaking up with her. It was too humiliating. And why talk about the breakup when she fully intended to get Alex back? "Nothing's happened. Everything's fine," she said, then looked out the window as if fascinated by the view of chimneys and cisterns atop asphalt and rubber-coated roofs.

Harry dropped to a crouch by her chair. He reached out and cupped her jaw, gently guiding her face back to his, forcing her to meet his green gaze. "Come on, Syd, you can fool anyone but me. We've shared this office for too many years. I left Boston and the very pretty Betsy Stevens because I sensed something was off with you. What gives, sweetheart? You and Miller have a lovers' spat?"

Sydney didn't know if it was Harry's casual endearment or the fact that he'd immediately guessed the source of her unhappiness, but her facade, such as it was, cracked. "He's dumped me, the bastard!"

Something flared in Harry's eyes, but Sydney, now that she'd blurted out the mortifying truth to her business partner, couldn't seem to stop the rest of it from rushing out, too, in a torrent of pained indignation. "Can you believe it? How could he do this? We complement each other in every way—our background, education, friends—everything. And he's dumping me!"

Rocking back on his heels, Harry stood and walked over to the window, where he perched his hip against the sill. With the afternoon sun coming in through the windows, his face was cast in shadows. His voice was equally somber. "I'm sorry, Sydney. I realize how that must hurt."

Sydney pressed her lips together to keep them from trembling. She hated the sympathy she heard in his voice. It made her want to bawl like a baby. She said nothing, fearing that was exactly what would happen. "But maybe," Harry continued as if he hadn't noticed she was about to flood their office, "Miller's finally realized that you're absolutely miserable with him."

"What?" she gasped. "What are you talking about? I'm not—"

"Cut the crap, Sydney. It's me you're talking to. Oh, I'll grant that you were damned pleased with yourself when the two of you first started seeing each other. But this past month or so? Come on. We both know it's not work and it's not the TLM account that's causing you to chomp down half a bottle of Rolaids for lunch. It's the stress of dreaming up the new thing that's going to keep Miller by your side."

"A woman always has to worry about that," she said sharply. "Otherwise—"

"Otherwise he'll walk out on you? Like your father did? Who's talking here, Syd, your mother or you? Maybe if you were with a guy who loved you, you wouldn't be obsessing about what you have to do to keep him. Don't you think it's time you found a guy *you* want instead of trying to please your mother?"

Sydney's temper flared. "I'm not with Alex to please Mother."

"Aren't you?" Harry fired back. "Then why does Hilary call you all the time, asking for a full account of where he's taken you, whom you've seen, whether he's bought you anything? Whose life is it you're living?"

"Mine. Mother has nothing to do with this," she

retorted, infuriated when Harry shook his head. "It's Alex's problem," she insisted. "Like a lot of men, he's just unwilling to commit, scared of taking the next step."

Harry laughed. "Miller's not scared of anything."

"You don't know him. Not like I do."

"Maybe not," he conceded with a careless shrug. "But I hardly believe that sleeping with him has given you any particular insight either, sweetheart. Especially if you can't see that if you go and do something as asinine as hitching yourself to Miller for the rest of your life, it'll be like living in Siberia. And Syd, you damned well hate the cold."

"Alex knows how to warm me up just fine, thank you," she purred. "Don't worry about me, Harry. This is only temporary. I'll get him back."

"Fine, whatever. Ruin your life. Just don't screw up the TLM account while you're at it," he warned as he walked over to his desk. "So what's on the agenda for this week?" he asked, picking up a stack of mail and sorting through it, discarding the topic of her love life like so much junk mail.

The feeling that she'd somehow disappointed Harry left Sydney oddly unsettled . . . and annoyed. What right did he have to criticize her, when for the past two years of their partnership she'd watched him go through a legion of women—all unsuitable? Irritated, Sydney straightened regally in her chair. "We have a meeting with a writer for *Architectural Digest* the day after tomorrow. I'm preparing an info packet for them now. The magazine would like to do a profile of the architect."

"And how about the artist TLM is looking to commission? Can we give them a name, some photographs?"

"No, Mrs. Miller hasn't found anyone she likes," she replied, frustration entering her voice. She'd suggested dozens of eminent artists. None had satisfied the old lady, who, in Sydney's opinion, gave a new meaning to the term "eccentric." It was ridiculous, really. Sydney couldn't understand why Alex indulged his aunt's every whim.

Harry's voice broke into her thoughts. "Hey, Syd, if you're free tonight, why don't we head over to Brooklyn? I found this great karaoke bar. . . ." He dangled the offer, an olive branch.

Was he remembering the last time they had gone out together? she wondered. Deciding to celebrate their landing the biggest and hottest PR account to date, the TLM Fund, Harry and she had gone barhopping. They'd ended up in a dive of Sydney's choosing, picked because the placard outside boasted the best karaoke in New York. High from the thrill of signing the contract, tingling from the memory of Alex Miller's cool, electric-blue gaze, and the certainty that he'd understood the unmistakable invitation in her own eyes, Sydney had taken to the small platform stage. There she'd belted out a sloppily enthusiastic, eyelash-batting, hip-swinging rendition of Elton John and Kiki Dee's 'Don't Go Breaking My Heart.'

The indulgent applause from the bar's crowd had been sufficient to keep her on the stage for several more tunes. Only after Madonna's "Borderline" did Harry lead her, flushed and laughing, out of the bar and into the wintry night, wrapping his arm about her waist and sharing the heat of his wiry body when she'd complained of the cold.

That night of belting out pop songs into the mike suddenly seemed eons ago. Ignoring the sharp pang of regret, Sydney reminded herself of what she really wanted—more than anything in the world: To be Mrs. Alex Miller. "I can't go out tonight," she told Harry, and her gaze slid away from his. "Alex might . . ."

When she looked back, Harry was already walking out the door "Right. I'm going home to shower and shave. Later, Sydney."

FIVE

Alex stepped out of the limousine on Broome Street and glanced up at the front window of the Alicia Kendall Gallery, where a sign hung from guy wires announcing the upcoming exhibit, "New Visions."

Though the gallery was officially closed until the opening later in the evening, Alex rapped his knuckles on the pane-glass door. The young woman sitting at the reception desk talking on the phone glanced over at him. She mouthed a few last words into the receiver before putting the phone down and hurrying over to unlock the door.

"Yes?" she inquired. "May I help you?"

"I'm Alex Miller."

"Oh, of course!" she said, stepping back to let him in. She held out her hand. "Hello, Mr. Miller. I'm Kyra Warburg, Alicia's assistant." Her smile warmed while she gave him the once-over.

Alex shook her hand, careful to keep his own smile polite. Kyra Warburg was very attractive, with straight, honey blond hair and almond-shaped eyes. But Alex had no desire to become entangled with another woman; the scratches left by Sydney had yet to fade completely. "I hope I'm not disturbing you," he said.

"No, not at all. This morning was a bit of a madhouse. We were rehanging a few pictures when the critic from the *Times* arrived. We had some other VIPs drop by too, but right now it's pretty much the calm before the storm. The opening's at six," she explained.

Alex glanced at his watch. It was just past three. "I promise I'll be out of your hair soon, then."

"Oh, please, take all the time you want," she protested, and a blush stole over her cheeks as she added, "I'd be happy to escort you through the exhibit."

Alex didn't plan to stay longer than necessary. He and his partners were taking the owner of an IT company the Miller Group had invested in to dinner at the Park Avenue Café. The company had just been the object of a friendly takeover, making the owner and the Miller Group both very much the richer.

"That's kind of you, but you must have last-minute details that need attending. If I have any questions. . . ."

"I'll be right here," she nodded. Plucking a stapled sheath of papers from a stack that rested beside a tall maroon-and-black glazed vase filled with forsythia, she offered it to him. "Here's our price list. If you have any questions at all, please don't hesitate—"

"Thank you, I won't." He tucked the price list under his arm, knowing, however, that it was doubtful he'd be consulting it.

He'd gotten good at this. Alex was able to cruise

through a gallery, take in the art on display, and reject it. Even with his aunt Grace making a preliminary selection, weeding out the shows and artists she knew would never suit, much of the artwork Alex had looked at over the past months fell into two basic categories—aesthetic babble and sensationalist dreck— art which none but art history PhDs and museum types could possibly care about.

Alex would be damned before he commissioned either sort.

He was donating the hospital wing as a memorial to Tom and Lisa, his deceased brother and sister-in-law. The art he envisioned for the space had to be about *life*. Messy, glorious, and all-too-precious life. He wouldn't settle for less. But from the looks of what was on the walls in these first two rooms, his latest foray into the New York art scene was doomed to be as fruitless as his earlier ones.

When Alex stepped into the third of the connecting rooms, however, a stirring of interest awakened inside him. For the first time, he felt as if indeed he was experiencing a new vision, as the exhibition boldly touted. Perhaps, just perhaps, this was it, what he'd been looking for. He stopped and gazed at the canvases aligned before him, vibrant fields of color bordered by bold, decisive lines. The paintings seemed ready to leap off the stark white walls. They pulsed with vibrant energy, with humor . . . with life.

There were six paintings, all by the same hand. Alex quickly saw that they were in fact a series of scenes depicting a city playground. Central Park, he guessed, though what the artist, Genevieve Monaghan (only by reading the typed label next to the painting could he decipher the scrawled "Monaghan" in the lower right hand corner of the canvas), had captured was universal. . . . A young girl jumping rope floated, suspended in midair, with her dark hair flying about her face, her arms rigid at her sides as her legs bent at the knees, free and clear of the jump rope's sweep. On either side of her stood two other girls, wielding the rope with intense concentration, their mouths open in midchant. Alex could almost hear their high-pitched voices.

He moved on to the next painting, which was as busy and riotous as the mob portrayed in it. Children, stripped down to underpants and padded diapers, raced on stubby legs through the arc of a sprinkler. Their rounded bellies shone pale and glistening in the afternoon sun. The artist, this Genevieve Monaghan, had caught it all—how the afternoon sun slanted, its rays penetrating the gushing spray of water, turning drops into prisms of light. And there, off to the side, the sinuous line of mothers and nannies seated on the row of wooden benches that encircled the playground. The women watched, some indulgently, others vacantly, their blank eyes and slumping shoulders testifying to the hot, endless summer day.

He liked how she'd captured the essence of this world through gestures and expressions: the bend of an elbow, the smile on a face. Her paintings showed a directness and candor as well as a refreshing sense of humor.

The next paintings were quieter scenes, away from the hustle and bustle of the jungle gym and sprinkler. Alex found himself smiling in recognition, remembering his nephew and niece, Jamie and Sophie, at this age. In the first painting, a toddler, no longer content to wait passively, reached with fingers splayed to grab a juice cup from an adult's hand. In another scene, the sweet, infinite trust of a child asleep, sprawled across his mother's lap, was brought to life. Alex marveled at the subtlety of Genevieve Monaghan's observations—the round swell of the mother's breast, which was the child's cushion; the mother's unconscious caress of her sleeping child, rubbing the small of its back as she chatted with her park bench neighbor.

Standing before the last two paintings, he noted that Genevieve Monaghan's keen eye had shifted once again. Iron gates marking the entrance to the playground framed these compositions. A long line of children snaked through them. On their faces Alex saw anticipation warring with impatience as they waited their turn to buy an ice cream from the Good Humor Man. Dollar bills peeked through grimy fists. Hands that would soon have a sugary glaze of melted ice cream coating them.

Alex felt a strange sense of regret when he came to the last painting in the series. Yet what Genevieve Monaghan had chosen to depict was a perfect ending, so wonderfully astute. It was a deceptively simple scene: the outraged fury of a toddler caught in the midst of a full-blown temper tantrum. Her back arched, her face distorted and bright red with tears streaming down it, and her mouth wide open to let loose what Alex knew must have been ear-splitting shrieks. The child's mother pushed the stroller, her own face set in grim lines, marking her frayed temper, her utter exhaustion. The people in the park parted like the Red Sea to make way for the shrieking child, and in their faces he saw smiles of compassion for both child and parent.

The day's outing at the park was over.

Alex turned, also ready to leave. He'd call Aunt Grace in the morning and have her contact this Genevieve Monaghan. But then, from the corner of his eye, he glimpsed a dark sea of colors floating in the next room. He pivoted so he faced the painting spanning the wall.

The haunting beauty of the work took his breath away.

His first impression was of a carefully controlled symphony of blacks and grays sweeping across the canvas. A second, closer look revealed the barest out-line of trees and a large, open expanse. Then he saw the woman—how he guessed that solitary figure was a woman he couldn't explain, simply knew it in his heart.

It wasn't easy to see her, shrouded as she was in the fog that rose from the ice-covered ground beneath her feet. He stepped closer still, hoping to discern more of her features. He couldn't, could only recognize the emotions locked inside her. Like the life imprisoned in this dark and icy landscape, they were growing, struggling to break free. There, under the sweep of soul-darkening gray, were flashes of new-born color: patches of pink, hints of green . . .

Change was in the air.

Something in the painting told Alex that the woman in it was uncertain, ambivalent, even scared. She seemed to understand that although the heavy shadows kept her from growing and changing, they also served as a kind of protection—like ice insulating tender shoots that uncovered might easily be crushed and destroyed.

Alex too understood about ice.

Hypnotized as he was by the dreamlike painting, he didn't know how much time had passed. He wanted to keep looking, to know this woman's secrets and see the colors inside her come to life.

He wanted. The strength of his desire was like a shock, jolting his system. Instinctively, Alex looked for the artist's signature. And there was the same bold scrawl he'd seen in the park series. Disbelief had him checking the label on the wall, and his breath rushed out in a low whistle of admiration. She'd entitled the painting *Day One.*

Late to her own opening, Gen could have kicked herself. Except that she was too busy hurrying up the steps of the gallery, threading her way past the crowd spilling out onto the stoop, clear plastic glasses of white wine in hand as they talked and people-watched. More people dressed in the requisite black on black filled the gallery.

Alicia must be thrilled, Gen thought. She couldn't even see Corey Dillon's paintings in this first room for the crush of bodies. Far more distressing, though, she couldn't see any of her family. Gen had assumed they would account for about 90 percent of the opening's guests—the running joke in the family was that the Monaghans en masse exceeded the population of most small towns.

She worked her way through the gallery rooms, smiling her excuses, when she inadvertently bumped a Prada handbag. The owner treated her to a frosty glare and returned to her conversation, her voice raised above the others. "Art's such a terrible investment these days. Besides, I haven't seen anything here that will match my interior. Let's go, Theo, we wouldn't want to lose our table at Cipriani's."

Unnerved by that snatch of conversation, Gen hurried on, thinking that she should have come in a T-shirt (black, of course) that read NOT YET READY FOR THE NEW YORK ART SCENE, except that she'd promised to wear one of Delia's designs and she couldn't let her sister down.

A cry of "Genevieve, darling! Where have you been?" had her smiling in relief. At last, a voice she recognized.

"Alicia," she said as she kissed the gallery owner's cheek. "I'm sorry I'm late. I was in the Hamptons, meeting a friend of Phoebe's. I thought I left in plenty of time but the traffic was—"

"That's lovely," Alicia replied, brushing aside Gen's excuse. "Come with me. I have something to show you that simply *cannot* wait." Then, taking Gen by the hand, she led her past the clusters of people who were drinking wine and nibbling on cheese twists. She stopped abruptly at the entrance to the next room. "Now, close your eyes until I tell you to open them."

"Alicia!" she protested laughingly.

"Humor me, darling. And by the way, you look wonderful, that dress brings out the russet in your hair and the green in your eyes. Now, will you please close those gorgeous eyes?"

Shaking her head, Gen did as requested. What had her family done now? she wondered. Had they managed to fly in Granny Jane from Portland? That would be something. Granny hadn't left the commune in decades.

Eyes closed, with Alicia's hand under her elbow guiding her, she walked hesitantly forward. The sounds in the gallery amplified now, she heard "Gen!" echo around her, the voices of her brothers and sisters, mother and father. Then there were shushing noises and muffled laughter. Her face split into a grin of embarrassed delight. Oh, Lord, what were they up to now?

"All right, you can look," Alicia instructed.

She was standing in front of *Day One*. More exactly, directly in front of the painting's label. Suddenly, the room around Gen shrank. Or maybe it was that the little red dot grew, blocking out everything else.

Sold.

She'd sold a painting . . . not just any painting, but *Day One*. Incredulous, Gen pressed a hand to her trembling lips.

"Congratulations, Genevieve." Beaming with pride and love, her father embraced her.

While Gen's family had failed to mobilize Granny Jane, all the other Monaghan kith and kin were present for the opening. There was her mother and father, as well as her eleven brothers and sisters, from Aidan, the eldest, to Tess, who was two years older than Gen. Then there were the wives and husbands, the babies, the aunts and uncles, the cousins, the boyfriends and girlfriends. . . . Gen felt like a well-loved rag doll, her cheeks bussed about a hundred times, her ribs slightly bruised from her brothers' crushing hugs.

Reaching Phoebe Hayes, who was chatting with Alicia, Gen offered her godmother a dazed smile. "Have you heard, Phoebe? I sold *Day One*."

"Isn't that what I told you would happen?" she asked before enveloping Gen in a fierce hug of her own. "I'm so happy for you. It's simply thrilling. Your first gallery sale. And snatched up before I could even open negotiations with Alicia." She rolled her eyes in mock outrage.

"Really?" Gen turned to the gallery owner. "It went that fast? Is the buyer still here? I'd like to thank—"

"The painting sold before the opening. A private collector," Alicia pronounced, looking supremely pleased with herself.

"So, I can't—"

Still smiling, Alicia shook her head. "Sorry. The client insisted on anonymity. Congratulations again, darling. Now I must circulate and drum up some more sales. Ciao." And she kissed the air near Gen's cheeks.

"Hey, kid, that's a heck of a funny look on your face considering you just unloaded a damned expensive piece of canvas," her brother Kyle teased as he came up and wrapped an arm around her shoulders.

Gen gave a breathless laugh. "I feel kind of funny. You know, weird," she admitted. "I didn't expect to sell *Day One*. I thought, perhaps, if I was extremely lucky, someone might be interested in one of the Park scenes. It's hard to explain. All my paintings have something of me in them, but this one," and she gestured toward the painting, "is far more personal. I guess I feel odd thinking that someone would want a painting that came from here." Her hand closed to a fist over her chest.

"That's exactly why someone would want the painting, Genevieve," her father said. "Because it comes from and speaks to the heart. Your mother and I were looking at the painting earlier with Phoebe. We're in complete agreement that it's your strongest piece yet. You're beginning to trust your wings. You'll be soaring soon."

Tears of happiness welled in her eyes. "Thanks, Dad. And thanks for coming. I can't tell you how much it means to me to have you all here."

"We wouldn't have missed it for the world. Now, tell me about this friend of Phoebe's."

"Mrs. Miller was great. The stories she tells. Do you know she and her husband actually met Matisse? Dad, you should see the studio. It's glorious. Banks of windows and *space*. It's a dream come true."

"Definitely surreal, imagining our little Genevieve

loose in the Hamptons." Kyle grinned and shook his head.

Gen shot her brother her prissiest look. "I'll leave the carousing to you and Nolan," she told him loftily. "I'm going to be much too busy painting."

"Hello, Aunt Grace? It's Alex."

"Oh, hello, dear. Did you get to the galleries?"

Alex smiled. Grace Miller, the Duchess of East Hampton, wasn't one to beat around the bush. "Yes, I did," he replied.

"And?"

Alex leaned back in his office chair. On his right were bookshelves, filled from ceiling to floor with books on economics, geopolitics, manufacturing, and an armful of biographies. He'd had to push the books deep into the shelves in order to make room for the framed pictures. There were crayon and marker renderings of ungainly, hairy canines, drawn by Sophie and Jamie, faithful recordings of their puppies' day-to-day antics. Nestled among them were photographs. Alex's gaze strayed to a silver diptych frame: On the left were Tom and Lisa on their wedding day. The picture opposite showed them cradling their newborn twins, joy illuminating their faces. He'd seen that kind of emotion in Genevieve Monaghan's work. "There was one artist who stood out."

"Oh? Which one was that?"

Alex's mouth quirked at his aunt's carefully neutral tone. "Hmm, let me see if I can remember the name. . . ."

"Alex," she said warningly.

"Monaghan. That's it, Genevieve Monaghan."

"Really." There was a slight pause. "Well, I always knew you had a keen eye, Alex. That sort of thing is in the blood, and you do take after Alexander in so many ways."

"Thank you, Aunt Grace. But as I know how much you love dealing with artists, I'll leave it to you to contact Ms. Monaghan."

"You didn't meet the dear girl yesterday, at the opening?" she interrupted.

He frowned, baffled by his aunt's words. What was with the "dear girl" thing? "No, I had a business dinner last night, so I shamelessly used my illustrious connections and dropped your name with the gallery owner. She agreed to let me view the show beforehand."

"I see." His aunt's reply was accompanied by the faintest of sighs. "Well then, you can meet her when you come out next weekend."

"She has a show in the Hamptons too?"

"What was that? Oh, no, from what I understand, yesterday was her first time out here. No, what I meant was that you could meet Genevieve *here,* at the house. The poor thing is in a terrible fix. She's lost her studio space. As I knew you'd choose her for the commission, I've decided to step in and help a promising young artist. I've invited Genevieve to come and stay with me."

"You've what?" he asked sharply.

"She can use Alexander's studio—it's been going to wrack and ruin, filled with cobwebs and whatnot.

Such a waste. She and I spent over an hour yesterday sweeping and clearing out old boxes. Already it looks more like it did when Alexander was alive. I can't wait to see art being made again under my own roof. Genevieve is ridiculously grateful. She's a charming young lady . . ."

Grace Miller continued talking. Alex's jaw was clamped too tight to interrupt. He could imagine only too easily how "charming" a needy, unprincipled artist could be to a susceptible old woman. "Aunt Grace," he managed at last, "I don't think this is a wise move. What do you know about this person?"

"I know everything I need to," she replied, her voice hinting at a stubborn streak that Alex knew ran a mile wide. "Now, don't try to talk me out of this, Alex. My mind's made up. Besides, I'm sure you'll find her equally charming. . . ."

A few minutes later, his aunt hung up with a cheery, "Good-bye, dear. See you next weekend." No sooner had the *click* of the telephone line disconnecting sounded, than he punched in Sam Brody's direct line.

"Brody."

"Sam, it's Alex."

"Hey, Alex, what's up? We still on for this week?"

"Absolutely. Listen, Sam, I was wondering whether I could ask a favor."

"Ask away."

"I'd like you to run a background check on someone."

"Sure. Prospective employee?"

"No," Alex replied, unconsciously reaching back to knead the knots in his neck muscles. "Aunt Grace has decided to take in a boarder. Her housekeeper, Tilly, won't be around and—"

"And you're concerned."

"Yeah." Alex gave a heavy sigh of frustration. "You know how my aunt is when it comes to taking in strays and championing causes. But the second I questioned the wisdom of opening her home to a virtual stranger, she got all snippy."

"The Duchess does like having her way. Listen, I'll be glad to do a check. I wouldn't want her getting hurt or taken advantage of. Have you got this person's name?"

"Yes. Genevieve Monaghan. Hometown Boston. She's an artist. We're offering her the commission for the hospital wing."

"She's that good?"

"Yes. But that's beside the point."

"Right. This Monaghan could be an even better con artist than she is a painter," Sam finished for him. "And Mrs. Miller would be a real easy mark. I'll have a report for you ASAP."

"Thanks, Sam. I owe you."

"No way. I love the Duchess too."

Alex replaced the phone in its cradle, feeling somewhat more in control of what had all the makings of a potentially disastrous situation. Nonetheless, he typed a series of numbers into his computer, the combination that would unlock the specially designed drawer in his desk for his private papers and records. When the lock released, Alex drew out the topmost file and opened it.

He stared at the white sheet of stationery, a bill of sale from the Alicia Kendall Gallery for the painting *Day One,* by Genevieve Monaghan. Eyes fixed on the receipt, he grabbed the telephone receiver once again.

Sam would run a complete background check, but Alex wanted to see for himself who this Genevieve Monaghan was. Up close and personal. Very personal.

The first mango of the season. The day had grown warm enough for Gen to appreciate the fruit's succulent flesh. Eyes closed, she imagined balmy ocean breezes as the fruit slowly dissolved in her mouth. The mango was a present to herself, part reward for her first sale, part consolation because her family had already left town. The loft seemed so empty with only Murphy for company.

She took another bite, her teeth closing over then tearing at the orange-gold sweetness as she angled her body so that the sticky juice landed harmlessly in the kitchen sink's scratched basin.

At the ring of the phone her eyes opened, but the deliciously messy mango won out. If it was important, whoever was calling would leave a message.

A man's voice reached her. "Ms. Monaghan, this is Alex Miller. I'd like to arrange a meeting with you. Please call me at the following number as soon as you receive this." The line went dead.

Ahh, so this was the favored nephew, Gen thought, taking another bite. The one his aunt thought hung the moon. At one point during the lunch she'd shared with Mrs. Miller, the old lady had laid her salad fork to rest on her plate of baby field greens and said, "I'm sure my nephew Alex will be contacting you shortly, Genevieve. He's the director of the fund that's offering the commission."

"Oh. So you won't be making the final decision in the commission?" Gen's lunch hiccupped unpleasantly in her stomach.

"Oh, I've no doubt he'll offer you the commission. Alex has excellent taste. Truly it's just pro forma at this point," she said, taking a sip of her white wine. "Still, it's important to observe the niceties, don't you think? And he is the TLM Fund's director, after all."

Gen had summoned an answering smile. "Uh, what does your nephew do, Mrs. Miller?"

"He makes money." The statement was accompanied by a vague flourish of her long, veined hand. "I'm not quite sure about the specifics," she admitted wryly. "All I know is he's very good at it."

"I'm sure I'll be delighted to meet him," Gen replied, pleased with how convincing she sounded. She couldn't imagine anything duller than someone who made money. Unless it was the performance artist who drew near-perfect imitations of dollar bills, then set out to barter them for goods. *That* was interesting.

So now as Mrs. Miller had predicted, the nephew was calling her. No, *summoning* her was more like it.

Gen sighed, resigned to following the prescribed rules of the art game. It was time to go and sell herself. That was how Gen viewed the task of promoting her work. She wanted to create, not peddle her art—her heart and soul—and she hated having to wow and impress potential collectors by opening her portfolio and then watching their faces as they examined her work. It was a most painful form of self-exposure, ending only when judgment was passed on her art.

And listening to the cool, clipped voice on her answering machine, Gen knew at once that Alex Miller was not a man easily impressed.

SIX

The address of Alex Miller's office was in midtown, which ruled out driving her car. It would take Gen a century to find a parking place, and the cost of a public garage would dip her checking account into a negative balance. Besides, this morning she'd lucked into a plum spot for the rusted-out Yugo, steps from the loft; Gen had adopted enough New York habits to understand she'd be a fool to give it up. And taxis were as prohibitive as parking garages. So that left the subway.

Unfortunately Gen missed the express train to Forty-second Street, and on Fourteenth Street a screaming match broke out between a gang of schoolkids who were blocking the subway car doors and the conductor, who was trying to close them. The shouting lasted forever. By which point everyone else in the crowded cars had joined in the fracas, a primer in multilingual cursing.

Gen had given up checking her watch by the time she climbed the stairs leading out of the Fifty-first Street station and into the hustle and bustle of Lexington Avenue. She caught the scent of sugar-roasted peanuts, pretzels, and hot dogs mixed with heavy blasts of bus exhaust. Heading west, she passed a street vendor selling Kate Spade and Prada knockoffs, and grinned as she spotted a bag identical to the one she'd bumped into at the gallery the previous night.

At Park Avenue her pace unconsciously slowed. Neck craned, she gazed up at the towering steel and glass buildings, noting how the sunlight blazed reddish-bronze against the endless sheets of glass.

The architecture of money and power.

Not her territory, but definitely the nephew's, as Gen had come to think of Alex Miller. She didn't know why, but for some reason she'd developed a vague animosity toward the owner of the cool voice on her answering machine. Probably because like the buildings all around her, it was designed to intimidate. Gen didn't respond well to people bossing her around, the result of having eleven older brothers and sisters, no doubt.

Passing men in business suits, Gen mentally sketched a composite portrait of Alex Miller. He'd have graying hair and carry a slight paunch from too many business lunches, she decided happily. Oh, and his face would already be sinking into fleshy jowls.

Alex Miller's office building was as imposing as the others she'd walked past. Constructed of black steel and glass, its front doors were large enough to roll a tank through. Gen checked in with the security guard at the desk, who asked to see her driver's license. The guard picked up the phone. "A Genevieve Monaghan here to see Mr. Miller," he said into the mouthpiece.

Hanging up, he motioned Gen to stand in front of a compact digital camera.

Seconds later he handed her a small photo printed on an adhesive label. Gen gave it a passing glance before sticking it over her left breast. Yup, she sighed inwardly. She looked like one giant freckle.

She stepped into an elevator equipped with a TV. An anchor for CNBC kept her company on the ride to the thirtieth floor, helpfully recapping the rise and fall of the NASDAQ. Gen tried to tune him out. After the chaos of the street, the interior of the elevator felt like a high-tech, stereophonic tomb. She longed to be back in the colorful confusion of the street. She didn't want to be here, meeting some stuffed shirt; wouldn't be here, except that she wanted to be as generous as Grace Miller had been with her, which pretty much ruled out insulting or ignoring Mrs. Miller's nephew.

Second door on the left, the guard had told her.

Plain, bold lettering marked the door. THE MILLER GROUP. Gen took a breath, plastered a smile on her face, and pressed the button. The door opened.

And Gen's jaw went slack as she stared stupidly into one of the most beautiful faces she'd ever seen outside of a museum. The man was gorgeous. All sculpted planes and perfect proportions, he rivaled Apollo, surpassed him with eyes the color of blue lightning, thrilling and dangerous. Her fingers instinctively curled as though holding a drawing pencil. Could she even capture such masculine perfection, do it justice? A wild thought entered her head: Thanks to her recent sale of *Day One,* she would have some serious money coming her way. Maybe she could ask him to model for her. The thought made her grin.

"Ms. Monaghan? I'm Alex Miller."

"Oh, damn. I was sure you'd look like a toad." She'd been certain, too, that he'd be middle-aged, but Alex Miller looked like he was only a few years older than herself.

Alex's brows shot upward and he laughed. This was certainly a novel greeting, he thought. He'd come to the door to meet this Genevieve Monaghan personally, hoping to catch her off guard. Yet instead it was he who'd been taken off guard and charmed in spite of himself. The woman with the wide, impish grin standing before him was clearly out of the ordinary . . . unusual and prone to the unexpected, he decided.

She was still staring.

Alex was used to stares. Women stared because of the way he looked. Women *and* men stared once they knew who he was—*that* Alex Miller, the one who'd made a pile of money. Being ogled no longer made much of an impression.

But Alex wasn't accustomed to staring back. Yet he realized he was doing exactly that, and quite intently, too, as he tried to match Genevieve Monaghan with the shrouded figure in *Day One*. Difficult when the woman standing before him looked far too young to have made such an extraordinary and powerful painting, let alone be the figure emerging from that dark, wintry landscape.

His gaze lingered. Her face was one of subtle colors, from the liberal sprinkling of freckles scattered across the bridge of her nose to the rise of her cheek-bones. Her lips were a soft, dusky pink. Bare of lipstick, they were nonetheless temptingly inviting. But it was her eyes that truly captivated him: they seemed to change from second to second, a shifting of blue, green, and brown. Alex was reminded of a poster that had hung over the foot of his bed throughout high school, the one constant in a passing parade of rock stars and Yankees players. He'd spent hours gazing at that aerial shot of the world, lost in the greenish browns of continents, the blue of oceans wide and deep. The world was there, in Genevieve Monaghan's eyes. For a moment everything else receded, except for his desire to spend the next few hours lost in their loveliness.

The ringing sound of the elevator being summoned, followed by the metallic slide of the doors shutting, had Alex abruptly remembering where he was. He cleared his throat and stepped back. "Come in, won't you?"

"Thanks."

"You had no trouble finding the address?"

"No. I'm really sorry to be late. There was a problem on the subway—" She broke off with a regretful shake of her head. "Actually, to tell you the truth, I seem to be constitutionally incapable of being on time. My mother claims she holds the grand record. I kept *her* waiting for ten days."

Biting back a smile, he gave a light shrug. "I had some reports to review anyway." Sam's report on the Monaghan family, to be precise. It had made for absolutely fascinating reading.

The time had flown by.

Alex stepped back, and Genevieve Monaghan brushed past in a baggy forest green sweater that fell over a straight ankle-length black skirt, and what appeared to be Converse high-tops, the faded red canvas coated with a spiderweb of paint splatterings. Her brown hair was in a topknot held in place by two lacquered chopsticks. A bulky red backpack, slung over her right shoulder, completed the outfit. She was tall, Alex thought appraisingly, and slender. He found himself wondering what her legs looked like.

Alex's secretary, seated behind her desk, was staring with open curiosity.

"Would you like some coffee, Ms. Monaghan?" he asked.

"It's Gen, and yes, thanks, I'd love some. Black, no sugar."

"Cathy, would you please bring us two coffees?" he asked his secretary.

"Certainly."

"Thank you," he said. Extending his arm toward a door at the end of a short corridor, he gestured for Gen to proceed.

Gen walked in front of him, feeling oddly unnerved. She told herself it must be the sleek sophistication of the surroundings. The hall's carpeting was so thick, she couldn't even hear her footsteps. Its walls were covered in what looked very much like a dove-gray ultrasuede. She willed herself not to reach out and run her fingers along it, and test its softness.

But no matter how polished the interior of Alex Miller's firm, she knew her nervousness was caused by the man himself. An extraordinarily handsome man who was walking silently behind her. When his arm reached around to open the door to his office and brushed her own lightly, Gen's heart skipped a beat.

Just as his office door swung open, another door off to the right opened, too, and a man thrust his head through the gap. "Alex," he said, and Gen caught the urgency in the man's voice, "I've got Bill Reynolds on the line. He has some questions. Would you mind?"

"No, I'll be right there, Robert," Alex replied. He turned to Gen with an apologetic smile. "This shouldn't take long."

"That's okay, I don't mind," she hastily reassured him. In truth, she was relieved to be given a chance to regroup. She wasn't used to being this aware of a man. Slipping her backpack from her shoulder, she added, "It'll be good for me to wait. A taste of my own medicine."

In response, the corner of Alex Miller's mouth lifted in a half smile that made his face, if possible, even more handsome—and made Gen's pulse go a little haywire. "Then if you'll excuse me," he murmured before leaving Gen alone in his office with the door slightly ajar.

Wow, she thought dazedly. Although she realized that such good looks were merely the result of a lucky scramble of genes, it was awfully hard not to be dazzled by such masculine beauty. Drawing a calming breath, she looked about her, curious.

The spacious office suited him, she decided. Understated and elegant, the furniture he'd chosen had the clean contours of the best in Italian design. A wide bank of windows faced eastward, and from where Gen stood she could see barges and motorboats chugging up and down the East River. To the north and south, she made out the crisscrossed spans of the bridges that connected Manhattan to the outer boroughs. Cars were moving along them at a rush-hour crawl. But it was the framed pictures crowding the bookshelves that had Gen's feet moving for a closer inspection.

In contrast to the orderliness of the rest of his office, Alex Miller's bookshelves were filled chock-a-block with drawings and photographs. This must be his family, she said to herself. The two blond cherubs, a young boy and girl, had to be Alex's children. Their features were painted from the same palette . . . and with a master's hand.

A beautiful woman with deep blue eyes and wildly curling hair smiled at Gen from a frame of burled wood. "And this must be his wife," she murmured softly, and was brought up short by the sharp stab of regret.

Get real, Monaghan, she admonished herself with a laugh. This man's in a whole different league from you.

Determined not to think about Alex Miller's private life, Gen resolutely moved away from the photograph of the woman and fixed her attention on the drawings lining the shelves instead. She examined them, her grin growing, loving their spontaneity, the joy and energy evident in each squiggle, slash, and cyclone whirl that made up the dog, the tree, the huge yellow sun—

"I'm afraid I'm running out of room."

Gen spun around. The door had opened—even the hinges were silent in this place. Alex Miller stood inside the threshold, regarding her with an inscrutable look on his face.

She felt embarrassment heat her cheeks. How long had he been watching her? She didn't want him to think she'd been prying, poking about his personal belongings. Her words came out in a hurried rush: "These drawings are fabulous. That's obviously an adored dog. Your children are beautiful, too," she added awkwardly, realizing anyone else would have mentioned the children first.

"Thanks. Jamie and Sophie definitely love to express themselves," he said and his voice was filled with tender amusement. He grabbed hold of the edge of the door and pushed it so that it swung shut with a quiet click. "And that's two dogs," he continued with a nod at the drawings as he walked toward her. "Radar and Annabelle. My present to the kids. Sophie and Jamie are twins, so I felt compelled to buy two puppies. Unfortunately, I can't take credit for how beautiful they are—" Alex was about to say more when a knock sounded.

Frowning at this latest interruption he turned around and went back to open it.

A woman's eager voice floated into the room. "Alex, darling! I decided to drop by on the way to a meeting with the writer for the *Digest*. I know, I know, I should have called, but I missed you so." And a tall, chicly dressed brunette swept into the office.

Then her gaze lit on Gen. "Oh!" she said, and her art-fully shadowed eyes widened in surprise.

Alex's secretary entered on the woman's heels, coffee cups in hand. Gen thought she mouthed "Sorry" to him but couldn't be sure.

Silence settled over the room. Just as it was growing awkward, Alex spoke, his voice bland as he made the introductions. "Sydney, this is Genevieve Monaghan, an artist whose work my aunt admires very much. Aunt Grace is hoping Ms. Monaghan will paint a piece for the Children's Hospital." To Gen he said, "Sydney Raines does public relations for the Miller Group as well as the TLM Fund."

Sydney Raines's handshake was like her smile: cool and perfunctory. Not that Gen was feeling overly friendly either. She found it off-putting that Sydney hadn't been in the room for thirty seconds and already she was firing off an unmistakable warning from her dark eyes: *He's mine.*

As if Gen had the slightest interest in an affair with a married man. It made her queasy even to contemplate causing pain to those laughing children in the photographs. She hadn't thought that Alex Miller would be the type of man who'd cheat on his wife.

"So Mrs. Miller has approached you about doing a piece for the hospital?" Sydney asked with the slightest trace of hostility in her voice.

"Yes, we've talked about it." Gen turned to Alex Miller. "I can see you're busy now. Perhaps another time."

"I was hoping you could show me some examples of your work," Alex said and from the cool challenge in his eyes, Gen realized he'd guessed how much she wanted to leave. "Especially as my aunt is convinced you're the artist we've been searching for. Of course, if you're not interested in the commission, I'm confident we can find someone else. . . ." Letting the sentence trail off, he smiled and gave a careless shrug of his broad shoulders.

Gen stilled. Was she going to jeopardize a wonderful opportunity just because she suspected Alex Miller of indulging in an extramarital affair? Of course not. What did she care about him? She wanted this commission because it would be an incredible opportunity to share her art with the public in a meaningful way. Instead of hefting the bag onto her shoulder, she bent down and pulled out a thick portfolio. She carried it to his desk, and unzipping the leather case, she spread it open.

"These color transparencies are of some of my recent work." Without sparing a second glance at either Alex or Sydney, she moved over to the windows and pretended to survey the scene below.

The next fifteen minutes passed with only the faint slap of vinyl sheets marking the time as Sydney and Alex studied Gen's portfolio.

At last Alex spoke. "My aunt is right. Your work is strong and evocative, perfect for the hospital wing." His words had the quiet ring of sincerity.

Gen turned away from the window to find his intense blue eyes fixed on her. Flushing slightly, she told herself that it was the knowledge that she was going to get the commission which was making her feel so warm and breathless. "Yes, I agree. Your work is very strong," Sydney offered.

"Thank you," she replied, unable to think of what else to say in the face of their praise.

Alex gestured toward a pair of chairs and a small sofa arranged around a kidney-shaped coffee table in the far corner of the office. "Won't you sit down?" he asked.

Gen chose one of the chairs, while Sydney and Alex sat on the sofa opposite her. Though Alex had initially lowered his lean frame onto the opposite end of the sofa, somehow Sydney kept shifting, inch by inch, until her long legs were almost brushing Alex's. A little closer and she'd be in his lap.

Seated across from them Gen could see why Alex Miller would be attracted to a woman like Sydney Raines. She was stunning and expensive-looking, with that high-end polish that came from weekly trips to the salon, monthly visits to the spa. Everything about her spoke of class and sophistication. Gen realized that Sydney was taking the opportunity to scrutinize her just as closely, but doubted that she'd draw the same conclusions. . . . Not if she was to judge by the small, satisfied smile she gave Gen before saying, "As I act as the liaison between the TLM Fund and the Children's Hospital, it would be helpful if I could have some background information to give to the hospital and to put into the press packet we're compiling." Sydney glanced over at Alex. "Would it be all right with you if I asked Ms. Monaghan a few questions?" Her voice had changed when she addressed him, taking on a husky, intimate note, as if they were alone in the room.

"I believe the decision's up to Ms. Monaghan," Alex said, inclining his head toward Gen. His blue eyes glittered with an unmistakable spark of challenge. She couldn't shake the feeling that he was toying with her somehow, like a cat with a mouse.

"No, I don't mind answering some questions," Gen forced herself to reply. Though she did. She prized her privacy. But Alex had said Sydney was in charge of the publicity for the TLM Fund, in which case she had a legitimate need for whatever information Gen provided. Somehow, though, Gen doubted her motives or interest were purely professional.

She waited while Sydney reached over and opened the slim attaché case that rested against the front of the sofa, and then pulled out a leather journal along with a silver fountain pen.

Pen poised, Sydney smiled. "Why don't we start with the basics? Would you mind telling me where you went to school?"

"In Boston, my hometown. I have a BFA from Boston College."

"Oh, what a coincidence. Alex and I went to school near there." From Sydney's tone, Gen instantly guessed what was coming next and resisted the urge to yawn loudly when Sydney supplied the name "Harvard."

"How nice for you both," she murmured under her breath, surprised at the quick flash of white when Alex grinned.

Sydney, jotting notes on gilt-edged paper, didn't notice the exchange between them. "So you grew up in Boston?" she asked. "Is your family still there?"

"Actually I grew up just outside of Boston. My mother and father live in Somerville. They still have the same house I grew up in. As for the rest of my family, my eleven brothers and sisters all live within a couple hours' drive. I've pretty much bucked the trend, coming to New York. . . ."

Gen didn't bother to continue.

Sydney wasn't listening. No doubt stuck on "eleven brothers and sisters," she stared, slack-jawed, as if Gen had just confessed to having an extra head hidden under her sweater. "How very, uh, *tiring* for your mother," she murmured.

"Oh, no," Gen contradicted cheerfully. "I'm sure Mom would have gone on having babies. She loves them. But our house only had four bedrooms. Things were getting a mite crowded by the time I came along. Do you need any information about my brothers and sisters, too?"

"No, no, that won't be necessary." Sydney paused. "Not unless they're famous somehow."

"Sorry." Gen shook her head mournfully. "Can't help you there. But none of us has ended up in the clink, so that's a relief. We are a little worried about Tessie, though. I guess she's what you'd call the black sheep of the family. Mom and Dad are good about hiding their concern. . . ." Lowering her gaze to her lap, Gen's voice became a fretful whisper. "We're worried it might be too late to save her. She's announced she wants to become an investment banker."

Alex's bark of laughter had Gen's chin snapping

up. Nonplussed, she stared at him, at the amusement shaking his shoulders. She'd been absolutely certain he would be wearing the same affronted expression as Sydney.

Sydney was staring at him, too, her lips pressed into a flat line, clearly displeased with Alex's reaction. "I guess that will do for now," she said coolly. "I can always contact you if I need more information. Oh, wait," she added, as if she'd suddenly remembered something. "I did have something I wanted to ask. When I was looking at the labels in your portfolio I noticed your paintings aren't very large. Given the dimensions of the new wing's atrium, the painting will have to be on a far more monumental scale."

"That's a good point," Gen said, reluctantly impressed. Sydney Raines wasn't stupid, she realized. Far from it. Indeed, she seemed extremely good at her job, and sharp enough that she'd caught an essential detail. "I do have a larger work that's currently on display at the Alicia Kendall Gallery in SoHo, but the transparencies haven't come back from the lab yet. *Day One* is eight by ten feet."

Listening to their exchange, Alex knew he could have interrupted and vouched for the visual impact of that particular piece, but he deliberately chose to remain silent. He didn't want Gen to suspect that it was he who'd purchased *Day One*. He didn't want her to know that he'd been so moved by her painting that he'd been compelled to buy it. That even as he'd written the check out to the gallery, he was already envisioning precisely where it would hang in his living room. In any case, experience had taught him that one learned more by listening than by talking. And he very much wanted to learn all he could about Gen Monaghan.

"The hospital piece will probably need to be even bigger than that," Sydney said, a hint of challenge in her voice.

Gen shrugged, unconcerned. "I assumed as much. But I've paced off the length of Mrs. Miller's studio. Its walls are more than long enough to accommodate either a large single work or a series of panels. Once I've hashed out the composition, I'll have a better idea what format I want to use."

"What?" Sydney said, her voice sharp with surprise. "She'll be using your aunt's studio?"

"Actually my uncle's. It appears Aunt Grace has invited Ms. Monaghan to live at the house and use the studio while she works on the commission."

"Do you mean to say she'll be living in Georgica *and* have free use of your uncle's studio? Doesn't this rather exceed the normal boundaries of charity, Alex?"

Gen's temper flared, annoyed at being talked about in the third person—something her parents had taught her was the height of rudeness—and insulted at being categorized as some sort of charity case, an undeserving one at that. "Not that it's either of your business, but nobody's *giving* me anything. I've already talked to Mrs. Miller about staying with her and have told her I'll be happy to work in exchange for the use of the studio space. I'm neither sponging nor taking charity."

Sydney's dark eyes narrowed on her. "And what sort

of work qualifications do you have?" she demanded, as if she had a right to ask. Upon hearing that Gen had been invited to live at Mrs. Miller's, her hostility had returned in full force.

Gen wasn't particularly interested in analyzing the reasons behind Sydney's animosity. She didn't care what Sydney thought of her. The only thing Gen wanted was to head back downtown and pack her belongings. Then afterward, she'd take Murphy out for a generous evening walk and start to bid her good-byes to the neighborhood as Murphy sniffed and peed along his merry way.

Still, Sydney's rudeness rankled. So with a tight smile Gen said, "Gosh, I'm sorry. I forgot to bring my résumé. But let's see. I've worked as a chambermaid, stagehand, short order cook, bartender, waitress, and auto mechanic. Which means I can clean, cook, hammer together a stage set, and do a lube job in twenty minutes flat. . . . Hmm, what else?" She pretended to think for a second. "Oh, yeah, I can also draw, paint, and sculpt. And I can weld like nobody's business. So I'm pretty confident I can handle whatever light housekeeping, errand running, and cooking Mrs. Miller needs while the paint dries on my canvases." For a second her gaze clashed with Sydney's.

Sydney turned to Alex. "Alex, this is utterly absurd. How can you allow—" But she didn't get a chance to finish her sentence.

"I think you've gotten all the background information you require, Sydney," Alex said smoothly. "I wouldn't want you to miss your meeting with the writer from *Architectural Digest*. Call me when it's over and let me know how everything went." He stood and Sydney, looking distinctly put out, rose too. Gen seized the opportunity to gather up her portfolio, shoving it into her backpack.

"If you'd stay a minute longer, Ms. Monaghan, I'd like to speak with you about my aunt."

Oh, brother, thought Gen, there goes that commanding tone again. Alex Miller speaks and the world obeys. Well, he was unfortunately doomed to disappointment. No way was she hanging around here. Shouldering her bag, she turned around just in time to see Sydney wrap her arms around Alex's neck and kiss him full on the lips. Unable to avert her gaze, Gen stood, a captive, unwilling audience.

The kiss would have continued, she knew, had Alex not pulled Sydney's arms down and away, and then stepped back out of reach. "Good-bye, Sydney," he said.

Sydney stared at him, her face a mask from a Greek tragedy. Then pivoting on her high heels, she said to Gen, "We'll need the painting very soon. I hope you can work quickly." The sound of her exit was punctuated by the thud of the solid wood door hitting its frame.

"I apologize for that."

"Apologize?" Gen asked, her voice cool with dislike. Tilting her head, she regarded him with a critical eye. Was the flush that colored his cheekbones from embarrassment, arousal, or anger? She found it mildly fascinating that she couldn't tell which it was. The man was obviously a master at hiding his thoughts and feelings from others. Abruptly recalling the photographs of his lovely wife and children, Gen decided it was far more likely that Alex Miller had no feelings for anyone other than himself.

"Sydney," he replied, a distinct coolness entering his own voice. "She's a bit high-strung and sometimes has a tendency to go overboard. By the way, I'm not married." A mocking smile curved his lips as he watched her struggle and fail to hide her surprise. "The woman in the picture there? My sister, Cassie. The drawings were made by my niece and nephew—*her* kids, not mine."

At his words, a thought slipped slyly into Gen's head, like a dangerous temptation. *Alex Miller is free, unattached.*

But of course that wasn't true. Sydney Raines couldn't have been more obvious in demonstrating her prior claim. So what he'd just told her meant nothing. Besides, Gen realized her first instincts about him had been right on the mark: Alex Miller was most *definitely* out of her league. She shrugged lightly. "Well, Sydney seems very capable at what she does."

Alex didn't miss the double entendre. He'd learned a great deal about Gen Monaghan in these forty minutes. He knew that she was clever and possessed a rich if offbeat sense of humor. He knew, too, that those beautiful eyes of hers were far too perceptive. Although she'd have had to have been blind to miss Sydney's theatrics.

He was still furious about the kiss, it being exactly the sort of unprofessionalism he'd been worried about. But it had been impossible to tell Sydney off with Gen right there. If he'd left with Sydney, both women would have assumed that he only wanted to go out and neck in private. After witnessing a kiss like that, Gen obviously assumed that he and Sydney were involved. The knowledge needled Alex more than he cared to admit. Why? asked a voice inside his head. Is it because you want to see whether you can get Genevieve Monaghan's eyes to change from cool and indifferent to the way they were when she first saw you—sparkling with that tantalizing hint of feminine interest? But that was a question he refused to answer.

Instead he said, "Yes, Sydney's quite capable. Still, you held your own against her quite nicely. I liked the creative touch you used in describing your family. It was especially intriguing to note which details you *omitted,* such as the fact that your father is an emeritus professor at Boston College. Or that your brother Nolan is a distinguished neuroscientist, and that your sister Alana, the architect, worked on one of the plans submitted for the World Trade Center Memorial. . . . Actually, every one of your eleven brothers and sisters is pretty damned brilliant."

"Yes, they are. But our parents raised us to make our way in the world without riding on others' coattails. Besides which, what Nolan, Alana, or any of my siblings has accomplished has nothing to do with my painting." Her brows drew together. "How is it you know so much about them anyway?" she asked sharply.

Alex acted as if he hadn't heard her question. "Of

course," he continued, "you also neglected to mention a few things about yourself. For instance, you're the only Monaghan to boast a criminal record. What was it again? Willful destruction of private property?"

"That wall in South Boston was soul-destroying." The words were out of her mouth before she could call them back.

"Unfortunately the judge didn't agree."

"The judge was a pompous, Beacon Hill snob who had never set a privileged foot near a low-income project in his entire life," she burst out. "I was trying to bring beauty and color to the neighborhood. Besides, I was only nineteen."

"Old enough to be tried as an adult," he replied coolly.

Her eyes narrowed angrily. "How do you know all this about me, about my family?" she demanded through clenched teeth.

His smile was hard. "I had a background check run on you. You don't think I would let you live at my aunt's otherwise?"

Gen looked around. Spotting her coffee cup on the table, she snatched it up and drained it. "The bathroom?" she asked.

"Excuse me?"

"I'll need to use the bathroom." She waved the empty cup at him. "I expect you'll be wanting a urine sample."

His expression turned glacial. "Don't be ridiculous—"

Gen ignored him as she replaced the cup on the tabletop. Stepping toward him, she shoved the loose sleeves of her sweater up above her elbows. Long and slender, the insides of her arms were dotted with tiny freckles. She peered at them, searching. "Sorry. It's awfully hard to see the needle tracks."

His angry gaze connected with hers. They stared at each other in tense silence. "You don't understand," he ground out.

She understood only too well—that Alex Miller *had* been toying with her. He'd sat beside Sydney, letting her ask Gen all those questions, when he'd had all the answers—in spades. And then he'd pounced.

Her heart pounding with righteous fury, she pulled the sleeves back down her arms. "You're right, I don't. I don't understand invading my privacy when all you had to do was *ask*. Instead like some grand inquisitor you summoned me here and waited to see whether I'd trip up."

"I won't risk my aunt being hurt in any way."

"So you investigate anybody who comes into contact with her?" she asked scathingly. Not waiting for his reply, she continued, "You know, when I had lunch with Mrs. Miller, she seemed awfully sharp."

"She is. She's also eccentric and given to flights of fancy. And generous to a fault."

"God bless her for that. Me, I'm not nearly so forgiving. In fact, I can't decide whether I loathed you more when I believed you an adulterer or now that I know you're a prying manipulator. Good-bye. It was interesting meeting you."

"We haven't discussed your fee."

She let her eyes widen as if shocked. "You mean you still want me to create a piece for the hospital?"

"I find your art exceptional."

"And I find your character offensive," she said, perfectly mimicking his cool tone. For a second she contemplated demanding a truly outrageous sum for her work, just to see Alex choke on it. But that would involve staying in his office a couple of seconds longer, so she tossed the idea. "I'm not interested in your money. I already informed your aunt that I'd be happy to donate the painting." She caught the swift frown that crossed his face and felt a sweet triumph that her gesture had taken him by surprise. Alex Miller could pry as much as he'd like—he still would never understand her. "I'll have her contact you when the piece is finished."

"That won't be necessary. I'll be coming to East Hampton quite often to monitor your progress on the painting."

Gen didn't believe for a second that was all Alex would be monitoring. "Nobody looks at my work without my permission."

"And you don't think I could persuade you?" he asked and stepped closer.

Suddenly the air in the Park Avenue office became charged with electricity.

Lord, the man was lethal, with a sexual potency that was a-thousand-percent proof. And the worst thing she could do was to let him see that she was even remotely affected.

"And with what could you possibly persuade me? Your winning ways? That pretty face of yours?" She shook her head and gave a light, mocking laugh. "Sorry. You might appeal to the likes of Sydney Raines, but I'm interested in more than a rich boy wearing a flashy suit." She shouldered her backpack and added, "But don't worry, no matter what I think of you personally, I'll make sure your aunt is well taken care of. Family is important."

This time when Gen turned to leave, Alex Miller didn't stop her.

SEVEN

Sydney was on her cell, talking as she climbed out of the cab, slammed the door, and strode down Twenty-third Street toward the chic Chelsea Hotel, where she and Harry had arranged to meet for a drink with the *Architectural Digest* staff writer and the architect who'd designed the TLM wing. Her agitated walk was faster than the clogged traffic around her. "Nancy, I've changed my mind about the tasting. We've got to reschedule. No, that won't do, I can't make it out during the week. It's got to be this weekend. Well, I guess it depends whether you care enough to keep me as a client, because if you don't switch my appointment, I will take every penny of my business elsewhere." Her tone relaxed at the response on the other end. "Yes, Sunday would be fine. Thanks a million, Nancy. You're the best." And Sydney flipped her cell closed.

As distracted as she'd been, her mind teeming with rearranged dates and revised schedules, Sydney nevertheless spotted Harry standing by the hotel's entrance. Dressed in an olive green suit that up close would make his eyes resemble an alpine forest, he was watching her walk toward him. Instinctively, Sydney's gait changed, slowing to enhance the swing of her hips. His reaction, a wide grin of masculine appreciation, was a soothing balm to her wounded pride.

"New skirt?" he asked by way of greeting.

"Barney's is having a sale," she answered. "Why?"

"Because I don't remember seeing it. And given the way your legs look in it, Syd, I'd need to make an appointment with the optometrist if you'd said, 'What, this old rag?' "

"You can rest easy."

He laughed and shook his head. "Not with you in that skirt, I can't. You don't mind if I walk a few paces behind, do you?"

Though Sydney knew Harry flirted as easily as he breathed, it occurred to her that it had been months since he'd directed that effortless charm her way. She'd forgotten how much she enjoyed it.

"Looks like we'll have time to enjoy a drink on our own," he said. "Wilfrid Seigel from the *Digest* is stuck in traffic and Alan Graves makes it a point always to arrive an hour late. I tried to reach you on your cell, but it's been busy. I was about to redial when I saw those gorgeous legs eating up the sidewalk."

Not even the fact that Harry had noticed her legs could mollify her this time. Her stomach cramped again, awash with a bitter mix of hurt and jealousy. "I was at Alex's office. He's found the artist he wants for the painting," she told Harry, her tone flat.

"Great, we can pass that along to Wilfrid."

"She was there when I dropped by." And Alex

hadn't even bothered to call and tell her he was meeting with Gen Monaghan. Consumed as she was by the thought, Sydney didn't reply as they passed through the doors held open by the hotel porter, who offered them a polite "Good afternoon."

Harry took Sydney by the elbow and guided her toward the softly lit bar on the left. A recording of Bobby Short singing Cole Porter blunted the background chatter of the couples who had already gathered and were relaxing on the plush velvet sofas, armchairs, and poufs while they sipped jewel-colored drinks. Harry chose a corner table where they'd be able to see anyone entering the bar and ordered two vodka martinis from the waiter. "So, whom did Alex pick?" he asked.

"A total nobody from Boston who looks like a scarecrow."

Harry's eyebrows rose in surprise. "And Miss Nobody's paintings, do they look equally dreadful?"

"No," Sydney said grudgingly. "Her paintings are beautiful."

"So is there some reason we should care about Miss Nobody's looks?"

"She's going to be living with Mrs. Miller."

"Ahh, now I see." He leaned forward, elbows resting above his knees, fingers knitted together. His voice pitched low, he asked, "So you think Miss Nobody might decide to compete for Alex?"

"Her name's Genevieve Monaghan," Sydney informed him, "and of course she will." What woman wouldn't? she added silently. "I'm going out this weekend. I already called Nancy at La Plage and rescheduled the tasting."

"What about the break you promised yourself before the curtains go up on Miller's party? Weren't you going to drive up to Maine and stay at that inn you discovered? The one with all the Shaker antiques?"

She shifted uncomfortably in her chair. "I'll reschedule the trip for after the party. There's too much to do right now anyway."

"Bull," he said, leveling her with his piercing green gaze. "We've got everything under control. All that's left are the usual odd jobs we could handle in our sleep. Why are you doing this, Syd, chasing after Miller? Listening to you, I'm not even sure what bugs you the most—that you and Miller have broken up or that someone else might get him."

"Why wouldn't that bother me?" she demanded. "How am I supposed to show Alex how right we are for each other if Genevieve Monaghan is there, who, when she isn't telling ridiculous stories about her ridiculously large family, will be painting a piece for the wing that Alex has built in memory of his own deceased family? How do I compete with that?" she asked, a betraying quiver in her voice as unhappiness welled up inside her. Her stomach cramped painfully. Instinctively she went for her purse, ready to dig out her Rolaids, Harry's knowing eyes be damned, but then she realized the pain was lower down in her stomach. Oh, God, she wailed silently. Just what she needed. Her life was falling apart and she was getting her period. Instead of popping a Rolaids, she reached for her martini and took a healthy swallow.

"You do so, Syd, by doing the best damned PR job Miller's ever had. A job which, by the way, I wish were ending next week instead of in two months. 'Cause then just maybe you could get over this idiotic obsession with Alex Miller."

Sydney opened her mouth to object but then saw that Harry's attention had shifted, his green gaze fixed on something behind her. "You can start following my excellent advice this very instant," he informed her as he rose to his feet. "Wilfrid Siegel's heading this way."

Gen discovered it wasn't difficult to settle into paradise.

She had a studio of her own and one of the most spectacular oceanscapes she had ever seen. She woke up every morning to a dawn that skimmed the sand and kissed the sea, lighting them with colors that blazed and glowed, capturing her imagination.

She knew people flocked to the Hamptons in the summer. They fell in love with the beauty of the setting and the ocean climate—sunny, dry days followed by nights cooled by ocean breezes—as well as for the glamorous social scene, a heady blend of billionaire moguls, bluebloods, and Hollywood superstars.

Gen fell in love with the Hamptons for the light.

It was a love affair that lasted from the first glimpse of rosy dawn until the very last glimmer had seeped from the sky, a time during which she sketched, painted, or simply looked, soaking up impressions, colors, and forms. When the light abandoned her, she would put away her art to sit and enjoy the calm of the star-studded evening with Mrs. Miller while the old lady sipped her glass of grappa, an Italian brandy that could also pass for kerosene. "So very good for the digestion, Genevieve, and I swear, it keeps the mind young."

Gen couldn't say for certain whether or not the grappa helped to preserve Mrs. Miller's mind, but her stories and reminiscences of artists, paintings, and sights rivaled Scheherazade's.

Mrs. Miller herself was a wonder. Gen delighted in the older woman's somewhat idiosyncratic rituals, which began each day with an 8 A.M. breakfast in bed. The tray that Gen carried up to her bedroom always held a bud vase, a pot of hot cocoa made from melted slabs of Belgian chocolate, a soft-boiled egg, a single piece of unbuttered toast, and a copy of *The New York Times,* which Mrs. Miller read while wearing white cotton gloves.

By the third morning, Gen couldn't resist. She asked Mrs. Miller if she might sketch her while at breakfast. Her reply won Gen's heart: "Why, certainly, my dear. Just don't paint me with egg on my face."

It was during one of these sketching sessions that Mrs. Miller, after daintily patting her lip with an indigo cotton napkin, said, "Have you been getting ideas for what you want to paint?"

"For the commission?" Gen asked, glancing up from the sketch pad to the older woman's lined face. The pencil in her fingers continued to fly over the paper.

"Yes. I noticed you've been doing a lot of cloud studies."

Gen nodded abstractedly. "There were some incredible ones just floating on the horizon yesterday and the day before. I'm pretty sure I want the composition to include some sort of landscape. When I drove by the site with my mom I remember thinking that with all that glass, the space will be filled with light. I'd like to work with that idea, so that when people look at the work, they're transported—at least temporarily—away from the hospital and their worries." A smile flitted over her face. "But to tell you the absolute truth, Mrs. Miller, right now I'm just kind of absorbing everything around me. It's so beautiful here. I won't start roughing-out the composition until I see the new wing again." Absently she worried her lip as she shaded the area beneath Mrs. Miller's bent elbow.

"I'm sure that can be arranged."

Again, Gen nodded. She'd call her parents once she figured out a date she could drive to Boston. "Can you tell me about this TLM Fund, Mrs. Miller? I've been wondering, does it have a specific mission? I thought I'd try to choose a subject that would connect the fund with the hospital in some way."

"Hmm, well, you should probably ask Alex about that."

She wouldn't be asking Alex Miller for the time of day, not if she could help it. Now that she'd been in Mrs. Miller's company she understood his wish to protect this wonderful and special woman. That didn't give him license, however, to resort to background checks on her and her entire family. Who did he think he was? she asked indignantly for the umpteenth time.

Frowning slightly as if concentrating on the ornate carving of the mahogany bed frame, an area she'd already finished, Gen asked, "And why is that? Because your nephew is the director of the TLM Fund?"

"No, because he *is* the TLM Fund."

The pencil in Gen's hand stalled. "Excuse me?"

"I really can't say more. Alex is a very private man. If you want to know about the TLM Fund, you'll have to talk to him. I believe he's coming out this weekend. Are you finished, dear?" she asked with a pointed glance at Gen's sketch pad. "I need to take my walk early. I'm spending the day kayaking with a group of conservationists and scientists to raise money for the wetlands on the South Fork."

"Oh! Yes, of course." Gen scrambled up, tucking her sketch pad under her arm and stuffing her pencils in the left pocket of her baggy shirt, a hand-me-down from her brother Benjamin.

"I'll pop into the studio before I leave," Mrs. Miller said.

"All right." Gen gathered up the breakfast tray in a distracted daze. What did Mrs. Miller mean, she wondered, by saying Alex Miller *was* the TLM Fund?

Curiosity consumed her as she carried the lacquer tray downstairs. Twice, she almost turned around to climb back to Mrs. Miller's room. But she knew it was pointless to question her further. She'd heard the decisive, brook-no-questions tone in the elderly lady's voice.

Well, didn't Paradise always have a serpent? she asked herself. And as it looked now, if she wanted to taste from the Tree of Knowledge, she'd have to talk to the Devil himself.

To Alex's chagrin he discovered that Genevieve Monaghan was as haunting as her paintings. The memory of her, of their meeting in his office, of the damning expression on her face as she'd roundly told him off, had preoccupied him; he couldn't get her out of his mind. This in spite of the fact that his days had been crammed with meetings and last-minute teleconferences, working out the details for the IPO—initial public offering—of one of their companies, Cybyte, a software developer that had designed and patented what promised to be the leading antivirus program on the market.

Preferring to be unavailable for comment when Cybyte announced its stock offering and the media frenzy began, Alex left the office early on Thursday, hitting the Grand Central Parkway at that magic moment when the road was virtually free of commuters. His partners could field the calls from the magazines and provide the necessary sound bites for Lou Dobbs, CNBC, and the other cable channels devoted to the business world.

Alex was far more interested in seeing those beguiling blue-green-and-brown eyes again.

He wondered how they looked in the morning light, just opening, her face still flushed from sleep.

He wondered which color shone brightest when she made love.

His silver Aston Martin made the drive from midtown to East Hampton in record time.

* * *

The layer of gesso she'd applied to the canvas had dried overnight. Gen had discovered that in this coastal climate everything tended to dry more slowly than in the studio in New York. This slight inconvenience, not being able to work quite as quickly as she was accustomed, was a price she was more than happy to pay.

Today she'd angled her easel by the open windows where she had a view of the main house, the garden bordering it, bright with peonies and late-blooming tulips, and the expanse of emerald-green lawn that led to the edge of Georgica pond. Of all the homes in Georgica Estates, some dating back to the 1890s, Gen considered the Miller house, with its weathered shingles, wide windows, and twin porches, the loveliest.

But what was truly breathtaking was its site. Built on a stretch of land at the southeast end of Georgica pond, the view out the windows facing the north was of the pond and the stately houses nestled around its perimeter, a scene of calm tranquillity. One only had to stroll to the opposite side of the house to see, not more than five hundred yards away, the dramatic, ever-changing, and eternally beautiful Atlantic Ocean.

Gen had tuned the radio to a public station out of New London, Connecticut. An aria from Rossini's *Barber of Seville* mixed with the sea air blowing in through the windows. Murphy lay flat on his side, legs straight out, dozing in the patch of sunlight that streamed in through the open door.

The background of the painting was taking shape. Gen's brush flitted over the canvas, laying down the burnt sienna that she was using as a ground, when suddenly Murphy lurched to his feet. With a single joyous "Woof!" he bounded out the door.

Gen heard the unmistakable slamming of a car door.

She tore after Murphy, knowing as she did that it was too late to stop him or even attempt a "Down, Murphy." She muttered a quick prayer that whatever friend of Mrs. Miller's had come to call had a strong heart and equally strong bones.

Alex had just slammed the car door and was starting toward his aunt's house when he heard a dog barking loudly. Looking around, he spotted an enormous gray dog running at him full tilt. Instinctively he braced himself. It skidded to a halt inches from him and before Alex could unfreeze his limbs, the dog, easily as tall as a Shetland pony, rose on its back legs. With a huge canine grin, it planted its front paws on his shoulders and proceeded to lick Alex's face as if he were a human ice cream cone.

But it was the sound of a strangely familiar laugh that had Alex staggering backward in shock. With the extra weight of the dog he stumbled and fell onto the ground. An *oof* flew from his lips as the dog landed, too, straddling his chest. The canine wash resumed.

That was the sight which greeted Gen. Pulling up short, she clapped a hand over her mouth. Really, it wasn't funny. But she was so relieved that it wasn't a deliveryman or one of Mrs. Miller's friends her dog had bowled over, she was giddy. . . . And she couldn't help but feel just a tiny bit gratified to see the om-

nipotent and far too handsome Alex Miller brought
low.

Way to go, Murph, Gen cheered silently and felt
her grin widen against her palm.

Deciding it was time to take pity on the poor man,
she said, her voice shaking with laughter, "Off, Murphy, right now."

With a morose look Murphy stepped off Alex
Miller's chest, leaving a smudged trail of paw prints
on what Gen knew must have been only seconds ago
a pristine, snow-white shirt. She bit her lip hard to
stop her snicker and then hazarded a glance at his
face.

Alex Miller was staring at her, his eyes glazed with
shock. Gen's amusement fled, replaced by bone-deep
fear. Could he have hit a rock when he landed? Was
he injured?

She dropped to her knees beside him as he struggled to sit up. "Are you all right?" she asked. "I'm
so sorry. It's my fault, I left the screen door to the
studio unlatched. . . ." Her excuse died away when
Alex closed his eyes and shook his head, violently, as
though trying to clear it.

Slowly he opened them again. His gaze fixed on her
then slid to Murphy. The dog, who'd been sitting,
stood and wagged his tail enthusiastically the second
he had Alex's attention.

"Sit, Murphy," Gen commanded. He sank back
onto his haunches.

"He's your dog." His voice sounded odd, strained.

It hadn't been a question but Gen answered as
though it were. "Yes, his name's Murphy. He's really

quite well trained, but as he's only two years old, there's a fair amount of puppy in him. He still loves to meet and greet. It's funny, though," she admitted, a slight frown furrowing her brow. "He's not usually this, uh, enthusiastic in saying hi, at least not until he knows a person." Suddenly convinced she sounded like some nutty dog owner, Gen fell silent. Only to realize with a start that she was sitting next to Alex Miller and that his face was very close to hers.

Unable to stop herself, she stared, mesmerized. He had a strong, aquiline nose and a mouth that was firmly sculpted. . . . Gen was filled with a sudden yearning to run her fingers over that mouth, learn the shape of his lips, trace their sensuous curve. What was she doing? She really was nutty. Insane. This man was all wrong for her, from *A* to *Z*, the last person whose mouth should fascinate her. And besides, he was taken. At that last thought, she flinched.

Coming to her senses, she realized that he was staring right back at her with an alarming intensity. Feeling ridiculously self-conscious, she raked her fingers through her hair, only to remember that she'd pulled it back in an elastic band.

This was all his fault, she decided.

Alex Miller was making her nervous, the peculiar light in his eyes positively unsettling. She couldn't understand why he kept looking at her and then at Murphy with that carefully blank expression on his face. Especially when she could feel the tension radiating from him. A terrible thought occurred to her. "Uh, you're not scared of dogs, are you?" she asked.

"No. I love them," he replied.

Gen's shoulders relaxed.

"What is he, an Irish wolfhound?"

She nodded. "I got Murphy from the shelter when he was just a puppy. The owners had bought him without realizing how much exercise wolfhounds require."

"You take him to Central Park."

"Yes." She eyed him quizzically. Maybe he did have a concussion and it was affecting his speech. Once again, his words had come out as a flat declaration rather than a question. But as she wasn't exactly eager to bring up any injuries her dog might have caused him, she decided to stick to a somewhat safer topic. "Murphy loves to run. The beach in front of your aunt's house is his favorite place now. It's a nice change for me, too. I can actually look at the scenery instead of having it streak by in a blur when I'm following him on my blades. Hey!" she cried, startled. Alex had dropped his head onto his knees with a soft groan. "Are you sure you're all right?" she asked anxiously.

Was he all right? Hell no. Alex felt as if he'd been walloped with a two-by-four to the head rather than merely being tackled by a hundred-plus-pound dog. He was still reeling, struggling to come to grips with the fact that Genevieve Monaghan was not only a painter whose art had the power to move him beyond words, a woman whose unique beauty and fresh charm triggered an undeniable response inside him; she was also his mystery woman, the Central Park speed demon whose laughter had lifted his heart. It was too much.

As he'd sped from the city to his aunt's house, his thoughts had continued to revolve around Gen. Thoughts that had quickly spun into sensual fantasies of seduction . . . of undressing Gen slowly, discovering exactly how many of those enchanting gold-dust freckles covered her. Of kissing every last one of them as she moaned in his arms and her eyes glittered with greenish-gold flames of desire.

Yet now that he realized exactly *who* Gen was, and recognized too the hold she had over his imagination, he wanted nothing more than to break her unknowing spell.

That was somehow the worst of it: Gen hadn't the slightest inkling of her effect on him, of her power. Because her power came from simply being who she was.

So he was stuck, smitten with a woman who wore button-down shirts and painter's pants that would have been baggy on Paul Bunyan. He was entranced by a woman who, when she wasn't telling him off, was deriving gleeful, sadistic pleasure from watching him get licked to death by a hairy dog in desperate need of mouthwash.

And it damn near terrified him that in spite of all this he'd be willing to do just about anything to have that smile wreath her face and see laughter light her eyes.

It occurred to Alex that the smartest thing he could do would be to jump into his car right now and drive away even faster than he'd come, putting as many miles between him and Genevieve Monaghan as possible.

Unfortunately his chance at self-preservation was snatched away by Aunt Grace's arrival. Her face flushed a glowing pink, her bare feet coated with sand, she'd clearly just come from her walk on the beach. "Why, Alex, dear. Whatever are you doing sprawled on the grass?"

"What is grass but to sprawl on?" he replied easily as he rose to his feet and kissed his aunt's cheeks.

Watching them, Gen felt an unexpected rush of gratitude toward Alex for having omitted Murphy's role in how he came to be on the grass. She didn't want Mrs. Miller to get the wrong impression about her dog.

"And why are you here?" Mrs. Miller demanded. "Today's Thursday."

"One of the joys of the computer age is that I can bring my work with me; one of the privileges of being the head of a firm is that I can leave when I want. No one but you to scold me when I play hooky, Aunt Grace," he said lightly.

Mrs. Miller made a *tsk*-ing noise and brushed at the dirt on his shoulders. "You've never played hooky in your life, although you probably should. You work far too hard. It's lovely that you're here, Alex, though I'm afraid it'll be just you and Genevieve for much of today and tomorrow. I'm off to go kayaking with the group for the South Fork Conservancy. Tomorrow I have a lunch followed by a committee meeting for the Hampton Classic. That charming friend of Sam Brody's, Ty Sheppard, has been nominated this year's chair." Turning to Gen she said, "I should be back later this afternoon, around five. Shall I pick up some groceries on the way home?"

"Oh, no, that's all right. I can do the shopping, Mrs. Miller. I've got the list already written out. But if you'll excuse me, I need to get back to my work. Come on, Murphy," she said, slapping her thigh. And Gen hurried away before she saw more of this side of Alex Miller's personality, and forgot to remember that she really didn't like him.

EIGHT

Alex rapped on the door frame hard enough to be heard over the classical music pouring from the portable radio. The dog, of course, had already noticed his presence and had risen from his post, his body poised.

As a precautionary measure, he said, "Down," in a low, gravelly tone. When the dog kept all four massive paws planted on the floor, seemingly content with wagging his tail so hard his entire body shook, Alex found himself grinning. Then, addressing Gen's pant legs and bare feet, the only parts of her that were visible behind the rectangular canvas propped against the wooden easel, he asked, "Do you mind if I come in?"

Gen's head popped around the edge of the painting. "Oh."

Not quite as warm a reception as her dog had given him, Alex thought ruefully. "I brought some food."

"Food?" she said in surprise, thereby confirming what Aunt Grace had told him before she left. "Make sure Genevieve eats something, Alex. She's spent the week making these delicious meals, each one more beautifully presented than the next. But then she neglects to eat them. I've come to the conclusion that she views cooking as a sort of still-life arrangement. Once it's done, she moves on to her next project."

"Yes, food," he said, echoing Gen. "Lunch was a couple of hours ago."

She glanced back at the canvas she was working on. "I guess I can take a break."

Alex watched her drop her brush into a can of water and wrap a plastic bag around her paint palette. Wiping her hands on a frayed rag, she looked with interest at the plate in his hand. "What have you got there?"

"What I assume must be your cooking, since it tastes delicious. Aunt Grace has an alarming tendency to burn everything she puts in a pot. She's gone through several fire extinguishers. Here," he said, holding out a plate filled with a cold roast beef sandwich, a potato and cucumber salad, and a bunch of red grapes. "A peace offering."

"A peace offering, huh?" she replied, taking it from him. "Well, I'm not really the type to hold grudges— although I admit in your case the idea has definite appeal." Flashing him a cool smile, she carried the plate over to the futon sofa and sat down. Raising her legs, she propped her bare feet on an upside-down milk crate, and with an expansive wave of her arm, said, "Go ahead, take a look around. I warn you, though, I did an excellent job of hiding your aunt's silver." She grinned mockingly and took an enormous bite of the sandwich.

"Your sense of humor overwhelms me."

She shook her head as her jaw worked. Swallowing, she said cheerfully, "No, that would be my dog. I see you changed your shirt. Think you'll be able to get the grass stains out of the other one?"

"If I don't, I'll send you the bill," he shot back dryly.

Laughter bubbling up inside her, Gen took another hefty bite of her sandwich to prevent its escape. In spite of her decidedly mixed feelings about Alex Miller, she had to admit she enjoyed his quick wit. Pretending to concentrate on her food—impressed to discover that he'd added horseradish to the sandwich, which gave it a wicked, nostril-searing kick, exactly what she liked—she surreptitiously watched him move about the studio, all the while trying not to notice how the cotton T-shirt he'd changed into clung to the muscles of his torso, or how very fine he looked in a pair of faded old jeans.

First he wandered over to her worktable and paused to look at her paints and brushes, charcoals and pencils. When he turned away, the angle of his head told Gen he was studying the long expanse of bare wall and the tall stool that she'd placed in front of it. The empty wall was where she planned to hang the canvas for the hospital commission. Gen had positioned the stool there so that at odd moments during the day she could sit and stare at the white emptiness, inviting images to float before her.

Next he walked over to the second worktable she'd set up. This one was covered with seashells, sea glass, bird feathers, rocks, and pieces of driftwood, objects that had caught her fancy on her beach walks with Murphy. While Gen found the objects fascinating, she grew puzzled when Alex continued to linger near them. Until suddenly it dawned on her: he was scrupulously avoiding the area near her easel, as well as the window ledge where the portrait she'd begun of Mrs. Miller rested. It surprised Gen how much it meant to her that he'd not only remembered but respected her declaration that her artwork was off-limits without her express invitation.

"I've been working on a portrait of your aunt," she said, with a nod toward the other side of the room. "If you'd like—"

"Yes, very much indeed."

She put the half-finished sandwich aside and went over to the window. "Here it is," she said, holding the sketch pad out to him.

He gazed at it. "It's terrific. You've captured my aunt perfectly, from the tilt of her chin to her white gloves. Tell me, though, why did you choose to draw her at breakfast? Because that's the only time she sits still?"

Alex's wry question had Gen laughing. "Yes, that was one reason. I also love how she understands what makes her happy, and that she starts each day surrounded by some of those things. One could do worse than follow her example."

Alex looked at her and a strange silence enveloped them, one that made Gen as nervous as a schoolgirl on her first date. There was such magnetism in his brilliant blue gaze. Drawn to it, she found herself suddenly wondering what it was that made Alex Miller *happy* . . . what gave him pleasure.

Sex. Hot, steamy sex was the answer that sprang unbidden into her mind. An answer that took her fertile imagination on a wild ride as she pictured Alex's leanly muscled body covered in a sheen of sweat. He was moving in sensual concert, hips flexing to a driving beat as his broad hands stroked and caressed freckled limbs. . . .

Oh, God! Panic-stricken, she reined in her shockingly vivid and, more important, appallingly inappropriate imaginings.

She nearly jumped out of her skin when Alex's hand reached out and grazed her cheek. "Are you okay?" he asked. "Something in your eye?"

Gen realized she'd been blinking, those erotic images burned into her retinas. It would be beyond mortifying if he guessed the true nature of her problem—one in which he'd had a starring role. "Yes, a speck of dust from the window," she lied, taking a hasty step backward. She squeezed her eyes shut. "There, all better," she managed with a bright smile.

"Thanks for letting me see this," he said, handing the portrait of Grace Miller back to her. "I'd like to buy it when it's finished."

Gen's shoulders relaxed at the turn of conversation. Art she could handle. "Sorry, it's not for sale. I'm giving the drawing as a present to your aunt, as a token of thanks for her generosity. Which reminds me, Mrs. Miller suggested I talk to you about this TLM Fund. You know, she said the most fascinating thing . . . that you *are* the fund. Mind giving me a little background information?" she asked sweetly, her eyebrows raised in open challenge.

Alex stiffened.

Ooh, but it did feel good to turn the tables on him. That was surely the reason for the keen sense of anticipation inside her, Gen told herself, not because she felt a growing fascination for this incredibly handsome and enigmatic man.

"That's what my aunt told you?"

"Uh-huh," she said, nodding. She walked back to the futon, dropping onto it. Leaning back against its frame, she stretched her legs out and crossed them at the ankles. "So tell me, how does one become a fund?"

Alex didn't reply immediately. Damn, he wished his aunt had been more circumspect about his involvement in the TLM Fund. No way was he going to explain to Gen why TLM had come into existence, that he'd created it in honor of Tom and Lisa, his deceased brother and sister-in-law.

Although Alex knew he wanted Gen, what he didn't want was her pity. Nor was he about to let anyone probe the painful memories that still haunted him. With a careless shrug, he said, "It's not a big deal. I made some money and put it in a fund."

She gave him a long look. "How'd you make it?"

"Initially? I traded. Then it was just a matter of adding to the original profits. I was lucky and made some good investments."

He made it sound ridiculously simple, Gen thought, as if netting what had to be millions was as easy as dropping pennies into a piggy bank. She didn't believe him for a second. Nor did she think his attitude was very common. She'd bet the majority of financier types would be braying about the fortune they'd made. "So you were into trading, huh? Isn't that interesting. I've done some trading myself."

"Really?"

She nodded. "Yup. I was a regular shark when it came to baseball cards. I still remember the day I suckered Nolan into giving up his Ted Williams for a Pete Rose. My finest moment."

"You're right," he said, grinning back at her. "That shows true killer instincts."

"Yeah, I know." She raised her hand to cover an exaggerated yawn. "I probably could have made some major bucks if I'd stuck with it. But really, I'd rather make art." Then, without skipping a beat she said, "So tell me, how come you're donating a hospital wing in Boston when you have no connection to the city?"

Perhaps it was because she'd posed the question out of left field, so to speak, that she was able to catch the sudden shadow that crossed his face, dimming the brilliance of his eyes. Gen felt the depth of Alex's pain like a visceral blow.

"Someone I once knew was born there," he said quietly.

She opened her mouth, but before she could whisper some woefully inadequate apology, the telephone rang.

The answering machine was on, as Gen routinely screened her calls when she was working. In a family of fourteen, it was an essential measure. Otherwise it would be impossible to get even a lick of paint on canvas.

She instantly recognized her mother's voice, her rapid delivery too. Tansy Monaghan hated getting cut off, so her messages were always spoken in a hurried rush, a race against the machine. "It's me, darling. I just wanted to tell you that the box with Bridget's present arrived this morning. I shook it lightly. Nothing rattling so I don't think the jars got broken. I can't wait to see them. I know she'll love them. We'll miss you this Saturday, sweetie. I'll call and tell you how it went. That's all for now, darling—oh, don't forget to eat. You're far too thin. We love you. 'Bye."

The tape clicked off and Gen lowered her gaze, studying her bare toes intently. But not before Alex said mildly, "That's an interesting shade of red."

"Excuse me?" It would have been nice if he'd pretended not to notice her embarrassment.

"Your face." He grinned. Seeming unfazed by her glare, he continued. "What is it you're missing, a party? Bridget's the chef, right?"

"I'm disappointed. You know my family so well. How could you forget Bridget's turning thirty this year?"

Ignoring her sarcasm, he said, "So why aren't you celebrating with your family?"

She rolled her eyes. "Because I'm in eastern Long Island and they're in Somerville, Massachusetts. Which is about a six-hour car ride that I'm not sure Hugo the Yugo can make. And I can't see hitchhiking with

Murphy being hugely successful, either. Bizarrely, Amtrak has a no-wolfhound policy."

"Ever hear of a plane? You could go and come back in the same day, and leave Murphy here."

"Ever hear of flat broke? No, I didn't think so," she said scathingly. "Come on, Murphy, it's time for our walk." And she brushed past him without a second glance.

Her lips had been trembling, Alex thought dully. God, what an ass he'd been. While he refused to feel guilty for asking Sam to investigate Gen and her family's background, firm in his conviction that his aunt was far too trusting when it came to opening her heart and her home, Alex hated the fact that now he'd hurt Gen with his arrogant assumptions.

He should have guessed that her finances were tight; it was far too soon for her to have received the check for the sale of *Day One*. Yet even when the check cleared, someone used to living within Gen's kind of budget, dependent on the sale of her art, didn't simply hop on an airplane to attend a birthday party . . . exactly what he'd cockily suggested she do.

Alex didn't like what that said about him. Above all, he didn't like what that made him in her eyes.

By the time Gen finished her walk, her usual buoyant sense of humor had been restored. The episode in the studio between Alex and her had merely brought into sharp relief how different two people's lives and worlds could be. Alex Miller's contained nothing that she coveted. Gen loved her life exactly the way it was, devoted to her art, to her calling.

Nevertheless she thought it best to avoid him as much as possible. There were a few too many things she liked about him and that piqued her interest. There was his philanthropy—mysterious though he was about it—his dry wit, and his obvious affection for his aunt.

But Gen was honest enough to admit that wasn't the real reason behind her decision. It was the powerful sensual thrill that coursed through her whenever Alex was near that troubled her most, and made her as wary as a wild animal scenting danger. She didn't understand her reaction to him. She'd never felt this way toward anyone else—not even Jiri, who knew her so well, and who shared so many of the same dreams and ambitions as she.

So while Gen could truthfully say that she coveted nothing that Alex possessed, she was increasingly and distressingly aware that what she desired was Alex himself.

A part of her longed to explore this heady attraction, yet she knew that the sensible part of herself would prevail. Like the lines to the pop song, her motto would have to be, "I do not want what I cannot have."

Perhaps that would help control her craving the touch of another woman's man.

As Gen washed the sand from her bare feet with the garden hose, the cold water turning her skin a bright red, she wondered about Alex's relationship with Sydney Raines. Did they spend their weekends together? Would Sydney be coming out this weekend? She found herself wishing that Alex's lover might materialize soon. Sydney's presence would force Gen to face reality: Alex was most definitely spoken for.

It was a truth that slipped all too easily from Gen's mind.

Where had Murphy wandered off?

Gen had been preparing dinner in the kitchen. A chicken curry simmered on the stove next to a saucepan full of fluffed basmati rice. Sautéed green beans with toasted almonds lined a warming dish, and Gen had bought gingersnaps to go with the passion-fruit sorbet Mrs. Miller adored. Murphy, who usually positioned himself in a prime spot where he could catch the bits of raw vegetables Gen tossed him, had vanished. She glanced around the terra-cotta-tiled kitchen and felt a horrible flutter of panic, like a mother who's lost her child.

He could easily have butted the screen door open with his head, she thought wildly. Taking a deep, calming breath, she reminded herself that the driveway was long and far away from road traffic. She would check the house and grounds first, she decided, then head down to the beach. She tried not to think of Murphy lost in the dark.

The house was quiet. She wasn't sure if Alex was around, or out doing whatever he did for amusement in the Hamptons. On the off-chance that he was in the house, she kept her voice a low, urgent whisper: "Murphy! Here, Murphy, come!"

When she neared the study situated off the living room, she heard the masculine voice she was coming to recognize so well. The door was open. Alex sat at the large oak desk, a cell phone pressed to his ear. The screen of his laptop was up, the computer making its distinctive humming noise.

She stepped inside onto the rich red of the kilim rug and gave the room a sweeping inspection. No, Murphy wasn't there, either, she thought. As she was about to retreat from the room, Alex held up his hand, gesturing for her to wait.

"Thanks again, Robert," he said into the phone. "I'm glad the press conference went so smoothly. Let's talk with Bill after the market opens tomorrow. Yeah, I'll be back in the office Monday. No, sorry, I'd love to join you for doubles but I'm flying to Boston for the day. Yeah, you can reach me on my cell if something comes up." With a press of the button, Alex ended the call.

He put the phone on the desk and leaned back against the chair. The windows were open behind him and the breeze gently ruffled his hair, which the light from the study's lamps had turned a burnished gold. "Are you looking for something?" he asked.

Gen would have preferred telling him that she was rooting around the house so she could steal the rest of his aunt's silver than admit she'd lost her dog. Then she heard it: the *thwack, thwack* of a tail slapping wood. Her disbelieving eyes found the source. Murphy lay underneath the desk, his head resting on Alex's feet. His traitorous eyes met hers and his tail thumped heavily once more.

"I'd have brought him back to you, but I enjoyed the company."

"How long—"

"Half an hour, maybe."

"I just can't understand it," she muttered to herself.

"You find it incomprehensible that anyone—man or beast—would seek me out?" he asked dryly.

Gen blushed. Though she hadn't intended it, that was how her remark sounded. "No, I simply meant that Murphy doesn't . . ." Her words ground to a halt. Did she really want to admit that Murphy rarely left her side? Did she really want Alex to know that her dog had formed some instant bond?

As if he understood that her sentence had come to a dead end, Alex spoke. "Actually, I was coming to find you. I've made arrangements for you to go to Boston this Saturday."

"Excuse me?"

"My aunt informed me that you need to visit the hospital wing. Saturday happens to be the best day for a visit. The construction crews aren't working so you'll be able to do what you need without the distraction of noise and dust. And in turn, you won't be getting in the way of the crew."

She crossed her arms in front of her chest. "What an amazing coincidence. Saturday is also Bridget's party."

"Is it?" he replied easily. "I'd forgotten. It also happens to be the same day I have a meeting scheduled with the hospital's director and chairman of the board. It's at 10 A.M. We'll leave at 8 A.M. and return in the early evening. If you find you have enough time to visit your family . . ." He shrugged.

She eyed him skeptically. She wasn't buying his

story for a minute. "And what do I do with Murphy?"

"Bring him on the plane if you wish."

"We're flying?"

He nodded.

"I don't have an airline-sanctioned crate," she said. Although thrilled at the prospect of seeing her family and Bridget on her birthday, Gen also felt a perverse triumph that she'd foiled his plan. He was really just a bit too high and mighty for her tastes.

"As I'm chartering the plane, I don't think a crate's required. A leash might be useful, though."

Gen couldn't reply. Her tongue had become a lead weight in her mouth, rendering her incapable of speech. Alex spoke of chartering a plane the way others spoke of going out and renting a movie for the night. Gen's mind was still grappling—unsuccessfully—with the notion of traveling on a private plane when his cell rang.

Alex picked it up. "Miller," he said and paused as the caller spoke. "Hello, Sydney. Yes, I am . . ."

Unwilling to eavesdrop on his conversation with his lover, Gen slipped away from the man who so effortlessly rocked her world inside and out.

NINE

Alex awoke at six in the morning and in the semi-darkness of his room rummaged through the dresser for his running shorts and T-shirt. This was the perfect hour to run in the Hamptons, when the roads that led past corn and potato fields and tall privet hedges, planted to screen the houses hidden behind them, were still empty and peaceful.

He walked silently down the hallway so as not to disturb his sleeping aunt and descended the stairs. At the kitchen sink he poured himself a glass of water. As he drank, his eyes strayed involuntarily across the backyard.

No lights shone in the studio. In his mind he pictured Gen's delicately boned face, the fan of her dark lashes against her cheeks as she lay sleeping on the futon his aunt Grace had told him the local handyman had moved into the studio. "I offered Genevieve the bedroom opposite yours, Alex, but she insisted she was quite happy sleeping out there. Such an independent-minded girl—not at all like those New York City lemmings," she'd added with a sniff of disdain for good measure, so Alex would know this was meant as a pointed reference to his previous girl-friends.

Aunt Grace was right, he thought, and took another sip of water, his gaze still riveted on the studio. Gen was different from those other women. He'd known her for less than a week and already she had a more profound hold on his thoughts than any other woman. And his fascination seemed to grow each time he saw her.

Out of habit, Alex left the house by the porch over-looking the beach, so he could have that incompara-ble first glimpse of dawn-lit ocean. He stood at the railing, taking in the wide sweep of sand, the roll of incoming waves—and froze as he spotted two dark forms bobbing in the surf. Everything inside him went still, except for the heavy thudding of his heart, which beat in sync with the waves pounding the shore. Only the bite of the porch's wooden railing against his palms kept him from thinking that this was but a continuation of the dreams and fantasies he'd had of her.

Gen and Murphy were emerging from the surf, the dog bounding through the water in great deerlike leaps, she timing her advance with the rhythm of the incoming waves. Alex was filled with an instinctive urge to rush to her aid that eased only when he saw how comfortable she was negotiating the opposing forces of waves and undertow.

When he tensed again it was for a different reason. She walked out of the sea like Venus at her birth, sleek, long-limbed . . . perfect nascent femininity. Alex had never beheld such a glorious sight.

Then Murphy gave a loud bark and shook himself vigorously, his long fur sending water spraying. Alex heard Gen's shriek as the water hit her bare skin. With a laughing reprimand to the dog, who had begun racing over the sand in crazed zigzags and circles, she bent down and grabbed a beach towel, wrapping it about her before scooping up the small bundle of clothes by her feet.

Gen trudged through the deep sand that was still cool from the night air, and stepped onto the wooden stairway that led right to the front lawn. The grass was prickly and wet with dew. The moisture plastered the sand to her feet. As she crossed the lawn in the direction of the outdoor shower, a flicker of movement on the porch caught her eye.

"Good morning."

Gen stopped in her tracks at the sound of Alex's voice. Luckily her arms were clamped tight about her towel. Though little good that did. Even from the distance of the porch, his gaze was a physical thing. Her skin tingled with awareness. And against the thick weave of the towel, her nipples grew taut and aching. She shivered.

"Cold?" he asked.

No, she wasn't cold. She felt like she was melting from a single fiery glance. With an effort, Gen pulled herself together. "Uh, have you been sitting here long?"

"Yes. It's beautiful here in the morning; the view's

always striking. This morning especially so. I liked your suit."

She decided to brazen it out. After all, she had no hang-ups about her body—at least she hadn't until three seconds ago. "Ahh, yes," she managed lightly. "That would be my birthday suit."

"And a more becoming one I've never seen. By the way, your mother's wrong. You're not too thin. You're beautiful," he said quietly. She felt his gaze slide over her and knew he was stripping her bare, seeing her as she'd been a few minutes before. Her heart pounded in her chest. "Still, be careful swimming alone. Much though I enjoyed it, I won't always be here to watch over you."

With that, Alex turned and headed back into the house, leaving Gen to stare after him. His words flowed through her like a warm, heady current. Had she acquired her very own guardian angel? she wondered bemusedly. One who, instead of wings, came equipped with a private plane? Certainly he had the fierce golden beauty of the Archangel Gabriel. And increasingly, when Alex looked at her as he had just now, Gen was sure she'd find heaven in the circle of his strong arms.

Alex strode through the house, leaving by the kitchen door. His hands still shook with the need to unknot that damnable beach towel and caress every inch of her damp, salty skin. To touch Gen until she writhed, needing him as much as he needed her.

He ran, pushing himself, making his heart pound and the muscles in his legs burn as sweat poured off his body. He ran as an act of will to control his unruly mind and body. He ran, but couldn't escape the memory of Gen's naked, glistening body rising from the sea.

Only the day before, Gen had wished that Sydney Raines might make an appearance, in the hope that her presence would serve as a physical reminder that Alex was quite unavailable.

It didn't take Gen long to regret her wish.

That very morning, Sydney announced her arrival with three short honks of her BMW's horn. Murphy, in the studio with Gen, barked back just as loudly. Luckily, Gen managed to grab his collar before he lunged out the studio door. Unluckily, Murphy's strength was such that he dragged her after him—a canine version of a Nantucket sleigh ride.

As they loped across the lawn, Gen, in a last-ditch effort, threw herself forward in a clumsy hug of a tackle, uttering a breathless, "Down, Murph!" in the hopes that the dog would obey. The fates smiled on her.

Sydney did not.

Dressed in a silk blouse, a short pleated skirt, ballerina flats, and a patterned scarf tied around her head to protect her hair from the wind, she looked as if she'd stepped out of the pages of *Vogue*. But seeing Murphy come hurtling toward her wiped any trace of a smile off her face. She stared wide-eyed at the pair of them, Gen and Murphy, both of whom were panting.

"What is that?" she said, pointing a finger at Murphy.

"My dog," Gen explained, still sucking in gulps of air. "Murphy's very gentle, just a little excitable when it comes to greeting new people. He won't hurt you."

Sydney raised her dark brows in a show of patent disbelief, continuing to stare at Murphy as if he were the fiend straight out of *The Hound of the Baskervilles.*

"Okay, Murph, I think it's time we got back to work." With a firm tug on the leather collar, Gen managed to pull the dog around in a semicircle. Seeing Alex, she faltered. Murphy didn't. With a happy "woof," he bounded out of her grasp, making straight for Alex.

This was the first time she'd seen him since she'd taken her morning dip in the ocean. And all she could think about was his thrillingly low voice saying, "You're beautiful." She couldn't help but wonder if he still believed that, especially when she was standing next to a woman as gorgeous and glamorous as Sydney.

Realizing that Murphy was about to jump on Alex, Gen tore her thoughts away from the land of impossible dreams. But before she could open her mouth, Alex raised his right hand. "Down," he said.

The dog skidded to a halt.

"Sit, Murphy."

Without hesitating, Murphy sank onto his haunches, his tail sweeping the grass.

"Good boy," Alex said. The sweeping redoubled.

Gen shook her head in disbelief. "That's amazing." Had Alex cast a spell on her dog? Though she hated to admit it, the whole obedience issue was a bit iffy with Murphy.

"Yes, amazing," Sydney echoed. "You have such a way with animals, Alex."

"He's a smart dog."

Alex's reply made Gen feel ridiculously proud. Few people recognized that quality in Murphy.

"You're here early, Sydney," Alex said.

"I decided to beat the weekend traffic and the horde of well-wishers. I wanted to be the first to congratulate you, darling. I'm so thrilled for you," she said with a wide smile. Her gaze flicked over to Gen. Noting her blank expression, Sydney said, "One of Alex's tech companies announced an initial public offering yesterday. The company's share price rose by more than three dollars by the day's closing." With an arch glance at Alex, she continued, "I spoke with Mark Rodgers, darling. His guess is that you netted fifteen million yesterday. I told him I was sure it was more than that."

Gen tried not to choke at the outrageous figure Sydney had named. Alex, however, simply looked bored, neither denying nor confirming her statement.

"Anyway," Sydney continued with a light shrug, "I thought that we might spend some time together and celebrate your latest coup."

When Alex leveled a long, inscrutable look at Sydney, Gen was left puzzled. She couldn't understand why he didn't seem more enthusiastic about his girlfriend's arrival. But then he said, "I have a lot of work to finish," and she realized that was undoubtedly the reason behind the tepid response.

Sydney must have interpreted Alex's comment in much the same vein. "Don't worry, darling. I promise not to distract you too much. Not unless you want me to, that is," she teased, an intimate smile playing over her lips as she linked her arm in his.

Now was definitely the moment to make an exit, before Sydney started demonstrating her powers to distract. "Well, it's been fun," Gen said brightly. "I'll see you around."

Alex waited until he and Sydney were in the study he used as a makeshift office. He leaned against the edge of the oak desk and folded his arms across his chest. "Sydney, you're making this really difficult."

"Good. I want it to be," she said, approaching until she stood close to him, the scent of her perfume enveloping him. "You never call me anymore, so what choice do I have?" Her eyes were huge, dark, and troubled. "I want to be with you, Alex, just like we were before."

He shook his head. "That's not possible."

"Why? Can't you see I'm miserable without you?"

"I'm sorry about that, but how do you think being ignored will make you feel, Sydney?" he asked. "Because that's how it will be. *The relationship is over.* I only said you could stay here at my aunt's because we have the tasting on Sunday. But that's it. There's nothing else between us."

"The Howards' party is tomorrow night. I thought we could go."

Striving for patience, Alex forced himself to count to twenty. "I'm not going to the Howards'."

"But Miriam told me—" Sydney had the grace to blush. She'd obviously been talking to Miriam Howard about him, keeping tabs.

"Miriam told you wrong," Alex said curtly. "I've changed my plans. I'm flying to Boston tomorrow. When I get back, I'm going to spend the evening with my aunt."

Sydney frowned. "Why are you flying to Boston on the weekend?"

"Gen needs to see the interior of the wing."

"But surely you don't need to go. She can travel to Boston on her own—" Her breath caught. "That's it. It's her, isn't it? You want *Gen*."

A champion at liar's poker, Alex kept his face impassive. "No, Sydney, you're wrong. There's nothing between Gen and me."

She was silent for a moment, her lips pursed into a thin, unhappy line. Then abruptly she said, "I'd like to come with you to Boston tomorrow. Harry and I finished writing the copy for the hospital's bulletin yesterday. I could use a couple of hours at the hospital to have a one-on-one meeting with Pru Trudeau so we can discuss any changes to the text. Then I'll be able to start on the revisions as early as Monday."

Jesus, Alex thought with an inward sigh. When was she going to quit? The problem was, Sydney had always been able to think on her feet. She'd given a perfectly plausible reason to accompany them. He couldn't refuse and at the same time accuse *her* of being unprofessional. Resigning himself to Sydney's presence tomorrow, he said tersely, "Fine, come to

Boston. Now if you'll excuse me, I have a conference call scheduled in five minutes."

"May I come in?"

Gen glanced over to find Sydney hovering in the doorway of the studio. She was looking warily at Murphy, who was lying at the foot of Gen's stool.

Involuntarily Gen searched for any signs that Sydney had been spending the past twenty minutes "distracting" Alex. It was impossible to tell. She was her cool and unmussed self.

Gen slipped off the stool. She'd been sitting on it, staring at the empty wall, trying to come up with images that might work for the hospital commission. But since her encounter with Alex this morning, she'd been unusually unsettled. And the image that too often appeared in her mind's eye was of Alex's face. Definitely the wrong thing to be dreaming about with Sydney here.

"Sure, come in."

Sydney took a tentative step inside, her eyes fixed on Murphy.

"Don't worry about Murphy," Gen told her. "He's busy with a bone. That'll be his world for the next twenty minutes or so."

"I'm not really a dog person," Sydney confessed, relaxing only slightly. "I know how much Alex loves them, though, so I guess I'll have to accustom myself." Her gaze flitted around the studio. "Do you mind if I look around?"

Gen shrugged and said, "Go ahead," aware that her tone was less than gracious. It was interesting.

She'd felt much more at ease when it had been Alex wandering around her studio—even though she'd still been angry at having been investigated by him. With Sydney, Gen had the decidedly unpleasant impression that she was being visited by a productivity inspector.

Sydney was circling the studio, taking in the various works in progress without making a single comment. Carefully bypassing Murphy, she came to stand by the stool Gen had vacated. For a minute she gazed at the bare wall. Turning toward Gen, she arched a dark brow. "I guess it's a good thing after all that Alex is taking time out from his weekend to fly you to Boston."

Prickling with irritation, Gen said, "It doesn't make any sense to begin the painting before I visit the wing. It's not often an artist gets to create a work for a specific site. I want to take notes on the light and get a feel for the proportions of the building. I would have been more than happy to go alone—I didn't ask him to do this," she finished somewhat defensively. It was true. She hated imposing on others. And what was worse, she had the sneaking suspicion that Alex had arranged the entire trip to Boston this weekend solely because he knew her sister was celebrating her birthday. Having Sydney inform her that he was forfeiting his weekend only made her feel worse.

"No, I suppose you didn't," Sydney replied. "But surely you've guessed how important this project is to Alex." She sighed, and a touch of sadness crossed her face. "The new wing has consumed so much energy and time, it's forced us to put a hold on other aspects of our lives. Still," she said, brightening, "I'm more than willing to wait to plan our future together if it makes Alex happy. He's worth it. But I'd appreciate it if you could do your best to complete the painting on time. I want every aspect of this project to proceed without the slightest hitch."

Gen jerked her shoulders in a shrug. "Sure, I understand."

"Thank you." Sydney smiled. "I hoped you would."

After Sydney left, Gen puttered around the studio aimlessly, unable to get down to work. Her mind was too troubled. She would have loved to lay the blame on Sydney's high-handed manner of asking her to get the painting completed on time. But that wasn't the problem. Gen understood that she was creating on a deadline. She knew, too, that once she was into a project, she could work practically around the clock, eating and sleeping in brief snatches while the paint dried on the canvas.

Which meant that she'd been lying to herself. It hadn't been Sydney's pointed reminder that there were time constraints involved. No, what had truly bothered her was hearing Sydney talk about her and Alex's future together.

That prickling feeling she'd experienced hadn't simply been impatience or irritation. It had been jealousy piercing like a needle into her heart.

TEN

Flying home aboard a privately chartered plane was a novel experience. Gen half wished she'd brought Murphy along, just for the once-in-a-lifetime thrill of being able to walk across the tarmac, her dog at her heels, and climb up the metal ladder, to have the pilot smile his hello as he directed them to a row of wide, comfortable seats. . . . Murphy would have gotten a kick out of it, she was sure. And she could have leaned over and whispered in his furry ear how weird it felt to be sitting—no, flying—in the lap of luxury. But Mrs. Miller had said she had a mountain of correspondence to catch up on and a slew of telephone calls to return, too. If she was going to be stuck in the house all day, she'd be glad to have the dog for company. Which left Gen to spend the entire trip, from takeoff to touchdown, with her nose pressed to the oval window.

Below her, the flat fields of Long Island were dressed in the vivid greens of their crops' tender shoots. She saw the bright aquamarine of swimming pools and the smattering of yellow, red, and pink flowers decorating the gardens of the properties below.

The plane banked, leaving the land to fly over the blue chop of the Sound. The sparkle of morning light glancing over the waves reminded Gen of Alex's eyes, a vivid blue enhanced by the white of his dress shirt.

For a second, she was tempted to glance across the aisle where Alex and Sydney were sitting. But she resisted the impulse and kept her eyes trained on the view below. She knew that if she succumbed, her passing glance would become a stare as she indulged in this growing fascination. She'd stare until she knew yes or no whether they were the type of couple who held hands. She could only be grateful that it was impossible, given the roar of the plane's engines, to overhear even a snatch of their conversation.

Gen hated this absurd envy that had sprung up inside her; she'd already lectured herself a number of times, always ending with: *Get a grip, Monaghan.* She was not a lovelorn ninny and she wasn't about to let her family see her behaving like one.

Gen found it much harder to ignore Alex and Sydney in the confines of the limo. As soon as they climbed in the leather and wood-trimmed interior, she realized belatedly that she should have volunteered to sit in front with the chauffeur. They could have talked about the Sox and how maybe, just maybe, the Sox would redeem themselves, at long last allowing their die-hard fans to wear their caps with pride. Instead she got an earful of Sydney talking about acquaintances of hers and Alex's. Eventually she managed to tune her out—wondering whether Alex, with his monosyllabic responses, was choosing to do the same.

The chauffeur had opted to avoid the traffic around the Callahan Tunnel, blocked due to a stalled car. As the limo wove in and out of the busy lanes along Storrow Drive, Gen stared out the window. It was a beautiful day, the kind of Saturday morning that brought everyone out to wander along the Charles River and soak up the warmth of the sun's rays. Gen glimpsed the sailboats and eight-men shells of the college sailing and crew teams practicing on the river, their white sails and hulls gliding smoothly, an Eakins painting brought to life. What a great day for Bridget's birthday picnic, she thought happily.

The limo exited the drive at Massachusetts Avenue and headed south toward Longwood, where the hospital was located. As they pulled up to the curb in front of the hospital, a gray-haired man dressed in a dark business suit approached them.

"Mr. Miller, Ms. Raines, hello!" the man called out jovially, his smile as affable as the purple bow tie around his neck.

"Hello, Dr. Williams," Alex said. "Dr. Williams is the director of the hospital," he explained to Gen. "Dr. Williams, may I introduce Genevieve Monaghan?"

Smiling, Gen extended her hand. "Hello."

"Ahh, Ms. Monaghan, the artist." Dr. Williams nodded as he made the identification. "We're delighted that you're creating a piece for the new wing. Ms. Raines faxed us information about you. We couldn't be more pleased that you're a Bostonian. And I hear your mother volunteers here at the hospital?"

That bit of information must have come from Alex, for Gen hadn't mentioned it to Sydney. "Yes." She nodded. "She's been volunteering for several years now."

"Excellent. Ms. Giovanelli, our director of community relations, will be sure to include that in the hospital's newsletter." Turning to Sydney, he continued. "By the way, Ms. Raines, Ms. Giovanelli asked if she might join you and Pru Trudeau in about an hour. She wants to pick that brain of yours."

"Of course." Sydney smiled.

"Good, good." Dr. Williams rubbed his hands in satisfaction. "Oh! Speak of the devil. Here's Pru now. Prudence Trudeau heads our development office," he told Gen as they turned to watch a woman bustling toward them.

"Good morning. Sorry I'm late," she said as she shook hands with the group. "Little League game for Jimmy. The cleats went a-missing," she explained, still sounding a little out of breath.

Gen noticed that Alex cast Sydney a hard look before turning his attention to Pru Trudeau. "I hope meeting on a Saturday hasn't inconvenienced your family, Ms. Trudeau."

"Oh, no," she reassured him, shaking her head. "Jimmy insists he always strikes out when I'm in the bleachers, so it's just as well. And I'm so eager to see the copy for the bulletin. Harry and Sydney have done a wonderful job."

Sydney's smile lost its stiffness. "I've got the draft

right here," she said, hefting her attaché case a fraction.

"Terrific. Why don't we grab some coffee before we head up? Oh, and Kathy Giovanelli and I reserved a table at the Riviera Cafe for brunch at eleven-thirty," Pru said, naming a chic and very expensive restaurant just off Harvard Square.

"I love the Riviera," Sydney pronounced happily. "We haven't been there in months, have we, Alex?"

Turning to Gen and Alex, Pru Trudeau said, "We'd love it if you could join us."

"Thank you, but I doubt Dr. Williams and I will be finished in time," Alex replied.

"I'm sorry, I'll have to decline too," Gen said. "I have a family gathering to attend."

"It'll be a girls' brunch then," Pru said cheerfully.

A flash of irritation darkened Sydney's expression, then it was gone. "Yes," she echoed. "A girls' brunch, though right now I would just love a cup of coffee."

"Off we go, then. It was nice meeting you, Ms. Monaghan."

After Pru and Sydney had left, Alex turned to Dr. Williams. "Why don't we take Ms. Monaghan inside the wing so she can get started."

"But of course. Ms. Monaghan, if you'll come this way," Dr. Williams said, extending his arm for her to precede him. "We'll go in the front entrance. That way you can have the full effect of the atrium's space. I think you'll be quite pleased at the construction crew's progress, Mr. Miller. We're right on schedule." He held open one of the wide double doors and with a courtly sweep of his arm ushered Gen into the wing.

Her feet came to a halt as she looked around.

The entrance to the wing was built of glass and steel ribbing. The space had obviously been conceived with the idea of infusing a sense of hope into those who entered. Like a cathedral of light, it soared to the heavens. Lost in admiration, Gen tilted her head back to peer at the rays of sunlight streaming in through the paned glass, her feet turning in a slow revolution.

Lowering her gaze at last, her eyes met Alex's. She'd felt him watching her. "It's spectacular," she said simply.

An indefinable emotion crossed his face. He gave a slight nod of his head, acknowledging her words.

"Yes, it is." Pride rang in Dr. Williams's voice. "Our new wing is going to be used for the hospital's rehabilitation facilities. This atrium will be the registration area, with the corridors that you see on your right and left leading to specially designed therapy rooms with state-of-the-art equipment and technology. The rehabilitation center will play a vital role in helping the community, as its facilities will be open to outpatients as well as inpatients. Thanks to Mr. Miller's generosity, we have the opportunity to make this one of the finest rehabilitation centers for our children in the entire nation."

Gen walked toward a freestanding wall that served as a focal point for the atrium, intuiting that this was the wall where her work would rest.

"Do you have everything you need?"

Alex's question had Gen turning around. "Yes," she said, slipping her backpack off her shoulders. "I've got my sketch pad in here. Can you tell me what's going to be in front of this wall?"

"Wilfrid Seigel suggested we use it as a waiting area for the families. He showed me a sketch—" Alex broke off, watching as Gen opened her sketch pad and drew quickly.

"Something like this?" she asked, handing it to him.

"Yes." He regarded her closely, his brows knitted together. "How did you know that the sofas would be arranged in an open circle?"

"Because it works, because it's right. A square formation would have been too cold. Circles heal." Gen shrugged as if stating the obvious. "What? Why are you looking at me like that?" she asked, unnerved by his penetrating gaze.

He smiled. "I was just wondering how you came to be so wise."

If he only knew, Gen thought. Right now she was feeling very far from wise, especially when his words, when the heat of his smile, made her giddy with pleasure. And reckless with want.

"If you've everything you need, Dr. Williams and I will leave you alone so you can work without distraction. The security guard can page Dr. Williams in his office if you have any questions. When you're done, have the driver take you to your family's house in Somerville."

Perhaps it was the effect of the heady warmth Alex generated inside her. Perhaps it was the stunning beauty of the building he'd donated and what it represented.

Whatever the reason, Gen found herself saying, "Would you like to come to Bridget's party? It's not fancy or anything. Just grilled hamburgers and hot dogs followed by an extremely vicious game of softball."

She was so lovely standing there, staring back at him, so honest and fresh. For a moment the rest of the world faded away. Alex needed more than a moment, though. All morning, he'd suffered through Sydney's chatter, alternately filled with resignation and frustration. By the time the limo was cruising along the Charles River, he was definitely ready to roll down the window and toss Sydney out. But somehow he didn't think he could explain tossing his supposed lover out the window to Gen.

He wished he could turn back the clock, to yesterday morning, when he'd seen Gen naked on the beach. This time he wouldn't hesitate to follow his desires and take this extraordinary woman in his arms. . . . And what would she have thought? That he was a two-timing son of a bitch. One didn't have to be a mind reader to tell that Gen believed he and Sydney were together.

Alex knew the smart thing would be to refuse Gen's spontaneous invitation to come to her sister's party, fabricate some excuse, keep his distance, and above all not indulge in this growing attraction he felt for her. But it was too late, his normal self-control already shot to hell. "I'd like that very much," he said quietly. "I'll do my best to wrap up my meeting with Dr. Williams quickly."

*   *   *

Scooting forward on the leather seat, Gen addressed the limo driver. "This is great. You can pull up right here."

"Yes, miss," he answered and steered the limo into an open space beside the tree-lined park.

It required only a quick glance at the people milling around and at the small children laughingly chasing one another for Gen to nod happily. "Looks like the gang's all here."

"How can you tell? There are only about fifty people."

Gen turned to Alex and grinned. "Yup, an intimate family affair. I think you and Phoebe Hayes, my god-mother, will be the only two non-Monaghans here. I hope this won't bore you. It's really a low-key affair—Oh! Thank you," she said, surprised to find the chauffeur had already circled the car and was opening her door.

Alex got out of the limo and stood next to her, watching the crowd of people mingling. Some of Gen's relatives had obviously just arrived, if the hugs and cries of welcome were anything to go by. "A party in the park," he said.

"Large, open spaces are a basic necessity in our family," Gen informed him cheerfully. "By the time Benjamin was born, Mom and Dad couldn't fit all the family and friends into the house. Now it's a family tradition. Spring-through-fall birthdays get the playing fields, winter birthdays get the hockey rink. Whosever birthday it is gets to be captain and pick his or her team."

"Was it your sociologist father who devised this plan?" he asked.

"How'd you guess?" She grinned as a sudden shout went up and the first wave of children and adults began hurrying toward them. "Brace yourself. Here they come."

Gen and Alex were soon surrounded and Gen was engulfed in the arms of a slim, russet-haired woman. "Gen!" she cried. "No one told me you were coming. I thought I was going to lose the game for sure without my best pitcher."

"No fear, Bridge. I got lucky and was given a ride here. Bridge, this is Alex Miller. You can thank him for what's bound to be a shutout game," she said, pointedly ignoring the chorus of loud jeers that erupted at her outrageous boast.

"Hello," Alex said to Bridget. "Happy birthday."

"Thanks—and thanks for the present, too," she said, nodding her pointed chin at Gen. "Sis, you're looking great. Must be the sea air—or something." She grinned.

Gen was about to reply when an older couple approached. With a broad smile she flew into their outstretched arms. "Mom, Dad, I'd like to introduce you to Alex Miller." Turning to Alex, she said, "This is my mom and dad, Tansy and Robert Monaghan." Her lips quivered, hinting at mischief as she added in a teasing voice, "I won't bother introducing you to all the others, especially since you already know everyone here so well. It'll be a cinch to guess who's who."

The little witch, Alex thought to himself, tempted to throttle her, and then kiss her senseless, both impulses impossible given that he was surrounded by a legion of Monaghans. Luckily for him, Gen's enormous family were obviously used to having to repeat first names to strangers, and so he was able to begin the daunting matching process.

The group began a disordered march across the playing fields to where the grills and coolers were arranged beside picnic tables covered in bright plastic tablecloths. Alex found himself walking next to Robert Monaghan, Gen's father. A tall, lean, silver-haired man, he wore slightly rumpled khakis, tennis shoes, and a tattered sweater that had suede patches on the elbows. The lines on Professor Monaghan's face did nothing to diminish the sharp intelligence of the blue eyes appraising him. "Tansy and I are extremely grateful that you were able to arrange for Gen to attend Bridget's party."

"It was nothing. As I told Gen, I had an appointment with the director of the hospital, in any case. I'm the one who's grateful. Your daughter is a remarkable artist."

"Yes." He smiled. "Gen discovered her passion early on. Her godmother, Phoebe Hayes, gave her a paint set for her fifth birthday. More than any of our children, she throws herself entirely into what she loves."

The memory of Gen laughing while her beloved dog sprinted madly over the sand flashed in Alex's mind. The corners of his mouth lifted. "Yes, I've noticed that trait also."

"Which is why I was so relieved when I approached your Harvard Business School professors. They speak very highly of you. I was especially struck by how often the word *principle* came up."

Alex's steps slowed. "You had me checked out."

Robert Monaghan shrugged. "So to speak."

Alex's gaze immediately sought out Gen, who was walking between her mother and a young woman whose name Alex hadn't caught. Gen was gesturing animatedly as she talked. "You might be interested to learn that your daughter was quite affronted when I ran a background check on your family, Professor Monaghan," he said mildly. "As a matter of fact, she's still enjoying her petty revenge."

A slow smile spread over Robert Monaghan's craggy features as he digested that piece of news. "I can well imagine her reaction. But as her father, I'm able to sleep much better knowing the kind of man you are." His gaze pierced Alex. "It's a tricky business, loving a child yet knowing that she needs her freedom—of all our children, Gen seems to need that the most. There've been many a night these past few years when I've paced the floor."

"I understand your concern, sir. New York can be a tough city."

"New York?" Professor Monaghan repeated, his blue eyes twinkling. He gave a soft laugh. "New York was the least of my worries," he replied enigmatically. "Well, that's all in the past. Now, would you consider doing an old man a favor, and keep this investigation business a secret between ourselves? Gen might very well decide to chew me out, too."

Alex grinned. "Of course."

"I'm indebted to you, my boy. Now, come and

have some food before we test your mettle as ball-player."

A short time later, Phoebe Hayes arrived. After kissing Tansy hello and offering Bridget her best wishes, she made her way over to Gen. "Is it true you've brought Grace's nephew?"

"Yeah, he's over there, talking to Nolan and Alana." Twenty yards of grass dotted with clumps of chatting family members separated them, but amazingly Alex seemed to hear her. He looked over, his gaze connecting with hers, and then turned, saying something to her brother and sister.

Gen realized he was excusing himself. She hoped she didn't sound as breathless as she felt when she said, "Here he comes. I'll introduce you, Phoebe."

Phoebe was a smart woman. She dispensed with a handshake, opting to kiss Alex on both cheeks. "I'm thrilled to meet you after all these years. I knew your uncle Alexander very well. He was a wonderful man. You're every bit as handsome."

Alex smiled. "Aunt Grace says you have a stunning collection of contemporary art. I've become quite interested in the field myself. . . ." His gaze slid back to Gen. For a second the rest of Gen's family seemed to disappear, leaving only Alex and her. Her pulse fluttered. *Lord, how could he affect her with just a look?*

Then Phoebe spoke, bringing Gen abruptly back to reality. "Darling," she said, her eyes shining with excitement. "I'm going to steal this young man from you. I'll give him back when it's time to play soft-ball."

Grateful that Phoebe had broken Alex's spell, Gen smiled. "By the way, do you play?" she asked him.

"These days? Only with my niece and nephew."

Heaving a dramatic sigh she said, "That's okay. We'll put you in left field," and had to bite the inside of her cheek when he scowled. Turning back to her godmother, she kissed her cheek. "I'm going to go chat with Mom. He's all yours, Phoebe."

"If only I were thirty years younger!" Phoebe declared in a stage whisper.

ELEVEN

Gen and her mother found a quiet spot beneath a maple tree. They sat cross-legged, laden paper plates balanced on their folded legs. Gen munched on her hot dog, her gaze flitting over the groups of people. Despite the number of loved ones assembled, her eyes always seemed to return to Alex, as if drawn by an irresistible force.

Next to her, Gen's mother forked a last bite of the potato salad Bridget had brought and patted her lips with a paper napkin. "Everyone looks like they're having a good time. Phoebe's positively glowing, dazzled by Alex Miller."

Gen grinned around a mouthful of hot dog. The two of them were still talking. Even from this distance she could hear Phoebe's peals of laughter. She wasn't convinced her godmother would be all that willing to part with Alex when the time came to play ball—which was probably how most women felt when it came to Alex Miller.

"Alex seems like a charming man," her mother said

in a tone that made Gen wonder if she'd noticed that her daughter couldn't keep her eyes off him.

"Yes." She gave a firm nod. That was absolutely undeniable. "He's interesting, too. I haven't figured him out—" Gen didn't get a chance to finish, for just then Bridget plopped down next to them.

"Thanks for the great party, Mom," she said. "So, spill the beans. What are you two whispering about? Or need I guess?" she added in an arch tone.

"Nothing terribly secret, Bridget. Gen and I were talking about how nice Alex Miller is."

"Nice?" Bridget's hoot of laughter was loud enough to turn several heads in their direction. "Nice doesn't begin to describe someone like Alex Miller, Mom. The man is gorgeous, divine . . . utterly scrumptious."

Gen bit back a laugh. Her sister, who'd taken over the family kitchen when she was twelve, reserved her highest praise for anything she considered tasty—but she had to agree with Bridget. Alex was definitely yummy.

Bridget caught her eye, grinning too. "He's a lovely birthday present, Gen. Thank you," and blew her a kiss.

She shook her head. "Sorry, Bridge. You're not getting anything nearly so fancy. Besides, he's already taken."

"Yeah?"

"Uh-huh," Gen replied, nodding. "He and a woman named Sydney Raines. They make a pretty dynamic duo. High society and all that."

"Really? How funny. He hasn't been looking at you

like someone who's taken. I have a hunch he finds you pretty darn delectable, kiddo."

Blushing furiously, Gen shoved the remainder of her hot dog in her mouth so she wouldn't have to reply, then nearly choked when her sister calmly added, "I think you should go for it, Gen. Lap him up with a little whipped cream and a dash of Grand Marnier."

"Stop teasing her, Bridget," her mother said calmly as she whacked Gen between her shoulder blades until her coughing fit subsided.

"I'm not teasing at all. This is some serious wisdom I'm dispensing, Mom. You've got to seize your chances while you can, sweetie pie. Men like Alex Miller don't come a dime a dozen."

"You were obviously given a few too many of those trite birthday cards this year."

"Nary a one. This advice is solid gold."

Attempting a swallow, Gen grimaced. "Yeah, well, I'll try to remember that next time I'm around some whipped cream."

"Good." Bridget gave an approving nod. "I think I'll let you and Mom go back to your whispering. I'm going to drag Tessie over to Alex and Phoebe. This'll be a dream come true for her. At last she'll be able to talk to someone who understands what she's saying. All those numbers and weird terms," she said with a mock shudder of horror. Rising to her feet, she brushed off her jeans and made a beeline for Tess.

"She must be eating leftover Valentine's Day cookies or something," Gen said, shaking her head as she watched her older sister. "She's chock-full of romance."

Her mother smiled. "You know, Bridget's advice isn't all cockamamie."

"Yeah, except that Bridge has got it all wrong. Sydney and Alex are definitely an item, Mom. Monogrammed towels and everything," she joked. "And besides, they're really well suited for each other."

"Sweetheart, your father's an academic. I don't have a scholarly bone in my body. Yet we've been happily married for forty-one years."

Gen gazed into her mother's face, still youthful despite the gray cap of hair framing it. "That's because what you and Dad have is something special and rare. I don't think there are too many loves like yours. And while I admit Alex Miller is handsome and smart and funny enough to turn any woman's head, do you know what I think he really needs? A friend. There's something about him that makes me think he's so alone. I could be a good friend to him, Mom."

Her mother's smile had her plump cheeks meeting her hazel eyes. She took Gen's hand and squeezed it tenderly. "If that's what you want, dear."

Gen nodded vigorously. "Yes, that's what I want." Then as if her mother needed convincing, she added, "Besides, I don't really have room in my life for anything but my art right now—except for softball, that is." She sprang to her feet as if her tail were on fire. "Come on, Mom, let's get these characters to play ball."

Nolan was too damned lucky, Gen thought sourly as she sat on the edge of the baseball diamond and glared at her brother, who was now infielding at second base. Last inning, he'd hit a double off her slider, driving in two runs and bringing the score to 4–3 in the top of the ninth.

Her team was up now. Bottom of the ninth, it was a do-or-die situation.

Gen got on base with a sneaky, perfectly executed bunt. But she was forced to cool her heels on first when both her mother and Delia struck out. Now Alex was up. In his other at-bats he'd had a walk and a pop-up that was caught by her father. He walked up to the plate, his dark trousers and white dress shirt totally at odds with the jeans and sweatshirts of the other players.

Gen uttered a quick prayer that Kyle, who was pitching, wouldn't send him diving into the dirt. Kyle played on a traveling team with his fellow police officers and wasn't the type to show anybody mercy.

As she'd feared, the first ball went straight at Alex's head. When he stood up, a smear of reddish dirt covered his front. Gen bit her lip while Alex calmly brushed himself off and took his stance over the plate. Kyle's second pitch had a spin like a gyroscope, twisting abruptly away from the plate as the bat went to meet it. The ball popped up for a foul. Thank God nobody caught it, she thought. Then before she could remind herself that this was only a stupid ball game, she cupped her hands to her mouth and shouted, "Come on, Miller! Take him down."

Alex lowered his bat, stepped away from the plate, and sent Gen a searing look that burned from thirty feet. With a roll of his shoulders he assumed his batting stance. Then Kyle was cocking his arm and hurl-ing a wicked fastball straight at him.

Which Alex promptly hammered into the far park-ing lot. Gen was so astonished she nearly forgot to run. As Alex tagged home plate, their teammates went wild, swarming them both. But what made Gen grin from ear to ear was the sight of her team slap-ping Alex on the back. Even the losers were atypically good-natured, contenting themselves with jibes about banning Gen from importing all-star players. But Bridget, after giving Alex a very enthusiastic smooch on the cheek, declared that from now on he had a permanent place on her birthday guest list.

There wasn't much time to linger after the game. Gen's nephews and nieces, cranky and teary from the excitement of the day, were ready for baths, dinner, and bed. She had only just managed to say good-bye to everyone when the limo pulled up so they could re-turn to the hospital and collect Sydney before going on to the airport.

"I love my spice jars, Gen," Bridget said as they stood next to the idling limo. "They'll be the center-piece of the restaurant. I'm so glad you came today and brought Alex." As she hugged Gen, her voice dropped to a whisper, "And don't forget what I said about seizing the moment."

"Sure, Bridge, I'll remember." She squeezed her sis-ter back. "Happy birthday, again. I hope I look as good as you when I'm your age," and laughed when Bridget stuck out her tongue.

A lump formed in Gen's throat as she embraced her

parents. " 'Bye, Dad, 'bye, Mom. I wish you could come see the studio—"

"Oh, goodness!" her mother exclaimed in a stricken tone. "That reminds me, I almost forgot to tell you. Jiri called. He tried you in New York, and became concerned when the operator said the number was disconnected. I gave him the number in Long Island."

Gen felt terrible. "I should have called him myself to tell him about the show and my new studio. I'll call him right away. He won't believe his ears when he hears I've been given a public commission."

"He sounded really eager to speak with you," her mother said.

"Oh, you know Jiri. He probably wants to talk shop and fill me in on how the directorship is working out."

"I think it's more likely he's realizing how much he misses you, Gen," Bridget contradicted her, her green eyes twinkling with her special brand of mischief. Aware that Alex was listening to the conversation, Gen tried for a casual shrug.

"Poor Jiri," Bridget continued, her tone sympathetic. "He's probably only now figuring out what he's lost in you—his right arm as well as his muse."

TWELVE

After Sydney's chilly greeting at finding Gen and Alex disheveled and dirt-stained, Gen volunteered to ride in the front of the limo. It didn't take a rocket scientist to figure out that Sydney wasn't very happy to learn that Alex had accompanied Gen to Bridget's party. The ride to the airport was made in tense silence. Gen breathed a sigh of relief when the limo pulled into the airport's entrance.

Gen let sleep claim her the moment the plane lifted off the ground. Indeed, the sunshine, her family's calorie-packed birthday meal, and the excitement of the softball game induced a sleep of the dead. She roused to groggy wakefulness only when the plane's wheels bumped, touching down on the tarmac.

Bleary-eyed, she stumbled after Alex and Sydney to where the Aston Martin was parked. Climbing into the backseat, she shut her eyes the moment the car's engine roared to life. Perhaps it was the downshift of gears, or Alex braking as he turned onto the graveled drive, but Gen awakened to the sound of Sydney's voice.

"Alex, please, Miriam Howard throws such wonderful parties." There was a desperate note in Sydney's voice.

Disoriented though she was, Gen nevertheless immediately sensed the tension crackling between Alex and Sydney, noted too the steely inflexibility in Alex's voice when he replied, "No," quietly yet distinctly. "I'm not going with you to the party, and I've already told you why."

"I guess some parties are more important than others," Sydney said. "I guess some people are more important than others. Very well, I'll go to the party on my own. I'm sure I'll think of something to say as an excuse for why you're not with me."

"How about the truth?" came Alex's drawled response.

Sydney stiffened as if she'd been slapped. Then as Alex pulled the car up beside Gen's battered Yugo, she swiveled in the seat to face him. "You coldhearted bastard," she hissed before scrambling out and slamming the door behind her.

"Damn," Gen heard Alex utter with a weariness so complete it made Gen's heart wrench.

She quickly shut her eyes, feigning sleep. It would only make things worse, more complicated, if she were to let on that she'd overheard their fight. While Sydney definitely wasn't Gen's favorite person, she had no wish to cause her hurt, and hated that she'd played an unwitting role in their disagreement.

A second later she heard the driver's door open then shut with a soft click. Before she could pretend to awaken, however, Alex had her own door open and was scooping her out of the backseat as if she were no bigger than a child.

She squirmed, making an inarticulate cry of protest—coherency next to impossible with Alex carrying her in his strong arms—but he ignored her protests, striding easily across the grass in the soft half-light of evening. "Relax, Monaghan, you struck out nine of your brothers and sisters today. You're dead on your feet."

"I'd have struck out Nolan, too, if he hadn't gone for that slider," she grumbled.

"You'll get him next time, Ace," he replied, laughter threading his voice.

She gave a halfhearted wiggle. "I can walk. Really. I'm awake now." In her heart she hoped he'd ignore her again. It felt so wonderful to be cradled in his arms, the warmth of his body seeping into hers, his scent, citrusy and slightly salty, making her senses swim. Surely she could indulge in a stolen moment of pleasure, just this once?

"You've got to be kidding. You were weaving your way across the airport parking lot like a drunken sailor. If I let you walk, you might fall and sprain your ankle. We're almost there, anyway. Just lie back and think of Murphy."

Gen gave a muffled snort. "You're a fool."

"Yeah, maybe," he agreed. "Definitely where you're concerned," he added under his breath.

Gen's heart squeezed at the softly spoken words. But before she could ponder the meaning of his cryptic remark, his arms shifted, loosening their hold. Gently he lowered her to her feet.

They were in front of the studio door. His hands grasped her shoulders, steadying her, and Gen was keenly aware of how close his leanly muscled body was to hers. His breath was a warm tantalizing breeze on her face. "Thanks for including me in the festivities today. You're lucky to have such a remarkable family."

Gen stared up at him, knowing as she did that despite the evening shadows, her secret yearning was plainly visible, etched on her face. Yet she was helpless to look away, or to break the connection between them.

With a crooked smile that tugged at her heart, he reached up and traced the curve of her cheek. Without another word, he turned and headed toward the house. She stared after him until he'd vanished into the shadows.

An hour passed while Sydney, holed up in the guest room to which Mrs. Miller always insisted on relegating her, rejected one outfit after the other. She absolutely refused to go downstairs until she looked in the mirror and beheld a woman who could bring men to their knees. She kept remembering how Alex had looked in the limo, happy and tired, with dirt streaks covering the front of his tailored shirt. He'd obviously been more than willing to grovel in the dirt for Gen.

Sydney couldn't understand it. There was no real contest—she was ten times more beautiful than Gen Monaghan. So why was he going to parties with Gen and meeting her entire family? He'd never been will-

ing to attend one of her mother's parties. In the midst
of slipping into an ivory dress that hugged her curves
like a lover, Sydney paused, frowning. In fact, the
only man who didn't seem fazed by her mother was
Harry.

Harry had been wonderful during the latest lunch
they'd endured with Hilary Raines. Throughout the
course of the meal, he'd deflected her mother's avid
questions about Alex Miller's TLM Fund with a smooth
aplomb, adroitly saving Sydney from having to reply
to her relentless harping.

All of a sudden, Sydney's thoughts veered to another memory of Harry. She heard his voice. It was
devoid of its usual teasing notes. *"Maybe if you were
with a guy who loved you, you wouldn't be obsessing
about what you have to do to keep him. Don't you
think it's time you found a guy you want instead of
trying to please your mother?"*

She shook her head, as if she might be able to dis-
lodge the memory. Since when had Harry become her
conscience? she wondered, annoyed.

Smoothing the dress over her hips, she focused on
her reflection, appraising it critically. The dress was
perfect, but the rest of her? While she'd been thinking
of Harry, her teeth had caught her lower lip, gnawing
it painfully. Her forehead was wrinkled with unhappy
lines.

With a determined effort, Sydney smoothed her expression and pasted a cool, confident smile on her
face. There, much better. All she needed was a little
lipstick, some blush and mascara, and she'd be ready
to bring Alex to his knees.

* * *

Upstairs in his bedroom, Alex, freshly showered, pulled on a pair of jeans and a dark blue button-down shirt. He left the shirt open, enjoying the ocean breeze coming in through the bay windows. The glass of whiskey he'd brought upstairs was sitting on the small end table next to an overstuffed chair near the windows. He dropped into the chair, grabbed the whiskey, and took a long, slow sip. The whiskey's rich, smoky, complex flavor reminded him of Gen. But hell, almost everything made him think of Gen, or of the countless ways he'd like to make love to her. She'd be like the whiskey: worth lingering over and savoring.

His aunt Grace was with her now, having volunteered to bring Murphy back to the studio. He knew Grace would be gone awhile, happily pumping Gen about the wing and her ideas for the painting.

He'd only barely resisted the temptation to join them. In the end resisting just because he wanted to be near Gen so damn much. Each time he was around her he had to restrain himself from taking her in his arms. He'd already succumbed once today, when he'd insisted on carrying her from the car to the studio— a flimsy excuse to press her body close to his and breathe in her light, flowery scent. The thrill he'd gotten holding her told him that the next time he touched her, he wouldn't be able to stop or content himself with stroking the velvety smoothness of her cheek.

His hunger for her shook him. Alex wasn't accus-

tomed to needing so much that it filled every fiber of
his being.

But with Gen, everything was different. Why, he
wasn't sure. Perhaps it was because she was so many
things to him already, perhaps it was because he liked
her, liked her sprawling, affectionate family. Hell, he
even liked her hairy monster of a dog. Ultimately, all
that mattered was the relentless desire that clawed
him whenever she was near.

And that was why he was still fighting it. He was
beginning to suspect that if he yielded to this all-
consuming need and made love to Gen, it still might
not be enough. Because from Gen he would want
more than just sex, he'd want—

Alex's thoughts were interrupted by the sound of
heels clicking against the hardwood floor outside his
room. The knock on the door had him turning away
from the mesmerizing view of the ocean waves outside his windows. "Come in."

Sydney looked like dynamite. The high-heeled sandals made her legs appear endless, and her ivory dress
left little to the imagination. It occurred to Alex that
life would be so much easier if he could transfer even
one iota of the desire he felt for Gen to Sydney.

"You look beautiful, Sydney," he said honestly albeit disinterestedly. He couldn't help it that these days
his tastes ran to bluish-green-eyed freckled nymphs in
paint-spattered clothes and high-tops.

Sydney's smile warmed at the compliment. "I was
hoping you might have changed your mind about
going to the party with me."

"Sorry to disappoint you, but no, I haven't changed my mind. About anything."

"Maybe this will persuade you otherwise," she murmured, her hips swinging seductively beneath her dress as she walked toward him, stopping within arm's reach from where he sat. Slowly she lifted the hem of her dress. Cut so it ended at midthigh, the dress didn't have far to travel up the length of her bare legs and over the flare of her hips before it was gathered at her waist.

Alex stared at the nearly transparent scrap of lace covering her mound. Raising his gaze, he met Sydney's eyes. They gleamed glittery bright with anticipation and arousal. Maybe she was so close to climaxing that she couldn't see the truth: she left him cold. Sydney was beautiful and erotically sexy. Yes, he'd grant her that and more but whatever they'd once enjoyed together was gone.

The fabric rustled softly as her hands shifted. Alex didn't even bother to look; from the slight shift of her body he knew she was shimmying out of that scrap of nothing then dropping the hem, so the dress resettled over her naked body.

"I'll be waiting for you, Alex." And she tossed the scrap of lace toward his lap like a parting gift. He didn't lift a finger to catch it. Light as air, it floated, landing silently on the floor near his chair. She pivoted on her heels and cast a sultry glance over her shoulder. "But don't make me wait too long for what we both want." Her smile was provocative. "My patience is wearing thin."

"Good-bye, Sydney."

He waited until she'd gone to drop his head against the back of the chair with a loud groan. Christ, this mess just kept getting stickier. Sydney still wanted him. He wanted Gen, but couldn't do a damn thing about pursuing her with Sydney playing her games, tossing panties as she paraded about as his lover.

Worldly-wise, Alex knew women's bodies. When he'd carried Gen in his arms, he'd felt that delicious, telltale softening in her body. If he'd chosen to, he could have lowered his lips to hers and tasted her. He could have learned her curves, the silky-soft texture of her body—she could have been his. But Gen wasn't the type of person to have an affair with him if Sydney was in the picture.

He rubbed his face with his hands. God, he hoped Sydney would finally get the message when he didn't come running to her pantyless side tonight.

The ring of his cell phone had him looking up and glancing around the bedroom in an effort to locate it. It was on the bureau. "Miller," he said, pressing the talk button.

"Hiya, Uncle Alex."

Alex grinned at the sound of his six-year-old niece's voice. "Soph! How's my blue-eyed daredevil?" he asked. He sat on the bed and lifted his legs up, crossing his bare ankles. All thoughts of Sydney and the trouble she was causing in his life vanished as Sophie launched into an enthusiastic description of the day's activities.

"And guess what, Uncle Alex? Me and Jamie jumped crossbars—what?" Alex grinned as he heard the faint voice of his sister, Cassie, then Sophie was speaking again. "Jamie and I," she corrected, "jumped cross-bars today. Pip was super and Topper—you won't believe what he did—a funny crow hop right after the jump. But Jamie stayed on him. Mommy says she's gonna—going—to cut back on Topper's grain, 'cause he's feelin' a little full of himself."

"Is that so?" Alex said, biting back a chuckle as he pictured the rotund and extremely placid twenty-four-year-old pony.

"So whatcha been doing, Uncle Alex? Did you go swimming?"

"No. I'm afraid I didn't get the chance. I had to go to Boston."

"Oh," she said with ill-concealed disappointment. Clearly Boston didn't rank as high as swimming on Sophie's list.

"But I got to go to a birthday party where there were tons of people. We played a game of softball and our team won."

This was definitely up Sophie's alley. "Really?" she said. "Whose birthday?"

"Well, it was the older sister of Gen. Gen's the lady who's staying at Great-Aunt Grace's while Tilly's away."

"Will we get to meet her?"

"Yes, she's living in Great-Uncle Alex's old studio. Gen's a painter. She makes beautiful paintings, Soph."

"Is she old like Great-Aunt Grace?"

Alex laughed. "No, she's about your mommy's age."

"Oh." Sophie paused. "What does she look like?"

Alex leaned back against the headboard. He closed his eyes, conjuring her, and there was a smile in his voice when he said, "Well, she's really pretty. With freckles and straight shiny hair. She has these neat eyes, Soph, that are blue and green and brown, all mixed up. When she smiles, it goes straight to her eyes. Oh, and she's got a dog named Murphy who's as big as you and Jamie," he finished.

"Wow! Do you think she'll let me play with him?"

"We can ask."

"Mommy, Mommy," Alex heard Sophie call out. She had yet to master the trick of putting a hand over the mouthpiece. "Uncle Alex got to play softball at a party and he has a friend named Gen and she's pretty and she has a dog! Can we bring Radar and Belle so that they can play with her dog? Please?"

"I think it's my turn to speak with Uncle Alex, pumpkin," he heard Cassie say.

" 'Bye, Uncle Alex. Remember to ask if we can play with her dog!"

"I will. 'Bye, Soph. I love you. See you next week."

"Alex?" Cassie's voice came on the line.

"Hey, sis."

"So, tell me about this pretty friend who has a dog."

Alex cleared his throat. "That's Gen. The artist who's going to paint the work for the hospital wing," he explained. "Her dog's a wolfhound. A beaut."

"My, my. And how pretty is Gen?"

"Very."

"And how does she feel about you, Alex?"

"I'm almost positive she thinks I'm pretty too," he teased.

"Alex," his sister said warningly.

"Okay, okay. How does she feel about me? Well, we kind of got off to a rocky start." A smile curved his lips as he recalled some of her barbs. He liked that she wasn't afraid to stand up to him or speak her mind.

"You mean she didn't fall head over heels the instant she saw you? A woman with brains."

"Very funny, Cass. Very funny."

"And how's Sydney these days?" Though his sister's tone was carefully neutral, Alex knew that she hadn't been especially taken with Sydney—or with any of his previous girlfriends.

"Sydney's around, but on a very limited basis. She still has to organize the party and the dedication ceremony."

There was a silence. Alex pictured his sister working through the implications of what he'd said. "Well, I can't wait to see how you're handling all this, Alex. You've definitely piqued my curiosity about this Gen."

"I think you'll like her, Cass. Her artwork is amazing."

"I bet Aunt Grace is thrilled to have her stay while Tilly's gone. How is Aunt Grace?"

"Great. We're going driving in about twenty minutes."

"In the Aston?"

"Yeah." He grinned. "I know she'd like me to let her take it out alone. But this way I can keep an eye on the speedometer. So, I'll pick the four of you up at the airport?"

"All four of us," Cassie repeated. "Though believe me, I'll have my work cut out dissuading Sophie from bringing Radar and Belle as canine playmates for that wolfhound."

Alex laughed. "And your efforts will be greatly appreciated, sis."

Sydney had positioned herself strategically, standing toward the back of the lavishly decorated living room so that she had an optimal view of every guest who passed through Dick and Miriam Howard's doorway. The house was now overflowing with people, but that hadn't stopped her from scanning each face, her stomach tightening in a painful knot whenever the face belonged to someone other than Alex. Already she'd popped a Rolaids from her beaded clutch and downed two champagnes, while around her people talked and laughed, some calling out a greeting to her. Her smiles and replies came automatically.

He had to come.

Why hadn't he come?

The plaintive demand rang inside Sydney's head, horribly and hauntingly familiar—a refrain whispered under her breath by her nine-year-old self as she'd stared out the window, waiting for her father to come for Christmas. She'd worked so hard to suppress the yearning little girl inside her—at that moment she almost hated Alex for causing her to resurface.

She'd been concentrating so hard on the faces of the people entering the Howard's home, willing them to morph into Alex's features, that the vivid green eyes staring back at her didn't register immediately.

With a surprised start she cried, "Harry!" as he reached her. "I didn't know you were planning to come tonight."

"Jeff and Nina invited me. I'd have told you I was coming but you clearly had plans of your own." He paused and his gaze swept around the room. "Is Alex with you?"

At Alex's name, her lips trembled. She shook her head, afraid if she spoke her voice would come out wobbly.

The hard glint in Harry's eyes softened. He cocked his head. "Poor baby," he murmured. The compassion in his voice was her undoing. The trembling descended to her shoulders then to the rest of her body.

"Ah, Syd, come here," he said, opening his arms. She stepped into them. His breath was warm against the shell of her ear as he made soothing noises. His hand, splayed across her back, moved in slow, hypnotic circles. "It's all right," he said quietly. "I'm here now. I'll take care of you."

Had she forgotten how it felt to be comforted? she wondered as Harry's warm strength seeped into her. She leaned into him gratefully, wishing she could burrow inside him. She inhaled deeply and closed her eyes.

"There now. Feeling better?" he asked. His arms loosened their hold on her fractionally.

She made a mew of protest and stepped closer. "Hold me, Harry," she whispered.

He looked at her, his handsome face solemn and strangely intense. "Sydney, don't you know that I'd do anything for you?" And his arms tightened again, drawing her flush against his rangy body.

The tender, unexpected words caused a swell of happiness, and a warm glow filled her. What would she do without Harry? she thought, ducking her head so her cheek was pressed to his chest. Beneath her ear she heard the steady thud of his heart. They stood entwined like this for a few moments, as if they were alone in the crowded room, while Sydney grew increasingly aware of how good it felt to be in Harry's arms. Of their own volition, her hands began wandering idly over his back, exploring the taut muscles beneath the fine cotton shirt. Traveling upward, her fingers toyed with his dark, curly hair and her thumbs brushed the lobes of his ear.

She was so close to him that she could feel the change in the rhythm of his breathing, feel his muscles tighten . . . feel his erection press against her belly.

Her heart hammered in recognition.

Slowly she tilted her head. His green eyes burned with a heat that seared all the way to her toes. "You want me," she whispered, awed by the revelation.

Harry smiled crookedly. "Eternally. But I'll live." He gave a small shrug. "I've become used to this condition."

He took a step back to put distance between them. But Sydney's arms were still looped about his neck. She moved with him, molding her body to his.

His breath came out a hiss. "Careful there, Sydney," he warned. "You're awfully close to the fire."

Indeed, the sudden heat coming in waves off his

body scorched her, set her own blood afire. She tried to swallow but couldn't. Her mouth had gone dry. "I need you to make me forget him, Harry," she whispered. "I want you to make the hurt go away. Please, Harry."

His gaze bored into hers. "I won't be a plaything for you, Sydney. Once I have you, I'm not letting you go."

Sydney felt a moment's hesitation. He looked so serious. But what if something went wrong? Harry was her partner. Together, with their complementary strengths, they made a terrific team, an unbeatable pair. If she lost him, she'd be losing so much: her business partner, her confidant, *her friend*. The enormity of what was at stake shook her.

"Scared, Syd?" Harry asked. He knew her so very well. He held her gaze, waiting for her answer.

She tried to swallow again. "Yes," she managed. "I'm terrified."

"Too scared to take a chance?" he asked quietly.

"Maybe—"

His expression altered, became shuttered. "I'm sorry to hear that. Have a good rest of the evening."

"—not," she finished.

His arms tightened about her. "Sydney," he whispered roughly. "Do you have any idea how long I've wanted you?"

She gazed into Harry's eyes. It was as if he was only now allowing her to see the depth of his desire. "I'm beginning to," she replied breathlessly. Her body began shaking once more, this time because her heart was hammering so. And then because it was Harry, and he wanted her, and, Lord, she wanted him with a sudden, desperate hunger, she said, "And Harry? Just to let you know, I'm not wearing any panties," laughing, delirious with happiness and excitement when his grip tightened convulsively around her.

"We, my lovely wicked witch," he growled, "are getting out of here—now."

It was nearly three in the morning when Sydney's BMW inched up the graveled driveway to the Miller house. Sydney sat curled in the passenger seat, facing sideways so she could clasp Harry's arm as he drove. By the dashboard light Harry's profile looked stern, his lips pressed in a straight line. He was still dead set against her decision to return to the Millers' for what remained of the night. He eased the car alongside Alex's Aston Martin, put the gear in neutral, pulled up the parking brake, and shifted in his seat. He looked at her silently.

"Harry, it'll be all right. I promise," she said, her voice quiet in the confines of the car. "I have to go back tonight. All my clothes and papers are there. And I've arranged for the tasting at La Plage at eleven. If I stay with you, I'll doze off in the caviar—because you know we won't be doing any sleeping." A smile curved her lips. Harry had been so aroused that Sydney had had trouble getting the condom over him—not just the first frantic, near-violent time, but each time they'd made love. Her body still tingled from the aftershocks of their passion.

"Why don't you reschedule the tasting?"

"I can't. A second rescheduling would ruin our

relations with Nancy. Then where would we be when our next client requested a catered party in the Hamptons?"

"I don't want you around Miller, where he can remind you of all the things you've spent years thinking you want. Alex is history. You're mine now, Syd."

Harry's possessiveness sent a secret thrill through Sydney. She hadn't expected him to act like this—but then again, so much of this evening was unexpected, like a wonderful dream. "Don't you trust me?" she asked, thinking that Harry would be right not to—it wasn't exactly easy to get over a man like Alex Miller. Even now, languid from the wild passion he'd shown her, a tiny part of her heart ached for Alex.

"Of course I do, Syd. It's just that—"

"Alex isn't interested in me, Harry," she said, and knew she was brave enough to say this only because of Harry's sweet, savage lovemaking. "He's said it again and again—and after last night, well, I'm not interested in him. But I have to go. Remember how you told me to do the best damn job I could with the TLM contract? This party for the Miller Group falls under the same rubric, Harry. I intend to do an outstanding job. So take my BMW back to Jeff and Nina's. I'll put my bags in Alex's trunk so when the tasting's over, you can pick me up at the restaurant." She leaned into him until her lips hovered next to his and whispered, "In the meantime get some sleep, lover. You'll need all your strength."

Sydney felt Harry's mouth stretch in a smile as he brushed his lips against hers. In a voice low and raspy with arousal, he said, "Could this mean you doubt my powers of recuperation?"

"Well, I don't know," she said breathlessly. "You haven't touched me in at least five minutes. I assumed you must be tiring—" With a soft growl, Harry pulled her closer, and kissed her ravenously.

Dizzy from his drugging kisses, wanting only more and more again of what he could give her, Sydney let her hand drift down to his lap. "Oh, Harry," she breathed against his smiling lips. "I am impressed."

"Good. Now, lift up your dress, Syd. Slowly. Mmm, yes, that's very good."

THIRTEEN

The house was quiet Sunday morning when Gen entered by the kitchen door. Her hair, still wet from her outdoor shower, was combed so it hung straight, brushing her shoulders and leaving two dark patches on her faded Red Sox T-shirt.

She brewed a pot of coffee, poured herself a cup, and grabbed a Granny Smith apple from the fruit bowl sitting in the center of the French provincial table. She crossed the downstairs with her breakfast in hand to enjoy it on the porch as she watched the clouds race one another. Murphy's nails clicked against the floor as he followed her. Pushing open the old wooden screen door with her hip, she held it as Murphy brushed past.

From behind, Alex's voice greeted her. "Good morning."

Gen swallowed a yelp of surprise. "Hi," she said, trying for a casual tone even though her heart had skipped about a thousand beats. She hadn't seen Alex since last night. But the memory of him gallantly carrying her in his arms was still fresh in her mind. She felt awkward and shy, like some naive bumpkin—aware that she was reacting out of all proportion to something that had no romantic significance at all.

Drawing a breath to compose herself, she turned and her heart took another acrobatic leap. Alex was lounging in the painted rocking chair, looking rumpled and sexy in jeans and an untucked button-down shirt. That his feet were bare and that his jaw was shadowed with light brown stubble did nothing to help her composure. It was unnerving how Alex seemed more good-looking every time she saw him—an achievement well nigh impossible since she'd already thought he was one of the handsomest men she'd ever laid eyes on. But her earlier appreciation had been that of an artist's. What made Alex so devastatingly attractive now was that she was beginning to like him so much as a man.

The thought made her stumble, hot coffee sloshing onto the back of her hand. She winced and muttered, "Ouch. Clumsy of me," then lifted the angry red mark on her skin to her mouth. Silently she chastised herself, You deserve to get burned, Monaghan, if you're foolish enough to contemplate playing with a fire as dangerous as Alex Miller.

"Are you okay? Can I get you something?" he asked. His eyes were riveted on her mouth soothing the back of her hand.

Gen immediately pulled her hand away. "No, thanks, it just stings a little." She sat down into the rocker beside his, bit a chunk out of her apple, and chewed vigorously, hoping that would normalize the situation:

two people on a porch, one eating an apple. No big deal.

So why was her heart still playing leap-frog?

"No swimming today?" Alex asked.

So much for normalcy, she thought as her cheeks flamed. She cast a sideways glance at Alex. He was staring at the shoreline where she and Murphy had been swimming the other day. "No, the water's a bit too rough for Murphy. I don't want him getting rolled."

Alex bent over and scratched Murphy vigorously behind the ear. Murphy's tail thumped in ecstasy. Sipping her coffee, she eyed him with a touch of pique that he'd won her dog over so quickly and that he could make her heart go *thump, thump* just as effortlessly. "How about you?" she said. "Why are you up so early? Lifeguard duty? Or reserving your seat for the peep show?"

"I had work to do. Though I admit the chance to see you naked was definitely enough to get me up." The corners of his eyes crinkled as he grinned wickedly.

Dear Lord, Alex was flirting with her and she liked it, she really liked it. Rattled, she blurted out, "So I guess Sydney's not an early riser," dropping his girlfriend's name like a ton of bricks between them.

Alex's grin lost its teasing allure. "I'm sure she'll be down for breakfast," he replied. "We have to go to a tasting at eleven."

"A tasting?"

"Yes, a restaurant is catering the party I'm giving next weekend. I'd like to invite you to it—though I'm afraid I can't promise you the excitement of a softball game."

"Oh, well, my family's parties are a bit special. Uh, thank you for inviting me." Inwardly Gen cringed, already imagining what the party would be like. A crowd of movers and shakers. She wouldn't fit in, wouldn't know what to say to them. And they, in return, would have nothing to say to her. "I'll probably be working, though. And, um, big parties aren't really my thing. Won't Sydney be going to the party?"

"Of course," Alex replied, a distinct note of frustration entering his voice. "Listen, Gen. About Sydney and me. Our relationship, it's not what you think—"

Gen had gone completely still listening to him, and only realized why he'd stopped when the porch door opened behind her. She turned and her stomach twisted.

Sydney walked toward them, dressed in a burgundy silk robe that clung to her shapely body. With her hair tumbling in dark waves about her shoulders, she looked incredibly glamorous, like a movie star from the forties.

"Good morning," she said. "I was just going in search of some coffee when I heard my name."

"We were talking about the party next weekend," Alex replied evenly, glossing over the fact that the conversation had assumed a far more personal note. "I've invited Gen," he informed Sydney.

"Oh." There was the tiniest pause. Then with a tight smile, she said, "I'll add her to the seating arrangement."

"Did you sleep well, Sydney?" Gen asked, desperate to switch the topic of conversation and avoid any awkwardness.

Sydney's smile relaxed into an enchanting curve. She shook her head. "Yes, but not nearly enough. I guess I'll survive, though." As if underscoring her lack of rest, she yawned delicately, raising her chin slightly to stifle it.

From her lower vantage point in the rocking chair, Gen looked up to see the pink abrasions marring the smooth skin along Sydney's jaw. No sooner had the words "beard stubble" popped into her head than, like a shot from a catapult, she bounded from her chair. "There's a pot of freshly brewed coffee," she said, brushing past Sydney as she headed for the door. "I've got to start Mrs. Miller's breakfast, but I'll be happy to make something for you as well, Sydney."

"Gen, you don't have to—" Alex began.

"That's what I'm here for," she interrupted, careful not to look back as with a yank of the screen door she slipped inside, leaving Alex and Sydney on the porch. Murphy, following her, nearly got his tail pinched in the door for his efforts. Gen didn't even pause to apologize to him as she fled from the man she'd come to want far too much, and from the woman lucky enough to have him.

After bringing Mrs. Miller her tray, Gen cloistered herself in the studio and tried to work. And failed.

It was a rare event when she couldn't block out the world and immerse herself in her art, but this morning it was she who was blocked. She blamed her low spirits on the weather. The clouds had become heavy and oppressive, turning the sky a dull, dismal gray, like an ugly, unwashed curtain shuttering the sun. As the light was all wrong, Gen couldn't finish her painting of Mrs. Miller's garden. Instead she dug out her sketch pad from her backpack and dragged her stool over to the worktable, where she laid out the notes and drawings she'd made of the hospital wing. She intended to make some preliminary sketches for the composition, but instead of scenes, shapes, or even colors, her mind drew only a frustrating blank.

She was scowling at the empty newsprint, cursing her inability to come up with even a smidgeon of an idea for the painting, when a knock sounded on the door. The speed of Murphy's wagging tail made it annoyingly easy to guess who was knocking.

She swiveled on her stool to face him. Alex, dressed for the city, had changed into sage-gray trousers and an ivory shirt—all pressed and freshly shaven. Her scowl deepened as Sydney's abraded skin flashed in her mind with a mocking, sharp clarity. Now there was an image she saw all too well.

"Yes?" she said impatiently.

His eyebrows rose at the sharpness of her tone. "I'm leaving. I wanted to say good-bye."

She shrugged. "Right. See you." She made to turn back to her notes, dismissing him, but then he spoke.

"Have I done something to annoy you?" he asked. Involuntarily she glanced at his face. His gaze, a penetrating blue, pierced her.

She returned it defiantly. "What could you possibly do to annoy me?" she replied.

"Good question." The coolness of his voice matched hers. "But obviously I have. I'd apologize, but from the look on your face, it's clear you're not going to bother to enlighten me as to what crime I've committed."

A wave of guilt flooded her. It wasn't Alex's fault she was plagued by this ridiculous jealousy; the problem was hers alone. She hated this feeling, how it turned her into a churlish wretch and made her act small and mean. She'd deal with it, master it, but she certainly wasn't about to explain the whys and wherefores to him. "Look, I really need to get back to work." She gestured to her drawing pad.

Alex's eyes narrowed and he looked as if he wanted to say something. From outside came the sound of his car horn honking impatiently.

"I believe you're wanted," she said silkily.

His mouth flattened into a hard line. "Good-bye, Gen," he said and was gone.

Disgusted with her childish behavior, Gen propped her elbows on the table, covering her face with her hands. But that only magnified the rumble of Alex's car and the crunch of tires rolling over gravel. Like a cruel taunt it reverberated throughout the studio long afterward.

The evening was a cool one, damp from the rain that the bloated clouds had eventually let loose. With Alex gone, the house suddenly seemed far too large for the two women.

"Let's sit inside, shall we, Genevieve?" Mrs. Miller

said after they'd finished dinner. "I dare say it's cold enough to warrant a fire."

"Nothing I love more than sitting in front of a fire," Gen said with a determined cheerfulness, for Mrs. Miller seemed in an uncharacteristically melancholy mood. After lighting the kindling beneath the logs and waiting for the flames to catch, their orange and blue tongues dancing around the wood, Gen rocked back on her heels and straightened. "I think I'll make a pot of tea," she said, dusting her hands on her jeans. "Would you care for some, Mrs. Miller?"

"No, thank you. Grappa's the thing to ward away the chill of a damp night."

Gen smiled. "A grappa and tea then."

When she returned to the sitting room, the fire was crackling hungrily. Mrs. Miller was seated on the sofa, staring into the flames. Gen set the lacquered tray on the narrow rectangular coffee table, then sat down at the other end of the sofa. "Are you feeling all right, Mrs. Miller?" she asked.

The older woman mustered a smile. "Yes, I was just thinking of Alex and how good it is of him to come out and relieve an old woman's loneliness."

"But surely he enjoys coming to stay with you. It's beautiful here."

"Genevieve, Alex is a handsome, thirty-three-year-old, unattached male," she said dryly. "He's more than wealthy enough to buy a house of his own where he can entertain his friends. Instead, he makes a point of spending his weekends with me. He actually *worries* about me." She sighed and her smile held a touch of sadness as she continued. "He reminds me of my own Alexander in so many ways. Both were men who put others' happiness before their own. I only wish my Alexander could have seen what a fine man he's become—though I swear, when I look at Alex now, it's as though I've taken a fifty-year step back in time."

"So there's a strong family resemblance?"

"Uncanny. Would you like to see some pictures?" Mrs. Miller asked, already leaning forward as if to rise from her seat.

Gen couldn't resist the elderly woman's patent eagerness, nor could she resist her own curiosity to learn more about Alex's family. "Yes, very much. I love family albums."

Mrs. Miller needed no further encouragement. She got to her feet and crossed the room to the paneled cabinet and opened one of the doors. From the bottom shelf she selected one of many thick albums. "This is the family album. The others are pictures Alexander and I took during our travels," she told Gen as she came and sat close to Gen so the album's pages lay across both their laps.

Then, with Mrs. Miller's wrinkled finger pointing, moving from one black-and-white picture to another, the stories began. The first pages of the album were devoted to Grace and Alexander Miller's wedding day. Gen saw Grace, some sixty years younger, an ethereal beauty in white silk, smiling into the camera with stars in her eyes. Next to her was a tall, blond man, dashing in his cutaway. From the smile on his face as he looked at Grace, Gen knew that this was Alexander Miller, Alex's uncle.

"And who's this?" Gen asked, pointing to another photo, which showed the bride and groom standing next to a man who bore the same, handsome features as Alexander Miller.

"That's Jack, Alexander's younger brother," she answered. "Jack was Alexander's best man. Look, here he is again with our wedding present."

Gen stared, entranced at the man with the laughing grin who held a beautiful German shepherd pup in his arms. "He gave you a puppy?" she asked.

"Yes." Affection filled her voice. "Definitely not your everyday wedding present. But that was Jack through and through. He made his own rules—Alex takes after him in that respect, too. Ajax was a marvelous dog. He lived to a ripe age of thirteen."

Mrs. Miller turned the page and Gen saw another wedding ceremony. "This was Jack's wedding," she said. "Alexander was best man, and I was Mary's matron of honor."

Gen found herself studying these photographs even more closely. So these were Alex's parents, she thought.

"Mary was a wonderful woman, strong and quiet," Mrs. Miller said. "She and Jack were so happy together." She turned to the next page and faded Kodachrome colors leapt out at Gen. "Ahh," Mrs. Miller said wistfully. "Here are the children—Tom, Alex, and little Cassie. We'd only just bought this house when Cassie was born. Jack and Mary and the children would come and summer with us. Here's Cassie at her first horse show at the Hampton Classic. She was six."

"The ribbon's almost as big as her," Gen remarked with a smile. Cassie Miller, her wide grin exposing several missing teeth, was holding the ribbon high in the air so it wouldn't trail on the ground. A little dapple-gray pony with thick braids stood next to her, looking sleepy.

"She was the short-stirrup champion, I believe. Oh, here's another one of Tom and Alex. This must have been the year they were the junior-doubles champions at the tennis club here. Those two were so close—none of that rivalry and resentment you often find in brothers. Alex idolized Tom."

"How old was Alex here?" she asked, staring at the picture of him, a renaissance angel of a boy with blond, wildly curly hair.

"I think about eleven. Oh, and this was taken a couple of years later, when the boys were in their teens."

Alex was on the beach, the Miller house in the background, jumping to catch a Frisbee in midair. He must have driven the girls crazy, Gen thought to herself, adding, Well, that hasn't changed much. She wondered, though, if Alex ever showed that joyful smile to anyone now. Sydney, when he's alone with her, holding her in his arms and making love to her, an insidious voice whispered in her head. Disgusted with her ridiculous obsession about Alex and his girlfriend, she thrust the thought aside.

Luckily, Mrs. Miller had turned to a new page. Alex's sister, Cassie, was decked out in a pale pink prom gown. She was hugging her father, whose hair was now threaded with silver. "Mary died shortly after this picture was taken," Mrs. Miller quietly informed her. "Jack was devastated when she was diagnosed with cancer. The disease spread so fast that she was gone from us in a matter of weeks. Then death took my Alexander from me. So many, many deaths in this family," she murmured sadly. With a sigh she moved on to the next page. "Oh, here's Tom and Lisa on their wedding day."

Looking at the photograph, Gen recognized it as the same one that had been in Alex's office. Another photograph showed the couple outside the church.

"Mrs. Miller, isn't that Concord, Massachusetts?" Gen had visited the colonial town too often not to recognize it.

"Yes," Mrs. Miller replied. "Lisa's family was from Boston, but they'd recently bought and restored an eighteenth-century farmhouse in Concord. They decided to hold the wedding there. Of course, Alex was best man at the wedding. He's giving the toast here."

A younger, laughing Alex, movie-star material in his severe black cutaway, stood raising his glass of champagne to the bridal couple, who were seated in the center of a long table, surrounded by wedding guests, their glasses also raised.

"They were a beautiful couple," Mrs. Miller said. "And here they are with their twin babies, Jamie and Sophie. My great-nephew and -niece."

Perplexed, Gen glanced at Mrs. Miller. "I must be confused. I thought Alex said Cassie was Sophie and Jamie's mother."

A shadow crossed Mrs. Miller's face. "She is. Cassie adopted Sophie and Jamie when Jack, Tom, and Lisa

were killed in a car accident almost six years ago."
Her lips trembling with suppressed emotion, Mrs.
Miller looked up from the old photographs to stare
into the fire.

Gen cursed her extraordinary ability to picture
scenes with such vivid clarity. Three members of a
family killed at once. How did one get past such a
devastating tragedy? "I'm terribly sorry for your
family's loss, Mrs. Miller," she said quietly.

"Thank you, my dear. Some deaths are especially
hard to bear—Tom and Lisa's particularly. But Cassie's
done a terrific job with the twins. They're happy,
carefree children. All four of them, Cassie and her
husband, Caleb, and the twins, will be coming next
week to visit."

"How wonderful for you."

"Yes." She smiled. "Genevieve, dear, you don't
mind if we stop here? I'd rather go to sleep thinking
of Cassie's upcoming visit than that sad period in our
lives."

"Of course," Gen reassured her.

Mrs. Miller closed the album and set it on the coffee table. "Now," she said briskly. "Tell me how your
work is coming along while I finish my grappa. How
is my portrait?"

"It's taking shape nicely," Gen said, more than
willing to follow the older woman's lead. "I think
you'll be pleased with it. A few more breakfasts and I
should be finished."

"I can't wait to see it." Grace Miller tipped the bal-
loon glass to her lips. "I think, however, that if I don't
wish to be drawn with horribly unflattering bags be-

neath my eyes, I should take myself upstairs and get a good night's sleep. This rain should help nicely." She stood.

Gen politely rose too. "I'll shut the windows and turn off the lights before I lock up."

"Thank you, Genevieve. Good night."

"Good night, Mrs. Miller."

Gen listened to the sound of Mrs. Miller's feet climbing the stairs, heard her muffled tread as she walked down the hallway to her room, the creak of hinges as her bedroom door was opened and then shut. Quiet descended, with only the pop and hiss of the fire to break the silence.

Minutes passed as Gen stared at the fire. But the album, a moving visual history of this family, was there in her peripheral vision. Finally, unable to resist, Gen leaned forward and pulled the album onto her lap, opening it directly to the page on which Mrs. Miller had left off, the one showing Tom and Lisa with their newborn twins. She looked at Tom and Lisa's eyes, how they shone with happiness and love as they gazed at the two tiny babes sleeping in their arms.

Slowly her fingers lifted the page, turning it, and there, inserted into the protective plastic sheath, was a cream-colored booklet with the words "In Memoriam" engraved on its front. Underneath, Gen read the names Thomas and Lisa Miller and the dates of their births and deaths. They'd been so terribly young, she thought sadly.

Her eyes drifted down the page and her breath caught in a gasp of recognition.

The printer had done an exquisite job designing the roundel. There, in the center of the page, entwined together, as though linked for eternity, were the initials *TLM*.

Gen stared at those initials, stared until she could no longer see, blinded by her tears.

FOURTEEN

By Thursday afternoon Gen had finally sorted herself out and come to terms with her feelings for Alex. Okay, she had a crush on him. And that was all right. Because after all, how could she not have a crush on a man who was not only gorgeous, sexy, and smart, but who also had a heart filled with pain and sorrowful memories? A man whose heart was in desperate need of healing?

Whenever Gen thought of the loss Alex and his family had suffered, she was humbled. Her family was huge and yet it had been spared any comparable tragedy. She could only imagine how devastated she would feel were one of her siblings to die; she could not imagine how shattering it would be to lose three of her family at once.

While she'd come to accept her crush on Alex for what it was—a totally understandable attraction toward an extraordinary man—she knew that she would simply have to vanquish the green-eyed monster that awakened inside her whenever Sydney was near. That shouldn't be too difficult, Gen reasoned.

Now that she understood the motivation behind Alex's generous donation to the hospital, she'd be busy creating a painting magnificent enough to pay homage to Alex and his family's spirit.

She was working in the studio when she heard the inimitable roar of Alex's Aston Martin coming up the drive. At the slamming of the car door, she smiled, not even bothering to stop Murphy as he sprinted outside.

A few minutes later, Alex appeared in the open doorway. Murphy circled about him, tail beating madly as he brushed against Alex's legs, welcoming him back into the pack.

"Hi," Gen said as he walked toward her. It was because of what she'd learned about him that he took her breath away, she told herself. All perfectly natural.

"Hi," he replied, a look of surprise on his face. He paused and cocked his head, regarding her closely. "What's up? Why the smile?"

Gen waved her hand airily. "Oh, you know the old saw 'Absence makes the heart grow fonder.' Hey! Where are you going?"

Alex had turned around, as if heading out the door. He glanced over his shoulder. "I figure I'm on a roll. I'll see you in about a month or so, Monaghan." Whistling, he walked out of the studio.

Her laughter bubbled out. She'd definitely missed his wit. She returned to her sketch, humming happily. Putting the finishing touches on her pastel drawing didn't prevent her from noticing that Alex was making repeated trips to and from his car, Murphy trotting loyally at his heels. Her curiosity winning out, Gen got up and went to stand by the open door. This time when Alex passed in front of the studio, he was carrying his laptop computer and a large file box.

"A bit of homework this weekend?" Gen asked.

Alex stopped walking. He shook his head. "Vacation work," he corrected. "Cassie and Caleb are leaving the twins here while Cassie competes in some horse shows. So I'm moving my office headquarters to East Hampton."

The thought of Alex staying at his aunt's for longer than a weekend visit had Gen's heart beating faster, her delight far outweighing any other pesky concerns—such as the fact that this undoubtedly meant Sydney would be around more too. Having Alex here would be a golden opportunity to start work on the idea that had taken root in her imagination since she'd looked at Mrs. Miller's family album.

"That's good to hear," she said, nodding. "I need a man."

Alex nearly dropped both the computer and the box of files.

She needed a man? The words echoed in his stunned brain. Had he imagined them, simply because he wanted her so damn much he was nearly shaking?

He'd spent the last four days in the city unable to get Gen out of his mind. Only to continue the torment by spending his nights in front of *Day One*, which now hung in his living room. He would stare at it, seeing more and more of Gen in the woman depicted there. And his hunger for her had grown apace.

Seeing the smile playing about her lips had the blood pooling in his groin. Alex only thanked God she hadn't said, *I need you,* or he'd have lost it right then and there.

"I'd be happy to oblige in any way," he managed calmly enough.

"I'll hold you to that," she told him, her eyes twinkling with that mischievous light he'd come to recognize. "When you've finished moving your headquarters, come on over to the studio. I'll show you what I want."

Alex returned twenty minutes later. He'd unpacked and changed into a pair of jeans and a T-shirt, wondering the entire time what Gen had in mind.

"Back so soon?" she said, laying her pastel stick down next to her drawing.

"I confess to being extremely intrigued by the 'need' you mentioned," he said, grinning at the laughter sparkling in her eyes. "Are you working on a new piece?" he asked, pointing to the drawing.

"Oh, just fooling around with some ideas for the wing," she said casually. Lifting the large sketch pad, she closed its cover, hiding the drawing from his gaze. "But I'm not ready to show them yet."

He nodded. "I understand."

"Thanks." She smiled.

"So is Aunt Grace out somewhere?"

"Well, today it's the tea for the Guild Hall patrons. Tomorrow it's the East Hampton Garden Club followed by the Friends of the Bridgehampton Library." She shook her head. "Your aunt is a remarkable woman. I'd collapse after a week with a schedule like hers."

"Yeah, she is," he agreed fondly. "Every year she seems to do more." Alex paused and fixed his gaze on her lovely, expressive face. "So you need a man?"

The question hung in the air between them. Alex saw Gen's eyes widen with a flash of sexual awareness. Then she was nodding vigorously. "Absolutely," she said, the beginnings of a grin playing over her bare and so very delectable-looking lips. "But I promise I won't make you do anything you're not comfortable with."

He stepped closer. "Oh, I have a pretty broad comfort range. I'm open to almost anything." Already he was thinking of the countless things he'd like to do to Gen. And as he firmly believed in turnabout, she could do whatever she pleased with his body. "What do you have in mind?" he asked in a voice grown husky.

"I want you to pose for me."

He blinked. "Excuse me?"

"That's right. I need a male model to draw from."

"You want to draw *me*?"

"Yes. I need a male figure for my painting and as you're the only male around, I thought I'd take advantage of your body. As you're far from hideous, you'll make a fine study."

He felt a grin stretch his mouth. Gen was the first woman who'd ever complimented him by telling him he was "far from hideous," as if he were half a step up from Quasimodo. He was still sorting out how he felt about being asked to pose when she said with a little sigh, "Well, I guess that's a no. It's okay, really, Alex. I'll ask one of the guys at the seafood shop or maybe one of the men from the landscaping company your aunt uses."

The very idea of Gen asking another man to pose had Alex stiffening in outrage. He could just imagine how they would react to a request like that, from a woman as beautiful as Gen. No way was he going to let that happen. "So do you want me naked?"

Gen's jaw dropped like that of a hooked fish, and a fiery blush stole over her, from the neckline of her ratty T-shirt all the way up to her hairline.

"Naked?" she repeated, her voice breathless. "No, no, that won't be necessary," she assured him hurriedly, only to pause, frowning, as a thought struck her. "Well, maybe in a couple of sittings, you could take off your shirt so I can sketch your torso and back—but the pants *definitely* stay on." Her gaze skittered away from his as, impossibly, her blush deepened.

Pleased at how flustered she'd become, he asked solemnly, "Are you sure? That way you could check out everything, ensure all the proportions are right."

Her gaze collided with his. Seeing the teasing smile on his face, her brows snapped together. "I highly doubt any part of you is as enormous as your ego," she said in a withering tone.

He gave her a roguish grin. "You'd be surprised."

"Jeesh." With an aggrieved sigh she rolled her eyes. "So are you going to do this or not? 'Cause I really need a man—"

"And I'm it," Alex finished for her.

* * *

It was a totally unnerving sensation, Alex realized, to be looked at this closely, with such intensity. Gen's eyes hardly ever left him as her graphite pencil flew over the paper. Saying she'd wanted to do a study of his hands, she'd seated him on the stool and then had him prop his elbows and forearms on the worktable so his arms wouldn't get fatigued from holding the pose. From the way her eyes moved, traveling over him, Alex had the impression Gen was taking in more than just his open hands. It felt like she was seeing everything, every pore, every line on his skin, every freckle, and then probing deeper still, as if her gaze could penetrate past his skin to the fibers of his muscles, to the density of his bones . . . to his very soul.

"You twitched again," she remarked absently. In the quiet of the studio, her pencil made a quick scratching noise as it moved in rapid, short strokes. She must be shading in an area, he thought.

"Sorry," he apologized. "This modeling stuff is . . ." He searched for the right word.

"Hard? Strange? Weird?"

"All of the above."

She smiled. "Yeah, I know. Few people realize how difficult it is to maintain even the simplest of poses. Whenever Jiri was in the mood to work from the model, he'd ask me." A wry grin split her face. "I remember feeling as if my body had turned into a giant pretzel after those sessions. There are people who love modeling, but I'm much happier on this side of the drawing pad." She flashed him a smile. "You're doing a great job, though. If you could just hold this position for a few minutes more, I'll be finished for today. Hands are the most challenging parts of human anatomy to draw. Yours are very expressive. Strong and lean. Nicely proportioned."

Although he was glad she liked his hands—as he intended to have them on her body very soon, touching her everywhere—Alex honed in on her earlier comment. "Jiri's the artist you lived with, right?" he said. "And you modeled for him? In the nude?"

"Sometimes," she replied, her hand moving confidently over the paper. "It really depended on what he was working on. Once, for an entire month, I was wrapped in burlap. In the painting it looks like I'm growing out of the earth. It's in the Tate collection now—probably the only way Genevieve Monaghan will ever hang in the Tate," she said with a light laugh. "Jiri did several nudes of me too, but those he didn't sell—No," she said abruptly. "Don't move. I need you to keep the fingers open."

Gen's sharp command had Alex realizing that his hand had clenched into a fist. And that he very much wanted to slam it into something—no, *someone*. He forced his fingers to relax, but the tension remained coiled inside him. "So just how close were you and Jiri?"

"Jiri?" She raised her eyes to his and gave a slight shrug. "He was my mentor and friend—*is* my friend," she corrected hurriedly.

"Was he your lover, too?" he asked softly.

Her left eyebrow arched mockingly. "Gosh, I'm surprised you have to ask. I'd have thought a background check as thorough as yours would have provided the juicy stuff too."

It took Alex a fraction of a second to calculate how to get what he wanted. He smiled. "Answer the question, Gen, or you lose the chance to draw this strong and lean and very expressive hand."

"Lord, you're like Murphy with a bone. No, that's not quite the analogy I want. You're just like a guy. Fixated on sex," she muttered. "No, we didn't sleep together. Sex wasn't important to our relationship. Jiri and I were totally involved in making art," she informed him coolly, but a slight frown marred her forehead as she studied her drawing.

Alex was willing to bet his bank account she wasn't even seeing it. "Why is it I don't believe you're telling the whole story?" he asked.

Startled, Gen looked up, surprise widening her eyes. And in them, Alex read the answer. "Ahh, I get it," he said, the strange tightness in him easing. "So Jiri wanted to sleep with you but you refused."

Her lips pursed in irritation. "Don't make a big deal out of it. I would have slept with him if I'd felt like it. I just didn't. Jiri understood."

"I'll bet," he murmured under his breath. Then, more loudly, he said, "So he's in Prague? No plans to return?"

"I can't imagine why he would. Being the director of the National Academy of Art is a pretty prestigious deal. He did call the other day but I was out. We keep playing telephone tag."

There was a short silence while Gen worked, totally absorbed in her drawing, and he sat, totally consumed by her relationship with Jiri Novak. "Do you miss him?" he asked abruptly.

"Hmm, what was that?" she asked.

"Do you miss him?" he repeated with a touch of impatience.

"Who, Jiri? Of course. I love him. He's an extraordinarily gifted artist. He was a fantastic teacher. Incredibly demanding," she added, her eyes still trained on her drawing. Finally, with a last critical look, she set her pencils aside. "There. I'm done." She closed the drawing pad. "You can relax now."

Alex straightened and slipped off the stool, shaking his hands out. But he was feeling far from relaxed. Hearing Gen say she loved Jiri had unleashed a storm inside him. He wanted to grab her and tell her she couldn't possibly love Jiri because . . . because . . . Alex's thoughts balked at supplying a reason. He didn't know exactly how deep his feelings for Gen went. But he knew he wanted her with a reckless need, and the thought of her with someone else was enough to make him gnash his teeth.

Alex took a slow, deep breath and told himself to relax. First of all, he was here, and Jiri, the genius artist, was way across the Atlantic in Prague.

And second, Gen hadn't given herself to Jiri.

Though she might refuse to acknowledge it, to Alex it was a revealing fact. No matter how wonderful an artist and teacher and friend Gen claimed Jiri was, something in their relationship was keeping her from taking it to another level. She must have sensed that what she felt for Jiri wasn't what she was searching for.

Which meant that Alex had to show Gen that the passion and joy inside her sprang from more than just her love of art. She'd said Jiri was a demanding teacher. Well, he would be an ever-so-generous one, Alex decided.

He looked at Gen, who was in the midst of putting her pencils back in their box. Feeling the weight of his gaze, she lifted her head and with a smile of thanks said, "That was great. Do you think you're up for doing more tomorrow?"

"Yeah, I'm definitely up for it," he replied, biting back a grin when her eyes lit up like a child's on Christmas morning.

"The poses won't be difficult," she assured him. "I just need your back and your, uh," she cleared her throat delicately, "your chest."

"Whatever your heart desires."

Whatever your heart desires.

Alex's words, spoken in that low-timbred, sexy voice, teased her, slipping slyly into her thoughts when she least expected them . . . though perhaps, in all fairness, she'd invited them. They were as seductive as the rest of him.

The drawings she'd done of him were before her. Studying them, she worried that she hadn't done a good enough job. Had she conveyed the strength and sensitivity in those elegantly tapered fingers?

She flipped to the following page and there was his face. She hadn't told him about that—that she was also sketching his face—worried he might freeze up on her, like someone posing for a picture, staring rigidly into the lens of a camera. She hadn't even decided if she would use Alex's face in the painting; the sketch had been pure impulse, her hungry artist's eye drawn to the sensuous line of his lips, the sloping angle of his nose. Once started, she couldn't stop herself from faithfully recording his slanting cheekbones, broad forehead, his mesmerizing eyes. . . .

Alex had been an excellent model. She'd sensed he would be. There was such a deep, watchful quality about him. He was a man who knew how to wait and control his impulses. He'd been remarkably good at keeping his hands open and relaxed throughout the session. There'd only been that one moment when he'd tensed in reaction. What had they been talking about?

Oh, yes, she thought, Jiri drawing her. She'd modeled for Jiri many times, sometimes in the nude, sometimes clothed. Neither way bothered her. Gen's parents had raised her to view the human body as a thing of beauty, never of shame. But baring her body was an entirely different matter than offering it in love.

Jiri hadn't understood the distinction, why she repeatedly declined his overtures. Finally, she'd seized upon the excuse that she was saving herself for her husband. Interestingly enough, Jiri had accepted that explanation—and for several weeks he'd amused himself by calling her his "chaste temptress."

Gen didn't regret that she'd lied to Jiri. Well, partially lied to him. She hadn't made any solemn vow to hold off on sex until she married—if she ever married. She just knew that when she made love, it would have to be with someone who made her feel truly special. Someone who understood her heart and soul.

* * *

The next morning, Gen whipped through the preparations for Mrs. Miller's breakfast, then carried the tray up the stairs with the finished portrait of her tucked under her arm. Mrs. Miller was already awake and had drawn the curtains so the morning light filled the bedroom. "Good morning, Genevieve."

"Good morning, Mrs. Miller, it's a beautiful day."

"Yes, I'll have to take my walk early. Now that the weather has turned warmer, the beach gets crowded on the weekends. I much prefer it when I can pretend it's my own private realm. What have you got there?" she asked, nodding at the drawing under Gen's arm.

"A present for you."

"What a lovely way to start off the day. May I see it?"

"Wouldn't you like your breakfast first?" Gen smiled.

"Certainly not. Art is food for the soul."

Setting the tray on the captain's sea chest at the foot of Mrs. Miller's ornately carved four-post bed, Gen placed the drawing in her outstretched hands.

She studied it in silence. "Genevieve, this is wonderful. I love it. I feel as if this is really *me,* my personality, from the crook of my wrist as I lift my cup of hot chocolate to the angle of my quite stubborn chin."

"I'm glad you like it," she replied self-consciously.

"My dear, I love it. As a matter of fact, I've just had an idea. I know you're caught up thinking about the composition for the hospital, but I was wondering whether you might be willing to do portraits of Sophie and Jamie when they come."

Gen barely stopped herself from dancing with excitement. How perfect. She'd been planning on doing sketches of the children on the sly. But this way, she could pull out her pad and pencils and draw them in a dozen different settings. "I'd be delighted, Mrs. Miller. Now let me give you your breakfast. I'm working on your nephew today. He's agreed to sit for me."

Mrs. Miller smiled as she poured the rich dark cocoa into her cup. "Did he now? Well, he's quite an impressive specimen, don't you agree?"

"He puts Michelangelo's *David* to shame," Gen said. "Sydney's a lucky woman."

"You think?" Mrs. Miller murmured into her raised cup.

Gen had told Alex that he could come whenever it suited him; her schedule was flexible. But his bedroom door had been shut when she'd brought Mrs. Miller's breakfast, and remembering the big box of papers he'd been carrying with his computer, she assumed he was still asleep. So when Alex's long shadow darkened the concrete floor of the studio a short time later, she glanced up in surprise from the sketch she was doing of a cluster of seashells and driftwood. "Oh, hi."

"Hi." Alex straightened from scratching Murphy's massive head. "That's some bone Murphy's got," he said, propping his shoulder against the doorjamb.

"I discovered the pet store in Bridgehampton. Like everything else in the Hamptons, they cater to outrageous appetites, Murphy's included." She nodded at the bone. "Anything smaller than that is gone in an instant."

"I came by to see whether you want me now." There was a slight pause, then Alex added, "For the sketch."

"Uh, sure. Now is great."

But when Alex walked into the studio, and Gen got a good look at him, she suddenly wasn't so certain this was a good time after all. He'd just come back from a run. His light gray T-shirt clung to the muscled contours of his chest in dark patches. Sweat had turned his hair into a helmet of dark sculpted curls, reminding her of a bronze sculpture she'd seen of a Greek warrior. He had the same powerful beauty—virile, elemental, and irresistible.

He came over to her worktable and the large studio seemed to shrink in size. Gen could feel the heat rising from his body, feel the very air stir with his breathing. Drawing a steadying breath she caught the musky male scent of him. Her pulse began hammering at the base of her throat.

"Is anything wrong?" Alex asked. His blue eyes glittered, intense and compelling, and very, very close.

Hastily she rose from her stool and moved so it stood between them. "No, no, I was just deciding where I want you," she said, using the first excuse that popped into her head. "Over here by the light." She gestured to the window. "The morning sun will highlight your skin's texture nicely," she said then bit her tongue before she could babble any other inanities.

He smiled, as if he could tell exactly how nervous

he was making her. "Well, that's good to know. So do you want me standing or sitting?"

"I'd like to do a few short poses of you standing, then a longer one of you sitting."

"Fine." His broad shoulders shrugged beneath the clinging T-shirt.

Imagining the play of muscles beneath the thin cotton had Gen's throat constricting. She swallowed hard. "Um, would you mind taking off your shirt?" she asked, appalled at the betraying huskiness of her voice.

He grinned mischievously. Grabbing the hem of his shirt, he slowly began peeling it off his torso.

Riveted, Gen watched as inch by inch his tanned body was revealed. Slick with sweat, it gleamed like gold in the morning light. Unconsciously biting her lip, she let her gaze travel up the thin path of dark blond hair to the shaded indentation of his belly button.

His stomach was all muscled ridges.

The shirt rose, revealing more damp, male skin. Avidly Gen drank in the faint lines of his ribs, the swell of his pectorals, the dark circles of his nipples, the muscled breadth of his shoulders.

The T-shirt slipped over his head and dropped to the floor, leaving Alex naked except for his black running shorts.

He was beyond anything she'd imagined.

Beyond beautiful.

Mere beauty had never made Gen feel this intensely, as if a fire were melting her insides, turning them into a liquid heat that pulsed low and deep inside her, beating in sync with the memory of his words, *Whatever your heart desires.*

Every thought flew from her head, except how his bare flesh would feel beneath her hands, hot and supple, and how she yearned to reach out and touch him, press against the warm resilience of his muscled flesh, and taste its slick saltiness on her lips and tongue. Worship it.

A soft, helpless moan escaped her.

At the sound, Alex's eyes, ablaze with a searing blue fire, locked with hers. She stared. He looked strong, predatory, and hungry. For her. He took a step toward her.

Some very remote region in Gen's brain ordered her to run for her life. Her rebellious body ignored the command; her feet remained rooted to the spot. Yet an iota of self-preservation remained. With a superhuman effort Gen managed an agitated flap of her hands. "I think this is a bad idea," she whispered. "A really bad idea."

Alex's smile widened and the pulsing heat inside her quickened. "Have I told you yet that you're a rotten liar, Genevieve Monaghan? This is the best idea either one of us has ever had," he murmured as his hands reached up to frame her face. This close, his eyes were hypnotic, the caress of his fingers on her skin mesmerizing, and the warmth of his breath carrying with it a hint of mint, delectable. Aware only that she was breathless with desire, breathless for him, Gen's lips parted.

He lowered his head, mouth hovering, his lips almost brushing hers. Softly he commanded, "Kiss me, Gen."

She never even thought of resisting as his mouth touched hers, settled, and lay claim in a kiss that was unlike any she'd ever experienced. . . . Indescribably delicious. That first touch, that first slide of lips learning and testing, was all it took for Gen to tumble headlong into a sea of need and want that only Alex could satisfy.

And satisfy he did. He seemed to know exactly how to kiss her, how to touch her. Every shift of his mouth, every thrust and parry of his tongue against hers, every glide of his hands over her body, thrilled, triggered brilliant fireworks of hot pleasure within her.

Caught in the fevered passion he aroused, she strained against him, the need to touch him consuming her. Her hands moved over his heaving chest. His skin was like satin warmed by fire. Beneath her open palm, his heart pounded. Wanting to feel that violent thudding against her lips, she pressed her mouth to the hard point of his nipple. His ragged groan of pleasure flowed through her like molten heat. And when his mouth descended to explore the sensitive region behind her ear, she went weak-kneed. Moaning, she clutched his shoulders for support.

God, he loved the sounds she made, the little whimpers that fell from her lips when he stroked her, learning the delicate curves of her body. The sweetness of her response scared him—he wanted her so damned much. And although he was trying to go slowly, to prolong their pleasure for an eternity or more, each cry, each shudder of pleasure had him shaking with the need to make her his.

Alex rocked his hips against her, letting her feel what she did to him. Her gaze flew to his. Her spectacular eyes were enormous. He imagined himself falling into them, drowning in their depths while he was deep inside her, touching her very womb, while she dissolved around him. His hands tightened, urging Gen closer still—only for them both to jump the proverbial mile when, from behind, there came the sharp rap of knuckles on the screen door, immediately followed by Murphy's signature bark. Added to the cacophony was the crash of the easel falling as Alex stumbled into it and the horrified gasp that came from the now opened door, filling the studio in a dreadful surround sound.

Oh, shit, Alex thought when he saw Sydney standing in the doorway. It was obvious she'd seen them locked in a fevered embrace. Even from here he could tell that she was trembling violently. What to say? Nothing, except that he was sorry that it had come to this.

"Sydney—" he began but before he could continue, Sydney raised her hand. Her shoulders heaved as she struggled to compose herself. "I brought the seating arrangement for the party. No one answered at the house, so I thought I'd try here—" her voice cracked in sudden anguish. Uttering a cry of "Oh, God!" she turned on her heels and ran from the studio.

Alex instinctively made to follow her, to ensure she was all right—hell, even offer to hold her while she cried or pummeled him until her anger and hurt were finally vented—but he hadn't counted on Murphy. With a loud, ringing "woof," the dog was off, chasing after Sydney. Beside him, Gen gave a stricken cry of "No, Murphy, no!" and dashed forward.

Alex grabbed her arm. "Gen, wait. I'll go."

Gen turned back toward him and his gut twisted. Her lovely, fine-boned face was pale, leached of color, and her eyes, which minutes ago had been bright with desire for him, were now glazed with shock. "No, I'll get him—he won't do anything but Sydney's afraid of dogs and she's been hurt enough; besides, it's all my fault," she choked out before wrenching her arm free and rushing outside.

What in God's name did she mean it was all her fault? Alex started after her, nearly breaking his neck when he tripped over the upended easel. Regaining his footing he ran out of the studio.

"Gen!" he called, looking wildly about the sun-drenched yard.

"She headed that way, down to the beach, hard on the heels of Sydney and the dog," a male voice answered, bringing Alex up short. He turned and saw Harry Byrne sitting on Aunt Grace's garden bench.

"Byrne," Alex exclaimed in surprise. "What are you doing here?"

"I came with Sydney. I was just finishing a phone call when she ran out. She looked upset."

"Yes, she was." Alex regarded him curiously. What the hell was going on? Why didn't Byrne seem more concerned about Sydney? Why hadn't he gone after her?

"From Sydney's expression I'm guessing this means it's officially over between the two of you."

"It's been over for a while," Alex answered impatiently. "What matters is that she's all right." He started to turn away.

Harry's voice stopped him. "Syd needs some time alone right now. She's like that. I'll take care of her when she comes back."

Something in his tone caught Alex's attention—the mixture of tenderness and calm determination. The possessiveness when he mentioned her name. For a long, silent moment, Alex looked at Harry, who leaned back on the garden bench, returning his stare blandly.

Sudden comprehension dawned, bringing with it an awesome sense of relief. "Jesus, I hadn't realized," he said quietly.

Harry gave a negligent shrug. "You weren't alone."

"No hard feelings?"

"No—not anymore, at least. Although I admit there was a dark period where I was seriously contemplating adding one more homicide to New York's crime stats."

"I appreciate your restraint," Alex said dryly.

Byrne shrugged. "Sydney would have hated visiting me in prison." Cocking his head, he regarded Alex intently. "So what about you, Miller? Do you still want Raines and Byrne on the job?"

Alex didn't hesitate. "Absolutely."

For the first time Harry smiled. "Thanks. Syd's done a terrific job organizing this party. I think your guests are going to be very happy. If it's just the same to you, though, I think we'll handle the remaining details at a safe remove. With Nancy Graves at La Plage to handle any hiccups, I doubt we'll have to stay for the entire evening."

"That would probably make the night less stressful for all concerned," Alex agreed, with wry understatement. "If I don't hear from you, I'll assume no news is good news."

Harry nodded. "That'll work." He rose from his lounging position on the bench. "Mind if I ask a favor of you, Miller?"

"Ask away."

"Would you sort of disappear for a while?"

Alex's brows arched in surprise, but his expression cleared when Harry added quietly, "I'd like to make it as easy as possible for Sydney to make a dignified exit."

And with that simple statement, it became obvious to Alex that Byrne understood Sydney in a way he never had—not even after months of going out with her. Harry clearly knew when to back off and give Sydney the space she needed, and when to step in and offer his support. No, Alex thought, he and Sydney had never even come close to this kind of caring.

Although she'd been little better than a royal pain in the butt these past few weeks, Alex was fond of Sydney. Now that it was well and truly finished between them, he hoped Sydney would see what she had in Harry Byrne. Though he wished he could go and find Gen, he realized that following both women down to the beach would only complicate the situation. He'd talk to Gen once Sydney had left with Harry.

More than happy to help Harry's cause, he made an elaborate show of glancing at his watch. "Damn," he said. "I just remembered I have a conference call scheduled with a California tech company. If you'll excuse me." He held out his hand to Byrne.

With a grin Harry shook it. "I'm glad I can like you now, Miller."

Gen ignored the stitch in her side as she wrapped her fingers around Murphy's collar and dragged him away from Sydney, who sat crumpled over her knees in the deep sand. Murphy had been trying to wedge his hairy muzzle into the space between the crook of her arm and her bowed head, no doubt trying to reach her face and lick her tearstained cheeks, as he did on the few occasions when Gen succumbed to a crying jag. As distraught as Sydney was, she didn't seem to notice Murphy's presence or even react when Gen pulled his wet snout away.

Gen stared at Sydney, feeling wretched herself, overwhelmed by guilt and a sense of perfidy. She'd kissed Alex, had moaned in his arms, reveled in the pleasure he gave her. What could she possibly say to Sydney to make this right?

Hoping she hadn't imagined that Sydney's sobbing had lessened, Gen nervously cleared her throat. "Sydney, I'm terribly sorry. I can't explain how this thing between Alex and me happened, but I know Alex would—"

Sydney raised her head. Even crying she was beautiful, her dark eyes magnified by the wash of tears, the bright flags of color on her cheeks contrasting with her flawless ivory skin.

"No," she said dully, swiping at her tears with the back of her hand. "You don't know Alex at all, but I do. I knew this was coming, that he'd find someone else, but there was this small part of me that kept hoping and hoping—" She broke off, her lips trembling. With a visible effort, she pulled herself together. "I don't understand what went wrong," she whispered. "We could have had everything. But he wouldn't commit. . . . He *can't* commit. And now it's really finally over," she finished sadly.

More than anything, Gen wanted to defend Alex, but she was hardly in a position to do so. Not when she'd done everything but beg for the magic of his touch. "Sydney," she tried again awkwardly, "Alex is a wonderful man. I'm sure if you talk to him, you can work this out."

"No." Sydney shook her head and rose to her feet. "No," she repeated more firmly, "because it will happen again. He'll never settle down with one woman," she said, a grim certainty in her voice. "You know, I suspected from the beginning that something would happen between you and Alex."

Gen opened her mouth to protest, to deny any "thing" between Alex and her, but Sydney was speaking again. "I understand why you've fallen for him. He's handsome and rich and a fabulous lover. I can't blame you—he must seem like Prince Charming to someone of your background."

At any other time, Gen would have immediately retorted that there was nothing wrong with her background, thank you very much, but under the circumstances she decided to ignore Sydney's condescension—she probably wasn't even conscious of her gratingly superior attitude.

"But take my advice, Gen," Sydney continued. "Whatever you do, don't be foolish enough to fall in love with Alex. And be wise enough to walk away before he breaks your heart." With a trembling hand she brushed at her still-damp cheeks, and sniffed. Suddenly something caught Sydney's attention and her gaze became fixed. She straightened, her posture becoming proud and erect.

Gen glanced over her shoulder, half expecting to see Alex coming toward them, and sighed in relief when instead she saw a dark-haired man. He waved and then stood waiting. Gen had the strange yet unshakeable impression that he would be willing to wait there indefinitely.

Sydney raised her arm, signaling that she'd seen him. "That's my partner, Harry. I guess we're leaving now. Good luck, Gen." She smiled tightly. "You'll need it."

FIFTEEN

Gen tarried on the beach with Murphy long after Sydney's departure. For the first time since her arrival in East Hampton, she was reluctant to return to her studio. She didn't want to risk running into Alex and having to deal with the stupidity of her actions—of that bone-melting kiss—especially since she was half convinced that it would only take a single glance at his sinfully handsome face to make her forget just how foolish she'd been and throw herself at him again.

Dumb, dumb, dumb, she recited in a self-chastising litany as she marched along the wide beach that stretched for miles and miles. Her leg muscles were ready to snap like worn-out rubber bands from having walked so far in the deep sand. Even Murphy was no longer gamboling about or frolicking in the surf, merely plodding by her side. As she walked, Gen kept her gaze trained on the sand beneath her feet, afraid to look out over the sun-dappled sea, knowing it would remind her of the color of Alex's eyes just before he'd kissed her. Which was why, in addition to mooning over Alex, she suffered the embarrassment of nearly bumping smack into him.

"Careful there," he said, reaching out to steady her, frowning slightly when she recoiled from his touch. "That was some walk you took. I was starting to worry about you." His eyes searched her face. "Are you okay?" he asked.

"Of course," Gen said, mustering a breezy and totally artificial smile. "I'm a big girl." Determined to avoid his gaze, she glanced around and realized they weren't far from Mrs. Miller's house. From here, the A-line pitch of the shingle roof seemed to rise out of the dune grass. She started toward it. To her consternation, Alex fell into step beside her. Didn't he know the meaning of the word "awkward"? she asked herself.

"We need to talk, Gen."

Obviously not, she thought, cringing at the very idea. "Sorry. I can't talk now. I need to make your aunt's lunch. And I have to put these away. My hands are beginning to cramp," she said, showing fingers stretched wide to hold the shells and stones she'd gathered. What she didn't mention, however, was that she'd been so preoccupied thinking of Alex's kiss and the thrill of his caresses that she couldn't even remember collecting them.

"My aunt's having lunch out today. And I can help you with those." He held out his open palms. Reluctantly she transferred some of her cache. With a hint of a smile he said, "There. Got any other excuses, Gen?"

Wishing she did, she settled for a frosty stare. "Actually, it seems to me the person you should be talking to is *Sydney,* not me."

"Sydney and I have already said everything that needed to be said," he replied evenly. "Listen, Gen, things hadn't been right between Sydney and me for some time. She knew it as well as I, and though I'm sorry she saw you and me together, at least she's finally accepted that what we had would never have worked."

The joy that burst into flame inside her at hearing Alex say that his and Sydney's relationship hadn't been working was quickly doused by a wave of self-reproach. After all, Gen had heard Sydney talk about her and Alex's future together. Today, she'd seen Sydney's stricken face awash in tears because that future was over. Gen hated the fact that she'd played the role of the other woman, that she'd let her wild attraction for Alex hurt Sydney.

"Well, I'm thrilled I could help you sort out your personal life. Whenever you need to dump a girlfriend, just give a call," she said sarcastically, relieved to find they'd reached the base of the shallow wooden stairs, which led up the dune.

"Wait just a damned second. I did not use you to dump Sydney," he said angrily.

"Fine, whatever, but that doesn't stop me from feeling rotten about the whole thing." Before Alex could come up with some palliative to soothe her conscience, she turned toward the stairs and motioned for Murphy to precede her. Following Murphy's wagging tail, she took the steps two at a time, all the while acutely aware that Alex was right on her heels. She knew that he wasn't going to let her escape to the solitude of her studio, where she could try to forget everything that had happened this morning.

Gen's ire mounted with each step.

She muttered a grim "Thank you" when Alex held the studio door for her. Murphy brushed past them, heading straight to his water bowl, and drank noisily, splashing water on the concrete floor, then ambled over to his bed, flopping down on it with a long-suffering sigh. Gen wished she could do the same with her futon, but she didn't think falling into bed would be the way to get rid of Alex. Quite the opposite.

Tired and guilt-stricken, Gen felt the tension grow inside her. A part of her was tempted to scream at Alex so he'd leave, another part wanted to beg him to look deep in her eyes and see how much she wanted him, how much she longed for his touch. As she wasn't about to succumb to either impulse, she decided that the best way to get Alex to leave would be to ignore him. The sheer novelty might throw him off balance. Gen doubted many people ever ignored Alex. He was too darned charismatic. Determined nonetheless, she walked over to her worktable. Opening her hands, she let the pieces of shell and rock clatter onto the plywood. She stood, head bowed, staring down at the exotic bounty she'd accumulated, her fingers lightly tracing their shapes and textures . . . acutely aware of Alex standing a few feet away.

Alex watched her with a mixture of frustration and tenderness. He was coming to know her, increasingly attuned to her voice, the flash of her eyes, the way she held her body. It made it easy to read the emotions coursing through her now. She was angry, nervous, and uncertain, but he refused to let her burrow like a hermit crab in her shell until he finally took the hint and left her alone.

No damned way.

He wanted her back in his arms.

He came and stood beside her, pretending he didn't notice that her muscles stiffened until she was as taut as a bow. "Here's the rest," he said, laying the other shells Gen had collected on the table.

"Thanks," she mumbled, without even sparing him a glance.

His eyes followed the clean lines of her profile. "Beautiful," he said quietly.

"Excuse me?" Her voice squeaked her inner tension.

You, he thought. "These shells and pieces of sea glass. Even these rocks, they're beautiful."

So much for being able to ignore him, thought Gen. He only had to say one word and her heart beat like a mad thing. Yet in her volatile mood, Alex's use of the word "beautiful" stuck in her craw. She realized she was spoiling for a fight. Spinning around to face him, she said, "So you find these beautiful, huh? Okay, pick one object from this table and tell me why it strikes you so."

Alex saw the challenge in the stubborn line of her jaw, the light of battle in her narrow-eyed gaze, and understood that this was some kind of a test, one she was sure he'd fail. Arching a brow in silent acknowledgment, he turned to the table and studied the different objects. At last, he picked up a dark oval-shaped stone. "This one," he said, holding it out to her.

Gen looked at the rock cradled in the palm of his broad hand. The color of gray flannel, it had two white veins running through it. It was a simple-looking rock, so plain one might easily overlook it. Intrigued in spite of herself, she wondered why Alex had chosen it over one of the shells or pieces of worn driftwood, whose colors and shapes were far more eye-catching. "Why?" she asked. "Why do you find this one beautiful?"

"Because it reminds me of us."

Gen stilled. "Us? What do you mean, 'us'? Like 'you and me'?" she asked, trying for a suitably scoffing tone.

"Yeah, you and me, us," he repeated. "Do you see these two lines?" he asked as his long index finger skimmed first one and then the other. "Look at how they start out so far apart. All this solid space separates them. And yet, here, in the middle of the stone, they come together . . . and join. And when they do, the line becomes thicker and stronger. Truer." He raised his head and looked at her directly. "I want you to give us a chance, Gen, so we can see if together we're like these two lines. I want to find out whether my hunch is right."

"Do you read tea leaves, too?" she demanded. "Look, we kissed. It was my fault—totally—I threw myself at you. It must have been hormones or pheromones or something. A momentary insanity. But one kiss doesn't mean you can start talking about any *us*. That's even crazier. You don't even *know* me. Look at you"—in her mind she thought of all the things Alex was: wealthy beyond imagination, brilliant, intelligent, handsome, and most important of all, awe-inspiringly generous— "and look at me. I'm a nobody from Somerville. I could never fit in your world. I'm not glamorous and sophisticated like Sydney. You can't—*oomph!*—"

Gen's words were stifled as Alex seized her in a rough, breath-stealing kiss, a kiss that brooked no resistance. Contrary to the core, Gen instinctively squirmed against the wall of his body, fighting the sweet thrill that swept through her the second his lips touched hers.

But she was no match for Alex. He already knew how she responded to his touch, to the stroke of his clever hands, and to the erotic rhythm of his tongue plundering her mouth. He knew just how to wring helpless shudders of pleasure from her. The assault he mounted on her senses was relentless, defeating every one of her defenses until with a helpless moan she arched against him, her body surrendering to his masterful touch.

It was as if he'd been waiting for her capitulation, for the moment she responded with a passion that rivaled his. He raised his head, ending the kiss. Dazed, Gen stared at him. Even with desire fogging her brain, she could see the fierce need glittering in his eyes, hear it in the harsh rhythm of his breathing, feel it in the tension of his body. Confusion filled her. Why had he stopped?

As though he'd read her mind, he said, in a voice low and rough with desire, "A single kiss from you and I'm more turned on than I've ever been in my life. So there goes your nothing-but-a-casual-kiss theory, Gen. And for your information, you hardly threw yourself at me. Not this time, nor the last. Get Murphy's leash."

She shook her head, desperately trying to clear it. She couldn't have possibly heard him correctly. "What?"

"The leash. Get it now."

Something in Alex's tone had her gaze flying back to his face. Determination was stamped on it. More confused than ever, she stammered, "Why—why do you want Murphy's leash?"

"Because I damn well need to show you something," he ground out, glancing around the studio. "There it is," he said, his sharp eyes locating the leather leash. He moved toward it, Gen following—his hand was wrapped around her wrist, not so tight that it hurt but she didn't kid herself that she could break free.

With a sharp whistle Alex roused Murphy from his canine dreams. The dog immediately leapt from his bed and trotted over to them. While Alex snapped on the leash, Gen, who'd managed to collect a few of her scattered wits, glared at his bent head. "Would you mind telling me where we're going?" she asked stiffly.

Straightening, he replied, "You'll see when we get there."

Infuriating man. He began leading her out the studio. "You could at least let me get my bag," she said, giving an experimental tug on her arm. As she thought, his hold remained firm.

"You won't need it."

Provoked by Alex's high-handedness, she snapped, "You know, you have some serious control issues. Does everyone just lie down like rugs for you to walk over?"

"Yeah, basically. You're the irritating exception."

"Good. Because I'm not going . . ." But Gen's words died away. Mrs. Miller was walking toward them.

"I was just coming to find you two," she said, her smile widening as she neared, doubtless misinterpreting the picture they made—Alex holding on to her arm, his other hand wrapped around Murphy's leash. "So you've finished with the modeling session for the day?" she asked.

Gen was surprised she wasn't incinerated on the spot from the fire that stole over her face. She wished she could mumble some excuse about losing the light, but that was not only lame, it was implausible.

"We're going to be gone for a while, Aunt Grace," Alex said. "Will you be okay on your own until tonight?"

"Tonight?" Gen squeaked, appalled. "I can't—"

"Of course I'll be fine on my own," Grace Miller replied, as if Gen hadn't spoken. "There's plenty of food in the house. And there's a biography of Martin Sheen on A&E. Don't you worry about me."

Gen slumped like a grumpy lump in the soft bucket seat of the Aston Martin. Alex still hadn't told her where they were going but she was beginning to recognize the back roads the Aston Martin was cruising down well enough to know that they were heading west, toward Southampton.

What could he possibly want to show her? she wondered, but was stubbornly determined not to cave in and ask again. She settled for casting him a baleful glare, but the effect was spoiled, rendered harmless by Murphy's shaggy body. He'd planted his two front paws firmly on the armrest and was panting as he stared out the windshield.

Just then Alex downshifted into a curve and his arm brushed Murphy's leg.

"Does Murphy always stand over the gearshift?"

"Yeah, he thinks he's helping with the navigating," she replied with gleeful obtuseness, smiling to herself when she heard Alex's grunt of resignation. Had he been anything less than an excellent driver, she would have immediately elbowed her dog backward to make him lie down on the rear seat. But, like everything else he did, Alex handled the powerful sports car with consummate skill. Indeed he drove so smoothly that Gen, in spite of her pique at being kidnapped by Mr. High and Mighty Alex Miller, found herself relaxing against the padded leather, and closing her eyes as the warm sunshine beat down on her face. . . .

She awoke when the car came to a stop. Blinking, she sat up and her eyes widened in surprise. "We're in New York," she exclaimed. "What are we doing— oh, thank you," she said as a doorman, dressed in a dove-gray cutaway with white trim and a matching cap with a shiny black visor, opened her door.

Gen scrambled out of the car and was barraged by

the sound of taxis idling and buses rumbling, both
honking in impotent rage at the daredevil bike mes-
sengers who responded with obscene hand gestures as
they threaded their way around the stalled traffic before speeding off.

To be assaulted by the city noise after the peace of
Long Island felt strange, Gen's disorientation all the
greater since she'd had no idea Manhattan was their
destination. Glancing around, she saw the dark stone
wall that enclosed a line of dense shade trees on the
other side of the broad, two-way street, and realized
they were on Central Park South.

Was this where Alex lived? Gen wondered, turning
around to stare up at the elegant art deco facade of
the apartment building.

Alex came around the car and opened its rear door,
handily catching Murphy's leash as the dog jumped
out and gave a huge body shake. Lowering his nose to
the sidewalk, he sniffed enthusiastically.

"That's a fine dog, Mr. Miller," the doorman offered.

"Thank you, George. He belongs to Ms. Monaghan," Alex replied, handing her the leash. "Would
you mind watching the car for me, George?"

"I'd be delighted to, Mr. Miller."

Alex turned to Gen. "Come on inside," he said and
she felt the beguiling warmth of his hand pressing
against the small of her back as he guided her into the
building. The bright opulence of the lobby, its glowing chandeliers reflected hundredfold in the floor-
to-ceiling mirrors, had her jaw slackening. Even the

marble checkerboard floor beneath her sneakers shone, waxed and polished, until it gleamed.

In the elevator, Alex pressed "P" and Gen fought hard to suppress a hysterical giggle. *Of course* he lived in a penthouse. Where else would someone like Alex live? A Central Park South penthouse was like living on Mount Olympus. "The view must be incredible," she murmured politely as the elevator began climbing rapidly.

Alex's lips tightened in irritation, even though he'd already guessed she'd use each and every trapping of luxury that surrounded him as a means to bolster her totally wrongheaded notion that she could never fit into his world. The very idea infuriated him, made him want to shake her. Of course the irony of Gen's ambivalence toward his wealth wasn't lost on him. Every other woman he'd dated had been hungry for the rarefied lifestyle his wealth guaranteed. Somehow he had to convince Gen that the differences in their backgrounds were inconsequential.

And the only way to do that was to show Gen what she meant to him. Which was why he'd brought her here, to his apartment, so she could see *Day One*. It was a decision he'd reached only two hours ago, back in the studio, a decision he'd rather have put off indefinitely. By letting Gen know it was he who'd bought her painting, he was letting her see the depth of his desire. Leaving himself vulnerable, open to hurt. Which, ever since the car accident that stole the lives of his father, Tom, and Lisa, he'd done everything in his power to guard against.

When the elevator door opened directly into his

sun-drenched apartment, he heard Gen utter an awed
"Oh, my God" beneath her breath. He watched her
fingers open, dropping Murphy's leash as she stepped
inside, moving toward the bank of picture windows
that overlooked the park. Then she faltered, perhaps
catching the flash of color out of the corner of her
eye. Slowly she turned and saw her painting, *Day
One,* hanging in solitary splendor on the opposite
wall.

His eyes fixed on the myriad emotions flitting
across her face. She looked astonished, overwhelmed,
and wondering, and most of all, scared at what finding her painting here, in his apartment, signified. Her
eyes grew huge and troubled, and so very beautiful.

"My painting," she whispered faintly. "You were
the one who bought it?"

"Yes. I went to the gallery before the opening. I saw
Day One and I had to have it." Alex fell silent as his
eyes roamed over the canvas.

Stunned Gen gazed at him, her mind grappling
with the discovery that it was Alex who'd purchased
the most private and personal work she'd ever created. He hadn't even known her then. What could he
have seen in her painting that would have compelled
him to buy it?

Alex's voice broke into her thoughts. "Let me tell you
about a woman I know," he said, and the quiet intensity of his voice combined with the compelling blue of
his eyes held Gen motionless, absorbing his words
deep into her soul.

"She's a woman I've known for months. An extraordinary creature who laughs as she flies like the

wind through Central Park, her dog racing by her side. I can't count the times I stood by these windows in the early morning, a voice inside me saying that if I went into the park, I'd have the chance to see her, cross paths with this ethereal sprite, and that something inside me would lift at having glimpsed her."

It was inconceivable. What were the odds? Gen opened her mouth, but couldn't find the words. It was all so unreal, so very improbable.

Alex watched her, a faint smile playing over his mouth, as if he understood her reaction. "It wasn't until I saw you with Murphy in Long Island that I made the connection, realized you were also the woman in the park. It was quite a shock. Once I got over it, I began to wonder whether serendipity wasn't involved. Because before I had even met you, I saw this." He paused and gestured to *Day One*. "And I had to have it. Your painting spoke to me, Gen, reached out to something inside me. I realize now it's because you put so much of yourself in this work. Like you, it's beautiful and passionate and haunting."

A flush stole over Gen. Shyly, she ducked her head, but his voice reached her, touching her like a velvet caress. "When I look at *Day One,* I feel you, Gen, your thoughts and your emotions. *Day One* is about a woman who's moving toward something unknown and potentially momentous. She has to choose between embracing the unknown or turning away and remaining safe, protected, cocooned. . . ." He paused and in the silence Gen raised her head, meeting eyes that pierced her soul. "I've sat in front of your painting for hours on end, imagining how incredible the colors in that woman's world will be should she decide to take that leap of faith. I know you'd like to pretend that you and I are too different to be together, Gen. But we're not," he said, his voice hoarse with barely restrained passion. "I want to see those colors come to life within you. I want to be a part of that. I want the woman who blades like a mad dervish, I want the woman who creates paintings of incredible beauty, I want the woman who walks naked out of the sea, I want the woman who moans so sweetly when I touch her. *I want you, Gen.*"

Gen tried to breathe. It was impossible. Her heart was hammering too loudly. Millions of thoughts flew through her head, each accompanied by an urgent warning: *It could never work, it will never last.* But how could she heed those cautions? How could she listen to reason when Alex spoke of serendipity and sprites and wanting her—not just Gen the artist, but every part of her?

She'd been wrong, she realized. Alex did know her, understood her in a fundamental way that no other man ever had. She'd always been a person who held herself somewhat apart, aloof from others, focusing exclusively on her art. But when Alex entered her life, something shifted inside her. Now Gen couldn't imagine what it would be like not to have him in it—not to feel that heady rush of pleasure when he was in the same room, have that delicious warmth unfurl inside her when he smiled. *She wanted that.* And more, she wanted to experience the feel of Alex hard and strong against her as he made love to her.

While Gen instinctively sensed that in giving herself

to him, she would be plunging headlong into unchartered territory, one look at Alex and she knew she wouldn't be traveling alone. He stood, hands shoved deep in his pockets, waiting for her response. The casualness of his stance was deceptive. She could practically feel the tension vibrating in him.

Wordlessly she came toward him, watching the hot flare of emotion light his eyes. Slowly, as if she were a wild creature who might abruptly shy away, Alex withdrew his hands from his pockets, then stood stock still. He was waiting for her, she realized. Gen stopped, mere inches away, the pull of desire so powerful she could hardly keep her body from swaying toward his, could hardly recognize her voice for the pounding of her heart. "Show me all the colors of the universe, Alex."

SIXTEEN

Her words still floating in the air, Gen raised a trembling hand, and stretched it out to him in offering. When Alex clasped it in his own, her heart felt as if it might burst free of her rib cage. His blue gaze never leaving hers, he lifted her hand, pressing her palm to his lips. The touch of his wet, open mouth against her skin was like a line of fire racing through Gen, melting her from the inside out.

She moaned softly.

The sound seemed to free the passion Alex had been holding in check. Swiftly, he shifted his arms and with breathtaking ease, swept her off her feet, gathering her so close that she could feel the thundering of his heart.

As he carried her across the room, Gen gazed enraptured at the chiseled planes of his face, at the curved lines of his firm mouth, committing every detail to memory.

The bedroom's blinds were drawn against the sun, giving the large room a golden sepia tone. The carpeting beneath Alex muffled his steps. Everything was quiet and hushed, except for the sound of their breathing.

He stopped in the middle of the room and slowly lowered Gen to her feet. His hands settled on her waist, even this lightest of touches searing her. Overcome with an uncharacteristic shyness, Gen glanced around, and her gaze landed on the massive platform bed that dominated the bedroom. The sight of it caused a flutter of panic. How many women had Alex slept with? she wondered suddenly, just as suddenly realizing she'd prefer not to know the answer. Her gaze ricocheted back to his face.

"You're not sure, are you, Gen?" he said quietly.

"No, no, I'm—" she stammered, embarrassed. Unwilling to admit her total inexperience, she said lamely, "I'm just not used to this kind of thing."

"I think I know how you're feeling. I've never been this nervous before. I want to please you so damn much, Gen," he admitted, his voice low and solemn.

"What?" she said, her astonishment chasing away her attack of nerves. "Are you kidding? I'm terrified I'll melt into a puddle at your feet just from your hands on my waist." At her words, the hands in question tightened possessively. Gen's breath caught, becoming a gasp of wanting.

Their eyes locked.

"Ahh, well," Alex murmured. "In that case, why don't we start from where we left off earlier?" And his mouth descended. She rose on her tiptoes, meeting him halfway.

It was a sweet fever that consumed them. Their

hands moved restlessly as their mouths tasted and tangled, fueling an urgent, unstoppable need. When Alex growled heatedly, "I want you naked in my arms," it set off violent tremors within her.

"Help me, Alex," Gen whispered, her voice shaking.

Alex was ever so accommodating. "My pleasure," he said and his hands shifted to the hem of her shirt.

Gen spared a panicked thought for the plainness of her underwear—a simple cotton bra with matching panties—but then he was sliding her T-shirt up her torso and over her head. Carelessly tossing the shirt aside, he went still. She saw the brilliant gleam in his eyes and felt the thrilling bulge of his erection against her stomach—unarguable proof that he was far from disappointed.

Gently, reverentially, he reached for her. His fingertips skimmed the swell of her breasts, which rose and fell with her breathless shudders. Moving with exquisite slowness he traced the line of white cotton to the front clasp of her bra. Her heart pounded as he unlatched the clasp and peeled the white fabric away. The bra dropped to the floor, unheeded.

His eyes feasted on her, taking in her slender torso and her heaving breasts, their dusky pink nipples tight with arousal. "I thought you were the most beautiful woman in the world when I saw you walking out of the sea. You're even lovelier up close, Gen. So delicate and yet so lush, I'm dizzy just looking at you," he whispered huskily. "Let me feel how beautiful you are, too."

Alex's hands covered her breasts, squeezing and fondling, and the sensation was so exquisite it made her as dizzy as he, made her ache for more. But as his head dipped toward her, hunger etched on his face, she said, "Alex, wait," aware that once his mouth touched her she'd be lost, utterly lost. "Your shirt. I—"

He paused. Heavy-lidded with passion, his eyes glittered in the half-light. Then his hands lightly stroked the undersides of her breasts, sending a shiver of pleasure down her spine, and he said, "Yes, my shirt, definitely has to go. Maybe you'd like to take it off for me this time?" His teeth flashed white in a smile of wicked invitation.

It struck Gen then, really struck her, the utter glory of being free to touch and kiss Alex. *He was hers.*

The thought electrified her. Desire lent speed to her fingers. They flew over his buttons. As the V of his shirt expanded, she drank in the sight of his broad chest, of his muscles quivering with sexual excitement. Leaning into him, she brushed the aching points of her nipples against his hot flesh.

A growl of need erupted from deep inside Alex. Wrapping his hands around the cheeks of her bottom, he pulled her flush against him. She moaned, feeling him hard and thick and straining just where she was dissolving and melting. He caught her moan, kissing her with erotic abandon, his tongue sliding in and out of her mouth to the rhythm of his hands squeezing her buttocks and his hips rocking against her cleft.

She was spiraling out of control, everything inside

her coiling tighter and tighter, ready to fly apart. Frantically her hands moved to his waistband.

At the touch of Gen's fingers grazing his naked stomach, Alex nearly burst. He was embarrassingly close to coming in his trousers, something that he'd managed to avoid even as a horny teenager. But then again, he'd never been this aroused in his life. He was dying to thrust himself into Gen, sheath himself in her slick heat, and claim her as his. The feel of her fingers undoing his belt buckle and working his zipper down over his rock-hard erection was enough to blow his mind—among other things.

The mere thought of her touching his straining cock had him growing, swelling even more. . . . God, she was so fine-boned, he thought with sudden concern, his eyes taking in her slender body, her small, perfect breasts. Would he hurt her? His disjointed thoughts ended on an in-drawn hiss as Gen pushed at the fabric of his trousers and his boxers, shoving them down his hips. His cock sprang free, pointing like a divining rod at what he craved more than anything in the world: *Gen.*

He stepped out of his trousers, simultaneously kicking off his loafers, and saw that Gen was transfixed, staring at his groin. "This is what you do to me, Gen," he said, his voice low and rough with desire.

Her eyes, saucer-round, flew to his face. Half dreading that she was going to run panic-stricken from the room, his heart did a joyous flip when that impish smile of hers lit up the room. "Why, Alex," she said in an awed stage whisper, "you don't look *anything* like the male models I've worked from."

His laughter burst forth. "Thank God for that."
Grinning, he realized that he was happier than he'd
been in years, and that his happiness was due to Gen.

As Alex stood before her, Gen knew she'd never beheld a sight as beautiful or as glorious as Alex naked
and aroused for her. She stepped forward until her
naked skin brushed his. She kissed him.

The sweetness of Gen's kiss shattered the last of
Alex's control. His hands swept around her. Scooping
her into his arms, he carried her to his bed and laid
her down. "It's my turn now," he whispered as his
fingers zeroed in on the metal buttons of her jeans.

Alex quickly dispensed with the jeans, but then had
to tamp down on the lust that roared through him
when only a scrap of cotton shielded Gen from his
ravenous gaze. Gen's pleasure was paramount to him.
He forced his trembling hands to tarry, slowly peeling
the panties down her narrow hips. His breath came in
a labored rush as inch by inch the dark triangle at the
apex of her slender thighs was revealed. She was so
incredibly beautiful, he thought dazedly. So beautiful
and so extraordinarily precious to him.

He touched her. His hands learned her delicate
curves, stroking and caressing Gen until she trembled
like a sapling caught in a tempest. Her body arched
and bucked beneath his touch, beneath the kisses he
rained on her as he whispered his approval. "God,
you're so soft and sweet, so very sweet. Like cream
dusted with cinnamon. These," he said huskily, his
fingers lightly teasing her nipples, "are like wild straw-
berries. . . ." Lowering his mouth to her breast, he

drew her nipple against his tongue, circling and lathing it as he suckled.

The hot pleasure of his mouth on her aching breasts had her clutching at Alex's shoulders, arching and pressing closer, offering him more. The pleasure spread, coursed through her, made her greedy. Her hands raced over him, glorying in his lean strength. Desperate for the taste of him, she pleaded, "Kiss me, Alex."

Lifting his head, Alex gave her a smile filled with promise. A smile that had her toes curling in anticipation when he murmured, "My pleasure." Instead of returning to her mouth, though, his lips blazed a trail southward, down the valley of her breasts and across the flat, shivery plain of her stomach. Breathless gasps escaped her as his tongue and teeth continued their exploration. Molten liquid pooled and pulsed, shooting off fiery sparks deep in her center. Gently, Alex's hands parted her trembling thighs. His fingers brushed her dewy curls, opening her.

At the feel of his finger gliding down her cleft and entering her, her breath caught then raced uncontrollably as the finger slid in and out of her again and again. Her muscles clenched around him, drawing ever tighter as his thumb began rhythmically circling and rubbing her clitoris. Then his mouth descended, hot and wicked, joining the erotic dance of his fingers. And the sparks inside Gen erupted in a glorious shower of colors. Exploding with pleasure, she arched into him, crying his name. As her body quivered with silvered aftershocks, he calmed her with languid caresses and gentle kisses. Slowly, slowly she returned to herself, only to realize that his seemingly lazy petting was stirring the wild need in her once more.

"Alex," she moaned, twisting in his arms.

"Shh, sweetheart, easy. There's no hurry," he murmured. "I want to go slowly with you. . . ."

Her eyes traveled over him. For all his calmness, there was a fierce tension in him. It was there in the taut line of his muscles, in the faint sheen of sweat that dotted his brow. And she knew he was holding back out of consideration for her. The thought made her heart sing. "But, Alex," she said, beginning to kiss her way across his chest, "I don't think I can go slowly. I want you too much. And something tells me you'd rather not wait, either," she whispered, as she slipped her hand around his penis. Lightly she stroked his engorged length, exulting when Alex closed his eyes, his entire body shuddering violently with need.

When her fingers traced the tip of his penis, Alex groaned deep in his throat. Rolling over, he pinned her. His fever-bright eyes locked with hers. "Are you sure, Gen?" he demanded huskily.

"Mmm, yes," she assured him. Raising her head off the pillow, she brushed her lips against his and murmured, "This time I want to see all those colors with you deep inside me, Alex," smiling when his erection pulsed against her palm. Above her, Alex reached for the drawer of his night table, opened it, and withdrew a foil packet. Levering himself up, he sat back on his heels, looking pagan and absolutely magnificent. Gen sat up, too, smiled, and held out her palm. He looked at her and hesitated.

"Uh, Gen, maybe I should do this . . ."

Her smile widened. "Please, Alex?" she asked. "I'm very good with my hands."

With a hoarse groan he shut his eyes. "I don't doubt it," he whispered.

"Please? If I promise I'll be very gentle with you?"

"Minx," he growled softly, handing her the condom.

At the feel of Gen's fingers smoothing the latex skin over him, Alex sucked in a ragged breath. God, she was right, she was good with her hands. Her touch was pure magic. Spellbound, Alex could barely breathe as her hands moved down, reaching the base of his cock. She was still holding him when she raised her eyes to his.

"Have I told you how beautiful you are?" he asked.

"You make me feel beautiful," she told him softly. "You make me feel beautiful things. Make it happen again for me, Alex."

More than happy to oblige, he clasped her hips, tumbling Gen backward, his body following hers. "Lift your legs and wrap them around my waist," he instructed. "Yeah, that's right, sweetheart," he breathed, a rampant urgency seizing him as the blunt tip of his penis pressed against her slick heat. "Now hold on to me," he whispered, his own fingers tightening reflexively around her hips. With a single thrust, Alex bore down and entered her, sheathing himself.

She flinched at the flash of pain and for a second instinctively struggled against the invasion. Above her, Alex stiffened and said, his voice tight with fierce tenderness, "Oh, God, sweetheart, you didn't say . . ." Then he was kissing her, stroking her, and she felt herself relax against him. "That's it," he whispered as she began to move against him tentatively. "I'm sorry it hurt. Let me make it better."

Alex was a man who kept his promises. The pain that flashed when he entered her soon disappeared, to be replaced by a dazzling array of colors and hues. He showered her with kisses that were lush and warm, like crimson velvet. She gazed into the saturated cobalt blue of Alex's eyes, while his hips rocked and danced with hers. His flat, pebbly nipples were dark, a rich, burnt sienna, and salty beneath her tongue. The feel of Alex moving rhythmically, deliciously inside her, over and over again, filled her with a sweet, liquid gold. The colors he gave Gen multiplied, grew more and more brilliant, as glorious and magical as a rainbow.

A piercing happiness filled her. Overcome, she climaxed, her body arching like a bow, crying Alex's name. With one final thrust, he joined her. Holding Alex's lean body close to her, feeling him shudder his release, Gen's eyes brimmed with tears. He'd touched something in her, she thought, a secret part of her. She was forever changed. Her lips curved in a smile that was bittersweet.

His eyes closed, Alex dragged air into his lungs, needing all his concentration to perform this simple act. The intensity of his orgasm left him dazed, shaken, perhaps a little afraid. He'd come with a force so strong, it had felt as if he were pouring his very soul into Gen's welcoming body.

Alex didn't bother kidding himself that he felt like this because he hadn't had sex in weeks. What he'd felt when he was inside Gen wasn't merely physical, the rush of getting his rocks off. No, it had to do with the profound awe and tenderness that filled him when he'd broken through her virginity, the fierce gladness that spread through him as he watched Gen's eyes grow enormous with discovery and her smile shine as her lithe body began moving in concert with his. It had to do with the soul-stirring pleasure he felt when she'd come, tightening around him and calling his name with such sweet desperation—as if he were the center of her world. It had to do with wanting to give Gen everything he had. . . . It had to do with never wanting to let her go.

It frightened Alex how important Gen had become to him—all the more so now that he'd touched her. And as his first instinct was to stay sheathed inside her, he forced himself to roll gently off her, despite her whimper of protest as he left her—despite his own aching sense of loss.

He couldn't, however, resist the urge to gather Gen close, settle her so that she lay with her head over his heart, her silky hair teasing his overheated skin. He couldn't prevent his fingers from skimming over her satin-smooth skin and gentle curves, couldn't stop the smile that spread over his face when he felt her breath fan his skin. His arms tightened their hold and he closed his eyes so he could feel her heart beating next to him.

Adrift in a sated semidoze, Alex came to consciousness by slow yet infinitely pleasurable degrees.

Opening his eyes, he found Gen poised above him, her legs straddling his thighs. Hands as delicate as angel wings lightly traced his features. Doubtless feeling the shift of his muscles as he smiled, Gen opened her own eyes to gaze into his. "I've wanted to touch you so much, for so long. Do you mind?" she asked in a hushed voice.

The idea of him ever objecting to Gen's touch had his smile widening. Shifting his head he pressed a kiss into her palm. "Do with me what you will, Gen," he invited. "I'm putty in your hands."

He watched her expression become eager, excited, and delightfully naughty. "Putty, huh?" she said and cast an arch glance at his erection, which had sprung to life the second he looked into her face. She shook her head. "No, I'd say we're looking at a different material altogether. One that's far more responsive. One I think I'd like to experiment with."

"Feel free to experiment to your heart's content," Alex offered huskily. Tracing the pale flesh of her inner thighs, his need soared as they clamped reflexively about him and he saw her nipples grow taut with arousal. Where he and Gen touched, he could feel her body warming, stoked by the same fire that consumed him. His hands moved closer to where he wanted to be the most. But before he could explore her nest of silky curls, Gen manacled his wrists, holding him at bay. With a smile she said, "I'm sorry, but I need you to lie back and stay very, very still." Dragging his hands back down to his sides, she added, "And no distractions, please. I need to concentrate here while I learn more about this material." Gazing down at his pulsing erection, she bit her lower lip, the artless provocation fanning the fire in him to flare wildly.

He wondered whether he might incinerate from lust.

Then even that thought was too much as Gen's gifted and stunningly talented hands closed around his straining cock, and he gave himself over to Gen's artistry.

Hunger and Murphy finally drove Gen and Alex from his bed a few hours later. The causes occurred simultaneously while Alex was pleasantly engaged in one of his own studies. He was scattering kisses across Gen's quivering stomach. One for every freckle he counted. By the time he reached the shallow dip on the inside of her hipbone, he was at 212. An impressive feat of mathematics, considering that Gen was being very, very distracting—moaning as her body undulated beneath his mouth and hands. But at 216, a foreign sound intruded, one that had Alex pausing and cocking his head. From the other side of the door came a single bark followed by a piteous whine.

"Murphy!" Gen exclaimed with the guilty horror of a mother who was late picking up her child at school. "He must be desperate to go out—and he's probably starving!" At which point her stomach chimed in with a rumble that put Murphy's bark to shame, and had Alex rocking with laughter.

Gen gave him a light punch on the shoulder. "Okay, yes, I admit it, I'm starving too," trying in vain to suppress her own laughter. "But I have definitely worked up an appetite."

"Well, then, let's feed you both—you realize, though, that this means I get to have a recount. Starting from the top," he said, grinning as he dropped a kiss on the tip of her nose.

Gen looped her hands around his neck and angled her face so that his lips landed on hers. Loving the taste and texture of him, she kissed him eagerly, unconcerned that she was perhaps being too obvious, lacking the sophisticated wiles to which he was no doubt accustomed. Yet even if she'd possessed those useful tricks and ploys, she wouldn't have bothered using them. Honesty was too important to her; the feelings Alex aroused in her were too precious. She wasn't going to sully them with pretense and silly games.

It was only after they'd rolled off the bed and were helping each other dress, a laughing, oft-interrupted process, that Gen noticed the painting hanging over the headboard. "My God, that's lovely," she said, gazing at the large oil landscape of marsh grasses bordering a dawn-lit pond.

"My uncle Alexander painted it. You recognize the view, of course."

"That's Georgica pond, isn't it? Your uncle captured the light perfectly. That filmy, golden glow as it hits the water is wonderful."

Slipping his hand around the back of Gen's neck, Alex stroked her sensitive skin. "Yeah, I love it. I've been out mornings when the pond looks exactly the way it does in this painting. You know, I've been thinking that I'd really like to have a kind of companion piece to this painting that I could hang here, over the fireplace," he said, pointing to the opposite wall.

Intrigued, she glanced at the fireplace, encased by a white marble mantel. Placed on the center of the mantel was a black lacquer vase filled with a tangled spray of branches. Though dramatic and calligraphic, the visual effect was also somewhat austere, at odds with the wealth of emotion, the love evident in each stroke of Alexander Miller's brush. Gen's brain whirred with possibilities, already taking in the dimensions of the wall and its high ceiling. "Would you want a landscape?" she asked, curious to know what Alex envisioned.

He glanced at her in surprise. "The subject matter is irrelevant. I've always thought what makes truly great art is what the artist brings to the work. . . . That was what drew me to your paintings, Gen. They come alive because there's so much of yourself in them—your spirit, your insight, your humor. That's what makes us want to look at the subject you've chosen as deeply and as generously as you have. That's what makes you such a powerful artist."

Gen swallowed the lump of emotion lodged in her throat. "Thank you. I think that's probably the nicest thing anyone's ever said to me," she said. It was true. And she knew she would treasure Alex's words forever. She smiled mistily. "I'll see what I can come up with," she whispered, sealing her promise with a kiss.

SEVENTEEN

As Alex's housekeeper had emptied his refrigerator of everything except a lone stick of butter, a jar of mustard, and a bottle of Sancerre, they opted to go to the park, where they bought six hot dogs, two for each of them, a bottle of water for Murphy, and iced tea for Gen and Alex.

Murphy was a forgiving soul. His tail wagged double time as he scarfed down his share of the hot dogs in two noisy chomps and then busied himself sniffing out the rich scents of Central Park and marking his presence for New York's canine world.

Content to follow in the dog's wake, they let Murphy's nose lead them where it willed. Their only desire was for each other. Alex and Gen walked hand in hand, shoulders brushing, heads inclined as they spoke in soft undertones or exchanged whispers with lips a feather brush to the ear.

At the boat pond, they bought a warm pretzel from a vendor then sat on a bench and tore the pretzel into thirds, Gen feeding Murphy tiny morsels at a time to distract him from chasing the pigeons and squirrels.

Alex's arm was extended along the back of the bench, his fingers idly stroking her shoulder.

"Is there any place you want to go?" he asked.

"Before we go back, you mean?"

Alex nodded. "Yeah."

"Hmm," Gen thought for a moment. "Well, there's the Met—I'd love to show you my favorite paintings—but I don't want to be away from your aunt Grace too long."

"Ahh, I see I'm not the only one who has a protective streak," he teased, squeezing her shoulder to draw her close and press his smiling mouth to her temple.

"Guilty as charged," she admitted, turning on the bench to face him. Her fingers sought his. "I can't help it. Mrs. Miller's wonderful. I'm so glad I've had the chance to know her. And if your aunt could see the two of us now, sitting on a park bench worrying about her, she'd throw her hands up in disgust."

Alex laughed. "You *have* gotten to know her."

Gen nodded, smiling widely. "Alex," she began shyly.

"Yeah?"

"There is one place I'd like to go—but only if we have enough time."

"We'll make the time. Where do you want to go?"

"Pearl Paint," she answered, naming one of the city's premier art supply stores. Leaning close she whispered, "I find myself greatly inspired . . . I need more colors."

His eyes twinkled. "Inspired, huh?"

She nodded. "Greatly." Leaning forward just a little more, she saw his blue gaze darken with desire. Her lips parted in invitation.

"Next stop Canal Street," he murmured then claimed her in a kiss that inspired them both.

Alex parked the Aston in a garage not far from Pearl Paint. Trying to park in that neighborhood would have been an exercise in futility. Furthermore, there was a high probability that the sports car wouldn't be waiting for them when they returned from Gen's shopping excursion. Canal Street was jammed solid with pedestrians and street vendors hawking their wares, yet seeing Murphy amble down the sidewalk had the most amazing effect on the people hurrying toward them: they parted like the Red Sea. "I've got to walk with Murphy more often," he said to Gen as they paused in front of the art store's double doors.

"Yes, he's like an ambulance without the sirens and lights," she said, patting the dog's shaggy head. "Hey, Murph, we're gonna see Bruno, so behave."

"Gen! Long time no shop! It's good to see you, kid. And Murphy, too, what a treat! So what are you in for today, beautiful?"

Gen grinned at Bruno. Bruno, Pearl Paint's manager, looked like a cross between Danny DeVito and Billy Crystal—short and wiry, with an irrepressible, near-manic energy. He'd been kind enough to take Gen under his wing the very first day she walked into the immense store, which for artists was more like Aladdin's cave. Bruno, an artist's encyclopedia with a Brooklyn accent, had become Gen's guide, pointing out specials and sales, offering advice on papers and canvases, brushes and glazes. She'd learned more wandering the aisles with him than she had from some of her teachers at college.

"Hi, Bruno. I love the shirt," she said, nodding at the puce Hawaiian print.

"Thanks. Check out the pants, too," he said, and came around the counter from behind the register to show off shiny, orange bell-bottoms. "Something told me this morning that I should go all out. I'm glad I did. You are looking more beautiful than ever. How about you and I go out—" Then, as if he'd suddenly realized that Alex was with Gen, and not just another customer who'd trailed in on her heels, he shook his head dolefully. "Damn! Missed again."

"And a good thing, too, Bruno. Donna might get a little put out." Turning to Alex, she explained, "Donna is Bruno's wife," and pointed to a bunch of color photographs taped to the front of the cash register. "That's Donna and that's their four beautiful kids. Bruno, I'd like to introduce you to my friend Alex Miller."

"Pleased to meet you," Bruno said, eyeing Alex from head to foot with an expression that told Alex he wasn't overly impressed. "You an artist?" he asked in a skeptical tone.

"No, 'fraid not."

Bruno grunted. "You know anything about art?"

"Enough to know that in five years, ten at the outside, artists around the world will be streaming in through these doors, like pilgrims visiting Mecca, because they've heard that Genevieve Monaghan will only buy her supplies from you."

Gen made a strangled sound of embarrassment at Alex's answer, but Bruno laughed, loud and heartily. "Damned straight they will be." Grinning he added, "You seem pretty smart for a suit."

"Thanks," Alex replied dryly.

"So, Gen, where have you and Murphy been hiding yourselves?" Bruno asked. "My dog biscuits have gone stale."

Her face still warm from Alex's outlandish praise, Gen was only too happy to switch the focus of the conversation to her dog. "I don't think Murphy worries about such niceties, Bruno. We've been on Long Island, working on a commission for Alex."

"A commission, huh? What sort of commission?"

Alex felt Bruno's dark eyes slice into him with renewed suspicion. He didn't mind Bruno's protective attitude toward Gen—not as long as Bruno was married with a passel of kids. "It's for a hospital in Boston," he replied. "The Children's Hospital."

Bruno's expression relaxed. "All right then. You bankrolling?" he challenged with a grin that Alex was beginning to recognize was very much part of his character.

Alex nodded. "Absolutely."

"All I need is some paint, Bruno," Gen interjected quickly.

Both men ignored her comment.

"This is your lucky day, sweets. I got some new linen canvas that's going to make you flip. Come and take a look," Bruno urged over his shoulder, already heading down the crowded aisle.

Gen instinctively laid her hand on Alex's forearm. He stopped and looked at her. "Alex, I really don't need a lot—"

"Oh, yeah, you do, and I want to give it to you," he said, his smile slow and wide and so beautiful she lost herself in it. He moved his arm so her hand slipped into his. Opening his fingers, he laced them about hers. "Get whatever strikes your fancy, Gen. Who knows where your explorations might take you or how they might inspire you?" His hand, warm and strong, squeezed hers gently.

And with that simple, most basic of caresses, Gen recalled all Alex and she had done together, all they'd shared, all they'd discovered. It would take gallons and gallons of paint, yards upon yards of canvas, for Gen to express what she felt for him.

Her heart fluttered when he dipped his head and caressed her lips in a feather-light kiss. "I like doing things for you," he whispered coaxingly, then with a wry grin added, "Besides, I don't want to annoy Bruno and wind up on his black list."

Alex needn't have worried about that, Gen thought an hour later when the three of them were back at the cash register. Bruno, busy ringing up item after item, was acting a whole lot friendlier toward Alex, having discovered that in addition to championing Gen's artistic career, the two of them shared yet another mutual passion: those damned Yankees.

While Alex and Bruno indulged in a brag fest over the Yankees' chances for stealing the World Series again this year, Gen did her best to look anywhere but

at the green numbers illuminated on the cash register's display. She was afraid she'd faint from shock if
she saw how much money Alex had spent. Still, the
thought of all those glorious colors and the rough-
textured weave of the canvas she'd be laying them on
made her feel as if Christmas and her birthday had
been rolled into one.

She couldn't wait to get back to the studio and
begin painting. Alex's niece and nephew were coming the next afternoon. She'd begin sketching them,
working out the poses she wanted for the hospital
painting. And when the light was gone, there'd be
Alex, she thought with dreamy happiness. Alex, who
made love like an artist.

Just then, something Bruno said filtered through
her reverie. She frowned, sure she was hearing things.

"Sorry, Bruno, did you say something about Jiri
just now?"

"Yeah. Jiri." He paused importantly. "Your Jiri. He
called and placed a major-league order."

Gen's face split into a grin. "Wow," she chuckled.
"Jiri really lucked out. The academy must have deeper
pockets than we thought. Why, the shipping alone
will cost a small fortune."

"Ain't that the truth. You'd have to be named
Onassis to afford it. But I'm not shipping the order to
Prague." His dark eyes gleaming with the excitement
of one imparting key information, he said, "Jiri said
he'll be picking up the entire lot in a couple of weeks.
Personally."

Mystified, Gen murmured, "How very strange. Why

in the world would Jiri be coming back to New York so soon?"

Bruno's thick eyebrows disappeared beneath his curly black hair. "Maybe 'cause he realized he needed something else besides a dozen or so cases of oils and gesso." His sharp gaze slid to Alex. "I'd keep a close eye on her, Miller, if I were you," he advised. "Else that rascal Czech might just spirit her away."

"Have you been sniffing Elmer's glue again, Bruno?" Gen teased. "It's far more likely that his gallery has snagged a prospective patron who's so eager to meet the renowned Jiri Novak, he's willing to foot the bill for a round-trip ticket."

"Yeah, that sounds like Novak's style," Bruno conceded with a shrug. "But then again, the one doesn't necessarily preclude the other, now does it, sweetie?"

After a brake-slamming halt in the traffic, Alex glanced over at Gen, and his mouth softened in a smile of amused tenderness. Dead to the world, she hadn't even stirred. They'd hardly made it out of the Midtown Tunnel before she'd succumbed to sleep. . . .

Just as she'd warned him.

They'd been standing with their bodies folded over the open trunk of his car, shoving the last of the boxes from Pearl Paint to make room for the final item: a thick roll of linen canvas. She'd turned to him with that little smile he'd come to love and said, "Alex, there's something I should tell you. Just so you don't take it personally or anything."

"Yeah?" He smiled, already intrigued by the possibilities.

"Yeah," she replied. "It's like this. In addition to arriving late for just about everything, I'm utterly incapable of staying awake in a car—or a plane, bus, or train, for that matter."

His smile became a laugh. "I'll try not to be offended. Actually, I'm relieved. I thought it was a damned effective ruse on your part, falling asleep on the way into the city. A neat variation of the silent treatment."

"Sorry, no. I'm not that cunning. Or clever. It's just something about the rocking motion when I'm sitting in a vehicle." She sighed and gave the plastic wrap protecting the canvas a final fond pat before stepping back so that he could slam the trunk shut. "No, the only way I can keep my eyes open is if I'm actually behind the wheel. Driving. So . . ." Letting the word dangle suggestively, she sent him a coy look and stretched out her hand, palm upward, her fingers wiggling.

"Nice try, Monaghan," he'd said with a wry shake of his head. He wished they were somewhere more private than double-parked outside Pearl Paint, so he could wrap his arms about her, taste her unforgettable sweetness, and then lower her down onto the warm shiny silver of the Aston's trunk. "Sleep away," he said, tossing the keys in the air and catching them easily. "You'll definitely need the rest, as I intend to provide hours of profound inspiration later tonight."

"Hours, huh? Then I really should drive—it seems to me it's *you* who'll be needing the sleep."

"Oh, I'm more than up to the task, I promise," he'd drawled huskily. "Don't worry about me. I'll have Murphy to keep me company. I'm sure we'll have a long, heart-to-heart talk."

Of course, Alex thought, when another deep, whirling snore emanated from the backseat, Murphy, too, was asleep—though not quite as sweetly as his mistress. Once again Alex's eyes strayed to Gen. She'd tucked a hand beneath her cheek, and her dark hair framed the delicate contour of her cheek. When she exhaled, an errant wisp danced over the tip of her nose. She looked so impossibly lovely that he was filled with an urge to clasp her tight and never let go.

He was stunned by the strength and urgency behind the impulse. Why did it feel like he was whisking a fairy princess off to his castle, where none could enter without his leave?

Unbidden, a name without a face popped into his head. Jiri Novak. Alex's lips flattened into a hard, determined line as he considered what he'd do if the artist made a move to get Gen back. No, there was no damned way Jiri Novak was going to get another shot at winning her. Novak had had his chance—and he'd blown it.

Of all the solutions to the potential reappearance of Jiri Novak, Alex's favorite was the one in which he squashed Novak flatter than a Long Island potato bug. The only problem with that particular scenario was, Alex knew how fiercely loyal Gen could be, and how impetuous, too. He didn't want to do anything that might drive her into Novak's arms.

Besides, what if the Czech was merely a self-absorbed artist, whose ego more than matched his prodigious talent? What if he contacted Gen solely to crow about some recent sale or brag about his position as the director of the National Academy? Sharing ideas and talking about the subject she loved most was an important part of Gen's life as an artist. Alex could never deny her that pleasure.

Which stuck Alex with a wholly unsatisfying option. It seemed that the only thing he could do was follow old Bruno's advice: if Jiri Novak did come sniffing around, he'd definitely be keeping a very close eye on Gen.

In the meantime, however, Alex intended to do everything he could to make Gen understand that she was his. Quickly he checked his rearview mirror—no, there were no lunatics about to ram him—then, leaning over sideways, he placed a kiss on her lips. They parted on a happy sigh.

Her eyes opened a fraction. "Mmm, I love the way you kiss me," she murmured with a sleepy smile. "Do it again later, 'kay?" she suggested before snuggling deeper into the seat and drifting off.

Shaking his head, Alex caught a glimpse of himself in the rearview mirror. He was grinning from ear to ear, the joy that was Gen easing the tension that had gripped him.

EIGHTEEN

Alerted to their return by Murphy's exuberant barking, Aunt Grace came outside to greet Gen and Alex. "Yes, yes, Murphy, I missed you too," she said affectionately as the dog gamboled across the lawn to squirm in ecstasy before her. "Although I wasn't expecting you back this soon."

"Soon?" Gen replied, giving the older woman a hug. It was shortly after 7 P.M. and the evening sky was awash with bold magenta and lavender streaks. "It feels as if we've been gone for days rather than mere hours. Come and look at the treasures in this trunk, Mrs. Miller."

Alex had backed the Aston so its rear end faced the studio. Aunt Grace peered into the open trunk. "My, you two have been busy."

"Yes, very busy," Gen echoed in a voice tinged with self-consciousness. She wondered what Mrs. Miller would say if she knew precisely how busy Alex and she had been—and doing what. Would she be pleased that she and Alex were together? Gen doubted Mrs. Miller would remain in the dark very long—she was far too perceptive. Then a sudden and horrible thought flashed in Gen's mind: perhaps Mrs. Miller would think she'd deliberately stolen Alex from Sydney. Would she be upset?

Quickly Gen ducked her head into the trunk and grabbed hold of a carton filled with tubes of acrylics and lovely new Grumbacher brushes and palette knives, all purchased by Alex. She swallowed and offered a silent plea: *Please, Lord, don't let Mrs. Miller think I'm some shallow fortune hunter.*

Hefting the carton in her arms she turned around and nearly plowed into Alex, who was back from his first trip to the studio and ready for the second haul. "Oh! Sorry!" she stammered, acutely aware of Alex's aunt watching them.

"Careful there, Rip," he cautioned, the husky timbre of his voice fueling Gen's uneasiness.

"Rip?" his aunt repeated, openly curious.

"Hi, Aunt Grace," he said, grinning. "Yeah, Rip. As in Van Winkle. I think Gen could sleep from here to California if given the chance." His grin became a smile, warm and intimate, as he returned his attention to Gen. "Here, let me take that."

She clutched it tighter. "No, that's okay, I've got it. I, um, need the exercise."

With a low rumble of laughter he stepped forward and lifted it out of her arms. "Save your energy for later," he advised in a soft undertone. Then without warning, he angled his head and planted a kiss just beneath her ear. One kiss became another as he leaned into her, his firm lips moving lazily, deliciously. . . .

A familiar thrill sped through her. Nerve endings

sizzling, she shivered, only to stifle a groan of dismay when Mrs. Miller said, "Alex, do stop nibbling on Genevieve. Otherwise I'll never get to see what's in all those boxes."

Alex's sigh of resignation fanned the shell of her ear. "Very well, Aunt Grace," he said, stepping back. "Though 'Man doth not live by bread only.' "

"I don't believe you're in any danger of starving," she replied tartly. "Which makes you a very lucky young woman, Genevieve," she added with what could only be described as a sly wink.

Gen smiled weakly in return. So much for Mrs. Miller remaining in the dark.

Okay, so maybe Alex's aunt wasn't overly upset by the new role Gen had assumed in her nephew's life. Either that or she was far too well bred to show it.

Gen didn't know why she was feeling so insecure. The three of them had just shared a delicious, thrown-together dinner. Alex had whipped up three fluffy, melt-in-your-mouth Swiss-cheese omelets that were seasoned with a hint of nutmeg to tease the taste buds. While Alex had whisked, poured, and flipped, Gen had toasted thick slices of whole grain bread and made a tomato and basil salad. Mrs. Miller, who had no culinary ambitions whatsoever, contented herself with arranging a wide ring of cherries around the left-over lemon pound cake Gen had baked yesterday.

The dinner conversation had been relaxed, without a single pointed remark to justify Gen's current un-ease. After they'd finished off the bottle of wine, Alex had helped with the washing up and then excused himself to check the e-mails from his office and call his sister to reconfirm her and the twins' arrival tomorrow. He would join Gen and his aunt out on the porch for a grappa as soon as he was finished.

Mrs. Miller was already out on the porch, eager to watch the stars come out. The kettle had whistled shrilly, yet Gen lingered by the stove, as if the chamomile blossoms for her tea could steep only there.

What was the matter with her? Why was she feeling so anxious? It was completely out of character. If she brooded and obsessed, it was about her art, not her life. But here she was, wracked with worries. Of course, she reminded herself, she didn't often have days like this one, either. A day, which now that she stopped to think about it, had had the kind of astonishing and surreal momentum of a tossed snowball that triggers an avalanche: a blink of an eye and the entire mountainside is transformed.

She'd awakened this morning as one person. By this afternoon she'd become a different one, fundamentally changed by Alex's lovemaking. Yet the earth-shattering experience of sharing her body with him wasn't the cause of her distress. All she had to do was look at him, hear his low voice, feel his body near hers, and she went tingly, her heart expanding until she felt as if she were floating on a cloud of happiness.

But what Gen hadn't realized or anticipated— because she'd never expected any of this to happen— was that being involved with Alex would entail so much more than simply *being* with him. And that was why her stomach was twisted in painful knots.

The rest of Alex's family was arriving tomorrow.

His sister, Cassie, might not be nearly as warmhearted as Mrs. Miller. She knew how jealous sisters could be when it came to their older brothers.

Then there was Alex's social and professional world, she thought, and the specter of his upcoming party rose ominously in her mind. It had been off-putting enough imagining herself mingling with the wealthy movers and shakers when she was just Genevieve Monaghan, the artist from Boston. Being scrutinized as Alex Miller's newest girlfriend was a thousand times more intimidating. They would no doubt expect to meet someone as polished and poised as Sydney. . . .

No, don't even go there, Gen told herself. She was *not* going to start comparing herself with Sydney. Nor was she going to start worrying about other people's expectations. And enough with the moping about. She was acting like a pathetic ninny and Mrs. Miller was probably wondering what was keeping her.

Gen closed the lid of the teapot. The tea was probably stone cold by now, she thought with disgust. Picking up the tray, Gen pinned a cheerful smile on her face and vowed not to think about how much she wished she and Alex were still in his apartment and that the rest of the world was far, far away.

Gen had poured Mrs. Miller's grappa and settled onto the cushioned wicker settee with her tea between her hands when Alex came onto the porch. By the soft golden light of the hurricane lanterns, she saw his smile widen as his eyes met hers.

"Is everything fine with Cassie and Caleb?" Mrs. Miller asked.

"Yeah. Cass sounded a trifle harried. It seems that

since the twins lost their campaign to bring the dogs to New York, they've decided they 'absolutely need' the rest of their worldly possessions, which is a bit more than can be crammed into two suitcases. But the flight's unchanged. The plane gets in at two-thirty at JFK. So with luck we'll be back here by five."

"Take my station wagon," his aunt offered. "You'll have more room."

"Thanks. You won't be needing it?"

"Well, if I have to go anywhere, I'll just borrow the Aston," she informed him breezily.

"On second thought . . ." Alex backpedaled hastily.

Mrs. Miller heaved a heavy sigh. "Oh, very well. I'll leave the Aston alone—although I've gotten very good at driving it, if I do say so myself." Turning to Gen, she said, "Have you driven it yet, Genevieve?"

"Unfortunately, no. Though not for lack of trying," she added with a small smile. "I imagine it's a truly fine machine to drive."

Mrs. Miller leaned forward and the candlelight caught the sparkle of excitement in her eyes. "Just wait till you feel it beneath your hands, Genevieve. All that power humming, responding."

Alex doubled over, seized by a fit of strangled coughing. Gen waited for him to stop before leaning back against the cushions with a grin. "Mmm, I've got goose bumps already."

"Right." Alex shook his head with exasperation that Gen imagined was only partly feigned. "That's it. I'm taking the Aston's keys with me. You two are terrifying me."

"Oh, Alex, really!" his aunt protested.

"Sorry, Mrs. Miller," Gen said in commiseration. "It looks like we're stuck with Hugo the Yugo."

"At least you can't try and break the sound barrier in that thing," he said, unswayed.

"Killjoy," she taunted, biting the inside of her cheek to keep a straight face.

"Sticks and stones," he replied easily. Bending over the tray Gen had brought, he lifted the grappa bottle by its slender neck. "Aunt Grace, would you like a drop more?"

"No, thank you, dear. I'll just finish what's left in my glass. The Martin Sheen special is on in fifteen minutes."

A comfortable silence settled over the porch as Alex unstoppered the bottle and poured himself some grappa. Snifter in hand, he walked over to the settee and sat down on the cushion next to Gen. The weight of his body caused hers to shift and her shoulder brushed his. All too aware of Mrs. Miller ensconced in the nearby chair, Gen straightened, her posture ramrod straight, and did her best to ignore Alex.

At least she tried to.

But then he casually lifted his arm and laid it along the back of the settee. His hand wasn't touching her. But perversely, that made her all the more conscious of him.

She sat there, wanting him so, she thought she might expire if she couldn't touch him. Hoping the night air would calm her, she drew in a deep breath, only to inhale the tantalizing scent of his cologne.

She was suddenly, intensely grateful for the porch's subdued lighting, certain the rush of desire she felt was stamped on her face, as damning as the *A* on Hester Prynne. In the quiet calm her breathing sounded unnaturally harsh. Hastily she lifted her cup to her lips and pretended to sip her tepid tea.

Surreptitiously she stole a glance at Alex.

He was staring meditatively into the pool of clear liquid at the bottom of his glass, watching it slosh gently back and forth. Raising the glass to his lips, he downed it. Mesmerized she watched the muscles of his throat work as he swallowed the fiery alcohol, and felt an answering heat flow through her.

Gen closed her eyes, secretly savoring the sensation. Next to her, Alex shifted again. Reaching forward he set the glass on the coffee table, and his hand, the one resting on the back of the settee, grazed her naked shoulder. Lust, wild and electric, sizzled through her.

She barely stifled her gasp.

Luckily Mrs. Miller chose that moment to rise to her feet. "It's upstairs for me. My program beckons. No, don't get up, Alex," she said when he made to stand politely. "You two stay here. It's a lovely night for star gazing. Good night, Genevieve."

"Good night," Gen replied in a voice that sounded far too tremulous.

Neither Alex nor Gen spoke as Mrs. Miller walked away. It was as if both were concentrating on the sound of her footsteps on the porch, the drawn-out creak of the spring followed by the sound of the screen door slamming. There was a brief silence, then the deliberate tread of feet marching up the steps.

Gen and Alex had gone up and down those steps so

many times now. . . . By the count of fourteen, their reaction was simultaneous. Explosive.

They reached for each other, Alex hauling her to him as Gen's hands tangled in his hair, dragging his mouth to hers.

They kissed as though starved for each other. Alex tasted like grappa, dangerous and potent. Her tongue dueled with his and she grew drunk with pleasure.

They touched, greedy to relearn curves and magic places. When Alex's hands streaked over her to cup her breasts and fondle them through the thin cotton of her dress, she arched against him in a provocative plea.

His lips left hers as he gasped for breath, gazing at her with eyes that shone bright with desire. He made a sound that was half laugh, half groan. "Christ, that was quite possibly the longest fifteen minutes of my life. I love my aunt. I love Cassie and the twins. Hell, I probably even love Caleb, my brother-in-law. But right now I wish they'd all just disappear."

"You do? Why?"

"I don't want to share you. And they arrive tomorrow. After that, things will be as busy as a three-ring circus."

Happiness flooded Gen. Knowing that Alex felt the same as she bolstered her previously failing courage, made the prospect of facing his family and associates much easier to bear. "A three-ring circus?" She smiled. "I'm sure it won't be that bad."

"Yeah, it will be. I was going quietly insane waiting for Aunt Grace to leave. God, you look beautiful in that dress. All evening long I've been thinking about touching you." His gaze fastened on her lips. He brought his mouth to hers and with the tip of his tongue traced its lush contours. She moaned, parting for him, inviting him in.

Alex didn't need a second invitation. With a low rumble of satisfaction, his tongue swept inside, rubbing against hers over and over again.

By the time their lips parted, his hands were roving over her possessively. Through half-lowered lids, he watched his hands move to the row of buttons at the front of her dress, freeing the material, opening it, exposing the gentle slopes of her breasts. The last button released, he pushed the narrow straps off her shoulders. The shiftlike dress slipped to her waist.

She shivered, but not from the cold. "Alex—"

At the sound of his name tumbling from her lips, he raised his head. His features were stark in the candlelight. "You're so damned lovely," he whispered hoarsely. "I'm dying here—God help me, I feel like I'll die if I can't touch you." His hands slid down to encircle her waist. His grip tightened, drawing her underneath him.

"No! Wait!" The words came out a stifled cry as Gen felt herself fall back onto the cushions. "We can't make love here on the porch! Your aunt—"

"Has the TV's volume cranked so she won't miss a word Martin Sheen utters," he finished, following her down, his hands already slipping her bunched dress down her legs. They streaked back up the length of her inner leg, setting off tiny explosions of pleasure, and then slowed so his fingers could graze her panties. At his touch, everything tightened inside Gen. Her hips rose in wanton invitation.

"Yes, that's it," he encouraged. His fingers massaged her in slow, wicked circles till her hips danced beneath him.

Inflamed, Gen grappled with the button at his waistband and jerked the zipper down, freeing him. He sprang into her eager hands, hot as silk warmed by the sun, hard as tempered steel. She closed her fingers around him, moving up and down, testing and teasing.

"Oh, Jesus, Gen." Alex groaned and shoved a hand into his pocket, withdrawing the small packet. With a frantic savagery, he ripped it open with his teeth. "Quickly," he commanded, pressing the condom into her palm.

Driven by the same mad need as he, Gen smoothed the latex over him in one hurried pass. Then he was positioning her, spreading her legs wide, and lifting them around his lean hips. Poised to plunge into her welcoming heat, his eyes locked with hers. "Time to see the stars, love."

And then he took her flying to meet them.

They abandoned the settee on the porch with reluctance, and only when the night air became too cold for them to ignore. Replete, with their rumpled clothes only partially refastened, Alex and Gen wandered arm in arm back to the studio. As they'd idly discussed their options, Gen had said that she didn't want to risk disturbing Mrs. Miller by going up to Alex's room. What she chose not to voice was her other reason for avoiding making love in his bedroom: she didn't want the memory of Sydney coming between them.

"I'll go wherever you want, sweetheart," Alex had murmured agreeably. "It doesn't matter to me. As long as I get to have my arms around you." As if underscoring his words, his arms had tightened about her as he'd pressed a kiss on her still-damp temple. "I'm never going to think of this porch in quite the same way," he'd mused, a smile in his voice.

Neither would she, Gen thought, and after they'd made love again in the studio, she knew, too, that she'd never forget a single one of his hushed endearments or his slow, devastating caresses as he rocked her into sweet ecstasy.

Afterward, they dozed, limbs entwined, and awakened to find their passion newly roused. Shifting, sliding, their parts became one again as together they found what they were seeking.

Exhaustion finally claimed them and they slept. At some point a sound penetrated Gen's slumber: Murphy's nails clicking as he walked over to his water bowl, lapped at it with his tongue, and then returned to his dog bed. She stirred enough to note that Alex and she had changed positions in the night. Alex's warm body was curled around her, spoonlike, his arms holding her even as he slept. His deep, even breathing fanned the back of her neck. She smiled as she recalled the dream she'd been having, a lovely dream in which warm breezes played over her skin. Now she knew where all that heavenly warmth came from. She wriggled backward for a snugger fit, loving the slight tickling sensation of his groin rubbing her bottom, sighing with pleasure when Alex mumbled something in her hair and pulled her even closer.

For several moments she lay awake, luxuriating in the happiness she'd found. So many firsts today, she thought, this one the latest in a string of profound discoveries. She'd never shared a bed before, and yet there was no awkwardness lying here with Alex, only a sense of rightness. Gen shut her eyes. Matching her breathing to his, she slipped back into sleep with a smile on her face.

It felt as if only minutes had passed when the telephone's ring jarred her awake. The studio was still dark. By the second ring panic had seized her. No one would be calling her now unless there was some kind of emergency. *Granny Jane?* Her grandmother's name was the first to spring into her mind. Oh, God, no, please no, she thought, terrified, already scooting toward the edge of the futon and grabbing the phone off the floor.

"Hello?" she whispered, her voice hoarse with sleep and fear.

"Hello, Genevieve, it's me."

"Jiri?" she said in blank astonishment. She sank back down onto the bed, instinctively adjusting her body as Alex's arm slipped around her, pulling her back, his hand cupping her breast.

"Yes. Genevieve, I have big news—"

With equal parts relief and annoyance, Gen interrupted him. "Jiri, it's only"—she paused and lifted Alex's arm to peer at the illuminated dial of his watch, then carefully lowered it so his hand lay over her breast once more—"quarter of five in the morning!"

Jiri made a sound like a verbal shrug. "I have meeting in one half hour and you get up soon anyhow. Listen, Genevieve, like I said, great news. They give me retrospective in Berlin next year."

Behind her, Alex shifted, pressing his groin into her. His hand began lazily massaging her breast.

"Mmm, that's wonderful," she said, a great deal more warmth infusing her voice.

On the other end, Jiri laughed heartily. "Yes. Only you understand how I feel. Berlin, a triumph! But, Genevieve, there's more. I have special surprise for you—I miss you. I miss you so much I plan special trip just to see you and tell you the surprise. I come to New York week after next."

Jiri's words registered only vaguely. The feel of Alex's penis jutting against her buttocks was too distracting to concentrate on a phone conversation. Still, she knew Jiri was pleased. With an effort she managed a cheery, "That's great. Call me when you get to New York, 'bye." She let the phone fall from her fingers.

"That was Jiri?" Alex's teeth grazed the line of her shoulder.

"Yes," she answered faintly, arching sinuously against him as she sighed with pleasure. Her sigh became a gasp as Alex flexed his hips, sliding his erection between her thighs. His hand traveled over her hips, then farther down till his fingers found her. He parted her slick lips, opening her, and she trembled for him.

"What did he want?" his voice breathed in her ear.

"Want?"

"Jiri." His teeth closed about her, nipping her neck lightly, as a stallion would his mare.

She whimpered in need and frustration. Why were they talking about this when he was doing such wonderful things to her body? "He's got a retrospective in Berlin," she gasped. "He wanted to share the news."

His fingers were inside her now, sliding in and out while his thumb rubbed her clitoris, exerting just enough pressure to drive her wild. Her inner muscles clenched about him as shocks of pleasure rocked her.

"That's all?" he murmured.

"All? Yes!" Teetering on the edge of her orgasm, she cried, "Alex, would you *please* stop"—half sobbing when his hand stilled—"no, I mean *talking*!" With a desperate whimper she moved against his hand. "Please, Alex, I need you inside me, loving me."

"Always," he promised huskily, kissing the hollow behind her ear. "Now, lift your leg over mine, sweetheart, and you'll get your wish."

NINETEEN

"**Y**ou're sure Jiri didn't say when he'd be coming to New York?" Alex asked Gen later that morning as they sat at the kitchen table.

Gen glanced up from the shopping list she was writing in time to see Alex tear his slice of toast in two and slip one half to a drooling Murphy. She sighed and gave a rueful shake of her head. Obviously if she wanted to maintain any control over these two males, she'd better lay down some ground rules—but for now she was too content to bother.

Picking up her cup of coffee she sipped the strong brew, her gaze lingering on Alex's face. Lord, the man was gorgeous, she thought. His hair was already dry from the outdoor shower they'd shared, its ends curling at the edge of his collar. Her fingers itched to run through it, feel its silky texture. The shirt he'd chosen was a deep azure blue that turned his eyes an almost exact match. He'd left the top two buttons undone, exposing the tanned column of his neck. She knew exactly how his skin would taste.

"So?" Alex prompted. He was looking at her with

his eyebrows raised in amusement. Obviously he'd been waiting for her to reply to whatever he'd said, and she'd been gazing at him as though struck dumb by love.

Love? Did she love Alex? No, no, she reassured herself hurriedly. It was too soon, too fast, and besides, she wasn't ready for that kind of complication in her life. But Gen readily admitted that she was very, very happy. Happier than she'd ever been in her life. The pleasure she derived from watching him, listening to him, simply *being* with him was bone deep and incomparably wonderful.

"Are you sure you put coffee in that cup, Monaghan?" Alex's voice broke into her thoughts. " 'Cause you seem a little dreamy-eyed." He nodded at the mug she held suspended in midair.

"What?" She looked at the object in question. "Oh, coffee. Right." She took a sip, swallowed, and said, "Now what were you saying?"

He shook his head. "Jiri," he repeated with exaggerated care. "When did he say he was coming?"

"Soon, I guess. Next week. Maybe it was the week after." She shrugged.

"Did he say why he was coming?" Alex asked.

"He's been offered a retrospective, which means he's probably coming to New York to meet with his dealer and the gallery that represents him. They'll have to go over his entire list and make sure they know where all his works are currently. You know, for loans and stuff." She took another sip of the bracing coffee. "Why are you so interested in Jiri?"

"Merely curious." Alex gave a casual shrug. "And he didn't say anything else?"

She put down the coffee cup and regarded him curiously. She couldn't understand this fascination with Jiri's comings and goings.

Could he actually be jealous? No, that would be ridiculous, she thought, discarding the idea immediately. What could Alex possibly be jealous *about,* especially after their lovemaking?

She cocked her head, a smile playing over her mouth. "You know, it's funny," she drawled, "but everything Jiri said at the crack of dawn this morning is a bit fuzzy in my mind. I wonder why." She pretended to think. "Oh, yes, maybe it has something to do with the fact that I was a wee bit distracted during the conversation."

"Only a wee bit?" A knowing and very cocky grin spread over Alex's face. "Gen, you wound me."

"Yeah, well, I'm pretty sore too," she returned lightly.

Alex's grin vanished. In a flash he was around the table and crouching by her side. He took her hands in his. "Damn," he swore softly. "I'm sorry, sweetheart. I should have been more careful with you."

Her heart squeezed tight at the worry in his voice.

Who could blame her if she *were* to fall head over heels in love with him? a little voice inside her asked. His obvious concern was so, well, darned adorable.

"It's not that bad. Just some interesting twinges and aches in rather unexpected places." Leaning forward, she touched her lips to his. "But like you, I have amazing recuperative powers. I'm certain that by tonight I'll be fully recovered."

Gen's ego got a definite boost from the immediate spark that flared in Alex's eyes, a hungry light of anticipation she'd come to recognize. Despite her undeniable soreness, she felt her body tighten in response.

His lips brushed hers in a second tantalizing kiss. "Maybe they'll be exhausted from the trip. . . ."

His family. They were coming today. Gen had almost forgotten. "Maybe your sister and brother-in-law," she said. "But your niece and nephew? They're six years old, right?"

Alex nodded.

"Then don't bet on it. They'll be totally wired."

His groan had her laughing. "What do they like to eat, by the way?"

"Mmm, let me see if I can remember. Oh, yeah. Pizza, pizza, and pizza. But we'd better wait until Cassie and Caleb are gone before we start spoiling Soph and Jamie rotten. Cass takes their nutrition very seriously."

"Soy burgers it is then," Gen pretended to write on her list.

Alex looked vaguely revolted. "I'm sure plain old hamburger will pass muster. I was thinking we could have a cookout after the beach. If the twins race around enough, they'll get tired. And if they're tired, they'll go to bed." He arched his brows.

"You have a truly devious mind. Or is it a one-track mind?"

"Both." He grinned at her with devilish charm.

"What time do you have to leave for the airport?"

"Around noon. Do you want to come along?"

"No, no," she said. "There wouldn't be enough room in the car."

"Chicken," he taunted softly.

"What are you talking about! I am not!"

He gave her a swift hard kiss. Grinning, he sat back on his haunches. "Are too," he replied. "You're a terrible liar, Gen. Everything shows on your face. Come on, 'fess up, you're terrified."

She couldn't help but laugh. "Okay, I admit to feeling a tiny bit nervous about meeting your family."

"Cassie's great, and Caleb's a vet. You'll get along fine. Believe me, meeting them is a cakewalk compared to what I went through at your little family gathering," he said, laying special stress on the word "little."

"What! They were totally accepting of you."

"Sure they were. But that didn't stop your father from letting me know how much he cherished his baby girl. It didn't prevent your sisters and brothers from giving me the third degree, and it sure as hell didn't stop Kyle from demonstrating that if he wanted to, he could decapitate me with a softball."

"Kyle's just supercompetitive when it comes to our family softball games. He wasn't trying—"

"Yeah, he was," Alex contradicted her cheerfully. "I should know. I used the same kind of tactics with Caleb. Come to think of it, I was probably even more heavy-handed."

"Has he forgiven you?"

"Pretty much," he said with a laugh. "After all, I let him marry my kid sister."

"Well, I still think it's better if I stay behind. I'm sure they'd like some time with you alone. And I want to get my canvas stretched and gessoed. Are you working this morning?"

"Yeah. There's a software company that's developing some programs with real potential. I've got to do a little digging and see whether their competitors have anything nearly as hot."

"And if they don't?"

"Then I make some calls double-quick and see whether we want to go into this solo or get a consortium together. So, yeah, that'll tie me up for most of the morning."

Then Alex would leave and be gone until late afternoon, Gen thought, her spirits sinking. She stole a glance at his wristwatch. It was just seven-thirty. She should start preparing Mrs. Miller's breakfast tray and then head to the studio—where she'd be apart from him.

Impulsively she leaned forward and asked, "Do you want to bring your laptop and papers over to the studio? I can clear off some space." Even as she spoke she felt a jolt of surprise at what she was saying. What she prized above all in her new studio was the privacy, the incredible luxury of working uninterrupted, with no one to distract her.

Alex appeared equally surprised by her invitation. Surprised and pleased. His eyes crinkled at the corners as he gave her a crooked little smile that did wonderful things to her insides. "I won't be disturbing your concentration?"

She shook her head. It would be far more distracting to spend the morning inventing a million excuses to go over to the house and wander into his study so she could look at him. "No, I'm pretty good at blocking things out when I work." She let her gaze travel over him. "And I do find you very inspirational . . ." she let her sentence trail off suggestively.

He grinned. "Well, I think it's really important to support the arts in every possible way I can." His voice took on a more serious note. "If I have to make any calls, I promise I'll talk softly."

"Don't worry, Miller, I'll tell you right away if you're bugging me. And I should warn you I may make some distracting noises myself when I stretch the canvas."

"I don't think that's what'll be distracting me." He rose, pulling her up from the chair with a tug of their clasped hands. He drew her close until she was flush against him. They stood melded, bound by a passion whose force neither could resist. Lost in each other, Alex's mouth settled over hers in a possessive kiss that made her pulse race and her heart yearn.

A movement at the edge of Alex's field of vision made him look up from the memo he was writing to his partners about I.Com, the start-up software company he'd mentioned earlier to Gen, in time to see her lean over Murphy, a fat paintbrush in one hand, a rawhide bone in another. Planting a kiss on his shaggy snout, she said softly but firmly, "Bed, Murphy."

The dog understood the bribe at once—but on his own terms. Alex watched him delicately pluck the bone from Gen's outstretched hand. Instead of carrying his prize over to his bed, however, Murphy, tail wagging, came over to where Alex was stationed. He brushed his shaggy body against Alex's shins, turned, came back for a second pass, then stopped when he was directly over his bare feet. Without hesitating, he sank down on them. Blanketed by his solid weight, Alex felt Murphy's ribs expand in a doggy sigh of contentment. Then, without further ado, he got down to the business of chewing his bone while watching his beloved mistress.

Damned smart dog, Alex thought, to figure out how to optimize his pleasure: Murphy now had a human tummy scratcher, a bone to gnaw, and Gen in his sight. For Murphy, life was definitely good.

Alex understood the feeling. He, too, was filled with a sense of contentment. And hell, he didn't even need a rawhide. All he needed was Gen.

The amount of work he'd accomplished this morning was surprising given the number of times his hands had slowed to a halt over the keyboard while his eyes sought her out. As they did now. Their gazes connected, hers filled with dismay.

"I'm sorry," she said, gesturing at Murphy with her paintbrush. "I was trying to keep him out of the gesso. For some weird reason, he always tries to stick his nose in it. Must be the smell or something."

"Don't worry about it. I've nearly finished with what I needed to do this morning. I don't mind wiggling my toes every so often if it keeps him happy. Gesso away," he encouraged.

"Thanks," she said, flashing him a grateful smile before turning back to the large stretched canvas that now hung on the wall. From the canvas's size alone Alex knew without having to ask that this was the piece she was painting for the hospital wing.

The glances he'd stolen of Gen this morning had been fascinating. He soon realized that she hadn't exaggerated one bit back in his office weeks ago when she'd rattled off all the things she could do—not if the ease with which she handled her tools was anything to go by. Solo, it had taken her about an hour to assemble the ten-by-twelve-foot stretcher, attaching the wooden strips with a heavy-gauge staple gun. Next, she'd measured out the canvas, cut it to size, and laid it over the stretcher. Using some type of wide-mouthed pliers, she'd then methodically worked her way around the stretcher, pulling the canvas tight over the wood and then stapling it into place.

When she'd first begun stretching the canvas, Alex had been tempted to offer her a hand. Luckily he'd been wise enough to keep his mouth shut. Gen obviously knew her stuff. And so he'd been able to sit back and enjoy the efficient and assured grace of an artist who clearly loved every aspect of her craft.

He hadn't expected her to suggest he bring his work to the studio. Although she was heaven in bed, his own wicked angel, he hadn't thought she was ready to allow him into the sanctum of her studio, where he might witness her wrestling with the creative process—pretty much the equivalent of being allowed to peek behind the magician's curtain. It moved Alex more than he could say that Gen was willing to share this part of her life, this part of her self with him.

It struck Alex again how different Gen was. She wasn't just different. She was extraordinary. And somehow even "extraordinary" seemed too dull a word to describe Miss Genevieve Monaghan of Somerville, Massachusetts, and his mouth curved in an unconscious smile. The way she'd given herself to him so naturally humbled him. He'd never been with someone so open, so free of artifice—in bed and out of it.

For instance, it hadn't even occurred to Gen to use Jiri against him. The majority of the women he'd dated would have sensed his jealousy right away and used it, dangling Jiri before him in the hopes of spurring his possessiveness. Not Gen. It wasn't because she was stupid or naive or some paragon of virtue. No, it was because she was graced with a forthright honesty and directness. She didn't use people or manipulate them for her own ends. Understanding this now made the possible reappearance of Jiri Novak less threatening; Gen wouldn't respond to him as she did if she were even remotely interested in her former mentor.

Alex wasn't sure how he'd gotten lucky enough to have Gen walk into his life. But he was beginning to realize that if she were ever to walk out of it, he would never be the same.

TWENTY

For once Gen didn't need Murphy's extra-sensitive hearing to alert her to Alex's return. Ever since the clock's hands had slipped past four-thirty, her ears had strained for the sound of a car coming up the driveway; she heard the rumble of the Volvo almost the same instant Murphy did.

As the last thing she wanted was for her dog to petrify two six-year-olds who were probably shorter than he, she'd taken the precaution of snapping Murphy's leash to his collar. Quickly she stepped on the end of it before Murph could bound out the studio.

"No way, buddy," she said. "We're going to try for dignified here."

Murphy gave a bark that to Gen sounded suspiciously like outrage.

"Hey, that doesn't mean we'll actually succeed," she replied. "But like Mom says, first impressions are important. So I'm going to see whether we can say hi without you toppling the whole family like a rack of bowling pins." Abruptly realizing that she would rather spend the next half hour lecturing her dog than walk outside and meet Alex's family, Gen shook her head. Jeez, she was a pathetic mess. Some first impression she'd make if they were to walk in now and find her babbling like a lunatic.

She definitely needed to get a grip—and on more than Murphy's leash. Wrapping the leash around her hand, she scratched the flat top of his large head. "Sorry to cramp your style, Murphy. I'm sure they'll like you fine. Well, here goes."

The sound of laughter and animated voices greeted her as she rounded the corner of the house, with Murphy's tail waving double-time as he picked up on the humans' excitement. All of the Volvo's doors were open. Her gaze immediately searched for Alex but found only his legs, the rest of his body swallowed by the trunk's maw. Suitcases lay in a growing pile by his feet.

Mrs. Miller's hearing was obviously as keen as Gen's, either that or she'd been keeping a sharp lookout for the car. She was already in their midst, exchanging hugs and kisses. Despite Murphy's wishes, Gen hung back, not wanting to interrupt as everyone said hello.

They made a lovely family, she thought, her eyes traveling over the group. She could see now that Cassie Miller was most definitely Alex's sister. Graced with the same arresting blond looks, fine bone structure, and lean athletic build as her older brother, Cassie had a timeless, ageless beauty—and what incredible hair, Gen added with a touch of envy. Falling down to the middle of her back, it looked like a cloud of pale gold. And, Lord, the twins had the same blond halos—cut short into corkscrewed curls that bounced wildly as they dashed around the talking grown-ups.

Gen had only time to ascertain that Cassie's husband, Caleb, was no slouch in the looks department, either—tall and broad-shouldered, his striking dark coloring a perfect foil for Cassie's blond beauty—when Alex's upper body reemerged from the car's interior and dropped two bulging backpacks, fuchsia and fire-engine red, onto the grass. Slamming the trunk door down, his eyes, radarlike, immediately fixed on Gen standing off to the side. Murphy, who'd been exceptionally patient up until that point, woofed joyously at Alex and lunged forward, dragging Gen willy-nilly after him.

"Wow! That's a cool dog!" one of the twins exclaimed as the other cried, "Daddy, Mommy, look at the dog!"

"Yeah," their father replied. "He's a beaut, all right."

Murphy had dragged her into the thick of things, so to speak, stopping only when he was in front of Alex. As her dog pressed his muzzle into Alex's hand, licking it, Gen gave the others a shy, breathless smile. "Hi, I'm Gen and this is Murphy. He, uh, really likes Alex."

"That's too bad," Caleb said and shook his head sadly. "Most wolfhounds I've encountered are pretty smart."

"Very funny, Caleb," Alex drawled. "Gen, this is my brother-in-law, Caleb Wells, who claims to have a degree in veterinary medicine."

Gen shook hands with Caleb, trying not to stare.

The man was really handsome. It was a good thing her vet wasn't this good-looking. She had a hard enough time getting appointments as it was.

"It's a pleasure meeting you, Gen. And he really is beautiful," he said, nodding at Murphy. "How old is he?"

"Two."

Caleb squatted on his haunches, bringing his tall frame down to Murphy's level. Murphy transferred his attention from Alex to Caleb. Caleb let him sniff his scent before giving the sides of Murphy's head a vigorous rub. The dog thanked him with a big lick across the face, making the entire family laugh. Caleb stood. "Definitely a smart dog," he pronounced.

Alex spoke. "And this is my sister, Cassie. Cass, this is Gen. And these two munchkins are Sophie and Jamie."

"Hi, I'm really pleased to meet you," Gen said, trying not to be disconcerted to find herself looking into three pairs of eyes so very similar to Alex's.

"You're the lady who paints and has baseball parties," Sophie said.

Gen laughed. "Yeah, I guess I am."

"Alex says you're a very gifted artist," Cassie said. "I'd love to see some of your work."

"Sure. Any time."

"I like to draw too," Sophie informed her.

"I know. I've seen your and Jamie's drawings of your dogs." Gen paused, searching her memory. "Radar and Annabelle, right?"

"Radar's mine, Annabelle is Sophie's," Jamie said.

"Well, your drawings are terrific. I could tell right

away that you love Annabelle and Radar. And how about baseball? Do you like that, too?"

"Yeah." Both children nodded enthusiastically. "We play a lot at home," Sophie told her.

Then Jamie asked, "Can we pet your dog?"

Gen instinctively looked at Cassie, who smiled and nodded slightly. "Sure," Gen said. "You know how to let a dog sniff you. . . ."

"Our dad's a veterinarian," Jamie informed her with pride.

"We help him tons," Sophie added.

Caleb ruffled their curly heads. "Yeah, they're my best assistants, and I only have to pay them in chocolate kisses. Kids, remember to be gentle with Murphy. And be prepared to get a big fat sloppy kiss."

For a few minutes, everyone's attention was fixed on the twins as they made Murphy's acquaintance. Gen relaxed as it became clear that the children knew how to behave around animals. In seventh heaven at finding himself the center of attention, Murphy's dark eyes shone as bright as the kids'. She smiled as she watched them stroking his shaggy fur.

"You've said hi to everyone but me," Alex said, his voice pitched low, for her ears alone.

Heart fluttering, Gen lifted her head and met Alex's eyes. "Hi," she uttered softly.

Alex's mouth quirked. "That's better," he said, reaching up to cup the side of her face. Holding her gaze, he slid his thumb over her bottom lip, tracing its lush outline. Gen's breath quickened. "Did you miss me?" he asked.

"Perhaps a wee bit," she managed.

"Ahh, Gen, surely it was more than a wee bit?" he murmured in mock dismay.

She bit back a smile. "I was very busy."

"So was I. Thinking about you. And thinking about tonight." Dipping his head, Alex touched his mouth to hers in a whisper of a kiss. When he drew back, his eyes burned with twin blue flames.

The man was utterly devastating, Gen thought shakily. He knew how to seduce her so effortlessly, with just a word, a touch, a kiss, expertly and artfully delivered. If she had any common sense, she'd be terrified by how powerless she was to resist him.

It was Jamie who broke the spell that Alex had woven. "Uncle Alex, look!" he cried excitedly. "Murphy knows how to shake his paw."

"Murphy's multitalented," Alex replied easily. "Let's get these bags inside so you can dig out your swimsuits. Maybe if we ask Gen nicely, she'll let us take him down to the beach with us."

"I'm sure there's nothing Murphy would like better." She smiled.

Her answer was greeted with shrieks of excitement from Jamie and Sophie and served to mobilize the group. As Alex and Caleb turned to deal with the luggage, Gen leaned over and patted Murphy on the head. "Thanks, pal, you did great. Just remember to be on your best behavior," she whispered. Straightening, she encountered Cassie's bright blue gaze. The smile that tipped the corners of her mouth told Gen that despite her whisper, Cassie had heard every word she said. For a second she and Cassie locked gazes, each taking the other's measure. Then as if reaching some private decision, Cassie's smile grew warm.

"Sorry to eavesdrop. It's fascinating listening to people talk to their pets. You should hear me with Orion, one of our stallions, before we enter a jumping class. I have a whole list of do's and don'ts for him. But I always have the feeling that his list for me would be twice as long, starting with, 'Just sit back and let me handle this,' and ending with, 'You got to work on this carrot thing. The supply's been real stingy lately,'" she finished wryly.

Gen grinned. "Yeah, it would be great to hear what they have to say. On the other hand, Murphy's pretty adept at getting his message across."

"According to Caleb, that means he has you well trained. Speaking of which—" Cassie's attention abruptly shifted. Reaching out, she tagged Sophie and Jamie, who were scampering about. "Not so fast, you two," she said. "I see two backpacks lying on the ground with your names on them. Time you showed Aunt Grace how strong you've gotten this year."

While Cassie expertly herded the twins toward their bags, Gen, feeling as if she'd just passed a major test, let out a breath that until then she hadn't been aware she was holding.

Thinking that Mrs. Miller and Alex would enjoy some time alone with Cassie and her family, Gen declined their invitation to join them on the beach outing, saying that she wanted to get a second coat of gesso onto the canvas and give it a chance to dry overnight.

The radio was tuned to an East Hampton station she'd found that played progressive rock. So while the Counting Crows sang about Picasso and Bob Dylan, Gen's brush danced in sync to the music's driving beat, covering the canvas's surface section by section with crosshatched strokes. When at last her laden brush had traveled over the entire canvas, leaving a uniform layer of the gesso in its wake, Gen let the brush fall into the half-empty tub and stretched.

A good day's work, she decided. And with the humidity as low as it was, there was a strong likelihood that by tomorrow morning the gesso would be completely dry. Then she could start roughing in the underdrawing for the painting, a process far more challenging than the merely mechanical application of gesso.

Gathering up the brush and gesso, Gen went to the sink and washed up, leaving her brush to dry on an old ragged towel. Next she put away her tools, and then set about tidying the rest of the studio.

She stepped outside and stood for a moment, drinking in the beauty of the late afternoon. The shadows had lengthened and deepened into wide swatches of lavender that lay against the emerald-green grass. The sky, tinged an orange-pink, was streaked with whisper-thin cirrus clouds. From off in the distance came the muted crash of the sea, and then closer, the sound of children's high-speed chatter mixed with the slower rhythm of adult voices.

She turned toward the source. And there strode Alex, carrying Sophie perched on his shoulders. Next to him was Jamie, who had the honor of holding

Murphy's leash. The others followed but Gen only had eyes for Alex.

In that moment she saw Alex differently . . . for the first time completely. She saw the joy in his face as, laughing, he answered Sophie, saw the care with which he watched Jamie lead her enormous dog. She saw the boundless love he had for these two children.

She looked and her heart nearly burst with everything she felt for him.

From across the lawn Alex spotted Gen standing in the doorway of her studio. She looked so incredibly right, standing there in her jeans and T-shirt, the weathered wood of the studio behind her. It made him want a lifetime of images of her smiling that special smile. His heart thudding strangely, he halted in his tracks and looked down at his nephew. "You'll need to let go of the leash now, Jamie."

"Can I race him?" Jamie asked.

"Yeah, but he'll be tough to beat. He really loves Gen."

"I want to run, too," Sophie said from somewhere above his head.

"Okay," he agreed and helped Sophie off his shoulders, setting her down next to her brother.

Jamie's fingers opened. For a second Murphy stood placidly, seemingly content to nuzzle Sophie, who'd dropped back down to earth. Then Gen, who'd guessed what Alex was about, stuck two fingers into her mouth and gave a sharp, piercing whistle.

Like a gray bullet, Murphy shot off with the twins tearing after him as fast as their small legs could carry them. The dog, of course, beat them by several body lengths. But then Jamie and Sophie were crowding around her, breathless from their race but still able to talk a blue streak. Gen was laughing and nodding as wet, wriggling dog and sandy kids vied for her attention.

Cassie, Caleb, and Aunt Grace stood next to Alex observing the scene. "I think I like this Gen Monaghan," Cassie said, rising up on her tiptoes to kiss his cheek.

Alex slipped an arm about her waist and squeezed it.

"Yes, Gen's a lovely girl," Aunt Grace chimed in.

Caleb nodded. "I agree with both Aunt Grace and Cass," he said. "So that leaves only one question, Alex."

Alex cocked his head. "Yeah? What's that?"

Caleb grinned and a devilish light sparked in his dark eyes. "How'd you get such a terrific girl to look twice at you?"

While Alex and the others showered and changed back into their clothes, Gen fed Murphy and then set about preparing their own dinner. She'd opted for a casual, kid-friendly menu: hamburgers, a potato salad as well as a green salad, brownies and ice cream.

The meal ended up being noisy, chaotic, and absolutely wonderful, the seven of them crammed around the porch's round table, rubbing elbows, talking, and devouring food. Agreement was unanimous that these were the best burgers ever, Gen's salads receiving an equally enthusiastic reception. When they moved on to dessert and coffee, the pace slowed, as if all of a sudden everyone became aware of how much they'd already consumed. Caleb and Cassie agreed to share a brownie, Caleb feeding her a bite at a time. Gen, who'd learned that they'd been married for almost ten months, found her eyes drawn to them, noting how their expressions softened whenever their eyes met. The love between them was palpable.

She felt Alex, who was seated next to her, stir. His body shifted, brushing her side, making her heart leap and her breath quicken—the same uncontrollable reactions she'd had each time he'd casually touched her during dinner. The man was fiendish—he knew exactly what he was doing, expertly orchestrating the tension between them, letting it build and build. Determined to show that she was no pushover, she retaliated, nudging him hard on the side of his calf with her foot.

He didn't even flinch, merely lifted up his arm and draped it along the back of her chair so his hand fell on her shoulder. As if unconsciously, he began caressing it in slow, lazy circles. She felt everything inside her go warm and fluid.

Across the table, Gen caught Caleb's knowing glance. With that teasing grin she was coming to recognize, he leaned back in his chair and looped an arm about Cassie and said to Gen, "That was a delicious meal, Gen. Thank you." Nodding to Alex he continued, "You're going to have a hard time beating a dinner as good as this one—no matter how fancy the restaurant is that's throwing your shindig tomorrow night."

Alex inclined his head. "True, but then think how many burgers you and I would have to flip."

Cassie looked across the table at her brother. "How many are coming?" she asked.

"Counting us, forty."

"Whew, that's a lot of CEOs under one roof," Caleb remarked.

Alex smiled. "They won't all be CEOs, or even CFOs. I mixed in some presidents and vice presidents too."

"Like Sam Brody," Mrs. Miller said with a girlish smile. "He's president of Securetech."

"Actually, Sam is Securetech's president and CEO. He'll be there. He's looking forward to seeing you all."

"Sam's great, Gen," Cassie said. "A very cool guy. He bought a filly of ours last year. He owns this security company." She looked across the table at Alex. "And before that wasn't he a bodyguard and a police detective?"

"Yes," said Alex, coughing into his fist. "I, uh, also made sure to invite Ty and Steve Sheppard."

"Yeah, Ty e-mailed me about it." Cassie nodded. "They're horse people," she explained to Gen. "Steve and Ty own a farm in Bridgehampton. They've bought a couple of our horses. And Steve trains Cassis, the filly Sam Brody bought. We're getting a ride up to Pound Ridge with them for a weeklong horse show. Caleb's partner, Hank, is meeting us there with the van."

"I never realized the horse world was such a tight-knit community," Gen said.

"Especially on the show circuit. Anyone else, Alex?" she asked.

He thought for a second. "Sam's bringing Lizzie Osborne as his date."

"Wait." Caleb grinned. "I think I remember her from the Garden. Is she the knockout? I only saw her from a distance, but man—*oof!*" he exclaimed as Cassie elbowed him sharply in the ribs.

"Yes, that most definitely describes Ms. Osborne," Alex said, the same male appreciation filling his voice. "From what I gather, though, Sam's holding his own in the ring."

"I didn't really get a chance to speak to her, but she's got to have a lot more going for her than great looks if Sam's bringing her. Unlike some men I know, he's not shallow," Cassie said pointedly.

Neither Caleb nor Alex appeared particularly contrite.

"Doesn't she own a stable in Bedford?"

"Yeah," Alex replied.

"I wonder whether she's in the market for a horse," Cassie mused.

With a chuckle, Caleb kissed her cheek. "My partner, Hank, hired Cassie because she's one of the best riders in the country. We had no idea that she can trade and deal with the best of 'em, too."

"Alex didn't get *all* the financial smarts." She smiled. "Well, this party will be fun. And with you there, Gen, we should strike a nice balance with the Wall Street types."

Gen mustered an answering smile of enthusiasm. She knew as little about horses as she did about corporate America. "Yes, I'm sure it will be loads of fun."

"Just make sure you check the seating arrangement," Mrs. Miller advised. "Sydney Raines might have inadvertently stuck you next to the only bore at the party."

"I'll make sure Sydney moves Gen to my table," Alex said.

Alex's words hardly registered. Gen had ceased following the conversation the second Mrs. Miller mentioned Sydney's name.

Oh, God, she thought in dismay, the food inside her stomach turning into a cold, leaden lump of dread. Of course Sydney would be there tomorrow night. Organizing the party for Alex and making sure it went off without a hitch was her job. Gen cringed at the thought of how awkward this was going to be, coming face-to-face with Alex's ex-girlfriend at the party. Party? This wasn't going to be a party, she decided, not when it had all the makings of a nightmare.

TWENTY-ONE

Gen's solution to handling the anxiety of the upcoming party was to block it from her mind. It was only a party, she reasoned, nothing more. With all those people about, she might not even have to speak to Sydney. And who was to say that Sydney wouldn't be just as eager to avoid her?

Despite her private pep talk and the effort Gen made to act her usual self, smiling and exchanging lighthearted jokes as the four of them, Cassie, Caleb, Alex, and she, washed the dishes and set the kitchen to rights, Alex must have sensed her underlying tension, the weight of his penetrating gaze landing on her frequently.

As soon as everything was put away in the kitchen, Caleb gave a yawn louder than the rumble of the dishwasher and announced that he was more than ready for an early night. From the gleam in his eye when he looked at Cassie, it wasn't terribly surprising when she blushed then murmured something about needing her beauty sleep for the party. While Alex ran upstairs to give Sophie and Jamie, who were reading a story with Mrs. Miller, a good-night kiss, Gen waited idly in the kitchen, absently straightening dishcloths that already hung neatly over the oven door rack.

When he reentered the kitchen, she was grateful for the energetic swishing of the dishwasher. It muffled the sound of her heart beating. Silently, he held out his hand and together they walked out of the house into a night whose sky glittered with a million diamond-bright stars. The majesty of the sky filled her with awe and a strange melancholy. An involuntary sigh escaped her lips.

"It's beautiful, isn't it?" Alex said and his hand tightened fractionally about hers. "You don't get stars like this in Manhattan."

"Not in Somerville, either," Gen replied wistfully. With a last glance at the celestial splendor, she pushed open the studio door and stepped inside, Alex following her.

She'd left a lamp on in the studio and its solitary light cast a honeyed glow over the space she'd come to love so much. Murphy, exhausted from his beach romp with the twins, was sprawled on his bed. He opened his eyes long enough to blink at them and thump his tail heavily before dropping his head back down with a sleepy snuffle.

Alex came up beside her and cupped his hand under her chin, slowly lifting it until her eyes met his. "Hey," he said quietly, "there's something the matter, isn't there? What's got you down, Gen? Is it the party?"

"Yeah, I guess." She tried for an unconcerned shrug. "Big social events aren't really my thing," she said. She fell silent, determined not to bring up Sydney. Not when they were here in the studio, near the bed where they'd made love, where they would soon be making love again.

"I understand how it might be nerve-racking, but a good number of the people at this party aren't just business associates. They've become my friends." He paused and his thumb arced over her lower lip in a slow, sensual caress. "I want to introduce them to you, Gen," he continued softly. "I think you might like some of them. And I admit that there's another reason I'd like you to come. It's a really primitive, Neanderthal impulse. I want to show you off, Gen, because you're witty, gifted, incredibly beautiful—and you're mine. Please come with me, Gen," he urged huskily.

How was he able to do this to her? What power did he possess that his words could move her so? Things were moving so dizzyingly fast in their relationship. Gen wasn't sure that she was at all ready for this next step, which would take her into Alex's super-rich, super-fancy life, but once more she was undone by his words: *And you're mine.*

The enormity of those three words simultaneously thrilled and terrified her. Emotions clogged her throat, making speech impossible. Desperate to show him how she felt, she swayed closer, her lips seeking his.

Their mouths mated, fused in passion. Alex's clever hands undressed her, peeling layers of clothes off her trembling body, feverishly dispensing with his own, letting the lot fall to the concrete floor in a ragged line as they made their way toward the futon. As one, they tumbled onto it and rolled, clasping each other as their tongues dueled and their hearts slammed. Landing on top, Alex sat up and opened his strong thighs, straddling her.

In the soft glow of the lamp, Alex drank in the sight of Gen's heaving breasts, her nipples tight points of arousal, her parted lips, moist and trembling, as she struggled for breath, and her eyes, those enormous blue-green pools, which minutes ago had been shadowed with worry, now glowing with desire. . . . With desire and something more brilliant, something utterly captivating. Alex's heart thudded loudly in his chest.

Beneath him, Gen moved restlessly, sensuously. "Come inside me, Alex."

Ignoring the need that roared through him at her whispered entreaty, he spread his fingers over the flat of her belly so that they spanned her slender waist. "I will, sweetheart. But tonight is for you. I want to take you places you've never been."

Slowly his hands began to glide over her silken skin. With a soft moan, she shivered, arching against his touch. Her eyes, weighted with passion, drifted shut.

Wanting to see that special light shining in her eyes, Alex commanded softly, "Look at me, Gen. I want to be in your eyes as I'm loving you."

Gen lifted the arm Alex had curled about her waist with care as she slid out from under its weight and eased off the bed. Rising to her feet, she turned to check that she hadn't disturbed him and then lingered, ever hungry for the sight of him, committing yet another image to her memory, to her heart. She took in the clean lines of his profile, the gentle curl of his thick lashes, the firm shape of his lips, somewhat softened by sleep. The lines on his tanned skin were relaxed, with only the faintest hint of the one that ran like a bracket near his mouth and the fan at the corner of his eye. His cheeks were shadowed now with dark blond stubble. Quickly she stepped away from the edge of the bed before she gave into temptation and stroked the beard-roughened plane.

As soon as she glanced in his direction, Murphy rose from his bed, tail wagging. Instinctively she put a finger to her lips before motioning him to follow her. By some miracle, Murphy obeyed her instead of going over and washing Alex's face for him. Silently she crossed the studio to the small bathroom closet where she kept her clothes. She pulled on some underwear and then slipped on a simple sundress, its pale rose color an almost exact match for the sky outside the studio's windows. Brushing her hair, she found it took more strokes than usual to untangle the knots—and caught herself blushing in the mirror as she thought of how and why her hair had come to be so very snarled.

Oh, Lord, the things Alex had done with her and to her. While Gen might not have a vast experience with sex, she knew with every fiber of her being that what she and Alex had shared last night went light-years beyond physical satisfaction. With every touch and lingering caress, with every kiss and glide of tongue and teeth, with every whisper and breathless gasp and moan, they'd worshiped each other body and soul. She'd never imagined that she could scale such heights while she lay wrapped in the arms of a man.

But that was it, wasn't it—the crux of the matter?

Alex wasn't any man.

He was the man she'd fallen hopelessly in love with.

It was a love that had been growing inside her. She wasn't even sure when it had started. Perhaps she lost her heart at the Children's Hospital, when she walked into the wing he'd built in memory of his brother and sister-in-law. But last night, as again and again she'd come apart in his arms, it was the feeling of Alex deep inside her, pouring his essence into her as he called out her name, which made her heart soar. And she had known that she belonged to him irrevocably, heart, body, and soul.

This love she had for Alex was so new and so infinitely precious, it frightened her. Staring at her reflection in the mirror she forced herself to admit the less than flattering truth: she was scared to say "I love you." Afraid that if she voiced her feelings, Alex might think that she was asking for a commitment he wasn't yet ready to make. Speaking the words might jeopardize the happiness she'd found.

She was being cowardly, she knew. But she also knew this impulse to protect her feelings was born from a real fear: her love might not be enough to surmount the vast differences in their lives; it might not be enough to keep Alex by her side.

She needed time to gain the confidence necessary to

vanquish her fears. Until then, she'd keep her love for Alex safe in her heart. Until the day came when she could say all that was locked inside her, she would spend her time showing him.

The presence of Cassie, Caleb, and the twins, whom Gen had come to regard as two blond-headed fire-crackers, full of mischief and spunk, made it impossible for her to worry over her tangled emotions about Alex or even her trepidation about the party later in the evening. She didn't even have a chance to fret whether anything in her wardrobe might be fancy enough let alone glamorous enough for the occasion. No sooner had she returned from a long morning beach walk with Murphy and was climbing the wooden steps up to the stretch of lawn when Sophie's distinctive, high-pitched voice cried, "There she is, Uncle Alex, there she is!"

Murphy instantly went into high gear, scrambling up the remaining steps. Gen heard a "Murphy, Murphy, hiya, boy!" followed by a loud *"Oof!"* and peals of laughter.

Gen raced to the top of the steps.

There were the twins rolling on the grass, laughing as if at some giant tickle-fest while Murphy licked their faces. "Uncle Alex, Mommy, Daddy, he's kissing us!"

"More likely he's washing your face, Jamie," Cassie replied calmly, her arms crossed, one hand wrapped around a steaming cup of coffee. "I noticed you did a pretty poor job of getting the maple syrup wiped off your cheeks. This is a mighty yummy breakfast for Murphy."

"Here, I can get him off," Gen offered hastily.

"Don't bother," Caleb said. "Murphy won't hurt them—these two are indestructible." He grinned as Murphy began licking Jamie's fingers, while Sophie, watching, succumbed to another bout of giggles. "Besides, this is probably the best bath they've had in a while."

Alex walked over to her. "Good morning," he said before kissing her, his lips moving over hers with just enough pressure to remind her of everything they'd done last night. He'd showered and shaved, and she inhaled the fresh scent of soap mingled with the citrus overtones of his cologne, which her senses now exclusively associated with Alex. Pleasure zinged through her, her toes curling in the damp grass.

He released her to stare deeply into her eyes. "I missed you this morning."

Did he know how much that simple sentence affected her? Striving for a light tone, she said, "I took Murphy out to run. With Sophie and Jamie here, a mellow, fatigued Murphy is definitely a good thing. I didn't want to wake you. I figured you could use the sleep. As you got so little last night."

His soft laughter fanned her cheeks. "You won't hear me complaining. Although maybe later this afternoon you and I could sneak off for a little restorative nap."

"That sounds tempting—and highly improbable," she added with a pointed glance at Jamie and Sophie, who'd finally gotten to their feet and were practicing the "shake" command with Murphy. "Besides, some of us around here actually work for a living," she added loftily.

"On a beautiful day like this?" he said in mock outrage. "That would be criminal. We were just talking about heading down to the beach after the grownups have ingested enough caffeine to survive until lunch. We're going to bring some balls and Frisbees and buckets with us."

"And don't forget shovels, too," Jamie chimed in, startling them both. "We're gonna make a humongous sand castle. Right, Uncle Alex?"

With an "I told you so" arch of her brows, Gen murmured pointedly about "little pitchers having really big ears."

Alex's lips twitched. "Right." He nodded at Jamie. "A humongous sand castle. So, are you as good at sand castles as you are everything else, Monaghan?"

After checking on her canvas Gen decided that maybe the second coat of gesso should dry a little longer. No sense ruining the painting by rushing things. Nevertheless, she packed her drawing pad, pencils, and pastels into her backpack, telling herself that at the very least she could make some sketches of the children at play.

Mrs. Miller declined their invitation to join them. She was going to take her morning walk on the beach and then drive into Bridgehampton for a hair appointment.

"Important to look your loveliest for Sam tonight," Alex teased.

Mrs. Miller blushed and called Alex an impertinent rascal—but Gen noted that she didn't exactly deny the charge. In spite of her trepidation, Gen realized that she was definitely intrigued by the prospect of meeting some of Alex's friends, this Sam Brody topping her list.

Organizing the six of them took some time—changing into swimsuits, gathering up beach towels, finding the twins' sunblock, getting a six-pack of water from the kitchen pantry, then locating a large tote bag that could hold all the paraphernalia—but at last, armed with buckets, shovels, and balls of various sizes, they trooped down to the ocean, Murphy dogging Alex's every step.

They chose a spot a discreet distance from the other families and couples and spread out their stuff in a large semicircle. Everyone peeled off their shorts and T-shirts except for Gen, who instead dropped down on her towel and began rummaging through her backpack, pulling out her drawing pad, box of pastels, and pencils.

"Hey, you're not planning to take this shirt off?" Alex said, squatting in front of her.

"Nope." She opened up her tin box and selected an HB pencil. "If I stay out in the sun too long my freckles multiply exponentially." Looking up, her insides melted at the sight of his leanly muscled chest. She willed her eyes not to travel south, fearing she'd start drooling if she hazarded a glance at the taut ridges of his abdomen, or the way his dark blue swim trunks were stretched tight around his splayed thighs.

Alex reached out and lightly fingered her shirt, one

of her brother Benjamin's discards, a threadbare white button-down that hung to midthigh, completely covering the tank suit she'd changed into. "Nothing wrong with a few more freckles. The more the merrier. I'm always ready to do a recount," he offered, his mouth curving into a slow smile.

Gen's body temperature soared as she remembered how she'd trembled and gasped while Alex counted and kissed his way into the hundreds. As casually as possible she reached for her bottled water and took a long, cooling sip. "Yeah, well, I also fry in the sun and I'd like to avoid looking like a speckled lobster tonight." With a nod toward Cassie and Caleb and the twins, who were down at the water's edge, racing in and out of the frothy surf, she said, "Go on with Murphy and join the others. I want to do some sketching."

Alex eyed Murphy and shook his head. "Looks like you're the consolation prize, Murph. Come on, boy."

He'd hardly turned his back before her fingers were reaching for her pad. Her eyes trained on Alex and his family, her pencil began to move swiftly over the paper.

It wasn't until a drop of perspiration slid down her face and landed on her sketch that Gen realized she was broiling. Time for a dip in the ocean, she decided. Then she'd get back to her drawing. She stood and yanked the shirt over her head and walked across the hot sand toward where the others were playing in the waves.

Alex was just emerging from the water, laughing and shaking his head. "No, I'm getting out for a while. That water's colder than—" Abruptly his gaze fixed on Gen and the rest of his sentence died away. His eyes burned hotter than the midday sun. Suddenly the scoop-necked black tank suit she was wearing seemed as risqué as a teeny-weeny string bikini.

Doubtless curious as to why Alex was standing transfixed, with the waves swirling about the backs of his thighs, the others turned. Raising her arm in a friendly greeting, Cassie called, "Hey, Gen, come and join us. Alex, being a city-boy wimp—"

Cassie's sisterly ribbing got no further, for Alex pivoted and dove straight into the next incoming wave. Surfacing, he sliced through the water in a fast, fluid freestyle.

"What's Uncle Alex doing, Daddy?" Sophie demanded, watching her uncle swimming off in the general direction of Portugal. "He said he was *freezing*!"

With a laugh, Caleb said, "Well, if I had to guess, pumpkin, I'd say something got him hot again awful quick."

Inspiration struck while Gen, Alex, and the twins were at work on their humongous sand castle. It came, like a bolt of lightning, right out of the blue, hit her with a searing flash of recognition. . . . Or maybe what struck her was seeing the shaft of sunlight falling on the three golden heads. And suddenly there it was, the picture she'd been searching for, the one she wanted to create for the hospital wing.

Set against the backdrop of this perfect summer day was Alex, crouching patiently beside Jamie and Sophie, his beautiful, strong hands busy digging, scooping, and patting, helping them build their dream castle. She rocked back on her heels, staring wide-eyed. Wasn't this—helping others to build and rebuild— exactly what Alex had done by donating the rehabilitation wing to the Children's Hospital? Wasn't he making it so that countless other kids could achieve their dreams?

Excitement gripped her. Her eyes fixed on the scene, feverishly memorizing details and making adjustments to the composition, she reached for her pad and pencils, lying on the towel by her knees. As unobtrusively as she could—desperate not to alert Alex or the twins—she balanced the pad on her lap and began to draw.

TWENTY-TWO

Gen chose another dress designed by her sister Delia to wear to the party. Actually there hadn't been any real contestants once Gen stood facing the contents of the small closet that held her decidedly unambitious wardrobe. The dress, a dark bronze, spaghetti-strapped affair, was deceptively plain-looking on the hanger. But oh, the magic of Lycra.

When Gen had first tried it on in her sister's Boylston Street store, she'd taken one look in the mirror, gasped, and said, "Uh, Dee, I don't think this is really me."

"That's because you have the fashion sense of a peahen. At some point in your development you decided that clothes are to put paint on. This, however," Delia had said with a thrust of her chin toward the figure-hugging dress, "is *not* a drop cloth. It's flirty, chic, and looks terrific on you. Take it with the other things and maybe someday you'll realize that you're living in New York City, where women pride themselves on dressing beautifully."

Which, of course, Gen never did. The little bronze

dress had sat untouched in her closet for the past year. But there really wasn't any alternative—even the dress she'd worn to her opening seemed too low-key for a party in the Hamptons. And there was no time to go out and buy anything. It was already six o'clock and Alex had said he wanted to leave at six-thirty. She really could *not* keep him waiting. With a nervous sigh Gen slipped the dress off the hanger.

Though Gen rarely went to the trouble of using it, at least makeup was something she could handle. After all, it was a lot like painting—building up hues, highlighting certain areas, working one color off another. She didn't bother applying foundation—she'd need an inch of it to hide her freckles anyway—instead concentrating on her eyes and adding a light blush to her cheekbones. Deciding that too strong a color on her lips would clash with the dress's metallic hue, she opted for a lipstick that had a hint of shimmer in it.

She looked okay, she decided, after smoothing the lipstick on. But the hair, it was all wrong hanging down like this. It had to go up so that the line of her neck and bare shoulders and arms would be emphasized. . . . What was that expression? Oh, yeah. In for a penny, in for a pound. If she was going to wear this thing, she might as well try and pull it off Delia Monaghan style rather than Gen Peahen Monaghan style.

She grabbed the only pair of high-heeled sandals she owned and pulled them on. Black, they weren't a perfect match colorwise, but at least Delia would be proud of her in one respect: they didn't have a single splattering of paint on them.

Leaving Murphy with one of his few remaining bones, she told herself she'd have to make a trip into Bridgehampton, to the pet supply store where she and Murphy had become loyal and frequent customers. Maybe Alex and the twins could come along. Sophie and Jamie would love all the dog toys they sold. She waited until she was sure Murphy was contentedly chewing away, took a deep breath, and wished herself luck.

Alex's heart was still racing when he pulled the Aston into an empty parking spot at La Plage, the restaurant he'd rented for the evening. He'd hardly been able to speak, let alone regulate his breathing with Gen sitting beside him, a vision of shimmery bronze and long, gold-dusted limbs. He'd kept his eyes fixed on the road leading to East Hampton's Three Mile Harbor, for fear that if he let himself look at those bare limbs for even a second, he'd drive off the road and into the middle of a cornfield. Caleb, chauffeuring Cassie and Aunt Grace in the Volvo behind them, would doubtless laugh his head off.

He turned the key, killing the ignition. "In case I'm too far gone when I finally get you alone later tonight, I just want to tell you that you're the most beautiful woman I've ever laid eyes on and that I want you so much I hurt."

Beside him Gen gave a startled laugh. "Thank you. That helps a lot. I was growing nervous with you glaring at the road in silence."

"Only way to get here in one piece," he admitted with a self-deprecating grin. "Believe me, if Aunt

Grace, Cassie, and Caleb weren't pulling in just now, I'd be seriously figuring out the logistics of sex in an Aston."

The sound of three car doors slamming reached them.

"Unfortunately this seems to be neither the time nor the place." "Which is too bad," she said, her bare shoulders rising and falling in a dramatic sigh. "I've always harbored this secret Bond-girl fantasy."

Taking her hand, he dragged his lips over her knuckles. "Would you consider a rain check, perhaps?"

"Definitely."

His entire body hardened at Gen's delightfully mischievous smile. With a shaky laugh he said, "Damn, this is going to be a long evening."

They joined Alex's family near the front of the restaurant, a white wooden building with large square windows trimmed in dark green. La Plage sat on the edge of the bay not far from the harbor. As they'd arrived with time to spare, the five of them decided to walk over to the railing to enjoy the view. Sailboats and powerboats bobbed gently at their moorings while a few gulls circled above. The evening breeze drifted off the water, carrying the slight tang of salt, diesel, and algae.

Although Gen's self-confidence had received the equivalent of a shot of B12 from Alex's obvious masculine approval, she was just as happy to be entering the La Plage as a group, among friends. The thought made Gen pause and smile. She'd truly come to regard Mrs. Miller as more than a heaven-sent benefactress and mutual lover of the arts—she was a friend.

And in spite of the fact that she'd known them for little more than twenty-four hours, she felt the same warmth and affection toward Cassie and Caleb. They were wonderful people: open, kind, and fun.

Mrs. Miller looked fabulously bohemian in a reddish-amber Indian silk tunic over white cigarette pants. Her pale silver hair had been curled and brushed back, so the fine bone structure of her face and the keen brilliance of her eyes were emphasized.

Checking his watch, Alex turned to his aunt and offered to escort her into the restaurant. "Champagne awaits, Aunt Grace."

Her nephew's thoughtfulness had Mrs. Miller smiling wistfully. "That sounds divine," she said, slipping her arm into his. "You can have him back soon, Genevieve."

"That's okay, Mrs. Miller. You keep him for as long as you want," she replied and had to stifle a giggle when Alex shot her a dark look. Turning to Cassie and Caleb, she asked, "Mind if I join the rear guard?"

Wearing a black cocktail dress, Cassie looked slim and sophisticated. With her riotous cascade of hair tumbling down her back, she also looked very sexy. Smiling she said, "Consider yourself our newest recruit."

"Stick with us and we'll lead you straight to the champagne." With a roguish grin Caleb extended his other arm to Gen and gave a happy sigh as she accepted it. "This evening is starting out fine, a gorgeous woman on each arm."

"I'd say we're pretty lucky too," Gen replied lightly. Like Alex, Caleb was dressed in a dark suit. Like Alex, he looked devastatingly handsome. A dark prince to Alex's golden god. But although Gen recognized Caleb Wells's devastating good looks, he somehow lacked the special aura Alex possessed. The special something that made her pulse flutter like the wings of a hummingbird whenever she looked at him. But that didn't stop Caleb from being utterly and devilishly charming. "You clean up pretty nice, Dr. Wells," she said in what had to be the understatement of the century.

"Oh, so you like the suit, too, huh?" He shook his head. "The mysteries of the female mind. I only agreed to wear it 'cause I figured it was the easiest way to get up close and personal with the caviar. You did say beluga, didn't you, Miller?" he asked, addressing the back of Alex's head. "Buckets of it?"

Ahead of her, Alex shook his head. "Yes, Caleb," he replied with exaggerated patience. "There'll be a raw bar, too. But if I were you I'd pace myself. One of the main courses is lobster."

"You know, Cassie, I believe I'm growing fonder of your brother every day."

Gen was in the midst of a lighthearted repartee with Cassie and Caleb when she heard a familiar voice greet Alex.

"Hello, Alex. Good evening, Mrs. Miller. It's so nice to see you again," Sydney Raines said.

Of course, the first person they'd see tonight would be Sydney, Gen thought. Suddenly she wished she were standing closer to Alex so that she could observe his expression as he talked to his ex-girlfriend.

Or maybe not. She really wasn't ready for this. Her steps faltered.

Then Caleb was giving her arm a reassuring squeeze, silently offering his support. He and Cassie were obviously aware of how potentially awkward this situation could be. And Gen realized that she'd walk over burning coals before doing anything to cause embarrassment to Alex and his family. Fixing her smile in place, Gen stepped forward.

Standing by the reception desk, Sydney looked sensational. On any other woman the revealing ecru halter dress might have appeared trashy. Sydney made it look Fifth Avenue elegant. She'd cut her hair, styling it in a short bob that framed the oval perfection of her face. Her mauve painted lips were parted in a bright, confident smile that didn't slip when her eyes met Gen's briefly. "Hello, Cassie, Caleb," she said, hesitating only slightly before adding, "Gen."

"Hello, Sydney," the three of them replied in unison. After which Gen was at a complete loss as to what to say next. Thus, she could have kissed Cassie's cheek for adroitly picking up the conversational ball.

"You're looking terrific, Sydney," Cassie said. "Obviously organizing this party for Alex has been a snap."

Gen thought she saw something like relief flicker in Sydney's brown eyes. "Yes, everything's gone so smoothly; working with a restaurant like La Plage makes all the difference. Harry and I will be extremely lucky if all the arrangements go as well in Boston this fall." She turned toward the man at her side and said, "Cassie, this is my partner, Harry Byrne. Harry, this is

Cassie and Caleb Wells, and this is Genevieve Monaghan."

Remembering that Harry Byrne had been present the day Sydney discovered Gen in Alex's arms, Gen's cheeks warmed with embarrassment. He too had to be aware of the undercurrents that were rippling beneath this seemingly relaxed meeting.

"Hello," she said, warily meeting his eyes as she stretched out her hand. But she saw only kindness and intelligence in their green depths as Harry smiled and shook it.

"Syd has spoken to me about your art," he said. "She admires it very much. I'm looking forward to seeing your piece for the Children's Hospital."

"Thank you. I only hope it will do justice to the space."

"I'm sure it will. By the way, I've heard you have a number of family members in the Boston area. Perhaps you'd like to invite them to the dedication ceremony?"

She smiled, grateful that he'd been so considerate as to think of her family. "I'd better ask Alex about that. Inviting the Monaghans is like inviting a small town."

As if by saying his name she had magically summoned him, Alex appeared at her side. "Definitely put them on the list, Harry," Alex said, taking her hand in his. "I've been making a few last-minute changes in the seating arrangements with Sydney. Everything looks terrific. You and Sydney have done a superb job."

"Thanks, Alex."

"I'm going to see Gen gets some champagne before everyone starts arriving. I'll make sure the waiter wanders over in your and Sydney's direction, too."

Harry flashed a quick, infectious grin. "He would be most welcome indeed. It was good to meet you, Gen."

Alex led Gen into the dining room. The decorator had obviously been asked to evoke the spirit of the restaurant's name, La Plage—"the beach." The walls were papered a soothing off-white and the large open room was illuminated by wall sconces and candles that bathed it in a soft, flattering light. But it was the ceiling that created the atmosphere: suspended above them were large, billowing canvas cloths draped to evoke summer clouds. The fabric swayed in the light the breeze coming through the open French doors that gave onto a patio.

She gazed at the circular tables decorated with artfully arranged majolica candelabrum and flowers. "Oh, Alex, this is beautiful. Did Sydney do all this?"

"Yeah. I knew she'd do an amazing job, she's a pro. But never mind about Sydney. I want to know about you." His hands framed her face as he regarded her searchingly. He brushed his lips against hers. "Are you okay?" he asked quietly.

Gen drew a deep breath. "I am now."

And she was.

Somehow Alex made the nerve-racking ordeal of meeting stranger after stranger easy. She'd been dreading being lost in a sea of investment- and business-speak, but Alex never failed to include some fact or anecdote when he introduced the men and women to her that allowed her to meet them on common ground. And he was right, she did like some of them—not only for the fact one man had grown up in Braintree, Massachusetts, a town not far from Somerville, or that another, who when he wasn't designing software programs made furniture using only eighteenth-century tools, but also because so many of these people clearly valued Alex's friendship, not just his business acumen.

One couple, who lived in New York and had adopted four racing greyhounds, had just left after swapping large-dogs-in-the-city stories with Gen, when suddenly Sydney appeared.

"Excuse me, Alex," she said, laying a hand on his sleeve. "I was wondering if I might speak to you for a moment."

Not waiting to hear whether Sydney would tack on "in private" to her request, Gen said, "I think I'll go out on the patio for a breath of fresh air."

Gen had excused herself too quickly for Alex to call her back. On the other hand, he knew how uncomfortable Gen felt, having to deal with Sydney's presence. She'd be okay out on the patio. A few minutes earlier he'd noticed Lizzie Osborne slipping through those same doors. Alex looked at Sydney and inclined his head. "Yes, Sydney? What can I do for you?"

"I wanted to tell you that Harry and I are leaving now. Your guests are all checked off. I talked to Nancy. They'll be seating people in about fifteen minutes."

"Thanks. You and Harry have done a fabulous job tonight. I've mentioned Raines and Byrne Consulting to a number of people already."

"That was really nice of you, especially after . . ." Sydney paused and he saw her throat work as if swallowing was suddenly difficult. "Especially after the way I've behaved these past few weeks. I'm really sorry, Alex. I acted like a complete idiot."

"Hey, don't be so hard on yourself. I'm just glad to see you looking so good. You have a glow about you I've never seen." He smiled. "You look happy, Sydney."

Her eyes met his and she blushed. "Yeah," she said softly. "It's amazing. I'm happier than I've been my whole life."

"Harry's a good man, Sydney. I hope everything works out for the two of you. You deserve it," he said and winked.

A surprised laugh tumbled from Sydney's lips as she remembered Alex saying that very thing during their breakup. "You're right. I do. If you need to reach Harry or me, call my cell. We'll be out of the office for a week. He's taking me to Maine," she said, her eyes sparkling.

"Maine, huh? I wouldn't have pegged you for an L.L. Bean kind of girl."

For a second her smile turned wistful. "I know." Impulsively she leaned forward and kissed him on the lips. "Take care of yourself, Alex," she whispered. "I hope you find what you're looking for."

* * *

Gen couldn't stop herself. As soon as she reached the torchlit patio, she turned around, her eyes glued to Alex and Sydney talking to each other. Too far away to hear their words, she had to rely on their body language. With every smile they exchanged, her heart grew heavier then plummeted as she watched them kiss.

"It's killing you, isn't it? You must be really stuck on him," a woman's voice said, not unkindly.

Gen whirled around. At first she saw nothing, only the orange glow of a cigarette burning. Then a woman stepped out of the shadows. "Sorry. I feel like some kind of creepy double Peeping Tom, watching you watch them. If it's any consolation, though, I came to a very different conclusion than the one you obviously reached. For instance, that kiss. You probably thought it was mutual. It wasn't. *She* kissed him. Believe me, that means Miller's not interested—at least, not anymore," she told Gen with utter certainty in her voice.

Gen cocked her head, regarding the woman curiously. "How could you tell all that?"

"My ex-husband. He taught me everything there is to know about men kissing other women. He was an expert in his chosen field," she said and took a long drag of her cigarette. Almost immediately she began to cough. Dropping the cigarette onto the patio, she ground it under her heel. "Nasty, awful things," she muttered. "Thank God I gave them up. I only bummed one from my friend Steve because I was a little freaked out about coming here tonight. And then to add to my nerves, my three-year-old daughter couldn't bear the thought of my date leaving her. I had to bribe her with two ice cream sandwiches before she'd let him go—which of course made us late. So I ducked out here, thinking this cig would be just the thing to settle my nerves. Now I've got a head rush like you wouldn't believe and with my luck I'll probably end up puking on my plate. At which point my date will laugh at me and tell me it's my own fault. And damn his golden eyes, he'll be right," she said, her voice filled with such comic resignation that Gen couldn't help laughing.

The woman flashed a quick answering grin. "Sorry again. I talk a *lot* when I'm stressed." Stepping fully into the light, she said, "Now that you know my entire life story, I might as well introduce myself. Hi, I'm Lizzie Osborne."

The knockout, Gen remembered Alex and Caleb had called her. The term didn't come close to doing justice to Lizzie Osborne's beauty. She had the kind of looks that make movie stars into idols. Gen smiled and held out her hand. "I'm Gen Monaghan. I'm pleased to meet you. So you're here with this Sam Brody I've heard so much about?"

"Yeah. I agreed in a moment of temporary insanity, brought on by Emma chirping about Sam day and night. I figured if she saw him she might stop talking about him. Not one of my smarter bets." She paused and glanced past Gen's shoulder. "Speak of the absolute devil," she murmured. "Sam's over there, talking with your Alex Miller. The woman's gone, by the way. Now that you and I have become such good, fast friends, want some really good advice?"

"Definitely."

"Don't let your fears destroy you," she said quietly, a shadow darkening her luminous eyes. Just as quickly it was gone, replaced by an impish light as she continued. "And since both your courage and mine could use a little boost, I suggest we snag some of the champagne that's floating around and then do our level best to torture the male species. What do you say, Gen?" she asked with a grin.

Gen found herself instinctively drawn to Lizzie Osborne. There was something incredibly appealing about her quirky sense of humor and her seemingly irrepressible spirit. Because it hadn't taken Gen more than these few minutes in her presence to understand that she used them to conceal a deep hurt.

With an answering smile, Gen said, "I'd say that sounds like a definite plan."

"Damn straight. Stick with me, kiddo, and you'll go far—and meet some great people, too. Let's go find Steve and Ty, two of my favorite people in the world."

"And where do I rank, Lizzie?" asked a man who'd stepped onto the patio, balancing three champagne flutes between his fingers. While the cut of his suit hinted at the solid strength of his body, he moved with a fluid, powerful grace.

Standing next to her, Gen saw Lizzie shiver and then stiffen, as if fighting an involuntary reaction. "Well, Sam, you might squeak into the top hundred if those champagnes are for me and my friend Gen. Gen, this is Sam Brody, my," she paused and cleared her throat, "date. Sam, this is Gen—"

"—Monaghan," Gen supplied.

"Pleased to meet you, Gen. Alex asked me to bring you this with his compliments," he said, smiling as he handed her a glass of champagne before passing the second to Lizzie. "So, Lizzie, I've made the top one hundred, huh?" Amusement laced his voice. "I'd say this calls for a toast."

"I hate to disappoint you, Sam, but those other ninety-nine people? They're rock solid. *Old* friend though you are, you'll never make it to the top." Sorrowfully she shook her head, her thick, reddish-gold hair sweeping her shoulders.

Sam Brody merely grinned and raised his glass. "To Lizzie, my very own Everest."

"Don't forget to bring your oxygen tank," Lizzie purred.

"And here I was hoping you'd offer a little mouth-to-mouth resuscitation—me being such an old friend and all."

"In your dreams, Sam Brody."

Gen sipped her champagne to hide her smile. Obviously Sam and Lizzie were engaged in some long-standing contest. A contest in which the stakes were very high. She wondered who would be the ultimate winner. Her musings were interrupted when a black-clad waiter stepped through the French doors to announce that dinner was served.

TWENTY-THREE

It was nearly two o'clock in the morning when the last guests left, calling out effusive thanks to Alex as they got into their cars and drove off.

After so many hours of playing host, seeing the final pair of taillights exit La Plage's parking lot was a relief. He'd begun to chafe, wondering why in hell everyone was hanging around when all he wanted was to go home, strip that sinfully sexy dress off Gen, and make love to her again and again until they drifted into oblivion.

Just then the object of Alex's fantasy yawned, only belatedly clapping a hand to her mouth. "Sorry," Gen said with a sheepish smile.

"Tired?" Not too, I hope, he thought, lifting his hand to stroke a strand of silky-smooth hair that had come loose from her chignon.

"And how." She nodded, smiling around another yawn. "It was a great party, Alex. I didn't know you could have so much fun without softball and hot dogs on the grill."

"I'm glad you enjoyed it."

"Yeah, I did." She rubbed the side of her face against the curve of his hand and blinked sleepily. "But I'm afraid this Cinderella desperately wants out of her party dress so she can hit the hay."

"What a coincidence. I was thinking along those very same lines." He stepped forward, allowing her to feel the heat of his body.

"Mmm." The sound came from deep in her throat. "You princes are all alike. Ply a girl with more champagne and caviar than she's ever seen in her life just so you can have your wicked way with her."

Alex grinned. "Guilty as charged. You game, Monaghan?"

She leaned into him, her supple body melting against him. "Absolutely."

"Then let's get the hell out of here," he said, grabbing her hand.

He should have guessed what would happen.

As the car tooled along the twisty East Hampton back roads, Alex taking care not to speed lest a stray deer jump out from the dense scrub oak that bordered it, an all-too-common hazard in this area, he and Gen conducted a post-mortem on the party. Perhaps because he was intent on scanning the road for foraging deer, he didn't notice at first that Gen's comments about the people she'd met were growing shorter and that her responses took longer in coming. It wasn't until he said, "You and Lizzie Osborne seemed to really hit it off," and was answered with complete silence that he glanced over. Gen was curled up against the car door, her hands tucked under her cheek. "Well, damn," Alex swore without heat and shook his head.

Not even Murphy pirouetting and whining with excitement at their return could rouse Gen. Maneuvering around the dog so he wouldn't bump Gen awake in his enthusiasm, Alex carried her to the futon. Bending, he dragged the coverlet back, and then lowered Gen down. Sleep made her boneless as a rag doll and she nearly toppled sideways. "No, love, let me get this off you first," he whispered, his hands already peeling the dress up her slender body.

His breath caught in his throat as he gazed at her lying there, fast asleep.

How was it that each time he looked at her, she grew more beautiful? How was it that every time he was near her he ached with the need to hold her and love her, knowing that when he did, the passion between them would burn sweeter and hotter than the time before? How was it that the sight of Gen Monaghan sleeping filled him with such tender protectiveness, made him want to wrap his arms about her again and hold her, not just tonight or tomorrow, or even six months from now, but for ever and ever?

For ever and ever? The thought rocked him with the force of an earthquake. Jesus, he was a hair's breadth away from falling head over heels in love with her.

Hands trembling, Alex pulled the blanket over Gen's body. Giving her a last, long, troubled look, he quietly left the studio.

Alex was still struggling to come to grips with his

feelings for Gen when the headlights of the Volvo pulled into the driveway. Caleb climbed out and made his way toward Alex. Murphy trotted over to greet him. "Hey, guy," he said quietly, patting him soundly on the shoulders. To Alex, he said, "You just get back?"

"Yeah. Dropping off the baby-sitter?"

"Uh-huh. Sweet kid. Definitely earned her baby-sitting stripes tonight."

"Is Cassie asleep?" At Caleb's nod, Alex asked, "feel like a drink?"

Caleb's shoulders lifted in a shrug. "Sure, why not? The night's young."

Neither man spoke as they slowly headed toward the dimly lit house, giving Murphy ample time to relieve himself. In the kitchen, Alex opened the wooden hutch and grabbed a bottle of whiskey and two glasses, then led the way out onto the porch. Setting the glasses down on the wicker coffee table, he uncorked the bottle and poured two fingerfuls in each glass.

"Thanks," Caleb said, taking the proffered glass.

Alex dropped into the chair next to Caleb's. Murphy, as if he'd been waiting for the two men to position themselves, sank down onto the floor between them. Caleb raised his glass. "Cheers," he said.

"Cheers." There was a moment of silence as both men sipped their whiskey. Then Caleb stretched out his legs and began rubbing Murphy's stomach with the toe of his shoe. "Gen asleep?" he asked idly.

"Yeah. Somewhere on Stephen Hands Path, Cinderella turned into Sleeping Beauty on me."

"Ahh." Caleb nodded. "I know both those ladies.

Sophie's a fan," he explained. "So Gen conked out, did she? Little too much champagne?"

"No, the car cast a spell on her." And she's cast a spell on me, he thought broodingly as he took a long swallow of the whiskey.

"Happens to Cass all the time."

"Yeah?"

"Yeah. Mainly when we're coming back from a horse show." He shifted in his chair and Alex could feel his eyes studying him before continuing. "So tell me, Miller. If you've got Sleeping Beauty lying in the studio, just waiting for your kiss, what the hell are you doing out here with me and a dog for company?"

That was one of the more annoying aspects of Caleb's southern drawl: it lulled you into thinking he was just another good ole Virginia boy.

Rather than spilling his guts, Alex merely shrugged. He should have known Caleb wouldn't leave well enough alone.

"Ahh, I get it," he said. "This is the scene they gloss over in the fairy tales. The one where the prince is scared spitless, wondering what happened to his world. 'Cause shitty though it was, at least it was *his* world."

Damn him for hitting the nail on the head, Alex thought, shooting Caleb a narrow-eyed look. "You have such an eloquent way with words. Pure poetry."

Unfazed by the sarcasm, Caleb grinned. "Thanks. I notice, though, that you're not denying the truth of my very eloquent observation." His voice changed, grew serious and kind. "Gen's worth falling for, Alex. She's bright as a penny, talented, and kind as the day is long."

"I know. It just—" He broke off and rubbed his hand over his face as he tried to describe what he was feeling. "It hit me so damned fast, like a—"

"Like a sucker punch," Caleb offered.

He nodded glumly—"Yeah"—and downed the rest of his whiskey in one fiery gulp.

Caleb leaned forward and snagged the bottle between his fingers and poured some more whiskey into Alex's glass. "You know, Alex, we could take the kids with us tomorrow to Pound Ridge. They can visit another—"

"No, no," he interrupted, shaking his head. "I *want* Jamie and Sophie here. Besides, having them around will give me a chance to figure this thing out while I get my bearings. Thanks, though." Raising his glass, Alex took a long swallow.

"You're welcome. You know, Alex, I won't ever forget how you helped me after I, uh, messed up with Cassie. I'd like to help you in return," he said quietly. "So here's some good advice, free of charge. Go back to your sleeping beauty. Wrap your arms around her and while you're holding her, think about what your world was like before you found her. Then try and imagine living without her. You'll be kissing her before long."

The following morning Gen was in her studio, drinking coffee from the largest mug she'd been able to unearth in Mrs. Miller's kitchen. She was frowning, not from a champagne-induced hangover, but from concentration. Putting the coffee mug down, she took up the Conté crayon and approached the canvas once more.

For the past hour, while Alex was in the house, keeping the twins occupied as Cassie and Caleb got ready to leave, Gen had been working on the under-drawing for the painting, lightly roughing in the composition, and then stepping back, studying it critically. Right now, she was most concerned with the proportions, that and the drama of Alex's and the twins' gestures as they constructed their fabulous sand castle. The poses and the position of their hands had to be just right, conveying expression and emotion to the viewer.

"Hey, Gen, can I come in?"

Gen's Conté stick stilled and she glanced over to the door where Cassie stood. Her preoccupied frown became a smile. "Of course."

"Wow, this place looks so different," Cassie said, looking about her with interest.

"It's a great studio," she said, picking up an old hand towel and wiping her reddish-brown-stained fingers with it. "There's room to do almost anything imaginable. Paint, sculpt . . ." She stopped in midsentence, aware that Cassie's attention was fixed on the canvas behind her.

"My God," Cassie whispered. "That's . . . is it . . ." Her throat worked convulsively.

"Yes," Gen said gently. "I made the sketch yesterday while you and Caleb were taking a stroll. Here it is," she said. Moving to the worktable, she handed the drawing pad to Cassie. Filled with a sudden anxiety, she asked, "You don't mind, do you? That I'm using the three of them for the painting?"

"Mind? It's perfect, Gen. Tom and Lisa would love it—" Her voice cracking with emotion, she pressed a hand to her lips. Her slender shoulders rose as she drew in a long, shaky breath. "It's perfect," she repeated. "Thank you, Gen."

"You're welcome," she said simply. For a minute, their eyes met, then Cassie's gaze returned to the drawing, studying it intently. Every so often, she would glance over to the canvas as if envisioning the finished painting. Finally she lay the sketch pad back down on the table. "Does Alex know?" she asked, turning to face Gen.

"About what I've decided to do for the painting?"

Cassie shook her head. "No, I wasn't talking about the painting. I meant about how much you care for him."

"I—I—" Gen stammered, feeling her face flame.

"It's there, Gen, in every line you've drawn," Cassie said gently.

Disconcerted, she picked up her coffee cup. "Alex is a handsome man," she mumbled, before burying her nose in the cup and drinking deeply.

"He's a heck of a lot more than handsome, and you know it. Most of the women he's been with have never bothered to look past the fancy veneer that surrounds him and see the real Alex. I think that's hurt him more than he's willing to admit. I love my brother, Gen. More than anything, I'd like him to have a chance at finding real happiness. I hope you do, too."

Before Gen could reply, however, Caleb's voice reached them. "Hey, Slim, we gotta get this show on the road or we'll be late for Steve and Ty." He stuck his dark head through the doorway. "Ahh, so you found Gen."

"Yeah, but I haven't gotten around to saying goodbye," Cassie replied as she and Gen walked over to Caleb.

"Busy having a girl talk?"

"Something like that." With a smile, Cassie turned and gave Gen a hug. " 'Bye, Gen."

" 'Bye, Cassie. Good luck at the horse show."

"Thanks. And good luck to *you*—remember what I said."

"Don't let the kids run you and Alex ragged," Caleb advised as he kissed Gen's cheek. "If you're in danger of collapsing from exhaustion, feed 'em pizza and stick 'em in front of the TV."

"Caleb!" Cassie exclaimed in outrage.

"What? I'm just providing an invaluable parenting tip. One we've used a couple of times when we suddenly needed a few minutes of privacy. Ain't that right, Slim?" he asked, his voice dropping to a suggestive murmur.

Cassie's cheeks bloomed a becoming shade of pink. "Extra cheese and sausage is their absolute favorite. Oh, and *Finding Nemo* works like a charm."

Gen stayed behind when Alex drove Cassie and Caleb and the twins to Southwind, the horse farm owned by Steve and Ty Sheppard. Although Gen would have really liked to see them and what was apparently a beautiful horse farm, she sensed that her presence would only delay the adults' departure. That, in turn, might be all that Jamie and Sophie required to start missing their parents before they'd even driven away.

Besides which Gen was grateful for a little time alone. It would give her a chance to mull over what Cassie had said to her in the studio about Alex. And as the house was empty, Mrs. Miller having waited to say good-bye to Cassie and Caleb before taking her morning constitutional, it would also be the perfect opportunity to vacuum the sand that had accumulated throughout the house.

Gen pulled out the vintage Hoover from the hall closet. Armed with a bevy of attachments, she attacked the downstairs rooms, sucking up sand and dust bunnies with a vengeance, her thoughts whirring inside her head as loudly as the powerful machine. Could what Cassie had said be true, that Alex had been hurt by the other women he'd been with? Could they really have been so stupidly ambitious—the sort of people who cared more for private jets and penthouse apartments than for what was inside Alex?

And what about Sydney's claim, that Alex wasn't capable of commitment? That he'd never stay with one woman? she wondered, bumping her way up the stairs, Hoover in tow, pointing the nozzle at every corner and crevice she encountered. From the way Sydney had described Alex's affairs, she'd made it sound as if he'd left a trail of broken hearts in his path. Was it broken hearts or broken ambitions?

Which was the truth? she wondered, realizing immediately that the truth wasn't necessarily black or white. It could be a shifting shade of gray.

With a slight frown, Gen yanked the Hoover over the top step and began vacuuming the upper landing. So, she thought, while everything she was learning about Alex only added to the complexity of the man, one thing was certain: her feelings for him. She was helplessly in love with him. And according to Cassie, she was practically wearing her heart on her sleeve— or, rather, on her drawing pad.

Was it really so obvious that she'd fallen in love with Alex? Gen wondered, unconsciously gnawing her lower lip. It must be. Cassie had looked at her sketch and recognized the truth immediately. . . . Oh, God, what would happen when Alex saw it?

To calm herself, she drew a long steadying breath, the air she inhaled carrying with it the lightest hint of citrus. Instantly she realized she'd unwittingly vacuumed her way into Alex's room. Glancing about, she felt suddenly shy, as if she were somehow trespassing.

Good Lord, she was being utterly ridiculous. It was only a bedroom. Nevertheless, she was glad Alex had left it as neat as a pin. She would vacuum and leave.

With the vacuum cleaner humming behind her, she worked her way across the bedroom, awash in sunlight streaming in through the bay window. Set at an angle to the window was a large, comfortable-looking upholstered chair. Her eyes strayed to the chair as she vacuumed, easily picturing Alex sitting there and gazing out at the blue expanse of ocean, and her mouth curved in a soft smile.

Her smile abruptly became a startled gasp.

Beneath her hand the nozzle jerked, while the vacuum's motor whined loudly in protest. Something was obviously clogging it. Pulling the wand out from beneath the chair, Gen lifted the nozzle.

He must have dropped a sock, she thought, as the half-swallowed white material vibrated madly. Automatically she stepped on the power switch. The room went silent, accentuating the awful pounding of her heart as with suddenly trembling hands, Gen freed the nearly transparent panties.

Her eyes closed. But that didn't stop her from seeing Sydney. Her cruel memory conjured the image of Sydney walking out onto the porch in a silk, claret robe, the ivory skin of her slender neck abraded with the marks of passion. She saw Sydney again—as she'd been last night at the party, dressed so beautifully, and gazing up at Alex with a wistful smile. She saw Sydney leaning forward to press a kiss to Alex's lips.

Her knuckles tightened around the vacuum cleaner's handle as jealousy and pain pierced her, cutting her to the quick. How could she survive this kind of torment? she asked herself as tears filled her eyes. The answer came from an unexpected source: Lizzie Osborne, her blue eyes filled with compassion and hard-earned wisdom, saying, "Don't let your fears destroy you."

Lizzie was so very right.

Gen couldn't go on like this. If she did, eventually jealousy and uncertainty would destroy her love for Alex. She had to believe in herself and she had to believe in Alex. Most of all, she had to trust that what they'd discovered together was real and lasting. If she didn't conquer her fears, their love would never stand a chance.

Squaring her shoulders, Gen lifted the nozzle and pulled off the attachment. Switching the machine back on to high, she gingerly picked up the scrap of white cotton and lace. Then, with a fierce growl that would have made Murphy proud and Lizzie Osborne get on her feet applauding, Gen let the Hoover have the panties.

TWENTY-FOUR

Homesickness struck the twins later that afternoon. As a veteran baby-sitter and an aunt herself, Gen had been expecting some kind of emotional meltdown from Jamie and Sophie. So it had come as a surprise when the kids returned with Alex acting upbeat and cheerful. But then she learned how savvy Uncle Alex was. After saying good-bye to Cassie and Caleb, he'd driven directly to the Candy Kitchen in Bridgehampton and treated Sophie and Jamie to a kiddie feast of grilled cheese sandwiches, ice cream, and licorice sticks. And since Alex was not only savvy but a soft touch, they'd next hit Penny Whistle, a toy store conveniently located across the street, and bought "just a few more" sand toys, as well as two kites, and two boogie boards so that Jamie and Sophie could be just like real surfer dudes.

But not even Alex's near-impeccable avuncular instincts could block out a sudden attack of longing for Mommy and Daddy. In Sophie's case all it took was something as inconsequential as a stubbed toe as she was running across the lawn—a hurt spunky little

Sophie would normally have hopped off with an "Ow! Ow! Ow!" But without the reassuring presence of her parents, her face crumpled. Her smile drooped like a wilted flower, her bottom lip trembled uncontrollably, and tears began slipping down her plump, sugar-smeared cheeks. Then came the dreaded wail of "I want my mommy!" And Gen, who along with Alex had rushed to Sophie's side, got a terrible sinking feeling in her stomach.

Her premonition proved correct. The homesick bug didn't take but a minute to spread. It turned out Jamie wasn't Sophie's twin for nothing—or her brother for nothing, either. He not only matched his sister, he upped the ante. Soon his shoulders were heaving in anguish as he cried, "I want my mommy and daddy, I want Radar! I want to go *home!*"

Simply because Gen had anticipated something along these lines didn't make it any less heart-wrenching, watching two six-year-olds dissolve into puddles of distress. A quick glance at Alex's face told her he was feeling equally helpless.

Thank God for Murphy, friend to woman, man, and six-year-olds alike. As the wailing and tears gathered steam, he pushed his way into the center of their small, unhappy circle and began licking wet, sticky faces, while his shaggy body wriggled against theirs, his curled tail beating back and forth for good measure. When it came to dogged determination not even Sophie's and Jamie's combined efforts could stand up against a hundred-pound wolfhound. First a hiccup interrupted the flow of tears, followed by an aggrieved but definitely happier cry of "Murphy, quit it!" and "Hey, that tickles!"

Gen's and Alex's eyes met over Murphy's shaggy shoulders. Gen winked, then quickly, before the kids could remember that they were disconsolate, she jumped to her feet. "Oh, my gosh, I can't believe it! I forgot I was supposed to take Murphy over to the groomer today!" she cried, slapping a hand to her forehead in an inspired touch of drama. Deliberately ignoring the kids she looked at Alex and said, "I have some shampoo, but there's no way I can wash Murphy all by myself. He's just got to have a bath. He's so stinky, I can smell him from here."

Alex rocked back on his heels. "Ugh, you're right. I guess I could help you, Gen, but I'm not sure about these two munchkins. Murphy's a really big dog—"

"We can help! Yeah, we can help," they shouted in unison. "We've given baths lots of times. Daddy taught us how. And Radar and Belle are almost as big as Murphy."

Gen looked unconvinced. "I don't know, it's a messy job. You'll get really wet."

"I know!" Jamie jumped up and down. "We'll put on our swimsuits. Then it won't matter if we get wet."

"Huh, that's an idea." Gen pretended to consider it. Shrugging her shoulders, she said, "I guess we could try it. Why don't you go get your suits on and I'll find the shampoo and dog brush."

The kids ran off, tears and toe forgotten.

Alex released a huge breath and stood up. "Thanks," he said with a crooked smile.

"My pleasure. Murphy's too," she added lightly. "Nothing upsets us more than six-year-olds crying."

He shuddered. "I'm with you there. I'll make sure Murphy's amply rewarded for his valiant efforts come dinnertime. You, however, deserve something more immediate." Angling his head, he settled his lips over hers in a leisurely and thorough tasting that left them both gasping and hungry for more. "Mmm," he said, coming back for a second helping. "Bedtime seems an awfully long time away."

"And we'll probably be so tired . . ." She sighed softly.

"Oh, I can think of a couple of activities that will reenergize us."

"Hmm, sounds interesting. What kind of activities?" she asked, rising on her tiptoes and draping her arms around his neck.

His blue eyes flared with desire. "I wouldn't want to spoil the fun by telling," he murmured, pulling her closer to his solid strength. "Let's just say that they involve lots of hands-on learning."

"Gosh, I didn't know you brainy finance types went in for that kind of thing," Gen teased breathlessly.

"Uh-huh." Alex nodded. "It's right up there with team-building. I'd say you and I make a pretty good team, Monaghan."

And so they did, Alex found himself thinking again and again over the course of the next few days as he and Gen, with occasional and much appreciated assistance from Aunt Grace, fell into a routine that began as soon as the kids scrambled out of bed. They worked well together. But in Alex's opinion, it was thanks to Gen that the twins' stay went so smoothly. She possessed a real knack for figuring out how to keep Jamie and Sophie entertained and absorbed. For instance, it was she who calmly suggested one morning that they go to her studio and draw when Jamie and Sophie succumbed to another bout of homesickness. "That's what I do when I'm sad. I make things, I make pictures of the things I love and the people I love. It helps me feel better," she told them with a simple honesty that had him tumbling that much more in love with her. "I have some paper and colored pencils you can use."

"At home we have markers," Jamie said with stubborn despondency.

Alex watched Gen bite back a smile as she reached out and ruffled Jamie's hair. "Trust me. These are way better than markers. Come on, I'll show you," she said, ushering them out of the kitchen.

Rising from his chair, he laid a hand on her arm. "Are you sure they won't be interrupting your work?" he asked.

She shook her head and smiled. "No, I have a feeling these kids have the same kind of focus as their uncle Alex. You know, intense and with an unflagging attention to detail."

"I hadn't realized you'd been observing me so closely."

"Intimately," she replied, her voice just husky enough to make the blood pound in his veins. "Besides," she added, "I bet you could stand to get a spot of work done on that software company you and your partner Glenn Powell were talking about at the party. Go on, hole up in your study for a while. We'll be fine."

She'd been right about that too. Alex and his partners had decided to open negotiations with the software company I.Com. Alex's IT expert, Glenn Powell, had been impressed with the Internet programs they were developing. As timing was crucial in the IT sector, the Miller Group would have to act fast. He hoped to set up a deal by the end of next week. Following Gen's suggestion, he spent an hour on the phone with his partners, discussing what I.Com would require in terms of management support, the kind of time projections they were thinking of, and what would be the Miller Group's optimal exit strategy for both them and I.Com.

After he'd finished, Alex, curious to see how Gen was making out, wandered over to the studio. Classical music poured out the studio's open windows to drift on the salty air. Mozart's *Figaro,* he thought, smiling unconsciously. The volume was loud enough to muffle the sound of his approach. Not even Murphy, happily gnawing on one of his beloved bones, glanced in his direction. That suited Alex fine, allowed him the chance to observe the artists at work.

Sophie and Jamie were lying on the floor, elbows propped, pencils clutched between their fingers, drawing with total concentration. Scattered around them were sheets of paper filled with bold figures and rainbows of color. Meanwhile Gen was ignoring them— that is, letting them create their drawings in peace, without interfering comments or suggestions. Her back to him, she was working on the painting for the hospital. Alex watched, feeling a thrill of pleasure that he was there, witnessing her bring life to the painting. Though there weren't many details in the lightish-brown drawing she was sketching on the white-gessoed surface, from where he stood, it appeared as if three figures, one large and two smaller ones, were grouped closely together. From the low horizon dividing the canvas he guessed that the scene was set out of doors. He was about to take an unobtrusive step closer when Jamie jumped to his feet, drawing in hand.

"Here, Gen, look at this one." At the sound of her name Gen turned around, a smile on her face. "I made a picture of you and Uncle Alex and Murphy. It's for you," he said, thrusting it at her.

"For me? Oh, Jamie, I'm so touched," she said, in a voice that wobbled. Dropping to her knees, she enveloped him in a quick, fierce hug. Releasing him, she cleared her throat and said, "I need to take a look at this."

"I want to look too! Can I, Jamie?" Sophie asked, already clambering to her feet.

"Yeah, I guess."

For several seconds, the three of them, heads bent, studied Jamie's drawing. Then Gen said, "It's a wonderful drawing, Jamie. I'll treasure it forever. Thank you. Can I put it next to the painting I'm working on, so I can look at it whenever I want?"

"Sure. That'd be okay. Now I'm going to make one for Uncle Alex," he said, racing back to his spot on the floor. Alex saw Gen smile, then brush a hand over her eyes, wiping away the telltale moisture.

To avoid the risk of Gen catching sight of him and realizing that he'd witnessed her and Jamie's exchange, Alex stepped forward, saying, "Wow, this looks like a real artists' workshop here."

His voice broke the spell of intense concentration, but not the twins' enthusiasm. They sprang to their feet, words tumbling from their mouths as they rushed to tell him about their drawings. And for the rest of the week, it seemed there was always some point during the day when Jamie and Sophie would wander into Gen's studio, head directly to the area where she'd laid aside a supply of paper and colored pencils specially for them, and settle down to work.

There was, however, one major drawback to the twins' weeklong stay, one that Alex hadn't anticipated. Gen and he were forced to spend their nights apart. For some reason he couldn't fathom, but nevertheless had to respect, she absolutely and adamantly refused to sleep with him in his bedroom. And in all good conscience, he couldn't chance Jamie or Sophie awakening in the middle of the night in strange surroundings and his not being there. Though they managed, after putting the twins to bed, to steal away to the studio for a few hours and lose themselves in the passion of their lovemaking, it was when Alex returned to his large, empty bed that he apprehended what it was he truly craved. What he missed, what he ached for: the sweet and profound joy that flowed through him when he held Gen in his arms.

* * *

Alex had arranged with Cassie that he would fly with the kids back to Virginia so that she and Caleb could drive with their partner, Hank Sawyer, and help with the horses on the return trip. When the day came for the twins to leave, Gen had to blink back tears as she crushed first Sophie and then Jamie tight against her. It was so hard to say good-bye. "You two keep drawing, okay? I want to see those ponies you told me so much about and that pond where the frogs live, and, well, *everything* you can think of," she said with a shaky laugh.

"Okay. And maybe you'll come and visit us. Then Murphy can play with Radar and Belle and meet Topper and Pip, too," Sophie said enthusiastically. "Uncle Alex can bring you. He knows where we live."

"I'd like that very much," she whispered, in a voice thick with emotion. It was amazing how quickly these two children had found their way into her heart. With a final hug she straightened and met Alex's warm gaze. His mouth was curved in a tender smile. What would it be like to carry Alex's child, to share with him the wonder and magic of bringing a life into the world with him? At the thought, a longing so acute pierced Gen, she had to bite her lip, stifling her cry.

As Jamie and Sophie climbed noisily into the backseat of the Aston, Alex reached out to stroke her hair. "Hey," he said softly. "Are you all right?"

Nearly undone by the gentleness of his touch, she pressed her lips together and nodded. When he continued to look unconvinced, she confessed tremulously,

"I'm lousy at saying good-bye, that's all. I'm going to miss you."

His hand slipped down her back and drew her close. "You mean, maybe more than just a 'wee bit' this time?" he teased, before pressing a kiss to her forehead.

Lord, if he only knew. Her throat was tight, clogged with emotions; she forced them back. There'd be time to tell him all she felt. "You'll be back the day after tomorrow?"

"Yeah. You know, I can easily switch my flight."

"No, no." Resolutely she shook her head. "Jamie and Sophie have been talking all week about jumping over those whatchamacallits."

"Crossbars," he supplied helpfully.

"Right. Crossbars. You need to see that feat. And I'll be able to get a lot done on the painting."

"And when I get back, I'll have you all to myself." As if sensing that she desperately needed levity to lighten the moment, he gave her bottom a playful swat, grinning wickedly at her squeal of surprise. "Get lots of rest, Monaghan," he advised. "I promise you, you'll need it."

TWENTY-FIVE

Gen spent the remainder of the day immersed in her painting. Spread over the worktable were dozens of drawings, all of Jamie, Sophie, and Alex captured in various poses. Yet she painted without even glancing over at them once. She didn't need to; their features were etched in her memory.

There were certain moments, rare and fleeting, when Gen created that she felt a wondrous synergy of mind, spirit, and body. Suddenly forms and lines flowed without hesitation or uncertainty from her hand to her brush. As she worked on the painting for the Children's Hospital, she experienced more than the glorious certainty of her artistic vision or the thrilling excitement of creating. This time love flowed from her. A love that filled her heart and that she poured onto the canvas. Hours passed and Gen painted.

The ringing of the phone broke her concentration. Thinking it might be Alex calling again, she snatched up the receiver without waiting for the answering machine to kick in. "Hello," she said breathlessly, as hungry for the sound of his voice as she'd been the first time when he called to tell her that he and the twins had arrived safely in Charlottesville.

"Genevieve, it's Jiri."

"Jiri?" she echoed in astonishment as she glanced out the window. The sun was setting. "Isn't it horribly late in Prague?"

"Yes." He laughed. "But I am in New York now. Don't you remember? I told you last time we talk on phone."

"Of course, I just lost track of the days," she fibbed, unwilling to admit that their conversation had flown straight out of her head. "So you're in New York? That's great. Have you seen your dealer?"

"Tomorrow," he answered. "Then I come see you. Gen, I have big surprise."

"Uh, Jiri, I'm out on Long Island. In the Hamptons."

"So?" She could practically see Jiri giving one of his eloquent, signature shrugs. "I rent a car."

"No, no," she said hurriedly. Jiri was one of the worst drivers in the world. The thought of him loose on the Long Island Expressway was enough to make her blood run cold. And then, if he managed to make it out to East Hampton without causing a major crash, there'd be all those Rollerbladers and joggers tooling down the roads, unaware their lives were in imminent danger. "Really, Jiri, you don't have to go to all that expense. There's a bus, the Jitney, which you can take. It's much cheaper. You can get on in midtown and go straight out to East Hampton. I'll meet you at the bus stop."

"Okay, I take a bus, you pick me up, I tell you big

surprise," he said so agreeably that Gen found herself staring in baffled wonder at the receiver in her hand. This didn't sound like the Jiri Novak she knew. Jiri had always been the kind of person who was happiest when he was making the decisions, no matter how minute. Maybe his position as director of the academy had given him a new appreciation for flexibility.

After agreeing that he'd call her once he knew which bus he was taking, he said, his accented voice gruff, "It will be good to see you, Genevieve. I have missed you in my life."

Touched, she smiled into the receiver. "Oh, Jiri, that's sweet. But it'll only take you about three minutes to remember how contrary and infuriatingly stubborn I can be. Of course, it works both ways. I'm so happy about seeing *you*, I've clean forgotten how aggravating you are."

With a laugh he said, "I will be on my best behavior. Then we shall see, no? Good night, Gen." She heard the soft click of the line disconnecting.

Smiling she shook her head and replaced the phone in its cradle, jumping in surprise when it rang beneath her hand. "Hello?"

"Hi."

Gen's smile turned dreamy at the sound of Alex's low voice. "Hi," she replied softly. "How are things?"

"Well, they'd be great except for the fact that I'm here and you're there. Which significantly downgrades the whole experience."

"Wow, that sounds like a real drag. Kind of like being stuck in economy class," she teased.

His quiet laughter rumbled in her ear. "Ahh, Gen, you're a tough woman to woo. Okay, how's this for a sweet nothing? What if I tell you that I'm going quietly mad because I want you so much? That these ten hours have dragged like ten years? That I'm sitting here with a goofy smile on my face because I'm finally hearing the sound of your voice?"

Closing her eyes at the delicious tingling sensation coursing through her, Gen gripped the phone tighter, lest it slip from her fingers. "That works," she breathed.

"Good. Now, what are you wearing?"

Her eyes popped open in surprise. "Excuse me?"

"Something incredibly sexy, right? Something that's going to drive me right over the edge. No, don't tell me," he said. "Let me guess . . . ripped blue jeans and a T-shirt, right?"

"Right," she echoed and then laughed when Alex gave a low groan.

"Ahh, Gen, you're killing me. Want to take 'em off real slowly?"

"Idiot," she accused, laughter still threading her voice. "Your aunt's about to walk in here; we're going to the movies in Sag Harbor. As liberal-minded as she is, I think that might shock her, seeing me buck naked having phone sex with her adored nephew."

"Damn," Alex said heavily.

She smiled, foolishly, gloriously happy to be having this ridiculous conversation. "Tell you what, Miller. Now that I know how much you *appreciate* this outfit, I'll be sure to wear it when you come home."

"Mmm." Alex's voice was a sexy rumble of approval. "And then I can be the one to take it off real slow."

"Whatever your heart desires," Gen said softly.

"That's a promise I'll hold you to." The teasing note was gone from his voice. Then, hearing Murphy burst into a loud canine welcome, he said, "Give Aunt Grace a kiss for me."

"I will. And what do I get?" she murmured provocatively.

"Me," he answered before hanging up.

Gen was only too happy to let Mrs. Miller drive. Still under the sway of Alex's effortless seduction, she wasn't sure she'd have been able to find Sag Harbor. It was only later, when she was sitting down in the dimly-lit movie theater beside Mrs. Miller, a tub of buttered popcorn between them, that she realized she'd forgotten to tell Alex about Jiri coming to visit.

Gen left for East Hampton early the next afternoon, so she'd have plenty of time to find a parking space in the busy town. From her various sorties and shopping expeditions, Gen had decided that East Hampton epitomized what made the Hamptons alluring to so many. It was simultaneously a picture-perfect, carefully preserved town that also happened to offer the height of consumer chic. One could stroll past a graveyard whose tombstones dated from the seventeenth century, lovely, gracious shingled homes and white-steepled churches, and then duck into Ralph Lauren, Coach, or David Yurman and do some serious credit card damage. Even East Hampton's smaller boutiques catered to bulging wallets; their prices left

Gen reeling with sticker shock. She was obviously in the minority, though, because she'd never driven to East Hampton without seeing the sidewalks crowded with well-heeled tourists and locals alike streaming in and out of the shops.

Fortunately Gen had gotten to know her way around the town and turned onto a side street where she found a space for the Yugo. She made her way back to Main Street and sat down on the wooden bench that marked where the Jitney stopped.

Jiri was the first to step off the gleaming black coach bus. The sight of his tall frame, his lean, ascetic face, his brown hair threaded with gray just a little shaggier than she remembered, had her face stretching into a grin. "Jiri," she called.

He dropped his black messenger bag and spread his arms wide. "Genevieve, my lovely Genevieve." He laughed, hugging her tight. Then relaxing his arms, he stepped back. "Let me look at you. The rich sea air must be good for you, Gen, you are looking lovelier than ever. And more of those charming freckles," he teased, touching the tip of her nose.

"You're looking fine yourself, Jiri. That's a fantastic shirt," she said, lacing her arm about his terra-cotta shirtsleeve.

"You like?"

"I like." She nodded. "It's very chic. Armani?" she guessed, knowing his passion for the Italian designer.

"Very appropriate, very Hamptons, I thought," he said, picking up his messenger bag and slinging it over his shoulder.

"Absolutely. Come on, I'll take you back home. We can have tea in my studio. Murphy's going to be over-joyed to see you."

Jiri groaned. "My new shirt will not survive a re-union with that beast."

"Oh, don't worry. He's gotten much better behaved."

"That would be a miracle."

They chatted about this and that, with Gen occa-sionally pointing out some of the famous houses—or people who lived in them—as they drove the four miles back to Georgica. But when she pulled into the driveway that led to Mrs. Miller's house, Jiri went quiet. He climbed out of the car and walked toward the house, its graceful lines bathed in the afternoon light. He stopped, and then turned in a slow circle. Gen knew he was taking in the ripples playing over Georgica pond, the different greens of the vegetation, the shimmering blue of the ocean. Still looking, he nodded and said quietly, "Okay, now I understand what brought you here. And you have studio, too?"

"Mmm." Gen nodded, pleased by the sincere ap-preciation she'd heard in his voice. "It's right this way. But let's make some tea first. And then I want to hear all about your upcoming show."

As they drank tea and ate slices of a raspberry loaf Gen had baked with Sophie and Jamie, Jiri kept rising from his stool to walk over and study her painting.

Standing before it now, he said, "Your colors have changed, Genevieve." He took a sip of black tea from the mug cradled in his hand and pivoted, looking at her quizzically as if trying to solve a puzzle. With his free arm he made a sweeping gesture. "So, this place, it has made you see differently?"

Gen smiled and shook her head. "No," she said. "Though it's beautiful here, and I love it. I've met someone, Jiri."

"A man?" he asked quietly.

"Yes." She met his dark gaze. "I don't know how to explain it except that he's changed me."

Jiri regarded her in silence and then turned once more to the painting. "The subject . . . well, it should be trite." His shoulders lifted in a heavy shrug. "But somehow it's not. You've succeeded where others would have failed, Genevieve. This work is strong and powerful and immediate. It has the joy and wonder of Marc Chagall. You feel these children's happiness, their pleasure in their creation. And this man, he's—" Jiri stopped and lowered his gaze to the floor. For a second he stood, head bowed. Then slowly his gaze returned to the figure of Alex. "This man, he's the one."

"Yes." Gen smiled softly. "He's the one."

Jiri came back to the table and sat down. "And it is he who commissioned the painting?" At her nod, he raised his eyebrow and smiled. "A rich man, then."

Gen laughed and shook her head lightly. "Alex could live in a tent and I would feel the same way about him."

The corner of his mouth lifted and he inclined his head in acknowledgment. "Yes, I suppose you would. Ah, Gen, I am happy for you." Reaching across the worktable, he took her hand in his. "You know, I had hoped . . . Well, maybe when you hear my news, it changes something in you, too," he joked.

Hoping to dispel the awkwardness between them, Gen squeezed his fingers briefly. "So tell me everything. You're going to have a show?"

His smile broadened, full of pride; suddenly he looked more like the Jiri she knew so well. "Berlin. Major retrospective, Genevieve . . . drawings, paintings, sculpture—*Alles!*" he said in perfect German. "Everything! They schedule it for late next year."

"Oh, Jiri, that's fantastic! Congratulations."

"Yes, fantastic. And fantastic for you, too. Listen, Genevieve, the National Museum in Praha, as soon as they hear about Berlin exhibit, they jump on—how do you call it?" Jiri paused, searching for the word. "Ahh, yes, bandwagon. They call me at academy and say they would like to have exhibit, too."

"You mean the retrospective would travel from Berlin to Prague?"

"Yes." Jiri nodded. "But as I am now director of National Academy, the curators say, Why not include artists I have taught, let public see contemporary dialogue of art and ideas. So, first name I give them is Genevieve Monaghan."

Gen laid a hand to her chest. "Oh, my God, a museum exhibit in Prague? This is incredible. I'm—I'm simply overwhelmed," she stammered.

"It's good, no?" He grinned back at her. Leaning forward, he took her hands in his. "Gen, I buy big apartment, right on the Vltava. Beautiful gardens five minutes' walk. Perhaps I stay at academy two years, three, tops. After that, Paris, London, we go where we want—even come back to New York, if you like.

What we had together, Gen, even when you behave as stubborn as a rock—it was important."

Gen felt her heart wrench at his words. "It was important to me, too, Jiri," she said softly. "I can't tell you how much it means to me that you want me to come . . . but I can't."

He pressed a finger to her lips. "No, don't say it. When I go back to Praha, I wait and I hope."

The light of the Aston's beams fell on his aunt's station wagon, and then picked up the space where Gen habitually parked her rusty Yugo. It was empty. Frowning, Alex pulled the car in beside it and killed the engine. He leaned over, grabbed the weekend bag he'd tossed onto the passenger seat at the airport, and slammed the car door shut behind him. He strode toward the house, its illuminated windows shining against the darkening sky.

Aunt Grace was in the kitchen, leaning against the counter as she talked into the phone. At the sound of the door opening, she turned with a squeak of fright. "No, no, Tilly, it's all right, just Alex giving me the scare of my life. Yes, I'll call you tomorrow and we'll finalize the plans. And congratulations again, dear," she said before hanging up and scowling at Alex. "Good Lord, Alex, you nearly gave me a heart attack! What are you doing here? You're supposed to come back tomorrow."

"Nice to see you, too, Aunt Grace," he said, dropping his bag by the door and coming forward to kiss her cheek. "If you ever bothered to use the security system I had Sam install, I wouldn't have been able to get within a mile of this place without you knowing it."

"Hmphh," his aunt replied testily, clearly not yet over her shock. "So, you didn't stay to watch Sophie and Jamie jump?"

"Cassie decided to move the twins' riding lesson to the early morning," he said and grinned, recalling how Caleb had informed him that Cassie had decided to take pity on her older brother and get him on the first flight back to Gen. He'd send her a big bouquet of flowers tomorrow. "After the jumping session, I hightailed it to the airport and here I am. I thought I'd surprise you."

"You succeeded," she said dryly. "And how did they ride?"

"If they keep at it, I think Cassie'll have some stiff competition in a few years. They're fearless, those two."

"The Miller courage," his aunt said fondly and they exchanged a quiet smile.

Alex cleared his throat. "So, uh, is Gen out somewhere?"

His aunt gave a tiny laugh. "I was wondering how long it would take you before you asked—about a minute and a half. Yes, she's having an early dinner with Jiri Novak before he heads back to New York."

Alex's smile died as jealousy, sharp as a knife, stabbed him. Aware that his aunt was watching him closely, he carefully schooled his expression. "Really? When did he come out?"

"This afternoon," she replied, crossing the kitchen. Opening the wooden hutch she pulled down a bottle of wine and held it up inquiringly.

"Whiskey, I think," Alex answered.

She carried the bottles over to the counter while Alex got down two glasses and rummaged for the corkscrew. After he'd poured her glass of wine, his aunt chose to resume the conversation. "Jiri's a charming man, I must say," she observed mildly.

Alex downed half his whiskey. "So you met him?"

She nodded. "Yes, when I came back from the Baroque concert at the church. He had the most wonderful news for Gen. She was positively glowing."

Upon hearing that the man Alex considered his rival could make Gen so happy, the knife twisted mercilessly in his gut. Jaw clenched he asked, "So what is this big news?"

With an insouciant wave of her hand, she said, "Oh, I'll let Gen tell you herself." And Alex bit back a growl of frustration. "In the meantime, I have some news of my own." She smiled at him expectantly.

As distracted as he was, thinking about what Jiri could have possibly said to Gen, it was a while before he took the hint. "And that would be?" he asked finally.

"Tilly's daughter has given birth to a little girl, Lucy Catherine. Mother and daughter are both doing fine," she announced happily. "I'm going to Connecticut tomorrow so I can give my baby present in person and see Tilly's new granddaughter. She's reserving a room at the local inn for me."

"How long are you going to be away?"

"A week or so. I have some old friends who live nearby whom I'd like to visit." She took a sip of her wine and set it down on the butcher-block counter. "My only worry is that I'll be leaving Gen alone here. I wouldn't want something to happen to her with only Murphy for company. Intelligent though he is, I don't see him picking up the phone and calling nine-one-one."

Alex spared a passing thought for how alike Gen and his aunt were: both were fiercely independent women who worried more about others than themselves. "That shouldn't be a problem," he replied casually. "I was thinking I'd stay out here while I ironed out the wrinkles of the deal we're negotiating with the software company I.Com. We have a meeting with them next Monday."

"Good." She smiled brightly. "And perhaps by the time I return you'll have used some of that indomitable Miller courage and told the girl how you feel."

Being told that he was basically a chickenshit by his aunt hadn't exactly improved Alex's mood. Especially since on the heels of that remark, she'd said she had to pack a suitcase for her trip to Connecticut and had left the kitchen before Alex could formulate some appropriately righteous retort. His aunt's observation was just a little too close to the mark.

But hell, he thought, jealous and annoyed, how was he supposed to tell Gen how he felt when she was off with Jiri?

Moodily, Alex nursed his whiskey. At least he had one friend, he thought, nudging Murphy's warm, snoring body with his bare foot. After changing into a pair of jeans he'd gone over to the studio. As he opened the door, Murphy had leapt out, dancing with happiness, overjoyed that Alex had sprung him from the confines of the studio. Deciding that such unswerving canine loyalty deserved a reward, he'd made them both steak sandwiches and poured himself another whiskey. Then they'd come out here, to sit on the front stoop and await Gen's return.

He heard the tinny cough of the Yugo coming up the driveway even before its lights penetrated through the dense foliage bordering the driveway. Murphy, recognizing the sound, jumped up, but Alex grabbed his collar before he could rush out in front of the approaching car.

Alex sat, tension coiled like a spring within him, and waited.

Gen's reaction eased some of the jealousy gnawing at him. She didn't even bother to park. The moment the headlights picked up the gleaming silver of his car, she slammed on the brakes. The engine was still dying a loud death when the door flew open and Gen scrambled out and started running toward the house.

He stood as she rushed toward him. "Alex," she breathed, ignoring Murphy's tail-wagging presence. He caught a glimpse of the gold-flecked sparkle of excitement in her hazel eyes and then she was launching herself at him, laughing as she flung her arms about his neck. He hauled her close, feeling whole once more as her supple body molded itself against his length. Her touch unleashed a maelstrom of desire in him. His mouth seized hers, kissing her ravenously. His hands swept down and grabbed the backs of her thighs, lifting her off her feet. Unhesitatingly, she wrapped her legs about his hips, and the feel of her open and warm and pressing against his erection had him groaning low in his throat. Holding Gen tight, his plundering mouth never leaving hers, Alex carried her to the studio.

It was only when they'd crossed the threshold that Gen tore her mouth from his. "Wait," she panted, squirming in his arms. Unwillingly Alex let her slide to her feet. "You've got to close your eyes," she said in a breathless voice.

Even as he obeyed, his brows drew together, disliking the coolness of the air as her body moved away from his. His remaining senses heightened, he heard the snap and rustle of fabric and then the sound of her footsteps again. Suddenly he caught the tantalizing, flowery fragrance of her scent as she drew near. His nostrils flared; he breathed deeply and shuddered as her lips lightly touched his.

"It's all right. You can open them now," she whispered against his mouth.

Curious, he did so, and saw that the Indian-print bedspread she used on the futon was now draped over the canvas, hiding it. "It's almost finished," she explained in answer to his silent query. "But I'd like to wait and show it to you then."

"So what'll you show me now?" he asked, his voice low and intense. The need to possess pounding with each beat of his heart.

Their eyes locked.

"How about this?" she murmured. Lifting the hem of her cotton shirt she pulled it up and over her head and tossed it on the floor. His mouth went dry as he watched her breasts rise and fall to the rhythm of her ragged breathing, her nipples tight, straining points against the thin cotton of her bra.

"That's a nice start. Go on."

Her eyes widened at the husky command. Then with a coy smile, she opened the front clasp and let the bra fall open. "Mmm, even nicer," he whispered, fisting his hands at his sides so he wouldn't reach for her . . . not yet, at least. "Got anything else to show me?"

Fire shot through his veins when her tongue swept over the lush curve of her upper lip. "I've been saving the best for last." Sweat trickled, pooling at the small of his back as she worked the buttons of her jeans. Baggy as they were, they slid unimpeded down her narrow hips and long slender legs. She stepped out of them and kicked them aside.

His heart thundering, Alex fixed his eyes on her panties. He took a step forward, backing her up against the wall. "Take 'em off," he growled softly.

She gave the tiniest shake of her head. "I was hoping you might like to do it for me. Would you?" she asked.

Gen's smile, as beguiling as a siren's, annihilated the last vestiges of his control. He dropped to his knees before her, his hands reaching and dragging the pink cotton down, then racing up her silken limbs to hold her quivering body as his mouth found her. She was wet and slick and exotically delicious. Greedily his tongue licked and probed and plundered even as she came, convulsing, her hands fisting in his hair, her cry of "Alex" echoing in the room. Nearly crazed with need for her, he rose, tearing at the front of his jeans. Reaching for her, he lifted her, pinning her to the wall. Helpless whimpers fell from her lips as he wrapped her slender legs around him, positioning the blunt tip of his straining shaft at her slick entrance. Capturing her lips, he drove his body deep into hers. Sheathed to the hilt, he knew at last he was home.

It wasn't until much later, hours, in fact, that Gen recovered enough breath to speak. Alex had been relentless. Wonderfully so. He'd made love to her again and again, as if he were claiming her body and her soul. Helpless to do otherwise, she'd given them freely, along with her heart.

Lying with her body draped over his, she lifted her head from his chest and gazed at his face. He looked sleepy and sated and simply wonderful. "Hi," she said.

His lips twitched. "Hi, yourself."

"I guess you missed me."

"Mmm," he said, his fingers lazily tracing the length of her spine. "I guess you could say that. 'Course, from that very fine welcome you gave me, I'd say the feeling was mutual."

"Mmm, I guess you could say that," she parroted, receiving a pinch on her butt for her efforts. "Ow!"

she protested, laughing as she swatted his hand and missed. "You should treat artists on the brink of international recognition with more respect."

"What?" He shifted, pulling himself and her farther up the pillows, so they were half reclining. "What's this about international recognition?" he asked.

Excitement energizing her, she sat up, tucking her legs beneath her as she faced him. "That's right," she said, and her face split into an ear-to-ear grin. "I, Genevieve Monaghan, am going to have my paintings exhibited at the National Museum in Prague, so please handle with care." A delirious giggle burst from her. "Can you believe it, Alex? The museum is doing a retrospective of Jiri's work—and they want to devote part of the show to other artists he's influenced. He came out on the Jitney today to tell me about it. Apparently mine was the first name he suggested. I, Genevieve Monaghan, am going to be gracing the walls of the National Museum in Praha," she crowed, leaning forward to kiss him smack on the lips, laughing when his arms encircled her and tipped her back onto his chest.

"That's pretty damned fantastic," Alex said as he hugged her close.

"Damned right it is," she whispered in his ear, so happy to be sharing this moment with him. Playfully she nipped his lobe and smiled as he shivered beneath her. Sitting up, she straddled his hips, her hands idly stroking the contours of his tanned chest as she continued. "Jiri said the curator, Tomas Kucera, is coming to New York next week and will be contacting me. Alex, I showed Jiri a transparency of *Day One*.

He really liked it. He was wondering whether you'd consider lending it to the exhibit—if the museum people like it too, that is."

"Is that all Jiri wanted?" he asked.

Startled, she glanced at his face. His gaze was intense and unwavering.

"Ah, so Novak would like more than just paint and canvas to come to Prague," Alex said softly.

Gen felt her cheeks flush uncomfortably. "It's nothing. Jiri's just fixated on the idea that I go and work in Prague with him—he'd regret it five minutes after I'd moved in," she added hastily.

"And what did you say to his idea?" he asked, ignoring her disclaimer.

She bit her lip. How should she answer Alex without making him believe that she was already planning their future together? What if he wasn't ready for that kind of commitment. "I told him I was touched."

"Wrong answer," he said flatly. "You should have told him you'd fallen madly in love with me and that there was no damned way you were going to Prague. That there was no damned way I'd let you go," he added fiercely.

His words were so close to what she'd said to Jiri, to what she hoped in her heart, that Gen gaped in stunned surprise. "Is that right?" she asked, trying to sound cool as her heart leapt wildly inside her.

"Damn right," he replied. Without warning, he flipped her over so she lay pinned beneath his solid, muscular length. His hands skimmed up from her waist to cup her breasts possessively. She was sure he could feel her heart racing against his palm as he fondled her, his fingers teasing the tight, aching buds of her nipples. With a soft moan, she arched her back. His eyes, inches away, burned like blue flames as he said, "Next time Jiri asks, tell him I'll lend the painting. But I get the flesh-and-blood woman. You are *mine*, Gen."

And then he set out to prove it all over again.

TWENTY-SIX

Alex and Gen spent the week indulging in the solitude Mrs. Miller's departure provided. They had the house to themselves. They had all the company they desired—each other. They wanted for nothing more. The days were loosely structured, and while the patterns shifted, the elements remained the same: they ate, they worked, they slept, and they loved. It was a perfect week and Gen had never been happier.

It was a week of learning, of joyful discovery.

With each day spent laughing and sharing, with each night spent lying in the magic circle of Alex's embrace, Gen grew more certain of Alex's love for her. In turn, her faith and confidence in her love for Alex gave Gen the strength to conquer the last remaining demons of doubt. Gen banished the specter of Sydney and the pall she'd cast over their relationship.

Emboldened and energized by her newfound courage, Gen rushed to finish the painting for the hospital. She needed to show Alex what he meant to her, and in Gen's mind, her art spoke more expressively what she felt than any hackneyed or clichéd words of love.

Whenever Alex was in the house, teleconferencing with his partners as they fine-tuned the business strategy for I.Com, the software company they were negotiating with, Gen would remove the cotton spread that still hung over the painting. She would work, pouring the love that welled inside onto the canvas.

From the curious looks Alex gave her after these stolen sessions Gen knew that he'd guessed her secret activity. Yet as always he respected her artistic wishes and refrained from asking to see how the painting was progressing; his restraint filled her with gratitude.

At last on Friday, a day when the sky was cloudless and the sunlight streamed in through the windows, Gen stepped back from the canvas and laid her brush down on the palette. Silently she contemplated the finished scene, imagining how it would look in the soaring space of the hospital wing.

Her stomach fluttering with nerves, she went in search of Alex.

He was in the study, seated behind the large oak desk, his attention focused on the computer screen before him. From the speakerphone Gen heard the voice of one of his associates. Not wishing to interrupt, she paused outside the doorway and gave herself over to the sheer pleasure of looking at him. Dressed in a white T-shirt that accented the bronze of his tan and the blond lights in his hair, Alex resembled a movie star far more than he did a financial wizard.

Then Alex reached out and pressed the button on the phone's console. "The restructuring plan sounds airtight, Mike. Cathy, can you fax me everything we've discussed? Great. Glenn, if either you or Mike need to get in touch with me over the weekend, I'll be here. Otherwise we'll meet at nine Monday morning. Okay, thanks, guys. See you." Pressing another button, he cut the connection and then stretched, rolling his shoulders. He stopped in midroll, as he caught sight of Gen hovering by the door. The smile that lit his face stole Gen's breath away.

"Hey there, beautiful," he said huskily. "Come here."

Nervous now that the moment had arrived to show him the painting, she stepped hesitantly into the office. She kept her hands behind her back as she approached Alex's desk, hiding the gauzy silk scarf she'd dug out of her closet.

"Have you finished your work?"

"I'm all yours." He nodded as boldly his eyes traveled over her body. From their scorching heat she could have been wearing a five-hundred-dollar transparent negligee, rather than a faded olive-green T-shirt and cutoffs.

"I'm glad." She smiled softly. "I have something I want to show you."

"Yeah?"

She nodded. "But you need to close your eyes first."

Alex's eyebrow cocked. "This is getting to be a very intriguing habit with you," he murmured. "One that definitely arouses the, uh, interest." The deep timbre of his voice told Gen that wasn't the only thing she'd aroused.

Gen did her best to ignore the quickening of her pulse. Nervous as she was, she wanted Alex to see the painting first. Afterward she could give him her body as well. She brought the scarf out from behind her back and dangled it from her fingertips. "Please, Alex?" she said, wanting the painting to be the first thing he saw when his eyes opened.

Time became suspended as he regarded her, his blue gaze probing. Then, with a smile both tender and amused, he shook his head and obediently closed his eyes.

Slipping around to the back of his chair, Gen wrapped the scarf around his head. Then, tugging a laughing, blindfolded Alex, who slowed their progress considerably by demanding a kiss every few feet, she led him through the house, across the lawn, and into the studio.

Positioning Alex in front of the painting so that when he opened his eyes the entire canvas would be within his field of vision, Gen stepped behind him. He stilled beneath her trembling fingers as she unknotted the scarf.

In a voice that shook with the force of her emotions she whispered, "This is for you, Alex." She stepped backward, pulling the scarf with her.

Alex had already intuited from the fine tension emanating from Gen that at last she was going to unveil her painting for the hospital wing. With his heart thudding heavily, he slowly opened his eyes. And beheld an image of himself he'd never caught in any mirror, his laughing expression tender and filled with the joy of the moment.

The scene Gen had depicted was instantly recognizable. It was the day when he and the twins had set out to build the biggest sand castle they could. There in the foreground, the castle rose, a tall and fantastic monument to the twins' unflagging enthusiasm. Sophie and Jamie stood next to Alex's kneeling self, pointing and exclaiming at their finished creation, pride and happiness shining in their faces.

With an innate sense of what would capture the imagination of the children coming to the hospital, Gen had rendered the castle meticulously. The moat, the high crenellated walls, the towers that stood at each of its corners, the seashells and branches the twins had chosen to decorate the fantastic structure— all the details were there. Even the texture was right, Alex thought in silent awe, wondering what Gen had mixed into the acrylic paint to mimic so perfectly the gritty texture of sand.

He knew that the visitors and patients who entered the hospital wing would stop just to gaze at Gen's painting. He knew that they would smile, gladdened by the precious beauty of a brilliant summer day in which two golden-haired children and a man shared a special moment together. They would look at the oceanscape Gen had painted for the background and be dazzled by the light that bounced off the incoming waves, their white frothy caps rendered with quick, daring flicks of Gen's paintbrush. They would gaze at the painting and behold a masterful symphony of colors and textures. And their hearts would be lifted by this vision of beauty, joy, and hope.

But for Alex, Gen's painting represented an even greater gift.

He turned to her. She'd been watching him, an aching vulnerability in the depths of her lovely eyes. As if she were as delicate as a flower, his hands reached out to cup her face. "You knew about Tom and Lisa," he whispered shakily.

"Yes." Her voice was hushed and solemn. "Your aunt showed me an album."

His shoulders rose as he drew in a long, ragged breath. "It still hurts, Gen," he admitted quietly. "Losing my father and Tom and Lisa so senselessly devastated Cassie and me. Tom and Lisa were just starting their lives together—Sophie and Jamie were only babies. Donating the hospital wing was my way of keeping Tom and Lisa's spirit alive and something I could give to Jamie and Sophie, too. Tom and Lisa would have been wonderful parents, Gen. They'd have loved watching Sophie and Jamie build their sand castles. They would have loved this painting." His throat tight with emotion, he swallowed, managing only a fierce whisper as he continued. "As for me, I can only say that I love this painting almost as much as I love you—" At Gen's sudden sob, Alex broke off. "Ah, sweetheart, *don't*. Don't cry," he pleaded as with infinite gentleness his fingertips caught the tears falling from her eyes.

"I can't help it. I'm so happy it hurts. I've never felt this way before," she whispered, smiling tremulously through her tears.

"Me neither. I never thought this would happen. You've changed my life, Gen." Wrapping his arms about her, he pulled her close and lowered his mouth, kissing her deeply. Then he was lifting her in his arms and carrying her to the bed and following her down. They made love to each other with hushed whispers and caresses that lingered, drawing broken moans and shattered sighs as their two selves became one.

Sunday arrived and with it the reality of the outside world began to filter into Alex and Gen's idyllic seclusion, suffusing the remaining hours with a bittersweet poignancy. In the afternoon they went for a walk on the beach. Murphy ran before them, sniffing at the intriguing scents, and in his bid to keep the beach pristine, devouring any picnic remains he happened upon. The hour was late enough that only a few straggling families and couples remained, and even they had begun gathering up their beach towels and folding their umbrellas before making the trek through the sand to their parked cars.

To Alex the sight was a forcible reminder of his own impending return to the city. Unconsciously his hand squeezed Gen's. "Damn, I wish I didn't have to go tomorrow. I hate the thought of being away from you. You sure you can't come with me? You could meet Jiri and this Kucera guy in New York while we negotiate with I.Com. I could duck out of the dinner with them—Glenn and Mike can do the honors—and you and I could go out. La Grenouille, maybe. You'd love the flower arrangements they do there, Gen. We'd have a nice meal, drink some champagne, and then go to my place, where you could have your wicked way with me."

"*My* wicked way with you? This from the man who did things to me in his Aston not even the producers of those James Bond movies would dare?"

"Only because they wouldn't have been able to fit a camera in that tight a space," he replied with a modest grin that had Gen laughing and poking him in the ribs. For a moment, they tussled in the surf, as carefree as children. Finally, breathless, flushed, and considerably the wetter for her wrestling match with Alex, Gen cried, "Uncle!" Slipping her hand back in his as they continued their stroll, she said, serious at last, "All that sounds lovely. But Alex, I know how hard you've worked setting up the I.Com deal. You should definitely go out and celebrate with them and your partners afterward. Besides, I can't—Jiri must have raved about the paintings I've done here, on Long Island. Kucera wants to see them. And Jiri says it's better to make Kucera come to *me,* that it's an important part of the curator-artist courtship dynamic."

Alex's jaw tightened. "Funny he should use the term 'courtship.' Tell me why he needs to accompany Kucera again?"

Gen cast him a sidelong glance and shook her head. "Because Kucera's English is a little spotty. Jiri's going to act as translator. And because he'll be going back to Prague this week and he wants to say good-bye."

Good-bye and good riddance, thought Alex, thoroughly sick of hearing Jiri's name. It was probably for the best that he wasn't going to be around when the Czech showed up tomorrow, because he wasn't sure he'd be able to conduct himself in a civilized manner. While he knew it was ridiculous and totally irrational to harbor any further jealousy toward Jiri, he still had an unshakable urge to plant his fist in Novak's face. And although he wanted Gen in New York with him, having her stay here would allow Alex to keep his surprise for her a complete secret.

Alex had made a private appointment Tuesday morning at Harry Winston, the Fifth Avenue jeweler. The little bit of string he'd used to measure Gen's ring size while she was fast asleep was tucked inside his wallet. He couldn't wait to see the look in her eyes when he slipped the engagement ring on her finger. After he'd proposed, that's when they'd really celebrate. His body hardened at the thought of making love to her, and knowing she was going to be his forever. So when Gen, with a pensive frown on her face, turned to him and asked, "Alex, you're not really bothered by Jiri coming out tomorrow, are you?" he was able to smile and say, "No, not as long as Jiri restricts this so-called 'courtship' to art."

Not even the heavy rain slashing at the windowpanes could dampen Gen's spirits Tuesday morning. Why care about a little rain when a museum curator had said he'd like four—count 'em, four—of her paintings for a major exhibit next year? How could a few measly drops from heaven steal her euphoria when the man she loved was coming home in a few short hours?

Happily ignoring the staccato beat of the rain drumming down, Gen sat at the kitchen table writing a shopping list for the dinner she was planning. Before leaving on Monday, Alex had mentioned going out to dinner to celebrate her meeting with Tomas Kucera. But Gen much preferred the idea of eating in, tête-à-tête. They didn't have to go to a fancy restaurant. She'd cook him a meal that would knock his socks off—the rest of his clothing she'd remove herself, she thought, giddy with anticipation.

Her pen poised in midair, she reread the list. Oh, yes, she should buy some more Belgian chocolate for Mrs. Miller's morning cocoa, as Alex's aunt was returning home Thursday. Gen smiled, realizing how much she was looking forward to the ritual of preparing Mrs. Miller's distinctive breakfast tray. Laying down the pen, she was in the midst of pushing back her chair to check and see whether there were enough eggs in the refrigerator when the doorbell rang. Murphy, who'd been dozing underneath the table, awoke barking.

It must be one of Mrs. Miller's friends coming to pay a call, that or a deliveryman with a package. In either case Murphy would be better off in the kitchen, Gen thought. She closed the swinging door behind her, ignoring his whine of protest.

At the front door, she instinctively peeked through the rectangular glass, but all she could see was a figure huddled against the driving rain. Not very threatening-looking, she decided. Pulling open the door, her welcoming smile died as her mouth fell open in surprise. "Sydney!" she exclaimed.

At Gen's voice, Sydney lifted her bowed head. Swiping her face with the back of her hand, she said, "Hi, Gen. Is Alex here?"

"No, no, he isn't," Gen stammered, staring at her in dismay. Sydney's face was awash not from the rain but with tears. She looked exhausted, her red-rimmed eyes testimony to hours of crying. Realizing belatedly that she was making her stand in the downpour, Gen said hastily, "Come in," opening the door wider.

Sydney stepped inside, only to turn and face Gen. She was already talking—indeed, her whole body vibrated with a horrible urgency. "I called Cathy, asking where Alex was. She said he'd be here."

"Cathy?" Gen echoed blankly.

"Alex's secretary," Sydney said impatiently. "I called his office assuming he'd be there. But Cathy told me he was coming out here. I drove all the way in the pouring rain and I really need to speak to him!" she cried, and a violent shiver wracked her body.

Sydney's patent desperation was beginning to affect Gen, too. A terrible sense of foreboding settled in the pit of her stomach. "I'm afraid he had an errand to run before he left. I'm not sure how long it was supposed to take—but I imagine he's on the road by now. You could try him on his cell."

"No." Sydney shook her head. "No, it's not something I can tell him on the phone. I need to talk to him. With the weather like this, and the traffic ghastly, it's going to take him *hours* to get here," she wailed and then pressed a trembling hand to her lips.

Whatever had happened to Sydney, it was bad, thought Gen. Really bad. She looked even more distraught than she'd been that day on the beach. She looked as if she was about to fall apart completely.

Laying a tentative hand on her arm, Gen said, "Sydney, what's the matter, what's wrong?"

Perhaps it was the sympathetic touch of another human, perhaps it was the obvious concern in Gen's voice. But the tenuous control Sydney had over herself crumbled. "I'm pregnant!" she blurted out, promptly dissolving into tears.

The room, the entire world, spun crazily, leaving Gen reeling. Her hand tightened, clutching Sydney's arm. "Pregnant?" she whispered dazedly.

"Yes. *Pregnant*. I don't know how it happened." Agitated, Sydney began to pace and her words tumbled out, tripping over one another in a chaotic, panicked rush. "I've never been so damned terrified—and so incredibly happy at the same time. I keep thinking of us having a baby together and I can't imagine a better father. He'll be so patient and generous. But the timing, the timing is terrible. I'm afraid he won't be ready. I'm not sure *I'm* ready. But Alex, I think he actually knew, at least on some subconscious level—at the party he told me I was looking so beautiful, that I was glowing. He was like the old Alex—I, I just can't keep this to myself any longer. I've been trying to screw up my courage—that's why I came here. . . ." Her shoulders shook as she succumbed to tears once more.

In spite of the crippling pain tearing through her, Gen managed, "Yes—yes. Of course you need to talk to Alex. Listen, Sydney, you can stay and wait—he should be here in a few hours."

"No," Sydney said tightly. Wiping her tears roughly with the back of her hand, she drew in a shuddering breath. "No, I can't stay that long. Harry would start to worry that I'd had an accident or something. I guess the thing to do is to come back later."

"Sure," Gen said dully, hardly listening anymore . . . as only one word Sydney had uttered truly mattered. "Alex will be here by then." With the stiff unnaturalness of a robot, she opened the door. As Sydney stepped forward, Gen looked at her. "Sydney, I'm—I'm really happy for you. A baby, it's a wonderful thing."

Sydney's mouth curved in a trembling smile and for a second her teary eyes shone with a luminous happiness. "I know," she whispered. "I just hope he'll know it, too." Drawing the collar of her trench coat up, she slipped around the door and hurried through the rain to her car.

Gen stood staring until the BMW disappeared down the drive. Shutting the door, she leaned against it. How strange it was to feel the solidity of the wood behind her when her world had just fallen apart.

Sydney, pregnant with Alex's child, oh, God, oh, God. The pain lashed at her in tempo with the words drumming in her head.

Alex was going to be a father. Tears began slipping from her eyes. He'd be wonderful. She'd seen what he was like with Sophie and Jamie: his endless patience and humor, the love that radiated from his eyes when he looked at them, the aching tenderness stamped on his face when he enveloped their small bodies in a hug. And he cared for Sydney, and Sydney in turn would fit so perfectly in his life. With a child to bind them they had a chance at finding happiness together. . . . They'd be a family.

But you love him! a voice screamed in protest. Yes, she loved Alex desperately. And that was why she was going to let him go. Because Gen loved him, she wouldn't put him in the position of choosing between staying with her and being with his child. Alex deserved to share every joyful moment—as well as the passing sorrows—that came with raising a child. In turn, the child growing inside Sydney's womb deserved to have a father who would be there for him. Gen knew she would end up hating herself if she were to come between Alex and his child.

And he loves you, the horrible voice continued relentlessly, the words like acid on her lacerated heart. Yes, Alex loved her. This last week he'd revealed the depth of his love for her in so many ways. He loved her so much he might even choose to stay with her, leaving Sydney to raise the child on her own. Gen couldn't let that happen.

Oh, God, she would have to leave, leave this beautiful place that over the past weeks she'd come to think of as home, leave without saying good-bye to Mrs. Miller, the woman who'd generously opened her house to Gen and shown her nothing but kindness. Just imagining what Mrs. Miller would think of such callous rudeness had Gen pressing her fist to her mouth and biting her knuckles hard, fighting pain with pain.

But there was no other way. Mrs. Miller wasn't due back until Thursday and Gen needed to be long gone by the time Sydney returned to tell Alex she was pregnant. A part of her wanted to run now, this very minute, grab Murphy and drive off. That wouldn't work, however. Alex was the sort of man who'd come after her, demanding an explanation. Which meant that she'd have to stay and face him and make sure that when she left, he would never want her back. She would have to hurt him.

Oh, God, she thought, and clamped her arm against her stomach as a wave of nausea ripped through her. Could she do it? Could she be that selfless? That cruel? Could she actually bring herself to hurt Alex and destroy his feelings for her? Could she willfully destroy Alex's love, what had become the most important thing in the world to her, so that he would be free to go to Sydney?

It was the only way. Her eyes squeezed shut, the agony enough to make her want to curl up on the floor and die. Instead she made herself stand away from the door. She couldn't succumb to the pain yet. Not when she had only a couple of hours to pack everything in the studio. And in that short time fabricate a story cruel enough to make Alex despise her.

Alex had told her she was a terrible liar so many times.

He was right. She was lousy at deception. But today she was going to rival the most talented of actresses. She was going to lie and desecrate something incredibly beautiful, something infinitely precious.

And she would be damned for the rest of her life.

It had taken longer than Alex had thought to find a diamond that came close to matching the beauty of

Gen's eyes. Luckily by the time he left the city, the rain had tapered off, so the rush hour traffic hadn't been more hellish than usual. He kept the Aston to a sedate-old-lady-on-a-Sunday-drive-after-church speed, his palms too sweaty with nerves to risk speeding. To calm himself he practiced his proposal to Gen.

He negotiated the rain-filled ruts as he drove up the dirt driveway to the house. Then he saw Gen's car and his brows drew together in perplexed surprise. She'd backed the car as close to the studio as possible.

He parked the Aston and got out, almost forgetting to grab the bouquet of wildflowers he'd bought at the roadside farm stand outside of Bridgehampton, which was lying on the front passenger seat. Flowers in hand he started walking toward the Yugo, his frown deepening as he neared it. The tiny car's interior was crammed with cardboard boxes. Then he spied one of her milk crates. Resting on top of one of the piles of boxes, the crate was stuffed with Gen's paintbrushes, her palette knives, the heavy-duty staple gun, and some rolls of masking tape.

What was going on? he wondered as he strode toward the studio, his jaw clenching as he tried to come up with a rational explanation for why all of Gen's worldly belongings were packed into her car.

The sight of Murphy, his mouth open in a huge canine grin, tearing out of the open studio door and galloping straight for him, momentarily eased the tension within him. Holding the flowers out of harm's way, Alex gave Murphy a distracted pat on the head, and walked inside.

A single sweeping glance was all he required.

The studio was bare of everything except for the furniture his aunt had moved into it for Gen's comfort. . . . Except for the painting she'd made for the hospital, its colors glowing even more vibrantly in the barren space.

She was standing by the futon stripping the sheets off. And though she must have known he was there, heard his and Murphy's approach, she didn't look over, merely continued with her quick, jerky movements, yanking the pillows out of their cases, and then folding the cases into quarters before dropping them on the other linens by her feet. That Gen ignored him, continued to fold the damned linens instead of flying into his arms, told Alex more than anything else—more than her car loaded with all her stuff, more than the jarring emptiness of the studio— that something was terribly wrong.

His voice held a sharpness born of fear. "What are you doing, Gen?" he asked.

She turned, her fingers gripping the last of the cases, holding it in front of her like a shield. "Oh, hi, you're back," she said, stating the obvious.

"Yeah. What are you doing, Gen?" he repeated, regarding her closely. "What's with all the stuff in your car?"

"Oh, that." A bright flush stole over her face. "Sorry," she grimaced. "That must have been something of a shock. I wish I had more time and could break this to you gently but I have to get to the city. Jiri's—"

"Break what to me? What's this all about?" he asked, crossing the studio to her. At his approach Gen stiffened, holding herself rigid. "What's happened? What's wrong, Gen?" he demanded, his voice quiet despite the tension mounting inside him and the strain he could practically feel vibrating off her.

Her gaze dropped to her hands fisted around the rumpled pillowcase. For a second she was silent. Then, with a shaky laugh she raised her head, not quite meeting his gaze. "Gosh, this is much harder than I imagined it would be. I guess the only way to put it is that yesterday I discovered that Jiri has certain qualities I never imagined. He stayed with me last night and was, um, wonderfully persuasive in making his case that I go with him to Prague." Her eyes strayed to the unmade futon bed and a vivid blush stained her cheeks. Seeing it, Alex felt the breath fly out of him as if he'd been kicked in the gut. Pain reverberated through him. As from a distance he heard himself say, "You slept with Jiri?"

Gen shrugged. "As I said, he was wonderfully persuasive. We, uh, really clicked. Anyway, I've reconsidered Jiri's proposal and I've agreed to go to Prague with him. With the painting for the hospital finished, it's a good time to move on. Jiri's bought an apartment with plenty of room for the two of us and Murphy too. I'm heading to New York now to meet—"

"How could you have slept with him?" he interrupted harshly. "What about us?"

"Us?" she echoed, frowning. "Oh, you mean the sex. Well, that was nice. No, actually, it was quite incredible. Quite an eye-opening experience," she added as she casually began folding the pillowcase in half. "But then again Jiri is so spectacularly creative.

No," she said, with a hard shake of her head. "There was never an 'us'—I realized that last night—thank God. What Jiri and I have goes much deeper than a summer fling. I've known him for years, we share the same passions—"

A cold fury erupted in Alex. His hands reached out to grab her, to shake her and damn her not only for betraying him with another man but for talking glibly about passion when he'd been about to lay his heart and happiness before her and ask her to marry him. But as he raised his hands he belatedly realized that he still clutched the wildflowers he'd bought for her. Stupidly he held them there, as if in offering, feeling like some pathetic fool.

For what seemed an eternity she stared at the bouquet. Then with a tight, artificial smile she said, "How pretty. But under the circumstances, maybe you should give them to your aunt. My car just can't fit another thing." Dropping the pillowcase she checked her watch. "It's getting late. I really have to go. Jiri—"

"You bitch," he said flatly. "I thought I loved you. Now I'm sorry I ever laid eyes on you. Get the hell out of here."

Alex kept his gaze averted, refusing to look at Gen as she brushed past hurriedly. Hurrying, damn her deceitful soul, into Jiri's waiting arms. In the awful silence, he heard her strangled whisper to Murphy, the scrabble of nails on concrete, and the quick fall of her steps as they left the studio. From the immediate rattle of the Yugo starting, he knew she must have run to the car. Just couldn't flee fast enough, could she?

Alone, Alex stood trembling with the need to lash

out, break, and destroy every last remaining object in the studio. But no damage he wreaked could ever match what Gen had accomplished with such cold and lethal efficiency. Without breaking a sweat, she'd played him for a fool and then left him with a shattered heart.

With a few choice words Gen had shown him that the love he'd thought was theirs was in reality nothing but a cheap illusion. Alex remembered how weeks ago he'd been sure that love just wasn't in the picture for him. It looked as though he'd been right after all.

Alex dropped the mangled flowers on the floor and walked out of the empty studio.

TWENTY-SEVEN

With a short, lethal chop of his forearm, Alex's racquet sent the black ball speeding like a bullet into the corner. Next to him, Sam Brody lunged, stretching out his racquet for a return, and missed the ball by a fraction of an inch. "Game and match," he panted, adding on his next breath, "Son of a bitch."

Alex ignored Sam's curse, as he'd been ignoring many things these past weeks. By sheer force of will he'd buried the pain of Gen's betrayal and then walled it off. He didn't particularly care that he went through his day-to-day life with all the emotions of a cyborg. He was doing whatever it took to survive. The nights, however, were pure torture. That was when exhaustion overtook him, and his defenses crumbled. The memories of Gen he'd thought were successfully buried would rise up. . . .

Alex started, abruptly realizing that Sam was speaking. "Sorry, Sam, what was that?"

Sam shook his head and passed Alex a water bottle. "As I seem to be a glutton for punishment, I was of-

fering myself up as a sacrifice. I'm free tomorrow for
another match."

"You think you'll have recovered by then?"

Sam laughed. "Very funny, Miller. Hell, thanks to
you I'm in peak aerobic condition. It's only my ego
that's bruised. What's it been, six weeks? And I've
won seven games off you?"

"Five games," Alex corrected, disregarding Sam's
veiled reference to the number of weeks that had
passed since Gen walked out of his life, leaving him
standing in the studio, his heart torn and bleeding.

"Right, five games. Like I said, it's only my ego. So,
you free?"

"I'll check my schedule with Cathy when I get back
to the office."

"And how about this weekend? Any plans? You
heading out to see the Duchess?"

In the midst of raising his water bottle to his mouth,
Alex froze. "No, I can't see Aunt Grace this weekend.
I'm busy."

"She misses you, Alex. She's hurting, too."

Alex flinched inwardly at Sam's quiet observation.
He'd tried, damn it. His last visit to Aunt Grace had
lasted a full three hours. One hour had been taken up
supervising the movers as they wrapped and crated
Gen's painting to transport it to the hospital. Hating
that he'd been duped into believing the emotion Gen
put in her art was real, when in fact it was the cruelest
of illusions, he'd been unable to look at the painting.
Instead he'd paced the totally empty studio—his aunt
having removed the last of the furniture—like a caged
animal, desperate to be free.

Once the movers had gone, he'd spent two hours in his aunt's house, seeing Gen wherever he looked. From the sad, knowing light in Aunt Grace's pale eyes, Alex knew she'd guessed he was lying through his teeth when he told her that unfortunately he couldn't stay any longer. There was a weekend house party in Montauk to which he'd been invited. No, he couldn't go back to East Hampton, not even for Aunt Grace.

"Tilly's there with her," he said, walking toward the door to the squash court. "I'll go out and visit when things quiet down."

"Alex, don't do this, man. For God's sake, hop on the next plane to Prague—"

Alex spun around. His voice low and lethal, he said, "If you value our friendship, you won't finish that sentence, Sam."

Sam looked at him in silence. "Sure, Alex. Whatever you say."

Turning his back on Sam and the pity he'd read in his eyes, Alex pulled open the door. "I'll call and let you know whether I'm free to whip your ass in squash again tomorrow. I'll see you later. I'm going to the weight room to lift."

As the door swung shut behind him, he heard Sam curse low and viciously.

Alex had regained his icy indifference by the time he made the ten-block walk from the New York Athletic Club to his office on Park Avenue. His secretary, Cathy, looked up from her computer screen and smiled as he entered the reception area.

"Hey, Cathy, here's your lunch." He held up the

white paper bag and jiggled it. "Chicken Caesar salad, hold the croutons, and an unsweetened iced tea with lemon, right?"

"I've got to have the world's best boss," she said admiringly. "Not only does he deliver, he gets the order right."

"That's me, a mind like a steel trap. Any messages?"

"Dr. Williams from the Children's Hospital. He was asking about the dedication ceremony."

Alex opened his mouth to tell her to call Sydney and let her field the doctor's questions, but then remembered that Sydney and Harry were still in Tuscany. They wouldn't be back from their month-long honeymoon until next week. With a terse nod he said, "Call him, will you, please? Oh, and can you check my schedule for tomorrow?"

"Sure. Would you like me to fix you a cup of coffee?"

"No, thanks, Cathy. I'm good."

Alex had just sat down behind his desk when the intercom buzzed. "Yes?"

"I have Dr. Williams on the line."

"Great, put him through."

"Hello?"

"Hello, Dr. Williams. This is Alex Miller returning your call."

"Oh, yes! Thank you for calling so promptly, Mr. Miller," Dr. Williams said. Pausing to clear his throat, he continued. "I was reviewing the guest list for the dedication ceremony and I was wondering whether you could tell me if Ms. Monaghan is planning to attend."

Alex squeezed his eyes shut and pinched the bridge of his nose, hard. "No, I'm afraid not."

"Oh!" Dr. Williams exclaimed in dismay. "This is awkward indeed. You see, I'm afraid I had no idea how generous a gift Ms. Monaghan was giving to the hospital when she dropped by yesterday. I was rushing from one meeting to the next and hardly did more than say thank you when she handed me the envelope. Of course, it's highly unusual to be handed that kind of a sum."

"Dr. Williams, are you certain this was Genevieve Monaghan? She's in Prague."

"Oh, I hadn't realized she was leaving the country. I see," he said, his voice heavy with disappointment. For a second there was silence on the line. "Mr. Miller, would you happen to have any way to contact Ms. Monaghan, get in touch with her somehow? Ten thousand dollars deserves a little more than a distracted 'Thank you so very much and good-bye.' " He gave an embarrassed laugh.

Alex's knuckles whitened around the receiver. "She gave the hospital ten thousand dollars?"

"Yes—and we haven't even started our capital campaign for the TLM rehabilitation center. I'm sure you can appreciate how awkward this is. . . ."

Alex wasn't listening. *Ten thousand dollars.* A child could do the math. *Day One* sold for twenty thou. After the gallery lopped off its 50 percent commission, that left ten thousand dollars. Gen had obviously taken every last penny she'd received from the sale of her painting and donated it to the hospital's rehabilitation center.

What the hell kind of game was she playing now?

And what was she doing in Boston, Massachusetts, when she was supposed to be pursuing her passion with Jiri in Prague?

"Dr. Williams, I'll have my secretary get back to you with that information as soon as possible," he interrupted smoothly.

He gave a hearty sigh of relief. "Thank you. I really appreciate—"

"Not at all, good-bye, Dr. Williams." Alex disconnected the line and then immediately dialed Sam's number.

He answered on the first ring. "Brody."

"Sam, it's me. Listen, how quickly can you get me the addresses of all Monaghans living in the Boston area?"

"Fifteen minutes, tops," Sam replied.

"Good. Can you call me with them on my cell? I'm headed for the airport now."

"What's up?"

"She's in Boston—or was, as of yesterday," Alex said, already rising from his chair and grabbing the jacket of his suit.

Sam didn't need to ask who "she" was. "Hell of a long way from Prague," he observed.

"Ain't it, though," Alex said. "What's more, I just found out from the director of the hospital that she basically emptied her bank account and gave it to the rehabilitation center. To the tune of ten thousand bucks."

There was silence as Sam digested that bit of information. "That's a pretty expensive conscience she's got. So I take it you think she's in Boston? What are you going to do when you find her, Alex?"

Alex paused, one arm halfway through the jacket's sleeve. That was a damned good question. "I honestly don't know, Sam," he admitted grimly. "Maybe I'm just a masochistic son of a bitch. Or maybe seeing her one last time is the only way I can really forget her. But something doesn't add up in all of this and I want to know why."

"Good luck," Sam said. "I'll call you with the addresses."

Alex soon learned what it was like to be a telephone solicitor. Sitting in the first-class lounge he systematically made his way through the list of Gen's family members, dialing the numbers Sam had provided. When he wasn't grinding his teeth in frustration at getting yet another answering machine, Gen's brothers and sisters were hanging up the second Alex said his name. Although her brother Kyle, the one who'd tried to decapitate him with a fastball, was a little bit more forthcoming: "I should have followed my instincts and taken you out that day at the picnic, Miller. Stay the hell away from Gen," he growled and then slammed the phone down in Alex's ear.

By the time Alex boarded the plane for Boston, he was steaming mad. What was going on here? They were all acting as if Alex were some kind of pariah who'd hurt Gen. Clearly whatever she'd told her family had been a pack of lies. Well, that was one more topic he'd bring up with Ms. Genevieve Monaghan once he got his hands on her—that is, if he didn't wring her neck first, he thought angrily, in his preoccupation not even realizing that for the first time in weeks, he was actually feeling something.

The taxicab pulled to a stop in front of Bridget's Cafe, a cheerful-looking restaurant with a red-and-white-striped awning, wrought-iron outdoor tables, and geraniums in the window boxes. A few couples were sitting at the outdoor tables, drinking coffee in white porcelain cups and enjoying the late-afternoon sunshine. After striking out at the senior Monaghans' home, leaning on the doorbell until at last he was forced to accept the fact that neither Gen's mother nor father was there, he'd gone through the list of brothers and sisters. Remembering Bridget's infectious exuberance and how close she and Gen seemed, Alex had decided that he'd try her next.

Leaning forward he handed the taxi driver a hundred-dollar bill, roughly three times the fare it had cost to bring him from the Logan Airport to downtown Somerville. "Wait for me," he said.

The driver eyed the bill. "Sure, mister."

Alex walked into the restaurant and guessed at once who'd done the art decorating the walls. He saw too the gaily painted ceramic canisters Gen had made for Bridget's birthday. They were proudly displayed on a shelf overhanging the maître d's station. As he approached, a man in a khaki suit left his stool at the bar. "Good afternoon. I'm sorry but the kitchen's closed right now. We start—"

"That's all right. I'm looking for Bridget."

"She's back in the kitchen. I'll—"

"Don't bother. I'm a friend," Alex said, already striding toward the back of the small restaurant.

As he pushed his way through the swinging doors, Bridget Monaghan looked up from the mound of egg-plants she was dicing. Seeing Alex, she scowled and her lips tightened in a grim line.

"Where is she?" Alex said without preamble.

"I wouldn't tell you if I were drowning and you had a rope. Jesus, you have some nerve, coming here. I should take this knife and cut off your balls for what you did," she hissed, holding the knife up.

"Get in line," he snarled. "You've got about half a dozen other Monaghans before you who want a piece of me. I don't know what kind of story Gen's fed you all, but I didn't do a goddamn thing to her. Why don't you tell me what heinous crime I'm supposedly guilty of," he demanded, pissed at being portrayed as the bad guy when it was Gen who'd ripped his heart to shreds.

He felt a bitter sense of satisfaction when Bridget Monaghan opened her mouth to reply and then snapped it shut. Her gaze dropped to the cutting board. "I don't know what you did," she muttered reluctantly. "Gen won't talk about it. Absolutely refuses— and we've all had a go at her these past weeks. But whatever you did, *boyo,* I can tell you it's made her bloody miserable. She's worrying us sick." She resumed dicing the eggplants with a vengeance.

Alex's brows snapped together. "What the hell do you mean by 'weeks'?" he asked sharply. He put a hand on Bridget's arm, stilling the knife. "How long has Gen been here in Somerville?"

Shrugging off his arm, she glowered at him. "I'd

say it's been about a month and a half that she's been wandering around, looking like death warmed over." She went back to her chopping.

Alex stared at Bridget's bowed auburn head, his heart pounding as if he'd just run a five-minute mile. "So she never went to Prague with Novak?"

She put down the knife. Reaching for the salt, she began liberally sprinkling the eggplants. "Why should she go to Prague?" she asked, frowning at him in patent confusion. Then her brow cleared. "Oh, you mean for the museum show? That's not until next year."

"No, that's not—Listen," he said urgently. "I have to see her, damn it all. You've got to tell me where she is."

Bridget raised her head. They stared at each other in tense silence. With a loud sigh Bridget shook her head. "All right. I'll give it to you—just remember, though, you didn't get this from me. And the only reason I'm giving you her address is that you look as freakin' wretched as she does. But I warn you, if you hurt her any more, I'll come after you—with about ten other Monaghans in tow."

"I don't know what's going on here or why Gen left, but I do know I'd take that knife of yours and slice my veins before I ever willingly hurt her," Alex said quietly.

The knife in question was promptly covered by Bridget's white apron as she leaned across the counter and planted a smacker on Alex's lips. "That day at the picnic?" She grinned. "I knew you were the one for her. Now for heaven's sake, get a move on. Go put the light back in my little sister's eyes."

* * *

Alex gazed grimly out the taxi window, taking in the dilapidated building. "You sure this is 1457 Chestnut?" he asked the driver.

"Yeah—the number's right above the door, see?" the driver said, pointing. "You want me to wait?" he asked eagerly, doubtless anticipating another hundred-dollar bill to add to his collection.

"No, that won't be necessary." Alex didn't know how long this would take. Hell, he wasn't even sure what this visit to Gen's would even accomplish. During the cab ride to what Alex had quickly surmised was one of Somerville's seedier neighborhoods, his initial euphoria at learning that Gen hadn't gone with Jiri Novak to Prague had subsided. The knowledge couldn't soften the cold, hard truth: she'd still walked away from him and from what they'd found together, as if their love meant nothing to her. But that somehow only made it more imperative that he get answers from her, answers to questions that kept piling up. And if Gen had lied to him about Jiri, he damned well wanted to know the reason why. Perhaps, just perhaps this time she'd give him an explanation he could live with.

Gen was sleeping, dreaming as she so often did of Alex. In the dream he was shouting, calling her name. It was awful, the terrible longing that consumed her at hearing his voice. He sounded so near and yet the dream wouldn't let her see his face. Desperate for even a glimpse of him, she unconsciously burrowed into the hollow of her tear-soaked pillow, as if she might delve deeper into her dream and find him. Only to sob aloud in frustration at the feel of Murphy's cold, wet nose poking her ear and then his tongue sweeping her cheek, bathing her urgently.

"No, no, go away. It's not time yet," she mumbled, flinging out her arm to bat him away. Turning her face into the pillow she tried to recapture her dream, the only place where she could be near Alex. His voice came again, but now it was accompanied by a heavy, insistent pounding. What was making that noise? she wondered, squirming in irritation as Murphy continued licking her.

But the dog was obnoxiously persistent. At last, groggy and annoyed, Gen sat up and rubbed her gritty eyes, wondering how long she'd napped. That her fists were damp from her tears came as no surprise—she woke up crying a lot these days. But her hands stilled as Gen finally registered the din coming from outside her apartment.

Somehow she must have conflated her dream of Alex with that cursed banging, she thought, sighing wearily as she swung her legs off the bed and stood. With an inelegant sniff from the summer cold that was sapping what little energy she had, she got up and crossed the small bedroom into the empty adjoining room, her progress hampered by a twirling, barking Murphy.

The pounding was coming from the front door. "All right, already," she yelled irritably as she bumped into Murphy once again. "Hold your horses, I'm coming."

Knowing her brother Kyle would strangle her if she didn't take the necessary precaution, she pressed her eye to the peephole, knowing too that she wouldn't be able to see a darned thing. The dim lighting of the hallway left it permanently shrouded. Double-checking that the security chain Kyle had installed was firmly in place, she unlocked the door and pulled it open a fraction, peeking her head around.

"Hello, Gen."

She stared speechless at the shadowed slice of him. Was it the lighting or were the planes of his face harsher than she remembered? She couldn't tell, her vision blurring as sudden tears welled, as her heart slammed painfully inside her breast. "Alex," she whispered.

"Open the door, Gen," he ordered flatly. "One of your neighbors has already threatened me with the cops and I don't feel like being hauled down to the Somerville jail. But I'm going to keep banging on this door until you let me in."

Gen hesitated. Could she bear having him in the apartment—not that she'd ever had a moment's peace since she'd spewed those awful lies to him. What was he doing here? she wondered. After what she'd done, she should be the last person in the world Alex would seek out.

She got no further in her confused thoughts. Alex, his voice colder by several degrees, said, "Open the damn door, Gen. You owe me that much at least."

Guilt piercing her, Gen went to remove the chain. But her hands trembled so she was unable to slide the chain's keep through the narrow slot. Agonizing seconds passed as she fumbled with it. Finally she freed it. Pressing her lips together to keep them from trembling, she stepped back, pulling the door with her. She was nearly knocked over by Murphy, who rushed into the gap to claim center stage.

Ecstatic, he greeted Alex. Standing to the side Gen watched them, listened to the obvious affection in Alex's voice as he stroked and patted Murphy, well aware she'd just sunk to a new low: she was envious of her dog.

Abruptly Alex's attention shifted and the impact of his blue gaze was like a blow. Afraid he would read the naked longing in her face, she dropped her gaze and stared at the scarred linoleum.

God, she wouldn't even look at him, Alex thought. She hadn't even said hello to him yet, only whispered "Alex" as she stared, her eyes enormous with shock—obviously unpleasant shock. *And you'd been thinking that she'd come flying into your open arms, you arrogant ass,* a voice mocked him. No, he'd only hoped. But here she was staring at that hideous floor like it was a Jackson Pollock. And he couldn't tear his eyes away from her. She was so thin, he thought, his heart constricting painfully. Slender before, now Gen seemed impossibly frail. Worry sharpened his voice. "What's the matter with you? You look terrible." He could have bit his tongue for that brilliant remark. Real suave, Miller, just what every woman wants to hear, he chastised himself, hating when he saw the flush of embarrassment steal up from the collar of her baggy sweatshirt.

"I have a cold," she mumbled to the floor and sniffed. "The medicine makes me woozy, that's all." She shrugged her thin shoulders.

Damn it, why wouldn't she look at him? What had happened to the proud woman who'd told him off in his office months ago? Gen looked like a ghost of her former self. If only she would look at him, meet his eyes. Frustrated, he said, "So, it seems you abandoned your idea of going to Prague. What happened? It didn't work out between you and Jiri?"

Listening to him, Gen tried not to flinch. His voice sounded so hard, she thought miserably. Well, of course it did, he hated her. "No, I guess it didn't. I—we thought better of it. How—when did you find out I was here?"

"Today."

Stunned, Gen's eyes flew to his face then ricocheted away when they collided with Alex's piercing gaze. "Today?" she echoed in disbelief.

"That's right. I got a call in New York from Dr. Williams at the hospital. He sends his many thanks for your very generous gift." He paused and out of the corner of her eye, Gen watched him turn, making a three-hundred-and-sixty-degree inspection of her dingy little apartment. "So you prefer to live here," he said with a sweep of his arm. "Than use my money. Even that repels you," he finished quietly.

"No, I just couldn't take your money, that's all," she whispered, tears clogging her throat. After the wrong she'd done, she'd had to make amends somehow. Giving the ten thousand dollars she'd made from *Day One* to the hospital wing had been the obvious choice.

Oh, God, she couldn't bear it, that Alex believed he repelled her. She wished she could tell him the truth, what really mattered. She loved him and without him it didn't matter where she lived or what she looked like—that ever since she'd driven away from Long Island she'd felt like death walking through the wasteland of her life. She hugged herself, vainly trying to quell the tremors wracking her body and to prevent herself from doing the one thing she most wanted in the world: to throw herself in his arms and beg his forgiveness.

She was trembling like a leaf, Alex thought. He ached with the need to touch her, to pull her into his arms, to hold her and make everything right between them. And yet here they stood, as awkward as strangers, reduced to stilted, meaningless conversation. Was this how it would end? he wondered in despair. God, what had happened to them, to her? Why had she left him to live in this sunless, oppressive pit of an apartment? he thought, casting yet another disdainful glance about the room.

Then abruptly Alex realized what really bothered him: she'd done nothing to the apartment. There were no tables covered with her extraordinary collection of findings. No canvases . . . nothing. "You're not even painting, are you?"

The unexpectedness of his question must have caught her off guard. She looked at him, pain etched in stark lines on her face. "I—" she began. "No, I haven't felt like painting lately." She turned her head, but not before he saw a tear slide down her pale cheek.

Instinctively Alex reached for her, but froze as Gen recoiled, stumbling backward to avoid his touch. The tension radiating from her had his shoulders slumping in defeat. What was he doing here? It was over. He'd been a fool to come. He hadn't learned anything, except that she didn't love him. And that was yesterday's news. "I'll give Williams your address," he said stiffly, "so the hospital can thank you formally for your gift." He turned toward the door.

Gen bit her lip, fighting the pain that slashed through her. Alex was leaving. He was leaving and she'd never see him again. In a voice that was tight with unshed tears, she whispered, "I hope the dedication ceremony goes well for you."

He didn't even turn around. "Thank you," he said distantly.

She'd told herself she wouldn't do it—not for anything. But as Alex's hand reached for the doorknob, she was unable to stop herself. "Please say hi to Sydney," she blurted. Her willpower in tatters, she continued. "Did she come with you today?" God forgive her, but she had to know—had to hear the words from his lips that he and Sydney were together again.

Alex clenched his jaw grimly. Damn it, why was she being so perverse, choosing now to carry on some stiff and banal exchange? He put his hand on the door. "No," he replied, pulling it open, "Sydney and Harry Byrne are in Italy, on their honeymoon. Good-bye—" He spun around at Gen's sudden, anguished cry.

She stared at him, her incredible eyes swallowing her face, which had gone a stark, chalky white. "What?" she gasped. "What did you say?"

Puzzled by her odd reaction, his brows drew together. "Sydney and her partner, Harry, are honeymooning in Siena. They left directly after they eloped—"

"No." Gen shook her head wildly. Her chest was heaving, her breath coming fast and erraticly. "Why would Sydney marry Harry?" A look of horror crossed her face. "You mean she wasn't pregnant with your— *oh, my God.*" With a heartrending wail, Gen crumpled to the floor.

"Jesus, Gen!" Panicked, Alex rushed to her side, scooping her into his arms, his terror mounting when he realized she was lighter than a feather. She was crying, her sobs wracking her body. Tightening his arms about her, he carried her across the room, to the half-open door on the other side, kicking it open with his foot.

Holding Gen cradled against his thundering heart, he swept inside the small bedroom, only to come to an abrupt stop in front of the most beautiful painting he'd ever seen. It was of a couple, naked and embracing, their bodies so close they became as one. The painting was of him and Gen.

He exhaled a long, shuddering breath. Drawing his eyes away from the painting, he gazed at Gen's tear-streaked face and felt more confused than ever.

And more hopeful than he'd felt in six weeks and a day.

He turned toward the bed and caught sight of Jamie's and Sophie's drawings, beautifully framed, hanging a few feet above the pillows. Other than Gen's painting, they were the only ornamentation in the spartan bedroom. Seeing that she'd cared enough to frame the twins' drawings eased some of the terrible ache inside his chest. He bent over the bed to lower her onto the rumpled covers, and when her fingers tightened, clutching him, unwilling to let him go, he instinctively pressed his lips to her flushed brow and murmured, "Easy, love."

As if hearing Alex's tender endearment was more than she could bear, , she hid her face behind her hands, and whispered brokenly, "Oh, Alex, I'm so sorry. I'm so very, very sorry."

Gently but no less determinedly he pulled her hands away. His eyes roved over her. "Why don't you try explaining what this is all about? It's something to do with Sydney, I'm guessing."

Gen nodded tightly. "Yes, you see, Sydney came to your aunt's house that day. She was looking for you and she was totally beside herself. Practically hysterical. I asked her what was wrong and she told me she'd just discovered she was pregnant—and as she wanted to talk to you, I thought you were the father. You'd only broken up a few weeks earlier." Her gaze dropped to her lap.

"Oh, Jesus," Alex groaned as things finally began to click into place. Reaching out, he let his fingers trace the damp smoothness of her cheek before slipping them beneath her chin, and lifting it so that their eyes met. "No, sweetheart, the baby is Harry's. I guess Sydney was panicking because they'd only been seeing each other for a few weeks. She never even mentioned that she'd talked to you." His mouth tightened and he shook his head. "I'd be furious with Sydney, but under the circumstances I can see how she might have been a bit distracted. And I never made the connection between her being pregnant and you leaving. I was so damn devastated that you'd left me, I wasn't thinking very clearly. Gen," he said softly, looking deep into her eyes. "Sydney and I had stopped sleeping together before I even met you."

Her eyes widened in disbelief. "What?"

Alex nodded. "I'd already ended the relationship before you came to the office. But Sydney refused to listen. She was convinced that she could, uh, seduce me back into her bed." Embarrassment had him clearing his throat. "I was in a stupid bind of my own making— I didn't want to fire her from the TLM account, but that meant I couldn't avoid her either, what with the arrangements for the party and the TLM wing."

"She made me think you two were practically engaged," Gen said, her voice quivering with outrage.

Alex cursed softly. "That was bull. I've never proposed to Sydney." Taking her hands in his, he said, "But I'm to blame for this mess, not Sydney. I wanted to tell you that there was nothing between Sydney and me, but I figured that with Sydney acting like we were lovers, you'd think I was some kind of two-timing creep coming on to you for the hell of it—after all," he smiled crookedly, "you didn't exactly have that great an opinion of me to begin with. So I decided to wait Sydney out. But I hadn't counted on how damned irresistible you were. Everything unraveled that morning when I was supposed to model for you. You looked at me and you were so beautiful, I couldn't stop myself from touching you the way I'd been dreaming of."

At Alex's words, emotions welled inside Gen. "I wish I'd known about Sydney, I felt so guilty thinking I'd broken up your relationship. I was jealous, too, of how perfect she seemed for you," she whispered. "But being with you and knowing that you loved me helped put my insecurities behind me. I knew that what we had together was real. Then, when Sydney came and told me about the baby, I realized it didn't matter that I was strong enough to fight my fears, because I had to let you go *anyway*." Her voice cracked in anguish at the memory of all that had happened, of what she'd done. The tears she'd fought to control rolled down her cheeks. "Oh, God, Alex," she cried, "I'll never forgive myself for the things I said to you— I only said them so you'd stay with Sydney and the baby. I knew that you were as jealous of Jiri as I was of Sydney. So I lied deliberately to hurt you and drive you away."

He touched his forehead to hers. "It worked," he admitted quietly. "It killed me to think that you'd used me and then gone off to be with Jiri. That's why I didn't come after you in Prague, because a part of me believed Jiri was perfect for *you*."

"Oh, Alex, no!" Gen cried. Her hands clasped the sides of his face as she whispered urgently, "From that first time together, I knew in my heart that I could never love anyone the way I love you. I haven't been able to live with myself, knowing how much I hurt you. I love you so much, Alex—"

"Shh," he said, his arms slipping about her, rocking her. His lips traveled over her, raining soft, healing kisses on her salty cheeks. His arms tightened their hold, the feel of her against him making him complete for the first time in so very long. "I know, Gen. I know you love me—I figured it out the second I saw this." And he nodded at the painting on the wall.

"It's called *Love,*" Gen told him shyly. "It's the only painting I've been able to make since I left you. I painted it for you, Alex, for that space above the mantel in your bedroom. It was the only way I could express how I felt—but then I knew I could never give it to you, never show you what you mean to me, because I'd destroyed our love."

"No, Gen, the love is still there." His mouth settled over hers, and his heart leapt at her familiar honeyed taste. "That's why I'm here. I tried to stop loving you, but I couldn't. As soon as I heard from Williams that you were in Boston, the wall that I'd built around my heart came tumbling down. I had to see you. I realized then that in spite of what had happened, I still loved you more than anything in the world. God, I love you, Gen," he whispered fiercely. "I love you so much. That day at the studio? I had a ring in my pocket—"

At Gen's sharp keen, Alex stroked the sides of her face. "Shh, sweetheart, it's all right; just listen," he said. "I was late coming back that day because I couldn't find a jewel half as beautiful as the light in your eyes when I'm loving you. And then I was even later because I drove like a little old lady, nervously rehearsing what I wanted to say to you. I'm not nervous now, Gen, because I know what it's like not to have you in my life. I know that without you I'm only half alive. Marry me, Gen. Come and make my life complete. Let me wake each morning to see the light shining in your eyes."

THE END

The deeper you dive,
the sweeter the reward . . .

NIGHT SWIMMING
by Laura Moore

When college offered an escape, Lily fled her hometown of Coral Beach and never looked back. Now a marine biologist, she must return there on a job to preserve the reefs that give the town its name. But going back means dealing with her past, her family, and worst of all, Sean McDermott. As a teenager, Lily passed through an especially awkward phase. Sean, attractive and self-assured, was her constant tormentor.

As mayor, Sean knows how important it is to maintain the town's natural beauty—and if the return of Lily Banyon is the price he has to pay, so be it. What's harder to disregard is the fact that Lily has grown into a smart and beautiful woman, as passionate about saving Coral Beach as she once was about leaving it. While working closely together, it becomes obvious to Sean that if he and Lily can put the past behind them, they could have a passionate future. . . .

Published by Ivy Books
Available wherever books are sold

*Subscribe to the new Pillow Talk
e-newsletter—and receive all these
fabulous online features directly in
your e-mail inbox:*

♥ Exclusive essays and other features by major romance
writers like Linda Howard, Kristin Hannah,
Julie Garwood, and Suzanne Brockmann

♥ Exciting behind-the-scenes news from
our romance editors

♥ Special offers, including contests to win signed
romance books and other prizes

♥ Author tour information, and monthly announce-
ments about the newest books on sale

♥ A Pillow Talk readers forum, featuring feedback
from romance fans...like you!

Two easy ways to subscribe:
Go to **www.ballantinebooks.com/PillowTalk**
or send a blank e-mail to
join-PillowTalk@list.randomhouse.com.

Pillow Talk—
the romance e-newsletter brought to you by
Ballantine Books